Maggie Mason is a pseudonym of author Mary Wood. Mary began her career by self-publishing on Kindle, where many of her sagas reached number one in genre. She was spotted by Pan Macmillan and to date has written many books for them under her own name, with more to come.

Mary continues to be proud to write for Pan Macmillan, but is now equally proud and thrilled to take up a second career with Sphere under the name of Maggie Mason.

Born the thirteenth child of fifteen children, Mary describes her childhood as poor, but rich in love. She was educated at St Peter's RC School in Hinckley and at Hinckley College for Further Education, where she was taught shorthand and typing.

Mary retired from working for the National Probation Service in 2009, when she took up full-time writing, something she'd always dreamed of doing. She follows in the footsteps of her great-grandmother, Dora Langlois, who was an acclaimed author, playwright and actress in the late nineteenth–early twentieth century.

It was her work with the Probation Service that gives Mary's writing its grittiness, her need to tell it how it is, which takes her readers on an emotional journey to the heart of issues.

Also by Maggie Mason

Blackpool Lass
Blackpool's Daughter
Blackpool's Angel

As Mary Wood

An Unbreakable Bond
To Catch a Dream
Tomorrow Brings Sorrow
Time Passes Time
Proud of You
All I Have to Give
In Their Mother's Footsteps
Brighter Days Ahead

MAGGIE MASON

Blackpool Sisters

sphere

SPHERE

First published in Great Britain in 2019 by Sphere

1 3 5 7 9 10 8 6 4 2

A CIP catalogue record for this book is available from the British Library.

ISBN 978-0-7515-7791-4

Typeset in Bembo by Hewer Text UK Ltd, Edinburgh
Printed and bound in Great Britain by Clays Ltd, Elcograf S.p.A.

Papers used by Sphere are from well-managed forests
and other responsible sources.

Sphere
An imprint of
Little, Brown Book Group
Carmelite House
50 Victoria Embankment
London
EC4Y 0DZ

An Hachette UK Company
www.hachette.co.uk

www.littlebrown.co.uk

For my sisters, Julie, Martina, Josephine, Felicity, Magdalene and the late, much missed and loved, Rosemary. I treasure and love you all with all my heart.

PART ONE

TAKING DIFFERENT PATHS

1902

ONE

Beth ached and her fingers felt stiff with cold as the February air cut its icy path across the field where she and her twin sister Babs were working. They had toiled since first light, clearing weeds so that Roman, who guided his beautiful shire horse, didn't plough them back into the earth to reseed. Beth hated the work, but Babs seemed to take it in her stride.

At thirteen years of age, they were both tall. Their raven-black hair had been left to grow and fell in ringlets almost to their waist. Their skin had darkened from being exposed to all weathers as Roman and Jasmine took them from county to county in the south of England, finding work where they could, from apple picking in Somerset to what they were doing now in Kent – preparing the ground for the spring planting of wheat.

'Eeh, Babs, I need a break. Me belly's giving me pain and I feel as though I'm going to faint.'

'It'll be your monthlies. I'll carry on here. You go and find Jasmine, she'll give you sommat to ease you.'

'Aye, she's sure to have sommat to help me. But by, Babs, at times like this I long for our ma more than owt. You don't reckon as she's forgotten us, does you?'

'Naw, Ma'd never forget us.'

They were quiet for a moment. Babs broke the silence. 'I can still see her face, Beth. I see it every time I look at you.'

'Aye, and me in you an' all.'

'Well, that stands as a truth seeing as though we're identical!'

They giggled at this and Beth's mood lightened as she walked over to where Jasmine was working a little ahead of them.

Jasmine had any number of potions that she concocted from the wild herbs she gathered. She called herself an earth mother, who was in touch with nature and used everything God provided to good purpose.

As Beth came up to her, she was greeted with open arms. 'Is it that you need my help, my darling? Your skin is pale, and yet your cheeks are too rosy red. You have a fever, no?'

Going into Jasmine's arms, Beth found the comfort she sought. 'Not a fever, Mama.'

'Ahh, the curse of us women. Come, I have a potion that will ease you. Oh, Beth, my darling daughter, if Mama could have your trials for you, I would.'

'I knaws that, Ma ... I – I mean, Mama.' The slip caused Beth a pain of a different kind – one of loss. A picture of her real ma appeared in her mind, mixed with the image of her sister Babs, and her heartache increased with her longing to be with the beloved ma they were stolen from.

They had only been six years old when gypsies, Roman and Jasmine, had taken them and, although they were happy, they still missed their real ma. Some of their memory of her was fading, but they tried to keep it alive by talking to each other about any fleeting recollections that came to them – their ma's tinkling laugh that lit up her eyes, her kindness and gentleness, and yes, her sadness and her struggle to keep a roof over their head after their da had been killed while working on building the Blackpool Tower.

Memories of their da had faded much more than those of their ma. And yet, when they did speak about him, it was with a warm feeling of love.

Brushing the painful thoughts away, Beth watched Jasmine dig into her satchel that was always slung over her shoulder – a bag that seemed magical to her and Babs as anything you needed Jasmine produced from it.

Roman called out to them, something about how they were getting behind and what was the hold-up.

Jasmine lifted her head and smiled at him. 'It is that our little Beth isn't well. I will see to her and then we will be forging ahead. Rest yourself in the meantime, my darling, it will be good for you.'

Roman smiled back. A handsome man, he had the typical good looks of the gypsy men, his dark weather-beaten complexion setting off his deep blue eyes. Jasmine was different. Though of the gypsy clan, she wasn't of Irish descent as Roman was but from a place across the sea called Romania. Her skin wasn't turned by the weather but was smooth and a lovely shade of olive brown. She had golden strands in her black hair and soft brown eyes with long lashes. She was beautiful to look at.

But not as beautiful as me real ma.

Beth gasped against the increased hurt this thought caused, but then as she took the nasty-tasting potion that Jasmine offered her, the struggle to keep it down took away all thoughts of yesteryear. But they came to the fore once more when she re-joined Babs.

Babs had never tried to settle in the way that Beth had, and often accused Beth of betraying their ma by accepting how things were instead of fighting them all the time.

'Has Jasmine sorted you then?'

'Aye, she's a miracle worker, but I wish she could make her potions taste better.'

'Well, you knaw what she says: if it taste's nasty, it's good for you.'

They giggled together.

'I wonder what Ma would have given us to ease us . . . Eeh, Beth, I wish as you'd agree to me plan. We could easily slip out at night and make our way back to Blackpool to find Ma.'

'Naw, Babs. You knaw that I want to find Ma just as much as you do, but we haven't a clue how to get back to Blackpool. It's miles from here. And even if we got there, how would we find Ma? Blackpool's huge.'

'I don't reckon that it's as huge as we remember it to be. We were only young 'uns but I do remember that everyone knew each other. So, as I see it, we'd only have to ask for Tilly, and anyone would knaw who she is and where she is.'

'That may be true, but you have to think about how we've naw money and we'd not be safe. We're two young lasses, and we'd be at the mercy of anyone who wanted to do wrong by us.'

'Jasmine and Roman have money. They keep it in that trunk under their bed with all our clothes. We could take that.'

'That would be stealing! Besides, how would you get it without them knawing?'

'You could do it right now. Look, Jasmine's with Roman again – she allus likes to be by his side. You could go to them and say that you need a lie-down. That would give you an excuse to go back to the wagon. I could keep Jasmine from following you. I'd say as I can't keep ahead of Roman without you, and then she'd help me, giving you time to get the money and hide it under our pillows in readiness.'

'Naw. I'm not stealing. And let this be an end to it, Babs. This is our lot. I've long accepted it, and if you don't, you'll allus be miserable. If we're meant to get back to Ma, it will happen. Now don't talk of it anymore, it unsettles me.'

'So, it's all right that Jasmine and Roman stole us from our ma, but not for us to steal from them. By, Beth, to say we're identical . . . That ain't what we are. Aye, we match each other in looks, but we are chalk and cheese in our nature. Well, nowt's going to stop me. One day I'm going. With or without you.'

Fear clutched Beth's heart. She knew that she hadn't the courage to run away, but didn't doubt that Babs meant to. *How will I bear to be apart from her?* 'Please don't go. Don't leave me, Babs, please!'

Babs stomped away from Beth and began to work ten feet in front of her. She didn't want to hear Beth's pleas as she knew they were aimed at undoing her resolve. *Well, not this time – I've had enough!*

In the past, Babs had made excuses for her more delicate sister, but as they grew older it seemed to her that Beth only accepted things as they were because the alternative would put her out. Beth liked the simple life and that meant letting things go on as they were, and not fighting to make things right.

Their ma's words were the reason that Babs hadn't taken the path that she wanted to take. 'Look after your sister, Babs. She needs you. You are the strong one.' *Well, I reckon that the best way I can look after Beth is to find Ma and get us all back together.*

With this thought, Babs's resolve deepened and for the first time, she knew that she could, and would, go without Beth.

Lying awake that night, Babs thought about their life with Jasmine and Roman. At first, she and Beth had fought against everything they suggested, feeling in their young minds that to be good and do what was asked of them would somehow mean they were being horrid to their ma. But whenever they became too upset, Jasmine would give them a potion and they would sleep. This broke down their resistance, and they gradually accepted and stopped their tantrums.

Life hadn't been unhappy for them. It had been hard, as from a young age they'd been expected to work. Sometimes in the fields with Roman, but sometimes going around the houses with Jasmine as she sold her crafts. She made the most beautiful things, such as flowers out of silk that looked real. Especially the tulips. Babs and Beth would help her in this too, as they wound strips of green material around a pipe clip – a fleece-covered length of wire, normally used by the ladies to curl their hair. Jasmine made the stems for her flowers with them. And she'd taught them to stitch in tiny neat lines too, a skill they used to hem the lovely aprons Jasmine told them were called 'afternoon pinnies'. These had long ties for tying around the waist and had a rounded edge. They weren't for doing the housework in but for ladies to don when serving tea to friends or to look nice and tidy for when their husbands came home from work. They were made of plain calico and Jasmine embroidered intricate details on them, from flowers to rows of varying sized cross-stitch around the edge, work that Babs loved to watch and tried to copy.

But though these thoughts gave her a nice feeling about life with Jasmine, and though she had to admit that she and Beth were loved and cared for, none of it lessened her longing to be back in Blackpool with her ma. *I have to go, I do. Aye, and right now.*

As she threw off the covers and quietly pulled back the curtain that surrounded the bed, Babs was stopped by the familiar sound of Roman and Jasmine sighing, moaning and whispering words of love. In this small gypsy caravan, their double bed was only feet away from hers and Beth's, though the drapes shielding it were of a heavy, thick velvet which gave them some privacy.

Knowing what was happening made Babs cringe with embarrassment, but she distracted herself by dressing quickly and focusing on her plans. At least the noise they were making gave her the comfort of not being heard herself as she took off her nightie and donned her thick knitted stockings, pulling her long calico dress over the underwear she'd kept on to keep her warm – something she often did on cold wintry nights.

When Roman's moans became more urgent and deepened to a guttural level, which she knew hailed the end of their lovemaking, Babs was at the entrance to the caravan. Putting on her coat, she turned and peered through the half-light at her beloved sister. A tear fell from her eye and wet her cheek. Brushing it away, she quietly unstrapped the canvas curtains and ran down the steps.

The cold night air, and the fear she felt, sent shivers through her body, and yet, filled with the urgency of the moment, she didn't falter, but bent down and took her boots off the pegs that were driven into the ground to hold them and slipped her bare feet into them, before scrambling around to the side of the caravan and lifting the latch to the larder. The creak resounded in the silence. Babs stiffened, conscious that sometimes when the act was over, Roman got up and went outside to relieve himself. If he did, he would come around to the side of the wagon where she was as it was closer to the hedge.

Crouching as near to the wagon as she could, Babs waited. Nothing happened. Her thumping heart settled a little, giving her courage once more. Hurriedly, she grabbed a newly baked loaf and a lump of cheese from the block Jasmine had bought from the farmer's wife. Wrapping these in her shawl, she ran for all she was worth.

By the time she reached the road, fear had a firm hold of her as every sound made her jump, even though she was used to each one – an owl hooting, an animal squealing as it fell prey to a predator, and undergrowth alive with moles and hedgehogs ferreting for food.

When she came to a junction, Babs was unsure of which way to go, but remembering that the road to her right led to the sea, she felt sure that was further south, so opted to take the road to her left, hoping that would take her north.

* * *

Shivering, Beth moved closer to where her sister lay, hoping to be warmed by Babs's body. When after a couple of moves she didn't meet Babs, she put out her hand. The sheet where Babs should be felt cold to the touch. Beth shot up. Every part of her tuned into the sounds of the night, hoping that one of them would tell her that Babs was paying a visit to the bucket outside. But none did.

As realisation dawned on her, a feeling of dread clawed at her as she felt a strong draught and heard the canvas curtains flapping in the breeze. 'She's gone, Babs has gone!'

The sleepy, mumbling voice of Roman asking, 'What? What is it that troubles you? Is it a nightmare that you are having, Beth?'

'Naw. Papa . . . Eeh, Papa, Babs has gone!'

A flickering brightness enhanced the shadows of the caravan as Roman emerged carrying a lighted candle. His nightshirt twisted around him, barely covering him. Jasmine followed, looking dishevelled as her hair, usually tied back in a neat bun, hung around her face in a messy mass of tangles. 'What is it that you are saying, little one?'

'Babs has gone, she's run away. She's gone to find our ma . . . Oh, Mama . . . I can't be without her, I can't.'

Jasmine scrambled towards her. Her arms held her close as her own sobs joined Beth's.

'No, no, please, no!'

'What? Gone? Be Jeez, why? For sure, she'll never make it to Blackpool.'

'Roman is right. Oh, dear God, is it that she is so unhappy? We love her, we have taken care of her – of you both. Why? Why?'

Beth wanted to scream that nothing they did could ever replace their ma. But all she could do was sob out her despair.

'I'll dress and take one of the horses and go after her. It is that she couldn't have got far. When was it that she left?'

'I – I don't knaw, Papa, she – she was beside me when I fell asleep.'

'Then I will ride north until I find her. Don't you be worrying, me little darling, I'll bring your sister home, so I will.'

Jasmine let go of her and went into Roman's arms. 'Please bring my baby back to me, darling, please.'

It came to Beth to say that Babs wasn't their baby and neither was she, and what a terrible thing they had done in taking them from their ma, but all she could do was to sink back down onto the bed and sob her heart out. *Oh, Babs, Babs, why did you go? How could you leave me? How?*

TWO

Tilly grabbed her shawl from the hook behind the kitchen door and picked up her basket. As she stepped outside, the early spring wind that cut across the south of Ireland's fells cut into her. Her heart was in her mouth. Today, she had to run the wrath of the hateful women of the village that nestled in the valley.

Not that individually they were hateful, but if a few of them were together, she became the evil British enemy who'd dared to marry one of their men.

The Irish hadn't forgotten what the British did to them, how they starved while landowners took taxes and rents from them that they could ill afford, nor how they held on to the North, splitting their country in two.

This wrath they felt came down on Tilly's head in the form of foul language and rotten vegetables being thrown at her. Those still agitating in Northern Ireland, who held their meetings locally, were particularly frightening to Tilly.

How Tommy braved it all, she didn't know, but he stood steadfast, protecting the farm he'd inherited, and as his wife, she had followed him from her beloved Blackpool to his native land.

Mostly she avoided going into the village, but the shop wouldn't deliver to her and often refused even to serve her, but she needed flour and salt and there was nowhere else to get it from. She had to run the wrath of the villagers and hope the shopkeeper would let her have what she needed.

Often, she bought these items from England when she visited Blackpool, but it had been six months since she last went. Each time she did, she wished with all her heart that she'd never left, but she loved Tommy and had said that she would be true to the maxim of where he lay his head, she would lay hers.

'Mammy, it is that I want to come too.'

Tilly smiled down at Ivan as he lay on the floor looking up at her. Now four years old, she thought of him as her little miracle. This was because she was told after she'd given birth to her beautiful twins, Babs and Beth, that she was too damaged to have more children. *Well, whatever ailed me must have righted itself, as this lad here is proof of.*

She'd not want to take him with her even if he could run when things got nasty, but with his twisted legs, the poor little mite had to be pushed in the special chair that she had made out of cane and that Tommy had fixed a frame and wheels to.

Around the house, Ivan crawled on his hands, pulling his legs along behind him – a truly uplifting sight as determination shone from him. 'Naw, you're to stay with your pappy, there's a good 'un. Mammy won't be long. Besides, the field has to be ploughed for the potato crop and your pappy cannot do it all on his own.'

Ivan pulled a face. 'Mammy, not safe on your own.'

Tilly's heart lurched. Ivan must have heard her and Tommy talking. 'Eeh, don't worry, lad. Mammy is fine.'

Sometimes she thought that God had given this son of hers the head of a much older child to compensate for his disability.

When he was born, Tilly had broken her heart at not giving Tommy a son who was strong and whole, who looked just like his father. Even in this last she'd failed as Ivan took after her in looks, with his dark curly hair and dark eyes, which painfully reminded her of her little Babs and Beth, her lost girls. But Tommy had lifted Ivan from his cot and fallen in love with him. 'Sure, he is me son, Tilly, and I will love and protect him. I'd have him no different. We'll call him Ivan, as that is a name that is strong, and will be helping him through life.'

Strong was something that Ivan wasn't. He ailed with everything brought on the breeze. If they had a cold, Ivan had a much worse one, which affected his breathing as it settled on his weak chest. Tilly feared for this adored son.

Tommy appeared at the door and bent and scooped Ivan up. 'It is that I need you to ride on Norman's back, son. Sure it is that horse never goes in a straight line without you. Come, let's get you in your warm coat and put your harness on you.'

Ivan giggled up at Tommy, and Tilly's heart filled with love for them both. The harness was Tommy's invention. He'd made it out of an old rein that had hung in the barn for years. Cutting the leather and stitching it so that it would hold Ivan firmly on the back of a horse had taken hours of work every evening. Sometimes Tilly had helped, and her basket-making tools had come in very handy for the job of getting the steel pins through the leather. These then opened and acted as a stud to keep the straps together.

Most of Tilly's time was spent making baskets. Back in Blackpool she was a senior partner in a shop with her friends, Liz and Molly, who ran the shop on a daily basis and helped to keep it stocked by making smaller items.

It was Tilly, though, who had the real talent. Taught at the knee of an old aunt who'd brought her up, she had skills that enabled her to turn the wicker and cane into many shades of brown and to weave intricate patterns, making beautiful chairs, shopping baskets and boxes. The latter would be turned into sewing boxes once they reached the shop, where Molly would apply her special talent of sewing beautiful silk linings into them, with many pockets to hold needles, pins and threads.

Tommy took all Tilly's wares to the dock once a month and they were shipped to Liverpool, where Dan, Liz's husband, and Will, Molly's husband, picked them up in a horse and cart.

Waving at Ivan and Tommy, Tilly walked towards the village. As she came to the first of the croft houses, she began to feel her nerves tickling her stomach. But all was quiet. Walking on, she grew in confidence.

It was as she reached the village centre that a stone whistled past her head and a woman shouted, 'Be Jaysus, you've a side to you, you English pig!'

'I'm not wanting naw trouble, I just need some supplies for me family.'

'Well, you'll not get them here, so you won't.' Tilly turned and saw Mrs O'Flynn standing in her shop doorway, her arms folded over her huge bosom.

'Please, Mrs O'Flynn. I'll pay double what the going price is, but I've naw flour to bake bread for me lad.'

'He's your punishment, so he is, and it's not for me to see that he's fed.'

Her desperate need made Tilly suppress the anger that this vile attack on her beloved son evoked in her. 'I've said sorry so many times for the wrong done to you all by me fellow English. What more can I do?'

'You can be for taking your scabby English presence from our doorstep! You're like a sore that is rubbed, so you are. A reminder to us of all we and our pappies afore us suffered, and are still suffering, but one day . . . aye, one day we'll rise up and be for taking back what is rightfully ours.'

Tilly had heard often about this planned uprising, and signs of it were everywhere as gangs of men met in churches and sometimes marched through the streets chanting in Gaelic, a language she didn't understand. She had been told by Tommy that they were inciting men to join them for when the hour cometh. And it wasn't just by marching that they showed their hate of the English, as they'd sometimes burn down property that was still owned by the English lords.

Turning back, Tilly held her back straight, showing all the courage she could muster as she strode away from the bigoted shopkeeper and the women who had gathered into a threatening mob.

As she turned the corner and went to pass by the last croft house, the door opened. 'Tilly, come in here. Be quick so it is that you're not seen.'

Shocked, Tilly looked at the beckoning woman, afraid for a moment that this might be a trap. 'Hurry yourself. Aren't I risking being tarred and feathered by that lot, if caught in the act of helping you?'

Once inside, Tilly waited, her insides shaking, making her feel sick. If a mob was waiting for her inside the croft, she'd not stand a chance.

'I'm not for meaning any harm to you, Tilly. It is that I don't agree with how the others carry on towards you. Och, I've not been for saying or doing anything about it for years, but I'm sick of their unjust ways, so I am. You couldn't help what was for happening in the past, nor the goings-on of today, with the high taxes, but they're not for seeing that. You're just like us, a farmer's wife, striving to help your man and feed your family. And God knows, it is that you have to shoulder more than any of us with your wee child.'

Still unsure, but grateful to hear a friendly voice, Tilly swallowed hard. 'Ta, them words mean a lot to me, Mrs O'Bryan.'

'Ruby. Call me Ruby, for that's me God-given name. Now, is it that you need flour? And did I hear right that you'd be willing to pay well for it?'

To Tilly's questioning glance, Ruby said, 'Och, I was for being on me way home when I saw what was happening and I heard it all, even though it was that I dodged around the corner.'

'Aye, I'll pay a good rate, and for salt an' all. I'm out of both.'

'At the shop you're looking at the price being a halfpenny for both; I'd be asking three farthings for them.'

'I'll take what you have, ta.'

'It is that I have a new bag of flour, but salt, I'll have to chip some off the block. Have you anything you can be putting it in?'

'Aye, I brought me salt tin with me.'

As Ruby chipped away at her block of salt, Tilly found her purse and the three farthings she needed. But then decided to give Ruby a penny, as she was taking a big risk, and Tilly knew she wouldn't be if she wasn't desperate for money.

When she put the penny on the table next to Ruby, Ruby snatched it up. 'To be sure, I'm not for having any change, so I'm not.'

'I'm not wanting any. I'd made me mind up to give you that. I'm really grateful to you, me lad needs his substance, as does me man.'

'It is for that reason that I am doing this. Poor wee boy.'

Tilly could see Ruby's hands shaking, and had the urge to hug her for the risk that she was taking. She could be judged as fraternising with the hated English, and be punished for doing so.

'I'm very grateful to you for helping me like this. Ta ever so much. If I can help you, Ruby, I will.'

'It is that I can get you what you need, but you must not be telling anyone. Don't be for asking me directly or speaking to me in the street. I will be for getting a message to you if I have extra that you can buy from me. Now, please see that you are for taking care when you are leaving so as not to be seen. There are those who would punish us, so there is.'

Tilly began to feel even more nervous and wanted to leave. 'That'll be plenty of salt, ta, Ruby. If you can scoop it into me tin, I'll be on me way.'

At the door to the little cottage, Ruby put her head out and looked this way and that. 'Be on your way. Go quickly, and may God bless you.'

Tilly almost ran down the hill to the farm. Her heart raced. Today she had met one of life's good people in Ruby, and she prayed that she wouldn't bring trouble to her door.

Once in her own home, Tilly looked around and saw not an inviting home that she shared with her beloved husband and son, but a prison. One that trapped her where she didn't want to be.

Feeling hemmed in, Tilly dropped her bag on the floor and ran outside. She didn't stop running until she got to the bottom field where she could hear the gentle tones of Tommy geeing Norman, his horse, along, and the giggles of Ivan. When they came into view, her fears left her. She smiled at the way Ivan was jiggled back and forth to the rhythm of Norman's gait.

When Ivan caught sight of her he clapped his hands. 'Mammy!'

Tommy turned. 'Me darlin', what're you for doing down here? Was everything for going well in the village?'

'Aye, it was, Tommy. I have me flour and salt, and should be baking bread for your tea, but I wanted to be with you.'

He came over to her and held her to him. He smelt of fresh air, and earth, and the fresh sweat of his labour. Her love for him overwhelmed her.

'Me lovely Tilly.' Lowering his voice, Tommy whispered, 'To be sure, if we were alone, I'd take you down right here in the field, such is the need you put in me when it is that you're in me arms.'

The words zinged through Tilly, filling her with a hunger belying the fact that he'd made love to her just this morning, taking her to the heights that had satisfied every part of her.

For she too wanted him at this very moment in the way he wanted her.

'Tommy, stop your antics, our son is watching.' But though she moved his hand from her breast, it wasn't what she wanted to do.

'To be sure, one day he'll know the feeling too, and I hope he does.'

A pain shot through Tilly as often she doubted that Ivan would ever lead a normal life. But she had no time to dwell on the emotion this thought evoked as a piercing scream sliced through the air. They turned as one and looked towards their son. Ivan sat safely on Norman, his face showing the fear that they both felt upon hearing the scream. Tommy ran towards him, but Tilly stood as if turned to stone as her mind tried to process who had made the terrible sound. *Was it Ruby? Did someone see me go into, or leave her cottage? God, naw! Don't let it be Ruby suffering for helping me!*

Tommy coming up to her, holding Ivan closely to him, broke her thoughts. 'Let us get to the safety of our home. Don't be afraid, Tilly, it is that it is nothing to do with us. Look, Ivan is for being a brave lad, so he is. We've to be the same for him.'

But when they turned, they were stopped in their tracks at the sight that met them. Plumes of smoke billowed from the thatched roof of their house. A swishing sound drew their attention. They looked up in horror as many fire bombs zoomed through the air above them. On landing, they exploded into a sheet of raging flames.

'Naw, naw! Why, Tommy? Our home . . . your home! How could they?'

Tommy didn't speak. A tear trickled down his cheek, leaving a silvery line through the smudges of dirt put there by his labours. Tilly reached up and wiped the tear with her thumb. Ivan copied her, his bottom lip quivering. 'Pappy, Pappy.'

'Don't be afraid, Ivan. Pappy is sad to see the home he was born in being destroyed by bad men, but we're not hurt, naw one can hurt us, I promise.'

Tommy held Ivan tighter. 'Son, it is that there are many bad men here. Me and Mammy will be for taking you to Blackpool in England where we can live in peace. One day, it will be that you can come back to the farm that is rightfully yours.'

Tilly couldn't help feeling a surge of happiness at this. 'Really, Tommy? You're ready to leave? What if they take your land and you never get it back?'

'For sure it is that they can never take what's really precious to me, Tilly, you and me little Ivan, but if we stay here, they may try. I'm fearful, so I am. I need to get you to safety. Let's sit a while till it is as the noise dies down and we know that they are all gone.'

'We should go into the barn to keep warm, Tommy.'

'No. What if it is that they plan to burn that too? They must be for having murder in their hearts, for how is it they burn a house when it is likely that you are in it? Come, we'll go to the top field as from there we can see what is happening.'

As they neared the far gate of the field they were in, they could hear wailing sobs. 'What's that, Tommy?'

But even as she asked, Tilly knew it was going to be Ruby. When they turned the corner, there, tied to the gatepost, was Ruby. Hardly recognisable, as her red hair lay in long strands at her feet, and her head, face and body were covered in tar and feathers.

'Don't be for coming near me. Go. Go now! Leave. Be for catching the next boat out of this country as they're baying for the blood of you all.'

'Oh God, Ruby, I'm sorry. I didn't believe that this could happen.'

'It is for being me own fault. I knew the consequences. I'll be all right, now that I've taken me punishment. But you're not safe. You must be for getting yourselves away.'

'I'm heartily sorry this has happened to you, Ruby. I'm not knowing what it was you did for me wife, but I thank you. Come, Tilly.'

'But we can't leave her like this, Tommy.'

'We have to. They'll send someone to her later, when they think it is that she's suffered enough. We cannot make her sacrifice be worth nothing by getting ourselves killed.'

As they walked away, Tilly felt like she was a traitor and desperately wanted to run back to Ruby and help her.

'Quickly, Tilly. It is that I dreaded this day and hid a tin with money enough to get us away. It is buried under the tree in the top field. We must get it and make our way to the dock in Dublin.'

Tilly knew the dock well but never had she been to it under such circumstances. Her heart was heavy and her body tired for they'd walked many a mile to get here and only getting a lift on the odd cart or two as they met traders and travellers who were kind enough, or desperate enough for money, to take them a few miles.

'Well, it is that I must secure our tickets on the next sailing, Tilly. Wait here with Ivan. Poor little chap is in need of our care, and we're unable to give it.'

Tilly knew what Tommy meant. Ivan was cold and hungry. But for all that, he was cheerful. It was as if he knew not to add to their troubles and slept most of the time but had a smile on his face during his waking hours.

When Tommy returned, he told her that they couldn't travel until the next day. 'It is that we'll go into the city and find a boarding house.'

'It is so late, Tommy, I won't find a shop open to buy something for Ivan. He needs clean nappies and food.'

'I know the way of it.' For a moment, Tommy was quiet. When he spoke, he had a solution. 'We'll go to the nuns, so we will. Me family has supported them this many a year, giving donations to their cause and gifts of food to grace their table. Sure it is that we will find help there.'

The nuns were as kind as Tommy had said they would be and soon, Ivan was bathed, fed and clad in the clean linen that the nuns had provided. They were offered a bed for the night too, but Tommy wanted them to be near to the dock, so they said their goodbyes and hailed a cab. Never had Tilly seen a cab in Ireland before, but Dublin boasted many of them.

The gentle rhythm of the horse's hooves as the cab took them to a boarding house lulled her to sleep – a fitful sleep that had her waking up with a start at the sound of the cab driver calling out that they had reached their destination.

In the morning they woke to a busy city with an air of joviality about it as folk called out to one another in their Irish lilt. Market stalls were being erected along the banks of the Liffey – the river that seemed to cut Dublin in two as it wiled its way through the streets to the sea.

In awe of the tall buildings built in a light-coloured stone that they passed, as the cab taking them to the docks jolted their bodies, Tilly didn't speak much and neither did Tommy. Ivan, still sleepy, snuggled into her. When they reached the docks, the sights and smells changed. The biting wind carried a tinge of saltiness and hung with the stench of fish and the folk, of which there were many, bustled about. Some in their quest to board the boat, others working, mending nets or loading cargo.

When they docked in Liverpool, after a choppy crossing that made her feel queasy but had Ivan giggling – especially when his pappy told him that it was a sailor that he was destined to be – Tilly felt a sense of happiness settle in her. Soon she would be home. Really home, not just paying a visit.

The shop she owned had a flat above it where she stayed when in Blackpool on business. It wasn't ideal but would do for her, Tommy and Ivan until they could sort out something that was more suitable.

Tommy was very quiet as they boarded the train to take them to Blackpool, as he had been from the moment that they'd left the nuns.

When they sat in the carriage and the countryside whizzed by, she asked him if he was all right.

'It is that I am feeling I'll never be for being right again, Tilly. That me own countrymen could do that to me . . . But I'm trying to come to terms with it and will do all I can to settle.'

'Ta, Tommy. It will be hard, I knaw, but if you try, you might succeed. Blackpool will welcome you. It's a town that welcomes everyone, and you'll soon feel at home and be able to live without fear.'

'I know, me lovely Tilly. And we'll all be together, that's all that matters. Me, you and our little Ivan. Nothing can be hurting us now.'

Tilly smiled as she looked at Ivan, lying with his head on her knee. She stroked his curls, watching them spring back as she gently smoothed them, but then she shuddered as if someone had brushed her back with a feather. Shaking the feeling and the thought that had come with it that one day, they would suffer a hurt too deep to bear, she took Ivan in her arms and held him close to her. *I'll not let owt happen to you, me lovely son. I promise.*

THREE

As the day dawned, Babs thought that she must have been walking for at least nine hours with very few stops. The low winter sun could hardly break through the heavy cloud. Feeling very tired, cold and afraid, she stopped next to a milestone and peered at the inscription: *London 18 miles*. Her spirits sank as a memory sent her back to her infant school in Blackpool and a classroom full of children excited to learn about the Queen. The teacher's voice came to her, telling them that the Queen's name was Victoria and she lived in London. One girl had asked if they could go to London to see the Queen one day. The teacher had smiled and said, 'London is a very long way. It would take a week by coach to get there.'

Sinking to the ground, Babs filled with despair as she realised that to walk that distance would take many weeks. It was a hopeless task.

Her feet and legs hurt. She had to rest.

Despite the dampness of the early morning fog, and the heavy dew, Babs sat down and curled herself into a ball, tucked her knees high under her chin and closed her eyes.

She ached to reach out and for Beth to be there to cuddle up to. *What have I done?* A tear trickled down her cheek. Loneliness engulfed her. But turning back wasn't something she could do. *I have to go on. I have to find Ma.*

Her thoughts went to the cosiness of the caravan. By now Jasmine and Roman would be stirring. They would know that she was missing. *Will Roman come after me?* Part of her wished with all her heart that he would, but still the spirit that had got her this far hadn't dimmed and she dismissed the longing. Instead she concentrated on remembering what she had set out to find.

Ma's face swam before her and an overwhelming love soared through her.

With the feeling came a new determination. Getting to her feet, Babs wiped her face on her sleeve and set off again. Wherever she looked there were endless fields dotted with hop driers – pointed buildings with the funny name of oasts. Sighing, she knew she hadn't yet left the county of Kent.

A sound in the distance made her stop her progress. She listened. The sound was distinctive now – horses' hooves galloping and coming nearer. This gave Babs hope, but this hope was mixed with fear. What if it was Roman? Just thinking it might be made her mind up. Crouching down, she rolled over, allowing herself to fall into a ditch. Water seeped over the top of her boots as she sunk into the soft surface, unleashing a stinking smell that made her want to heave.

But still, she didn't want to be seen.

The sound of the horse grew louder. Babs knew it was very near now. Keeping her head down, she prayed the rider hadn't seen her before she'd hidden in the ditch. But as it slowed and came to a halt, she knew that he had.

'Who's there? Why are you hiding? Come out.'

It wasn't Roman. The voice was very posh. Keeping still and quiet, Babs prayed the man would go away. 'Hey, what are you doing?' The voice was above her now. When she looked up the face peering down at her didn't look unfriendly, nor did he look angry.

'My dear girl, why are you down there? You're soaking wet. Climb out at once. Here, give me your hand.'

Once she was out, Babs could see that the person she had thought was a man was a boy not much older than herself. 'Eeh, you had me worried then, you speak with a funny tone. I thought you were a magistrate or sommat.'

'Ha, me? I have a funny tone? You're from the North, aren't you? I know that accent. Whereabouts exactly?'

He didn't say how he recognised her speech, nor did he make fun of her, or treat her differently because of it. Babs liked him and felt comfortable enough to tell him her business. 'I'm from Blackpool, and that's where I'm headed. Have you an idea which way it is?'

'I know that it is a long way from here. My parents go there on occasion. Meant to make Mama better. She has a perpetual cough. But it takes them days to get there, and Papa has a good team. But you're walking . . . You're running away from somewhere, aren't you? The poor house, is it?'

'Naw, I'm not! I'm just lost, that's all.'

'Well, I'd take you home with me, but you stink. What are you going to do?'

'Walk. I'll get there sometime, I will.'

'Well, I must away. There's a farm just over yonder. One of the only ones around here that's not tenanted to my papa, but I happen to know the farmer needs to take someone on. Why not make for there and try your luck? You might be able to save what you earn to take a train part of the way.'

'Ta, I will.'

With this, the boy mounted his horse, touched his cap and galloped away, leaving Babs feeling strangely bereft as despite what he'd said about her stinking, her heart had fluttered when she'd looked into his eyes. A strange feeling, but one she knew she would never forget.

Through the dimness of the approaching dawn, Babs could see the lights of the farmhouse in the distance. The sight renewed her strength and gave her the momentum to venture further.

When she was near, the smell of cow dung vied with the smell of damp hay. There was no one about and the light she'd seen was coming from an upstairs window. Everywhere looked uncared for. A plough stood in one corner of the farmyard, rusting away and with a growth of weeds around it that told of it not having been used for a long time. The stables to her left held no horses, and the smell coming from them suggested that fresh hay hadn't been laid for a long time.

Babs thought to seek some warmth in the barn to her left until she heard anyone about who she could ask for work.

She followed the cobbled path that led to the barn. Everywhere was clothed in shadows. Once inside, she saw a pile of sacks; picking one off the top caused a cloud of dust to rise which made her cough. Shaking it, she used it to dry her legs, then seeing a wooden ladder leading to the loft, she climbed up, hoping to find a place to rest. Once up there she was relieved to find sweet-smelling hay and to feel the warmth of this enclosed space. Stripping off her boots, she turned them upside down to dry, then took off her coat. The hem of her frock was wet, so she turned it up then settled down to rest.

A rough hand shook Babs awake. 'What the blazes does you think you're doing, eh?'

Babs squinted through the beam of sunlight that filtered through the skylight above her. 'I didn't mean naw harm, mister, I were just resting meself.'

'Where've you come from? You sound Northern, and yet look like a gypsy.'

'I – I'm looking for work, I'm on me travels to Blackpool. I want to get to me ma.'

'Blackpool, you say? That's a few days' ride from here. And you're walking? I can't see you ever making it to Blackpool. Let me look at you in the light.'

Dragging Babs over the floor until she was under the skylight, the man peered down at her. Babs could see he was unshaven, and she could smell his stale body odour. As he stared at her, his very cross expression gave way to a smile that showed his yellowing teeth. 'You're a pretty young thing. I might take advantage of you landing in me barn. It's been a good while since I laid with a woman.'

Fear zinged through Babs. 'Naw, let me go! Don't touch me.'

'Touch you? I'll do more than touch you.'

Spit came from his mouth as he said this in a different voice to the one he'd used when he'd found her. Babs knew the tone. How often she'd heard it from Roman as he'd looked at Jasmine in a certain way and suggested it was time that they turned in. Not long after, she would hear them making love. But this dirty-looking man wasn't talking of making love, he was wanting what Jasmine told them they should be careful of. It had been when they had started their bleeding. 'It is that the men will lust after you, my beautiful girls. But we won't take you to the grabbings. Not ever.'

The grabbings, she knew, was a gypsy tradition. She'd been at fairs when it had taken place and thought it barbaric as young men looking for a bride grabbed the girl that he fancied and kissed her. If he managed that – and sometimes he'd beat the girl to accomplish it – then she had to marry him.

Jasmine had gone on to tell them what she'd called a story of the birds and the bees and had said that men did that to women to make babies, but even if not for that reason, just because they had an urge in them to do it that they couldn't deny.

'I'll scream if you touch me and bring the farmer to you!'

'I am the farmer.' With this he pushed Babs till she was lying down. 'Now, take off your clothes, and let me watch you.'

'Naw, I won't! I don't want to! Leave me alone!' With this she kicked out at him.

Pain shot through her head as the man grabbed a handful of her hair. Her gasp disappeared beneath the sound of his curses. 'You bloody swine! You'll fucking do as I say, but I'm not one to fight for what I need, I'd rather pay.'

Holding her so that she could hardly move, his voice softened once more. 'I'll pay you good, girl, and I'll feed you, and yes, take you on and set you to work for me. You'll be set for life. How does that sound, eh?'

Babs's fear screamed from her as she forced his hold to loosen and sat up. 'Naw! Naw! I just want to leave here.'

The blow sent her reeling back. The weight of him crushed her. His hand was up her skirt, his stinking breath gasped over her face, his spittle dropped onto her cheeks. Babs retched. 'Leave me, please, please, leave me alone!'

But the man wasn't going to give up. She felt him fumbling, while his full body weight was on her. Babs thought that she would die if she couldn't take a breath soon. But then a pain shot through her and she knew he was doing that thing to her.

Babs freed her arms from his grip and gouged at his eyes. He hit her again, but the blow that he gave her didn't stop her. However, when he grabbed her hair and banged her head on the ground, she weakened.

His shape above her became hazy; his movements meant nothing to her now, nor the sound of his deep guttural moans. As the light beaming on her began to shimmer and then fade, a darkness descended and took her into its depth.

Two days had passed since Babs had come to. She'd been horrified to find that she was bound to the main beam of the barn.

As she awoke now, she pulled herself to a sitting position. She gave her arm a tug against the restrictions of the chain that held her, feeling the soreness caused by the fruitless action as she peered through the darkness. The only light she'd seen since being awoken by the man she called the 'Brute' was when the sun beamed through the skylight. By this happening, she'd counted the days from when she'd come to after she had fainted. When it shone again, it would mark her third day in this hayloft.

Fear vied with her hunger, as Babs felt her stomach gnaw and protest at not being fed since her first day when she'd eaten the bread and cheese just before finding this barn. The Brute had only given her a jug of water, and that was now gone.

Her limbs were stiff and painful. In her despair she called out in her mind for her ma, for Beth, and yes, for Jasmine and Roman. Her eyes were sore and swollen from crying. Her nose was blocked. Lying back down, Babs begged of God to help her and willed the sun to come as its warming rays would give her a little comfort.

FOUR

On the morning of the third day after Roman left, he returned alone. 'It is that I have ridden further than Babs could have possibly walked, but I was for not finding her. I asked of strangers, but no one has seen her. I'm sorry, me little darling, but I daren't stay away any longer, as it is that we will get behind with our work and then the farmer won't pay us.'

'No, no, I can't bear it! Why? It is that we treated her well. Oh, Babs.'

'If it was in her to leave, we were never going to hold her. We've not done anything other than love her. If that wasn't for being enough, then that is how it must be. We are still for having our beautiful Beth. We are to help her through her loss and be taking care of her now.'

Beth didn't react, though she wanted to. Something inside her had died. She knew that she could never have left Babs, and this thought made part of her feel cross and want to slap Babs for doing what she had. But mostly she felt a deep sense of grief and shock. *It can't be possible that I will never see Babs again. She'll come back, I knaw she will. And maybe . . . Maybe she will have Ma with her.*

At this thought, Beth felt some of the coldness that had clawed at her insides release its hold on her and a tiny bit of hope took its place. Always seeing some good in every situation was a trait she'd had since birth. But so was her reliance on Babs. They were each one half of a whole and without her sister, she didn't think she could ever be happy again.

Babs didn't know how long she'd slept, but the longed-for sun was now beaming down on her again. Lying still, she listened. Voices! She wasn't mistaken, she could hear voices, she was sure of it. Hope entered her. She tried to call out, but only managed a croaking sound that rasped her dry, sore throat. The voices became louder. It sounded as though an argument was going on. Straining to listen, Babs heard a man shouting. 'I tell you, I'll not wait much longer. I want my money. I want what is rightfully mine, Cecil.'

'You've got no rights. You've never lifted a finger to help on the farm, while I've toiled away at it trying to make something of it.'

'Toiled? Toiled? The place has gone to rack and ruin, man. There's not a barn that's in good order, nor a field that's ploughed. The cattle herd has all gone. You've brought the place to its knees.'

'And you haven't, eh? Swanning off to your learning and leaving it all to me to do. Mother and Father must be turning in their grave.'

'They would if I had left college, when they worked hard to put me there. You said you'd manage with the help of Bob. You did for a long time while Dad wasn't able to work. Why not now? I always said you were a lazy bugger. Well, it's going to stop. I'm putting my half up for sale, and I'll help you to find somewhere to live nearer to me where I can keep an eye on you. I'm haunted by what might be happening to you, now that you haven't got Bob. At least he used to let me know now and again that you were all right or if you needed something. Now, I'm forever having to come out here and I haven't got the time.'

'Of course I'm all right. And you can't force me to move. Look, come up to the house and let's talk. Things have changed. The cattle got sick and had to be slaughtered and I had to let Bob go – he was passed retiring age anyway. I've tried. I really have, but it's beating me.'

Fear that they would walk away spurred Babs on and despite her sore throat, she forced out a sound that was more like a moan than the scream she wanted to give.

'What was that?'

'What?'

'That sound. It came from the loft.'

'Well, there's nothing there that can make a sound, it must have been the beams creaking. The whole barn's ready to collapse if you ask me. Look, John, I need more capital. You have to countersign for the release of some of the trust to me. I'll make things right with that, I promise, and then you'll get all that's due to you.'

'No . . . listen, there it was again. There's someone in your loft, man!'

Hope soared inside Babs, giving her the strength to call out for a third time. At last, though she could hear the Brute protesting, the hatch opened and a head and shoulders appeared. 'Is there anyone there?'

'Aye . . . over here. Help me.'

'What the blazes! Christ! Cecil, there's a . . .' The man began to rock violently. 'Stop! What do you think you are doing? I'll fall, Cecil! For God's sake, man.'

Babs watched with mounting terror as the man tried desperately to find a hold. When his hand finally clutched part of the chain hanging from the beam, a relief swept over Babs. She watched his face bulge and redden with the extreme effort it took for him to pull himself into the loft. 'You bloody idiot, Cecil. You don't change, do you? You could have killed me!'

'You shouldn't meddle in what doesn't concern you.'

'My God! You've got a girl up here . . . What . . . Christ! What's going on, man?'

Babs was shocked to hear a loud sob, followed by crying that was akin to wailing. 'I was lonely. I didn't mean to. She came looking for money and shelter, and I made her pay for it, that's all. You won't do anything about it, will you, John?' The crying became louder. John ignored it.

'Who are you? Are you hurt? Oh my God, you're chained! Cecil, you're mad! What have you done, man?'

The Brute didn't answer, but his crying became louder as the man approached Babs. 'Don't be afraid. What's your name?'

'B – Babs.'

'You're safe now, Babs. I'll get help for you. I'm sorry. I – I . . . my brother, he, well, he suffers with mental problems. I'll release you.' Turning, he shouted for Cecil. 'Where is the key to this padlock? Tell me now!'

As the Brute's sobs turned to screams, John told her to try not to be afraid, that he would be back for her. With this, he crossed back over to the ladder and started to descend. Babs wanted to ask him not to leave her, but she could only watch as he disappeared. Her body began to shiver. The Brute now sounded like the madman his brother had said he was.

To think these two men were brothers didn't fit at all. The Brute was rough-shaven and dirty, with yellowing teeth; his skin was swarthy, and his hands marked by rough callouses and filthy nails. The only thing the men had in common was their fair hair and blue eyes. John was clean and smart. Babs thought he looked like a doctor or something, with his white collar and dark suit. His face was clean-shaven, and his smile revealed lovely even white teeth.

John's voice – what she'd call a posh voice – drifted up to her. 'Cecil, Cecil, calm down. It's all right. I'll sort this. Just stop crying. Have you taken your pills? Cecil, please. Try to get a hold of yourself, man.'

Cecil's crying slowed, and gradually died to a moan. 'Help me, John. I've done something very bad. I've been a very naughty boy again. You shouldn't have left me, John.'

'I had to. You were . . . well, you were managing. I'm no farmer, Cecil. You know that. I have to follow my calling. Now, let's get you inside the house, and then you can tell me where the key is, and I'll free the girl and take care of her.'

'I've been a bad boy, John. They'll put me away again. I don't want to go away to that place. Don't let them take me, John. Please!'

'It's me that's been bad. I should never have left you. I should have cared for you and given up on my dream. Anyway. We'll sort everything, I promise. Now, come on. Come into the house.'

Babs heard no more protests. All went silent. The fear that had given way to hope returned once more. She tried to think what she would do if it was Beth who was ill and had done something terrible. Would John try to save his brother? Would he help her? A fresh tear fell on her cheek for she knew if it was her and Beth, she'd do everything she could to save her sister. *Oh, Beth, I wish I'd never left you.* A pain of loss struck Babs's heart, making her bow her head and bend her body forward with the weight of her distress.

It wasn't long before she heard someone in the barn below her, and then John called out and some of Babs's fear lifted. His voice didn't sound as though he was going to do other than help her. 'Don't worry, it's only me. I have the key. I'm coming up to free you.'

To Babs, John looked like a god when his head appeared through the hatch and the sun caught the highlights in his fair hair.

'Don't be afraid, everything will be all right.'

She could only stare up at him as he stood in front of her. She didn't know how anything could ever be all right again, not now she'd had that thing done to her.

Her arm cried out against being released as the pain of movement fought against the stiffness that had settled in it.

'Let me rub it for you, it will bring the blood back into it. How long have you been here . . . No, don't be afraid. I – I . . . Oh God, Cecil hasn't . . . Has Cecil done things to you?'

Babs had cringed away from him at the word 'rub'; now she nodded to his question.

'No! Dear God, no!'

'Help . . . me. I – I want to go to me ma.'

'I'll help you. Come on, try to stand.' When she couldn't, he lifted her. 'It's barbaric what has happened to you. I'm so sorry. Let's get you down and clean you up. Then you can tell me why you're here, and how you got here. I can guess what has happened to you, and I'm so sorry. My brother, well, he's not well in his mind. He can go for a long time acting normally, but then has a kind of breakdown, when he doesn't know what he's doing, only that he wants to do it. I'm dreadfully sorry.'

Feeling safe, Babs snuggled into him, desperate for some kindness and loving contact from anyone, and he was showing her that. These last days, she'd grown up in a way that she hadn't wanted to, but now she felt like the young girl that she was. Her sobs were those of a child.

When they reached the house, Cecil was nowhere to be seen and she didn't ask where he was. John sat her on a kitchen chair. All around her was messy and dirty. The table was piled high with magazines and all manner of discarded, dirty plates, with half-eaten food with mould growing on it, and mugs with tea that had formed a skin. A loaf that looked like a stone was to the side of her, and this too was mottled with dark blue mould.

A stale smell clogged her nose, and as she glanced around, the same chaos and filth was everywhere. The stone floor was matted with mud, and the stove looked as though it hadn't been blackened for a long time. Remnants of food having boiled over stained its doors. The sink and draining board were piled high with dirty pots, and the dresser was sagging under the weight of everything imaginable that had been dumped on it, from a horse's harness to an old horseshoe and a host of tools. But despite it all, to Babs it felt like a home.

This was the first time she'd stepped inside a kitchen since she'd been six years old and she'd heard the sound that haunted her dreams – the front door of the home she and Beth had shared with their ma clicking shut behind them.

The scene weighted her heart with sadness as she saw herself in her mind's eye, holding Beth's hand on one side, trying to reassure her, and holding on to Ma's hand too, as Ma told them that they had been made to leave their home and were to seek help from the gypsies.

Tears of a different kind fell down her cheeks at the memory. Her fear was still with her, but it was now flanked by her longing to be back there. To be held by her lovely ma, and to know and understand why. Why her ma had left them with Jasmine that night. Yes, she was ill, but she'd been able to speak to them. She'd said she'd come for them later. But she hadn't. *Oh, Ma . . . Ma.*

'Here, drink this. Take it slowly now. Just sip it.'

The water cooled her burning throat and helped her to control her crying.

'That's better. Now, do you want something to eat, or shall I get you a hot bath first? The stove is lit, so it won't take long to warm the water. There's always a tub of it warming on the other stove in the scullery.'

Babs let everything happen; she didn't agree, or disagree to anything. Even after he'd taken her into the room that led from the kitchen and where he'd lit a fire and set a bath for her, she didn't protest and when he told her to undress, she just did it.

When she removed her frock and stood in her under-shift, John shook his head. 'Dear, dear, you're bruised and sore. I'm so sorry. The bath water will sting but is the best thing. Once you're clean, I'll give you some soothing ointment to apply. In the meantime, I'll leave you so you can have some privacy and see if I can find something for you to eat that hasn't gone off. Then we'll see what has to be done.'

'Don't leave me.' The words of fear just came from her and were the first she'd uttered.

'You'll be all right. Cecil is sound asleep and won't wake. His medication does that to him, and I gave it to him before I came back for you . . . I – I can see that my brother has hurt you badly. I'm so sorry. Look, I'll hum while I search and prepare something, then you will hear my voice and know you only have to call out and I'll come running to you.'

It was as he'd said – the water did sting her open sores – but at the same time, it soothed her. One thing Jasmine was always keen on was that they and everything around them should be clean at all times. This had seemed funny at first as when she was little in the playground at school, gypsies were always spoken of as being dirty and scruffy.

The thought of the little girl she had been in her former life sent Babs reeling back to the past again. Faces that had been so much in her life but had gradually disappeared came at her. One she was sure was a lady called Martha. An old lady, who she remembered was like a granny to them. She could recall too going to this lady's house for tea after school as her ma was at work. A warm feeling filled her, and she remembered that she and Beth had loved Martha, but now she could hardly bring a true picture of her face to her mind, nor anything that happened with her, other than eating their tea. Then Aunt Liz came to her. Aunt Liz had a lot of kids. They were funny and she and Beth loved to go there and play with them, but Aunt Liz disappeared. The words 'moonlight flit' came to her. She didn't know who said them, but knew it was what Aunt Liz had done.

As she leant back and closed her eyes, her da came into her mind. Her lovely, smiling da. Her world had been wonderful before he'd died. Ma had said that he'd fallen off the tower that he was helping to build. *Oh, Da, Da . . . if only you hadn't had to die.*

'How are you doing?' John's voice came to her through the door. 'The water must be getting cold now.'

'I'm all washed, ta.'

'I've found a towel and, some of my late mother's clothes for you. As you are tall and she wasn't a big woman, they should fit. Anyway, they are better than the ones you had on. I'll throw them into the room for you.'

With this, Babs eased herself out of the bath, picked up the towel and gently dried herself off, trying not to cause herself too much pain.

As she donned the garments, the silky knickers felt strange to her skin. She'd always worn the wincyette ones that Jasmine had made. The liberty bodice was fleecy and warmed her as if it was cuddling her. The skirt was navy and fitted her waist perfectly. Falling to her ankles, it was made of wool and felt soft on her legs. The twinset was also made of soft wool. Grey in colour, the jumper had a bibbed-shape neckline that was embroidered with little daisies, and the cardigan had the same embroidery around the cuffs of the sleeves. Babs thought it very pretty and not at all old-fashioned, and all fitted her well. When she was ready, she felt like a different person as she patted her damp curls into some kind of order. Somehow, she felt she'd grown up. All of her time with Jasmine and Roman, she'd been treated like a grown-up in the work they'd had to do, but had still felt like a child in the way that Jasmine fussed over them and loved them.

Yes, she could admit to herself that Jasmine and Roman had loved her and had tried to do their best for her. And even though she was going to tell of how they stole them from their ma, she didn't want anything bad to happen to them.

'Can I come in?'

'Aye.'

'Well! You look so much better. How're you feeling? I've cooked eggs for you.'

'Better, ta. But that brother of yours is a beast. He wants locking up. He did bad things to me.'

John looked shocked and embarrassed.

'He did that thing as men do to women that makes them have babbies. I don't want to have a babby.' With this frightening thought, Babs's tears came again.

'Oh dear. I'm so sorry. I don't know what to say. Come and eat and tell me how you came to be here.'

How he could be so calm when her world was so horrible, Babs didn't know. She wanted to scream at him as nothing seemed to ruffle him.

The eggs tasted good. And even though her stomach churned with the revelation that had occurred to her, she enjoyed every mouthful.

'Now, tell me, Babs, why you are here, and where did you come from?'

In that moment, Babs decided that she wouldn't tell the whole truth. She didn't want to go back. She wanted to fulfil the promise she made to herself and the silent promise that she'd made to Beth.

'I come from Blackpool. Me ma's there and I want to go back to her.'

'Blackpool! But that's miles away from here. How on earth did you get all this way from home, and how old are you?'

'I turned thirteen on me last birthday. I were forced down here by gypsies. I ran away from them and they've long gone now. I had nawwhere to go and took shelter in that beast's barn.'

'My brother isn't a beast. I know he has done beastly things to you, but he doesn't always know what he is doing.'

'He did knaw! He said he pays for it, but that I were better. You should get him locked up. It ain't safe for him to be around others. He didn't care about hurting me, only getting what he wanted.'

John looked shamefaced. 'I know. I will do something now. I hoped that I could help him to lead a normal life by leaving him to manage the farm that our father left us, but when I see how he has let it all go to ruin since his farmhand left, I want to pull out and have my share in cash and make some arrangement to take care of him. Now, after seeing what he is capable of, I'm going to get him committed to an asylum. But that's as far as I want the law involved. I couldn't bear to let him go to prison. If you had a brother or sister, you would understand.'

Babs didn't say anything. She didn't want John to know she had a sister. It would complicate things as she would have to tell him where Beth was. 'If you help me get to Blackpool, I'll not tell about owt as went on here.'

'It isn't that simple. I have a responsibility for you. You need to be examined by a doctor. Look, I'm training to be a doctor, and I have friends who are qualified and would help me out. Would you let one of them take a look at you, to make sure you're all right? They wouldn't report anything.'

'Naw. I told you, the only way I won't say owt is if you get me to Blackpool. Me ma'll take care of me.'

'Where does your ma live? What's her address? I'm not sure you're telling me the truth. I can't imagine gypsies bringing you all the way down here. Did they tie you up? Force you, or what? I think the best thing is to get you cared for medically, and then to take you to the nuns. There's a convent in Maidstone. The Sisters of Mercy. They take care of orphans and girls who have fallen by the wayside.'

'Naw! Naw, I just want to go home to me ma. Please. Please. Just give me me train fare and you'll never hear from me again.'

'I can't do that. My conscience wouldn't let me. I know that a lot is said about Blackpool being an exciting place that everyone wants to visit and for someone like you, young and alone, it must seem like the answer to your prayers. But it isn't. You're just a child, you need caring for. And the nuns are the ones to do that.'

Babs felt at a loss. What could she do? She could try to run away again, but what if she came across another beast of a man who would use her like that Cecil had done? Sighing a deep sigh, she knew she had no choice. *Oh, Ma, one day I'll get back to you, one day.*

FIVE

Having had no time to write to Liz and Molly, when Tilly walked into the shop that she was part owner of, after walking from Central Station, Tilly was greeted with shock and delight. It was good to feel the love of these two women who were like sisters to her.

'Tilly! By, lass, what blew you in? It's never an ill wind, that's for sure.'

Tilly couldn't answer this from Liz, as both she and Molly had almost knocked her over with their rush to hug her. There was a fusion of Molly's lovely red hair and Liz's fair curly locks with her own raven-black curls.

Being held in this way was what Tilly needed more than anything the world. With love, friendship and a trust that came from the past the three friends had shared.

'Eeh, was it an ill wind? What's wrong, lass? Awe, come through to the back. And this is little Ivan! He's beautiful. Hello, little one. I'm your Aunty Molly and this is your Aunty Liz. Has your ma told you about us?'

Ivan gave Molly a tired smile but didn't answer her.

'Awe, is he shy?'

'Naw. He's just at the end of his tether. A lot has happened to the poor lamb. Can you shut the shop for half an hour, Molly, and then I'll tell you all about it?'

Tommy had a different idea. 'Do you think it is as we can get settled first, Tilly, me wee love? Only, as you say, Ivan's for being overwhelmed with the suddenness of all of this, and what he saw before we left.'

'Aye, you're right, Tommy, love. We'll go up to the flat, girls, and come down in a while. Or, I tell you what. It's eleven now. How about you come up when you close the shop for dinner, eh?'

At this, Liz suggested that before they did, she would go to get them all fish and chips. 'You both look all in and'll have nowt in the cupboard upstairs.'

'Ta, Liz. That'd be grand.'

'And I'll pop a pot of tea up to you in five minutes. We've allus got the kettle on in the back kitchen, as you knaw.'

'Ta, Molly. Eeh, I miss you girls when I'm not here. But I'm not going away again. Sommat happened that's forced us back here. It's a lot for Tommy, and for me little Ivan to take in. But with you two by our sides, we'll get through, won't we, Tommy?'

'Aye, it is that we must. We've a new life to make, that's for sure. Now, away up the stairs, Tilly, Ivan is a heavy load now he's turning into a little man, so he is.'

Ivan giggled at this, and the sound warmed Tilly. Though bringing Tommy and Ivan to Blackpool wasn't caused by her, she somehow felt guilty about it. Especially as it was the answer to her dreams, but a nightmare for Tommy, and a strange world for Ivan.

* * *

The fish and chips tasted the best that Tilly had ever had. She savoured the flavour of the fried potato when she bit into it and had to wipe her mouth as the vinegar that had been sprinkled onto the chips ran down her chin. She wanted to giggle with her joy at being home, but she felt sad too for Tommy and all he'd lost, which she now related to Liz and Molly.

Liz expressed her sadness, but also gave hope. 'Eeh, Tilly, it beggars belief, and I'm right sorry for you, Tommy, but you'll be all right here. Naw one'll hound you and Tilly. Neither will they damage what belongs to you. But what d'yer think you'll do, Tommy? That's if you've had time to think about it.'

'I've had a few ideas, as it was that. I was expecting something like this, so I was for stashing a good bit of money away in one of those private banks, and keeping some ready cash, that we were able to get before we left. I'm hoping it is that it will be possible for me to put a deposit on a small holding if I can get a bank to loan the rest to me.'

'We're going to see Mr Fellows,' Tilly told them. 'Me solicitor who helped me when Martha left me that money and got this shop all sorted. He knaws a lot of folk who have connections in and around Blackpool. You remember, he helped me friend Florrie and her Reggie get settled on Lord Clefton's estate. And them coming from the workhouse an' all.'

'It is that we need land that is for having a house with it, Tilly.'

'Aye, we will, Tommy, but if we don't find some land with a house already on it, we can build one. Ha, not me and you, but builders can. I knaw a lot of builders an' all.'

'Is it that you know everyone in every trade, then?' Tommy asked.

'Naw. But me Arthur were a builder, remember?' Tilly marvelled at how she remembered her dear Arthur every day of her life, but not with the pain it used to give her. Now, she remembered him with a sort of settled love, knowing he was happy for her, and that she was living her life in a good and happy way. Not in the way she did when he first died. She shuddered at the memory.

'Eeh, we should light a fire. It's nippy up here. Your coal house out back is still full, and there's some kindling out there an' all. I'll see to it.'

'Ta, Molly.' Tilly didn't say it was her memories that had made her body shudder, but now Molly had mentioned it, she realised that it was chilly in this almost bare front room of her flat.

While Molly busied herself and Liz and Tommy chatted, Tilly looked around the room. She'd never bothered to furnish it fully, and the sofa and chair she had in this large bay-windowed room looked lost and soulless. There were no ornaments or dresser, and only an old occasional table with a cloth to cover its flaws provided a surface for their cups.

The flat had a kitchen, which again was sparsely furnished with just a central table and four chairs, a sideboard for her pots, and a stove and sink. No frills to make it look cosy. She did have a double bed in her bedroom, but she'd have to sort something out for Ivan to sleep on.

Tilly looked over at her little son. He was propped up in the chair, and as usual had a smile on his face as he watched Molly strike a match and light the kindling.

'So, me lad, what d'yer think of your first fish and chips, eh? Your mammy was raised on them, as everyone in Blackpool is.'

'Mmm. I'm for liking them, Mammy. I'll have them every day, please.'

They all laughed at this.

'That one's got an old head on his young shoulders, Tilly. He knaws what to say to please you.'

'He has, Liz. He's a good 'un. And I knaw as he loves you two already.' With this, Tilly remembered that she hadn't yet asked after Liz's husband, Dan, or Molly's husband, Will. 'So, Liz, how's your Dan? Is he doing all right on his stall?'

'Aye, you knaw Dan. He could sell snow in Iceland.'

They laughed again, and Tilly began to relax. Even Tommy looked at home now and was laughing with them all.

'And your Will, Molly, and your lads, Gerry and Brian?'

'They're all fine. Will's reet proud of the fact that Gerry and Brian love to work with leather like he does. The three of them make some lovely things out of the offcuts that Will brings home from the saddlery. I was going to show you on your next visit to see what you thought as I think they're sommat we could sell in the shop.'

'What sort of things?'

'Well, one that I love. They covered an empty wine flagon with leather – it looked like the flagon was wearing a jacket. It's eye-catching and sommat as the rich folk as come to Blackpool would love. Especially for their red wine that has to be kept warm.'

'Eeh, you've a knowledge of wines now then?'

'Naw. Ha, I haven't touched a drop since that Christmas when . . . Oh, sorry, Tilly.'

'It's all right. Neither have I. You were right when you said it would only take a drop to send me back into me drunken ways. I'm still ashamed of that Christmas, when I had too much and showed meself up.'

'Well, isn't it that something good came from it?' Tommy winked as he said this.

'Aye, Tommy, me wee Ivan. The best present I could have had.'

Ivan giggled. 'Mammy is for saying that, then she says the next will be when me sisters come home.'

'By, lad. Are you sure you're only four years old? Look at the size of you!'

'I am, Aunty Liz.'

This response brought a huge smile to Liz's face. 'Eeh, he warms your heart. You were sent for a purpose, lad. Your ma could never be sad while she has you. So, you knaws all about your sisters then?'

'Yes, it is that Mammy says that I look like them and that one day we will find them, because they are lost.'

'You do look like them. The minute I saw you, I knew you were their brother. And aye, they were sommat. The prettiest little girls, and so lovely.'

Again, a silence fell.

'Eeh, lass, I'm sorry. It's me putting a dampener on things now.'

'Naw, Liz. I want me twins talked about. I want you all to remember them and chat about their antics. Through you, Ivan will come to knaw them. And that's a good thing.'

Tommy changed the subject. 'Well, I think it is that I need to be getting to the furniture store to be buying a bed for Ivan. Will you excuse me, ladies?'

'Oh, I have a spare bed. My Will could bring it round tonight for you. It's a small one that Will made for our Brian when he wanted out of his cot and to be like his big brother in a proper bed. He's long outgrown it, and it's been stacked away for this good while. I made a mattress and bedding to fit it. It would be perfect for Ivan.'

Ivan clapped his hands together and gave Molly a lovely smile.

'Say thank you, Ivan, lad. What has Mammy allus told you? That we must allus thank folk for gifts they give us.'

'Ta, Aunty Molly.'

With this, Ivan had sealed the ready love that Tilly could see both Molly and Liz had given him. Calling them aunty had pleased them both.

'Well, it's time we opened the shop again, so we'll get going and let you rest a while. I'll get Will to bring that bed as soon as he's back from work.'

'Aye, and as the shop ain't busy, and we're on top of the orders for baskets, I'll pop down to Ma Robinson's shop and get a few provisions for you. I'll keep them down here till you're ready to come and get them.'

'Ta, Molly, and you, Liz. You're the best pals a girl could ever wish for.'

Closing the door on her friends, Tilly turned to Tommy. 'Eeh, Tommy, what d'yer reckon, lad? Can you settle?'

'Come here into me arms, so I can show you how much I can, me little Tilly.'

Tilly knew that look in Tommy's eyes.

She glanced at Ivan and saw his eyes were closed. He looked so peaceful and happy. Even in sleep, Ivan looked happy.

Looking back at Tommy, she saw a look of sheer love in his eyes.

'It is that lying with you and loving you will dispel the last of me doubts, me Tilly.'

'Aye, I've heard some excuses from you, Tommy O'Flynn, but that one's blackmail if ever I heard it.'

'It is, me darling, for at this moment, I'd tell you anything to get you into this new bed that only you have slept in. It needs christening, so it does.'

His tone, and the look in his eyes, sent a rush of feelings through Tilly. She took his hand, and with her fingers on her lips to indicate they mustn't wake Ivan, led him to her room, which he was soon to make theirs.

Taking their clothes off was a frenzy of tugging, pulling, kissing and giggles. The more they tried to be quiet, the more they collapsed into a fit of laughter.

But when they stood in front of each other, the giggling stopped. They gazed into each other's eyes and reached out to one another.

'Me little Tilly.'

'Tommy, me lovely husband.'

Being held next to Tommy's naked, firm body transported Tilly to a dreamlike place where no one could intrude. His kisses touched the heart of her and lit a flame that she had to have extinguished. Only Tommy could do that.

When he gently pushed her to lie on the bed, she went willingly and lay receptive and loving as he came down on top of her. As he entered her, she felt as if she would explode as wave after wave of exquisite pleasure built to a crescendo that ricocheted through her. 'My Tommy. My man. I love you.'

The feelings couldn't be sustained as she could tell that Tommy was at the height of his passion quicker than he'd ever been, but it was so right that he should be as it matched her own instant release.

Afterwards, they lay in each other's arms speaking words of love and Tilly knew from that moment that her Tommy was going to be all right. He would build a new life here in Blackpool and she would pick up her old one – making baskets to sell, having good times with her friends around her, but above all, praying every day that her girls would return to her, as now she was where they would begin to look.

A few days later, with the March winds whipping the promenade and the waves of the sea crashing from a great height, Tilly and Tommy caught a tram to Bispham, where Mr Fellows, Tilly's solicitor, had his office.

When they arrived, they sat across from him with his large oak desk between them. Mr Fellows listened to their tale and commiserated with them. 'I know a lot of influential people who fear an uprising in the South of Ireland. A lot admit to their fathers' treatment of the Irish farmers being very shoddy. One of my friends has refused his inheritance of a large house and acres of land over there as he doesn't agree with what his father did.'

'For sure, if he has a good mind, he should take it and lead the way. Give his tenant farmers a good deal with their rents and help them to thrive. That is a far better way than to turn his back on them.'

'Actually, I agree with you, Mr O'Flynn.' Mr Fellows smiled.

'Tommy, please. And if it is that it isn't too late, then tell your friend that what Ireland is needing is a few good landlords.'

'I will. Now, what can I do for you both?'

Tommy outlined his plans and told Mr Fellows the budget he had.

'Well, now, that's a tidy sum. And you were very astute to protect it how you did. I will need to ask around, but I don't see a problem. I do know of one place. A client of mine. He's getting on in years now and passed being able to upkeep his land. He used to have livestock but has long sold them off. It will need a big investment of money and effort, but it used to be a grand farm turning over a very good profit. I could talk to him.'

'That sounds just what I'll be looking for. How many acres?'

'A fair few, Tommy, but I don't know the exact figure. I would say about three hundred acres.'

Tilly leant forward. 'Is there a house with it, Mr Fellows, and is this man likely to want to sell?'

'Yes, Tilly, there is a house, but you'll have to use your imagination to think of it as a home. It has been neglected for a long, long time.'

'But what of the owner? Where is it that he would go?'

'The answer to that is surprising. You see, he has had a long-standing courtship with a woman who lives in Preston. It started when they were in their forties. He's never married, and she's a widow, who would never agree to marry him if she had to live on his farm with him. He has long said that if he can rid himself of it, he would, and he'd go to her.'

'Eeh, that's lovely. It makes me feel as though we'd be doing him a favour, instead of offering for his home.'

'You would, Tilly. But don't get too excited. What old Bert says isn't always what he does when it comes to it.'

When they left the solicitor's office, Tilly felt full of hope. 'By, Tommy, it's as if that place is made for us. And in Marton an' all. Mind, I'd have a ways to travel, but I can handle a horse and trap now, so I'll have to buy one and use that.'

'Ha, it is that you can, Tilly. Better than any man, I'd say. I used to love to see you coming along the lane when I were in the top field.'

'That was 'cause you knew as I had your snap tin full.'

'Aye, and if Ivan was asleep in the trap, a chance of a tumble in the grass, too . . . Them days will be for coming back to us, won't they, Tilly?'

'Awe, don't get mawdling, Tommy. 'Course they will. Naw doubt there's a top field on that land, and I'll be visiting you for a romp!'

'Och, me Tilly. You're a grand lass, so you are. And I love you with all me heart.'

'And I love you, me Tommy. Nowt'll ever alter that. And we'll make that love real wherever we are – top field in Ireland, or bottom field in Marton.'

They giggled at this.

'Right, we'd better get a cab and get home. Little Ivan was excited to be stopping with Molly and Liz, but I don't like to leave him too long.'

They hailed the first cab to come along. As it took them along the promenade, Tilly looked out and felt the love for her home town consume her. How could anyone not love the crashing waves of the sea, the liveliness of the traders calling out, and the music of the Wurlitzer? She was home. Home where she belonged. In her beloved Blackpool.

SIX

Clutching the small valise that John had packed with a flannel, soap, a spare pair of silk knickers and another blouse, Babs looked up at the huge building in front of her. Latticed with black beams, it looked lovely.

'Come on, I promise you'll be all right here.'

Not answering John, she followed him up the path, every step on the gravel that crunched under the tread of her boots deepening the dread inside her.

'I will check with the nuns that you're all right, and if . . . well, if there is an outcome from what my brother did, then I'll make sure the baby is cared for. I have an aunt who will see to it.'

None of this had any effect on Babs. It was all beyond her imagination. She had nothing to compare it with – not what life would be like inside this convent, nor what it would feel like to have a baby. None of it. And she wanted none of it. *I should tell him now. Tell him about Jasmine and Roman and me lovely sister, Beth.* But she knew he wouldn't believe her. He'd questioned her for a long time before he'd made up a bed for her on the sofa of a room at the front of the farmhouse. A lovely room that seemed as though it didn't belong to the rest of the house, despite smelling musty, as if it had been shut down for a long time. But she'd stuck to her story that she'd come from Blackpool.

It was when he asked her for her address, and to describe Blackpool, that she'd not been able to convince him. When she told him what she could remember of the streets with houses each side and of the tower that was so tall she had to lean right back to see the top of it, he'd said she could have seen those in pictures, as he'd seen the same himself. Then he said that if he wasn't so afraid for his brother, he would take her to the police, but what he was doing by taking her to the nuns was protecting them both.

When the door opened a little woman stood there. Only her face showed as the rest of her was clad in a flowing robe from the top of her head to her feet. She smiled sweetly and Babs began to feel a little better.

They followed her inside where they were met with an overwhelming smell of wax polish and a stillness which made Babs feel as if they'd left the outside world behind. Dark oak beams formed a criss-cross archway above them, and red carpeted stairs with a highly polished banister went off to the right of them. A sort of sideboard stood on the wall to their left, again polished until it shone. On top of it was a small white cloth on which stood a gleaming brass crucifix.

The nun seemed to glide rather than walk and a jingling sound followed her every step. Babs saw that this was made by a string of beads with another crucifix attached to it, which hung from her waist. This was knocking against a large key on a shiny silver chain that dangled next to the beads. There were no questions asked when John told them the lie that he'd concocted to protect his brother: 'My brother and I found this young girl sleeping in our barn and I have brought her here to be cared for. She doesn't seem to have anyone and won't tell me how she came to be on our farm. She made up a story that is so unbelievable about coming from Blackpool.'

'I'll take you to the Reverend Mother.'

Babs wanted to protest, but her mouth had dried and she felt in awe of her surroundings which, in a strange way, crushed her spirit and clothed her in a shyness she'd never experienced before.

When the nun tapped on a huge oak door with a brass knob, an unfriendly voice snapped, 'Come.'

The voice matched the stern-looking woman who sat behind a huge desk glaring at them as they entered. Babs's nerves clenched her stomach. Tears stung her eyes. She looked towards John and sensed that he too felt nervous in the presence of this formidable woman.

Dressed from the neck down in the same black and white robe as the little nun, she didn't have a flat veil but a huge, stiff, hat-like white veil that jutted out at angles and reminded Babs of the paper windmills that Roman used to make for her and Beth when they were little. He would fold stiff paper and attach it to a stick. They'd loved running with these and seeing the paper swirls whirl in the wind. A nervous giggle, which she tried to suppress, came out as a hiccup and resounded around the room. The woman's neck stretched, and her eyes bore into Babs, sending shivers of fear through her body.

'So, what have we here?'

'Her name's Barbara.' John told his story of finding her in the barn. Then he coughed. 'There's something else, Reverend Mother.'

'What? What else is there to know about this waif?'

'I – I, well, I think my brother may have . . . You see, he is ill in his mind. He doesn't see wrong from right. If he wants something, or to do something, he forces it to happen. Babs, I mean, Barbara has said that he raped her . . . But, he has a simple mind and I'm not sure that he did . . . I mean, he wouldn't know what he was doing. I'm taking him into an asylum later today.'

'By the look of her – overdeveloped for her age – I would say it was more likely that she seduced him. Is that right, girl? . . . Oh, there's no use shaking your head at me, I've seen it all. Harlots who protest their innocence. You look typical of that kind, girl!'

'Naw . . . I—'

'Don't speak unless you are spoken to. And remember, lies don't get you anywhere with me. No doubt you are now pregnant and regretting your actions and seek to lay the blame at a poor sick man's door. Well, none of it will wash with us here. You will learn to repent your sins, not deny them. And when you have, and not until then, we will help you to lead a better life. Understand?'

'B – but I'm naw sinner, I—'

'Believe me, girl, one day you won't stand in front of me and protest your innocence when you are clearly guilty. One only has to look at you to see what type of girl you are.'

Suddenly, Babs became aware of her body and how her breasts were bigger than Jasmine's were, as were Beth's, and how their hips curved, making their waists appear tiny. An image of her ma appeared in her mind and she knew that she and Beth looked just like their ma had. A distant memory came to her of men calling out things to, and whistling after, her ma and how her ma would blush and hurry on.

The Reverend Mother addressed John. 'The only truth this girl seems to have uttered is that she comes from the North. Her accent tells me that. I once met a young nun who came from up that way and she spoke the same common slang until it was beaten out of her.'

John's head turned towards Babs and as she met his eyes, she saw his shock at these words. She wanted to plead with him to help her, but he looked away and stared ahead.

'Well, you can leave her with us, Mister . . . ?'

'Redman. John Redman.'

'And what is the full name of your charge?'

'Oh, I don't know. What's your surname, Babs?'

'I – I don't knaw.' Babs didn't want to tell them that she went under Jasmine's surname, Petrilona. Not that she and Beth ever needed to tell anyone.

'Don't lie, girl! Mr Redman, I'm beginning to think we have a runaway on our hands. Probably from an orphanage, or a workhouse. You say that she wouldn't give you any information of where she's from, apart from some ridiculous story she obviously made up? And now she's being cagey about her name. I think she needs dealing with and in a very severe way so that she learns she cannot continue to lie to us. In the meantime, we will list her as Smith. Barbara Smith.'

Next to her Babs felt John shift uncomfortably. Once more, she wanted to beg him to take her away from here, but she felt as though someone had turned her to stone. She couldn't move or speak up in her own defence. She'd spoken the truth – neither her nor Beth could remember their surname.

'Reverend Mother, may I leave my address with you? I would like to be informed of Barbara's welfare and, well, if she does have a child, it will be related to me and I want to take care of it.'

'Oh, you have no need to worry about such things. Her welfare will be safe in our hands. We are Sisters of Mercy and devoted to caring for others – which of course takes in their spiritual well-being, something we take pains to instil in all our girls. And if what she has done results in the birth of a baby, then that is taken care of too. We have a list of childless couples waiting to take our babies into their homes. You need to get on with your life. It seems to me that you have enough of a burden taking care of your brother, you don't need any more encumbrances.'

'But—'

'I think you should leave this harlot with us now and just forget you ever met her. It's for the best, believe me. Her type can drag a man down with them. You look to me as if you have your feet firmly planted on the right path and your action of caring for your brother, and even for this girl who has done wrong by him, shows you are a decent man. Continue on the road you are travelling and put this experience behind you. We will pray for you and for your brother. Good day, Mr Redman.'

John hesitated for a moment, but then turned to leave.

'Naw, naw, don't leave me here, John, don't!'

'Quiet! How dare you bring your sins into my office where there is nothing but purity. Sister Anne, please take this girl to the bathroom at once and prepare her to be purified. She will soon learn that a clean life is the only one we will tolerate here!'

The fear in Babs increased. Her heart thudded against her chest at these words. She couldn't imagine what being purified would feel like, but instinctively knew it would be terrifying. The dread in her, struck her dumb once more. She made no further protest even though she felt an urge to scream and scream.

John turned to her. 'Be good, Babs, please. This is the only solution for you. If you behave, I'm sure you'll be all right. Goodbye.' He turned then and addressed the Reverend Mother. 'Thank you, Reverend Mother. I will make enquiries after Barbara and hope that you will furnish me with details of how she is. You see, I feel, despite what you have said, that it is my duty to do so. And I beg of you to reconsider what happens if there is a baby. I cannot bear to think of a relative of mine going to strangers.'

'I will consider your request, Mr Redman.'

With this, John bowed his head and left. As he did, Babs felt her last hope was gone, and that she'd been cast to the devil, for she saw the Reverend Mother as just that – a she-devil.

'Hand her over to Sister Brenda, Sister Anne. Tell Sister Brenda that this one needs cleansing more than any girl we've ever had here.'

'Yes, Reverend Mother.'

When they were out in the hallway, a surprising thing happened, and one that compounded Babs's fear.

'I'm sorry, little one, I will pray for you.'

Babs looked into the pale blue eyes of the little nun and was shocked to see tears swimming in them.

As she followed Sister Anne, she had the feeling that she was walking the plank, something she and Beth had read about in *Robinson Crusoe*, a book that one of the farmers' wives they'd worked for had given to them. They both loved reading, and had mastered the basics within a short time of starting school in Blackpool before they had been taken.

Their learning developed with reading books such as *Robinson Crusoe* and they had taken it in turn to read it to Jasmine and Roman. Both had enjoyed it so much that whenever they could, they'd bought other books for them to read. Babs's favourite had been *Adventures of Huckleberry Finn*. She'd loved reading how Huckleberry got in and out of scrapes and had always wanted to be like him. It had been this book that had given her the idea of escaping and having adventures as she searched for her ma. Never in a million years did she think that she would land where she was, or go through such horrific things.

After passing a lot of doors and seeing no one, the unnerved feeling that Babs had became deep trepidation and the thought of why the Reverend Mother had seen her as dirty and needing to be washed clean mystified her. She was clean. And was clad in the clean clothes that John had given her the day before.

When they reached the end of the long corridor Sister Anne turned to her left. In front of them now was a steep staircase. This one was covered with a thin woven carpet. 'Nearly there now.'

Her 'nearly there' took them to the top of these stairs, then onto a landing from which another set of stairs led. Babs's tired legs began to ache, but Sister Anne skipped up them in a sprightly way. When they reached the top, they were faced with another long corridor with many doors leading off it. It was a relief to Babs when Sister Anne stopped at the first one. 'Here we are.' The door she knocked on had a brass plate at eye level, which read 'Clinic'. Again, a harsh voice shouted, 'Come.'

Sister Anne seemed nervous as she opened the door. The look she gave Babs was one of pity. Babs's throat tightened.

Inside, they were met by a big, fat woman sitting at a table, an open book in front of her. She looked up from what she was reading and stared at them.

Her veil told that she was a nun, and yet, she wore the uniform of a nurse. Her veil was different again to Sister Anne's and to the Reverend Mother's. Covering her hair, as the others did, it was pleated to the crown of her head and then billowed out into huge folds of starched cotton. The nun's ruddy-looking, fat face was squashed into the tightness of the veil, making it bulge. Her eyes were what Babs would call beady. Small, and yet piercing as they stared out from baggy sockets.

'Oh, another one! And where did you get her from, Sister Anne? Don't you think I have enough to contend with? I've five girls about to birth, and three in the sick bay with a fever, besides all of those in various stages of pregnancy! No doubt this one is another holding a bastard in her womb, through her sinful ways. Who is she?'

'Barbara Smith. Reverend Mother says she is to be cleansed, more than any girl we've ever had in our care, Sister Brenda.'

'Did she now?' Sister Brenda's face lit up with a gleeful expression. 'Well, we can do that, I'm sure. In fact, I will do it myself so that I know it is done properly. I won't ask you why she needs it. I can see she has a defiant look, and her whole appearance smacks of her being a harlot. Yes, I'll enjoy washing that out of her. You can leave her with me, Sister Anne, thank you.'

Once the door closed on Sister Anne, Sister Brenda's face looked as though she had been given a present. She smiled, a non-smile as it didn't reach her eyes, or hold any kindness, but looked rather like she was savouring what she had in store. 'Well, now. A cleansing is it. I tell you, my girl, you will beg of the devil to leave you by the time I have finished with you. And that stubborn look you have is very pleasing to me, as I will enjoy turning it into one of complete submission, and all with the instruction of the holy Reverend Mother!'

This she said in a way that sounded like an insult to the Reverend Mother and caused every limb of Babs's body to begin to tremble, weakening her until she felt she would faint.

'Follow me!'

Babs, who felt that she could hardly put one foot in front of the other at this moment, didn't only cry out in her mind for her ma and Beth, but for Jasmine and Roman too. *Why did I do it? Why did I leave? What chance did I stand? Oh, Ma, help me, help me!*

But no help came, and Babs found herself being led into a bathroom and told to strip. Not daring to defy this ogre of a woman, she did as she was bid, while Sister Brenda shouted orders for buckets of water to be brought in immediately.

Two girls came in carrying the buckets, which they emptied into the large round tub that stood in the corner of the room, giving Babs a sidelong look as they passed her that told of their pity for her.

Both looked older than Babs and she guessed they were around sixteen or seventeen. They wore dark green frocks which fell to their ankles, the full length of which was covered by a navy pinafore of the type you put your head through and tied each side of your waist. Their hair was pinned back into a bun and each wore a mobcap. They gave Babs the impression that they were terrified of Sister Brenda as they moved as though they were scurrying, desperate to avoid her.

'Hurry up, bring more!'

While this was going on, Sister Brenda donned a thick brown apron which covered the white one she already wore and rolled up her sleeves. Babs took in the bar of carbolic soap and scrubbing brush that stood on a wooden stool next to the tub and prayed that the brush wasn't going to be used on her, but as she did, she had the sinking feeling that it would be. Her imagination wouldn't give her what the stiff bristles would feel like. Her breath caught in her lungs as she stared at it.

'Get in!'

Babs didn't move.

'I said, get in!' With this, Sister Brenda reached out and grabbed Babs's arm, gripping it so tightly that Babs cried out with the pain it caused.

'Do as I say!'

Unable to resist the force of the woman, Babs was flung towards the tub and crashed into it. The tub rocked on the bricks that it stood on. Babs grabbed the sides of it to steady herself, then stepped onto the smaller wooden stool that stood beside it and climbed in. The icy-cold water stung her feet.

The bathroom door opened, and the girls appeared again. One kept her eyes lowered but the other looked up at Babs, who now had both feet in the water and was standing shivering from head to toe. She had a pleading expression in her eyes as if begging forgiveness as she obeyed the sister's instructions and doused Babs with the water.

The impact took Babs's breath away.

'Sit down, girl!'

Babs opened her dripping eyes and saw that Sister Brenda was talking to her. Not wanting to, but feeling compelled to obey, she lowered herself. Thankfully, her body had adjusted to the cold and the feel of the water touching her bare bottom wasn't as bad as she dreaded. Grasping her knees as she couldn't straighten her legs, Babs waited, fearful of what might happen next.

The second girl stepped onto the small stool. Babs looked up at her, but the girl avoided her eyes.

'Go on! What're you waiting for?' Sister Brenda's voice bellowed out. The girl cringed but then lifted her bucket high. A whimper that Babs wasn't conscious of making came from her as she bowed her head and braced herself for the onslaught of yet another bucket full of cold water to be thrown over her.

'Emma, no! Don't!'

Babs looked up at the sound of this desperate cry from the second girl. As she did, she saw Emma turn and throw the contents of the bucket.

A gasp followed by a cry and then the clattering of the bucket falling to the floor had Babs staring in disbelief as she registered what had happened.

Sister Brenda's eyes stared out of their fleshy sockets. Her body, soaked from head to toe, shivered uncontrollably. Shocked gasps came from her.

'Oh, Emma, girl, what've you done?' A wail of distress took Babs's attention and she looked towards the girls huddled together in the corner of the room. Emma was sobbing. 'She had it coming to her, Rita. She's a brute. I – I couldn't throw it over the girl, I couldn't.'

Emma's voice seemed alien to the looks of her. It was a posh voice, which didn't fit with the surroundings, the way she was dressed or with what was happening.

'You wicked girl! I – I'll kill you for this!'

Instead of cringing away in fear, Emma took herself out of Rita's embrace and stood up straight. An air of defiance was in her expression as she answered. 'Just try! You are the wicked one. And you deserved what I did. How can you be so cruel to this poor young girl?'

'How dare you speak to me like that and in that tone? Get out! Get out both of you! And just you wait, you'll rue this action! You mark my words.'

'Come on, let me help you out of there.' Babs couldn't believe the bravery of Emma, who now stood on the stool again and was extending a hand to her.

'Leave her alone!'

'No! I'm taking her with me. This treatment is barbaric and I'm not standing for it anymore!'

Sister Brenda had fully recovered now and though she still shivered with cold, she moved forward and grabbed Emma and flung her across the room. Emma's head smacked against the far wall. Her body slumped to the floor.

Rita's screams filled the room, blocking out all conscious thoughts, leaving Babs feeling as though she'd descended into hell. She stared at Emma, saw her head was slumped to one side and watched the trickle of blood run down and into her ear before the sight was blocked out by the huge body of Sister Brenda as she lunged towards the hysterical Rita.

It was the sister's raised fist that spurred Babs into action. In a flash, she stood and leapt towards the sister. She landed on the woman's back, grabbed her neck and kicked with all her might, digging her knees in as hard as she could.

'Get off! Let go! My God, you girls are going to pay for this!' Her sudden jerking movement caused Babs to drop to the floor. A vicious, stinging kick landed in her ribs, taking her breath from her and leaving her feeling weakened and unable to fight back. The second kick made her retch.

'You filthy tyke!'

But these words disappeared beneath an even louder, blood-curdling scream which hailed a rush of cold air. Looking up, Babs saw Rita had somehow climbed up to the window above the tub and was pulling herself up to it. Realisation of what she had in mind had Babs frantically trying to remember how many steps she'd climbed to reach this level. The answer had her calling out, 'Naw! Naw!

But Rita disappeared amidst the terrible noise of Sister Brenda's scream joining that of Rita's, before both trailed off into a silence.

Sister Brenda bent over the tub, her body shaking as she wailed, 'Why? Why? Dear Lord, aren't I tasked with enough? Oh God! Oh God!'

Babs had heard the saying 'God should strike them dead' and at this moment she wished He would do just that to this wicked woman.

The door burst open, taking the thought from her. A white-faced Reverend Mother came through, followed by three other nuns. One was a weeping Sister Anne, the other two wore nurses' uniforms and veils identical to Sister Brenda's.

'What happened? Sister Brenda, for the love of God, what happened? I was on my way up when I saw Rita hurtling past a window. Sister Joan ran back down and I . . . Oh, no! Emma! Emma!' Stepping over Babs, the Reverend Mother went over to the unconscious Emma. 'Quick! Help her. One of you nurses, help her now!'

Nothing seemed real to Babs, not even Sister Anne's voice as she knelt down beside her asking. 'Are you hurt? What happened? Did Rita jump?'

Babs could only nod.

'Don't ask that one! She'll only lie. She caused it all. Rita didn't jump. She pushed her!'

Finding her voice, Babs cried out against this from Sister Brenda. 'Naw, naw, I didn't. Emma threw the water . . . and – and—'

'Liar!' Sister Brenda's face screwed into an ugly mask as she spat these words at Babs. Babs couldn't believe her ears as what Sister Brenda went on to say was so far from the truth: 'She threw the water! She took the bucket from Emma and threw the water over me. Then when Emma went to stop her, she . . . she pushed her. Rita tried to intervene, as I was in shock, but . . . Oh God have mercy on her for what she did. The little vixen g – grabbed Rita! I'd opened the window earlier to let in some air. Rita was pushed and landed against it. I – I . . . Oh, Reverend Mother, I saw her lift Rita's feet. I dashed forward, but Rita was gone in an instant. I – I grabbed that one, and I admit that in my anger I threw her across the room. She's a devil, a murderer!'

'Naw, naw, she's lying! Emma will tell you!' Babs turned, desperately seeking to see that Emma was all right, but the sister attending her turned and shook her head.

'You'll hang! Do you hear me? You'll hang, and I'll testify so as you do!' With this, Sister Brenda began to sob. 'Oh, help me, help me! I cannot bear it, I can't. Two of my girls, and to see such carnage!'

Matron took charge. 'Sister Elizabeth, tend to Sister Brenda. And Sister Anne, get that slut locked into a solitary room. I'll send the gardener for the police. We need her to be removed, and now! Get her out of my sight!'

Babs looked around her, at the accusing faces, and then towards the deathly white body of Emma. A tear for this lovely girl seeped out of the corner of Babs's eye. She couldn't cry for herself or take in that all believed that she had killed Rita and Emma, for surely, both were dead, but she prayed. *Help me. If you are really there, God, please help me.*

SEVEN

Tilly walked down the promenade, pushing Ivan in his basket chair. She was on a trip to Dan's stall. She hadn't visited it in the six weeks she'd been home and though she'd seen Dan on a couple of occasions, she hadn't really caught up with him and been able to ask how he was.

Tilly had met Dan before Liz had got to know him. He'd offered her help when she was down on her luck and needed to have an outlet for her basket work. 'You can pitch up next to me, lass. Spread a blanket out and put your baskets on it. I reckon with the quality of your wares, you'll bring trade to me stall.'

This had been just after Jeremiah had died, and Tilly was homeless. But Tilly hadn't made it back to the stall the next day, or for a long time after, as she'd taken to the gin to drown her sorrows, then been arrested and judged as insane. She shuddered now at the memory of the horrid place she'd landed in, but she was glad that it had brought Liz back into her life as Liz too was an inmate after having suffered a terrible tragedy and temporarily losing her mind.

Together they'd become strong again and made it back to Blackpool where Liz met Dan. They were such a happy couple now.

'Hello, Tilly. By, it's good to see you, lass. And the young 'un an' all. How are you, Ivan, me lad?'

'I'm going to be getting a new toy, Uncle Dan.'

Tilly marvelled at how quickly Ivan had accepted her special Blackpool friends as his aunts and uncles. And Dan was special. It had been he who had given herself and Liz their first chance, when he'd shared the cost of the pitch they had on the prom back then.

After Dan had a few words with Ivan, Tilly asked, 'How are you, Dan? I've brought you a bite to eat. Liz sent it. I told her I was going to take advantage of this nice weather and take me little Ivan out for a walk and she made good use of me.'

'Aye, it's a bonus to have it like this so early in April; makes me work a lot easier when the sun shines. So, I take it that you're not here because you want to be, though I'm grateful for the snap.'

Tilly laughed. She'd forgotten that the men called their sandwiches snap. 'Of course I am, you daft apeth. I've bought a billycan an' all with some hot tea in it. I'll stop a while and have a cuppa with you. How's trade?' Tilly looked around Dan's stall. It always fascinated her, laden as it was with all sorts of knick-knacks. From shoe brushes, to ornaments and kitchen utensils, Dan seemed to carry every line of stock you could imagine.

'I miss having you all with me, lass. But I'm reet proud of how the three of you are doing. Liz loves her work in the shop and being involved in making the smaller baskets.'

'Yes, it worked well when we were all here with you, but the weather played havoc with the cane and willow. I was glad when Liz and Molly consented to go into a shop.'

They sat down on a couple of old stools that Dan kept behind his stall. 'You have a nice set-up now, Dan. This structure that holds up the canvas shelter looks very sturdy.'

'It is. It keeps me dry, and cool, but it can never warm me when the cold snap comes. I feel the cold more every year.'

This reminded Tilly of how much older Dan was than she and Liz. He was a good ten years their senior.

'So, apart from going for a walk and bringing me snap, what else brings you meandering down the promenade?'

'Two things, Dan. I've to call on a chap who's designing a house along the way there. He has some rich clients and wants to show me some drawings of a vase he'd like me to make, and the situation it will be in. Eeh, I've not done owt like this before, I feel nervous about it.'

'I would an' all. You should have brought Molly or Liz with you. I don't trust no blokes around you, Tilly.'

'Eeh, Dan, don't say that. I can handle meself. I hate to be thought of like that. I'm a business woman on a business meeting.'

'Well, you be careful. How far is it? I can come with you. Pauline'll watch me stall; we often keep an eye out for each other's, when nature calls.'

Pauline had the stall next to Dan's. She sold embroidered cloths, some of which Tilly wanted to buy, as she was trying to make the flat homely, even though they may not be there long.

'Talking of Pauline, Dan, will you watch Ivan a mo for me? I'll pop along and do a bit of shopping at her stall.'

'And not mine then?'

'Ha, I will actually – them fancy jugs. I like them. They'd stand on me dresser. How much are they?'

'Threepence for the pair, to you, Tilly.'

'Ta. Wrap them for me, I'll be back.'

At Pauline's stall, Tilly bought a matching set of runners for her sideboard, antimacassars for her sofa and the new chair she'd bought, and a full tablecloth. 'Ta, Pauline. By, you're nifty with that needle of yours. These are lovely. I love the roses you've stitched on them.'

'Ha, I do it in me sleep now, love. You're very welcome. I love me stuff to go to them as I knaw.'

Getting back to Dan, Tilly stood a moment at the sound of Ivan giggling. Dan had a puppet on his hand and was acting out a scene with him, talking to the puppet and then throwing his voice so it seemed as though the puppet was talking back to him. 'Another one of your party tricks, eh, Dan? By, what with your piano playing, and now this, you're a one-man show.'

They both laughed and Ivan joined in with them. A lovely sound that warmed Tilly's heart. 'Well, I'll get on then. See you in a while, Dan. I'll pick up me purchases when I return.'

'Righto, Tilly. Now, mind what I said.'

The house wasn't far from Dan's stall, which was in the garden of a similar house. Many of these houses were only occupied for a short while in the summer, and their owners rented part of their front gardens to traders. It was exciting to walk along and to hear them all calling out, vying for custom. Ivan clapped his hands with joy as one trader stepped forward and gave him a big sugar mouse in a triangular paper bag. 'Ta, how much?'

'Nowt, lass. Your young 'un has made my day, with his cheery smile on this grey afternoon. My pleasure.'

Tilly smiled. Ivan had that effect on everyone. Well, most folk, if they could see beyond his disability. Bending and tucking his blanket around him, she kissed his cheek. 'Wait till we come out of this house before you start on that, Ivan, lad. I don't want your fingers all sticky.'

'I'm for thinking to keep it so that you and Pappy can have some. You can hit it with your rolling pin. It made me giggle when you broke that stick of rock, Mammy.'

'Aye, it shot everywhere. And that's kind of you, me lad. I'm partial to sweet things. I'll enjoy that. I'll have his tail.'

Ivan laughed then looked very cheeky. 'And I'll be having his bottom!'

'Ivan! You rude thing.' They both giggled and Tilly swelled with love for her son. Two little girls came to her mind, but she didn't dare dwell on the picture. She'd never get through this coming interview if she did.

The designer had been into her shop previously and introduced himself as Malcolm Stanley. A funny name, Tilly had thought, as it sounded like two Christian names.

When he opened the door, he greeted her with a flourish, which made Tilly giggle. Ivan copied him, which nearly undid her.

'Oh, you came! Come on in. I'm so excited to show you what I have in mind. Don't mind the builders and watch your step. Through here. Come into my grand creation . . . The conservatory! Isn't it divine?'

Tilly knew she was giggling as much from relief as anything else, as Dan had unnerved her. She was glad she hadn't allowed him to come with her, as she wasn't sure how he would take to someone like Malcolm.

'Now. I have a vision of this huge vase standing right there! I will fill it with pampas grass, so it has to be made of wicker. I want something like this.' Malcolm unrolled some drawings. Excitement shot through Tilly as she gazed at the twisted design. 'Eeh, that's grand.'

'And you think you can make it?'

'I would love to try, but aye, I reckon I can figure it out.'

'It has to be exclusive, I don't want any more being made. Just the one. It is to be unique. And, if you can do that, and I am happy with it, there will be other commissions for you. I'm thinking of a chair there. Something that wraps around you when you sit in it. What do you think?'

'If you draw it, I will make it. I made this chair for my son.'

'Really! Well, little man, you have a very clever mummy.'

'Mammy. She's me mammy.'

'Oh?'

'He was born in Ireland. He has their way of talking.'

'Charming. Charming little boy. Lovely smile. You should have his portrait painted. I know someone who would love to paint him.'

'That'd cost a lot, wouldn't it?'

'We could do a deal. My friend is a wonderful artist. He would do the painting for you, if you gave me a special rate for what I order.'

Tilly liked the idea. 'I'll let you knaw. I'll make the vase and tell you the price, then you can tell me if that's near to what your friend would charge.'

'Done. Now, when could you have this done for me?'

'Give me a week.'

'Wonderful, darling. A week it is.'

With this, Malcolm almost danced to the door to open it for her. 'I simply love it when everything starts to come together. Goodbye, you two. I'll see you in one week.'

Once outside, Tilly felt as though a whirlwind had blown through her. She couldn't help but have a smile on her face.

'He was for being a funny man, Mammy. All sort of flouncy, like my rag mule. Papa says he's flouncy.'

'Floppy. Mule is floppy, but aye, lad, you're right, flouncy is a good word to describe Malcolm. Well, let's get home. I've me work cut out, but eeh, I'm excited. I love to turn me hand to sommat different.'

Tilly had a lightness to her step as she walked back to Dan. 'That went well, Dan. I reckon as I've got meself a good commission there.'

'Naw one can resist you, Tilly.'

'Eeh, it's nowt to do with me skills then? Cheeky. Anyroad, I'll allus be safe around the Malcolms of this world. He was lovely.'

'Oh? Well then, I shouldn't have worried. I nearly came after you. I was going to give you another five minutes.'

Tilly felt relief that he hadn't done so – though she would have loved to see his face on meeting Malcolm.

'Well, young Ivan, I'll say me goodbyes to you. Shake me hand, as that's what men do.'

Ivan put his hand out, chuckling as Dan shook it. With his other hand, Dan slipped the puppet into Ivan's chair. 'Now, you practise with that, lad, and come Christmas, me and you'll put on a show. How's that?'

'I'd be loving that, Uncle Dan.'

'Good lad.'

Dan had a tear in his eye as he said this. He was obviously moved by Ivan's plight. Tilly didn't let herself think about it, as if she did, she'd never cope. Ivan had a good life. He loved folk, loved to make them laugh. It came to her how intelligent he was too. She'd ask Molly to give him some lessons in reading and writing as she knew he could master it. It would open up such a lot to him. He loved her to read to him, a skill that Molly had taught her when they'd first met. Once more her mind went back to her twins and how proud she had been to have them start school. Both had been exceptionally clever. She hoped with all her heart that Jasmine was taking care of them and allowing them to go to school. But then she pulled up this thought with a start as she realised that if they had been to school, they would be leaving very soon and taking up work positions. At this thought, she couldn't stop the tear that escaped from the corner of her eye.

'Mammy, are you sad?'

'Naw, lad, I'll be all reet.'

'What's "reet", Mammy?'

'Oh, it's a way the Northerners say "right". I used to say it all the time, but it slips out now and again . . . Well, here we are. Did you enjoy our walk, lad?'

'I did, Mammy. Especially playing with Uncle Dan. I love Uncle Dan. Oh, and the man called Malcolm was for making me laugh.'

'Me too. Flouncy Malcolm.'

They both giggled at this and the moment had passed for Tilly. She could cope once more; she had to for the sake of little Ivan. He needed a happy home and a happy mammy, not someone moping over the past. *Not that that stops me. Oh, me little Beth and Babs. I long for you every day, me lasses.*

'You're back then? How did it go?'

'Oh, it were grand, Liz. I've a real challenge on and I'm really looking forward to it.'

'Eeh, how someone can get so excited over making baskets and things, I'll never knaw. I love doing it, but for you, ever since you've been knee high to a donkey, it's been such a big thing in your life. I reckon as it'd break your heart if owt happened and you couldn't work with your cane and willow again.'

'It would. It would be like cutting me right hand off. It's kept me going at times, Liz. It's been a saviour to me and you.'

'Aye, it has. We'd have never have got out of that asylum without your skill. By, I still think of them chairs we mended – well, you did and I helped. They were falling to pieces and you made them like new.'

'Aye, that were a terrible time for us, but it had its compensations. I met me Tommy, and we made a difference to the inmates' lives.'

'We did. We should go back and visit one of these days. See if Gertrude's still there and if she's all right.'

'Aye, we'll do that. Dan said ta for his snap, by the way.'

'Eeh, they say the way to a man's heart's through his belly; it is with that one. He could eat a house could Dan.'

Scooping Ivan up, Tilly carried him upstairs. 'You're getting to be a lump, Ivan, me lad. I'll be glad when we move into a house and I don't have to take you up and down stairs all day.'

'Sorry, Mammy, I'll try not to grow, so I will.'

A funny feeling shivered through Tilly. 'Naw, don't say that, lad. I want you to grow. I want you to be a big strong man like your pappy.'

She snuggled him into her. She wanted to hold him like this forever, and was sorry that she'd complained now, even if it was in jest. For she knew that if she had to carry him when he was twenty, she would do. And, she told herself, there was no reason why she shouldn't as the sea air was doing Ivan good. He had a lot less trouble with his breathing, though his legs and other problems hadn't improved. Sighing, Tilly got on with the job of changing Ivan and making him comfortable.

Tommy came in at that moment. 'Hello. Aren't I the lucky one! Me two favourite people in all the world waiting to greet me.'

Kissing his offered lips, and waiting while he kissed Ivan, Tilly asked, 'Any news?'

'No. The solicitor is fed up with me, so he is. He said he is still negotiating, but that everything is looking good. The old man is sorting things out with his lady friend. It seems now that it's come to it, she is not for being so keen.'

Despite this meaning a potential disappointment, they both laughed.

'I can't blame her. It's a lot to go from seeing your man when you want to and having him under your feet.'

'Oh, and is that what I am now as I'm not working?'

'Aye. You're under me feet, and I love you being so.'

'Is it sure that you are? Haven't you been gadding about today and meeting posh men from London then?'

'I have, and a lovely man he is too, isn't he, Ivan?'

'He's a flouncy man, Pappy. He does little dances and waves his arms like this.' Ivan put his arms up and did flapping movements with them.

Tommy smiled a knowing smile. 'Oh, it's flouncy that he is. Well, that's for making him a very nice man, I'm sure. Kind and gentle. It's glad I am that you both made his acquaintance.' With this, Tilly saw Tommy visibly relax and she wondered at him being a little jealous. Well, she'd have to reassure him, as she didn't want him unsettled in any way.

'No more talk of flouncy men. I'm going to the chippy for our tea. I've had naw time to cook today.'

At this both her men clapped their hands. Tilly smiled. *It seems me men are settling in well to Blackpool. Thank God for fish and chips.*

EIGHT

Babs lay awake. The darkness around her never eased much, day or night, for the cell she sat in only had a small window very high up, making her think she was in a cellar. There were four others in the cell. Older women who were all a comfort to Babs.

During the day they talked about their lives. Two were prostitutes; another had been caught stealing food from the market stalls, and one, who just sat in the corner night and day, the women told her was known as mad Lilly, who lived on the streets as a bag lady, and was glad to be brought into the prison every now and then, for the warmth and the food. She never spoke, just sat picking at her clothes, or rocking backwards and forwards. Sometimes she would get distressed and start to pull her hair out and to wail in a horrible way that frightened Babs. But the prostitute called Sally would calm her.

Sally and her mate, who had the funny name of Pixie, were a lively pair. 'When the assizes are on, you watch us get off and be set free. Always happens. We know most of the judges, you see. Ha! We've slept with them and know what they like. They fear us exposing them. This is just a little rest for us, ain't it, Pixie?' Sally had said earlier. This had prompted Doreen, the thief, to say that when she got out, she might join them as it seemed they'd got life sorted.

'Don't you believe it,' Pixie had said. 'We don't have it good. A lot of the men treat us rough; I've had many a beating. But it's a living. We've got a decent pimp and a nice flat. We can't grumble.'

Babs hadn't known what a pimp was and was shocked to find out it was a man who controlled the girls and that they had to give him half of what they earned.

Doreen, Sally and Pixie were kind to her and believed her story. Both Sally and Pixie had said they'd had dealings with the nuns at that convent, which is where they'd met. Their stories made Babs realise how circumstances beyond your control can drive how you end up living your lives, as each of these women had been raped when just a bit older than she was. They'd held her in their arms when she'd told them of what had happened to her at the hands of Cecil.

'Well, if you're having a baby because of it, you might get sent to another convent till it's born and then have to do whatever sentence they give you.'

Babs had asked if they thought she would hang. None of them had reassured her that she wouldn't. 'Just tell them your story and stick to it. That's all you can do, love,' Sally had said. Then she had taken Babs in her arms again and rocked her as she'd cried uncontrollably.

The thought of being hanged haunted her day and night. More so in the night as she lay awake, like now, and listened to the gentle snores of the women. A terrible fear encased her, and her body shook. Trying to make herself feel better, she thought of Beth, and wished with all her heart that she hadn't left her. She should have waited until she was older, when she might have known more about the ways of the world and looked after herself better. It might have been that Jasmine and Roman would have agreed then to take them back to Blackpool.

A picture of her ma came to her, as it often did. Always it was as she was when they last saw her, happy and dancing, then that would be spoilt by her falling to the ground. If only she could remember her surname. That would help her to get folk to believe her about her ma. This had been her quest for most of the time in here. She remembered that all the children had been asked to stand and say their name and where they lived on the first day of school, but that was the only time she could remember using it. *I must have known it then, though*.

She thought of Beth standing next to her. Beth had been so shy that she couldn't get the name out, and she had stood and said, 'Me and me sister are twins.'

'We know you are, and once you give your names, I will pin a badge on each of you so that I know which is which. Now, do you want to tell me what each of your names are.'

'Aye, this is Beth – she's Elizabeth really, but Beth is what Ma and Da and everyone call her.' When she told the teacher her own name, the teacher had asked for their surname. But though Babs had gone over and over this scene in her head, she couldn't remember what her answer had been.

She wondered if Beth remembered it and wished with all her heart that she could ask her.

'Come on, lazy bones. The porridge is here. Get stuck into it and fill your belly, girl.'

Babs woke with a start. She couldn't remember falling asleep. But memory came back to her now of the dream she'd been having that Beth was ill and calling out for her, and the feeling of desperation she'd felt in the dream wouldn't leave her. Beth needed her. There was something wrong. *Oh, why did I leave?*

Two days later, Babs was shocked when one of the women wardens came to fetch her. She looked towards Sally. 'You'll be all right, love. It'll be a solicitor, or a doctor, they only fetch you for one or the other.'

Taken to a small room with just a table and two chairs in it, Babs was greeted by a man who told her that he was a solicitor and that the court had appointed him to her case. He was about the same age as Roman and had a nice face – rounded and smiley. His hair was thinning and combed straight back; it looked dark from the oil he'd used, but his waxed moustache that curled upwards at each end was ginger.

His greeting was friendly, and made Babs feel at ease. He said his name was Mr Drayford, and that it would be his job to prepare a defence for her. 'You'll appear at the assizes first, and they'll set a date for your trial. There's not many as young as you who go through the court on such serious charges. But let's make a start, Barbara, by you telling me exactly what led to you being accused of murder.'

He didn't interrupt her and when she'd finished her tale, he looked through his papers. 'You said that two girls died? Well, I've only been told of one. The one who it was alleged you pushed out of the window.'

'Emma didn't die? They . . . well, I thought . . .'

'No, there was only the one death. Though the girl it is alleged that you pushed towards the wall is mentioned on the charge. She lost her baby as a result and you're facing a charge of grievous bodily harm towards her.'

'Naw, I didn't harm her, I didn't! She'll tell you. It were her who threw the water at Sister Brenda and Sister Brenda as threw her against the wall. And naw one killed Rita, she just jumped! Please believe me.'

The solicitor was quiet for a moment. 'I will try to contact Emma. The statement from the convent says that she was discharged. They had her previous address, but they believe the family moved and they say they don't have her current one. I'm not sure why. I will pay a visit to the convent myself to see what I can find out. I want you to know that I believe you. But I have to warn you, Barbara, that it will be hard to convince a jury to do so without Emma's testimony. You are calling a nun a liar and a bully and that isn't the impression that nuns give. They are looked on as holy women doing God's work and making sacrifices. You're not in a good position at all.'

'If you believe me, won't it mean as others do an' all?'

'No, for the reasons that I have explained.'

'Will Sister Brenda have to tell her story in the court?'

'She may be allowed to just write it all down.'

Babs was silent at this. Nothing seemed fair. But then the question came to her that haunted her every hour. 'Will I hang?'

'No. You are too young. That's not to say that capital punishment – hanging – won't be the sentence, but if it is, you will be reprieved. The law is being looked at and should be changed, but in the meantime the sentences on anyone under eighteen aren't carried out. You will go to prison, though, and it will be a long time before you're freed. Have you no family? There's none listed.'

'Aye, I have a ma and I were trying to get to her when this farmer bloke held me in his barn and . . . well, he did things to me.'

'Oh? Tell me about your mother and this man, what happened?'

Babs readily told him of her ma but found it difficult to tell him about Cecil and what he did.

'Don't worry, I understand. And I think we should get you examined by a doctor. I'll make sure that is arranged. Now, I am happy with your story regarding what happened, but it says in your notes that you won't say where you came from. How did you become separated from your mother? Where have you lived? Are you running away from somewhere? I have to know all this, otherwise everything else you tell me, or the jury, will not hold any substance.'

'What's substance?'

'They won't believe anything you say. We have to know your story from the beginning.'

Babs thought about this. Something inside her didn't want to get Jasmine and Roman into trouble, but she could see how important it was that she told Mr Drayford everything. Taking a deep breath, she started from the time she and Beth were stolen.

'But that's preposterous! And sounds like something you have read in a book. Can you read?'

'Aye, I can, but what I say is the truth. They're camped at Butterworths Farm near to Maidstone. Me sister's with them.'

'Let me write that down. *Butterworths Farm* . . . Dear me, there is so much for me to check and sort out that I will have to ask for the trial to be set a good few months ahead. I'm sorry, Barbara, but that will mean you're here, or wherever the judge places you, for a good while yet.'

'Naw! I can't stand it, I can't. I want to go back to Jasmine and Roman. I'll not run away, I promise.'

'I won't be granted that. Not with gypsies. They are notorious for disappearing. I doubt that I will find them where you say they were even now. The moment gypsies think there is trouble coming to them, they are gone.'

Despite all she'd been through telling Mr Drayford everything that had happened, Babs had remained strong, but the truth of what he just said hit her hard and took her strength from her. Tears rolled down her cheeks.

'Don't despair, child. I will do all I can. I plan to look up the records for twins born in Blackpool in 1891, or thereabouts, and see if I can locate your mother. There's always hope. And I can tell you, when I believe a client, I pull out all the stops to help them. It just takes time, that's all.'

'Ta, Mr Drayford.' This was said through her sobs. Now she'd let go, she couldn't stop. Mr Drayford rang the bell that was on the table between them.

'Oh, crocodile tears, is it? Well, girl, they won't wash with us, nor with Mr Drayford. We've seen it all, haven't we, Mr Drayford?'

'Maybe not quite all, Miss Perkins. This youngster is a little different. And it doesn't do to put everyone you come across in the same basket. There's a lot of different circumstances that bring people to where they are.'

'Oh, well, if you say so, Mr Drayford, but I know the kind that are brought in here. They're all the same. Tough as old boots until they think they have someone with a soft heart to listen to them. You need to watch out for them.'

'Good day, Miss Perkins.'

'Good day to you, sir.'

'Goodbye, Babs. Keep your chin up, this could all turn out right for you.'

'Huh! That'll be the day. On a downward path this one, you mark my words.'

Mr Drayford let Miss Perkins have the last say. As he walked away, Babs wanted to shout after him to come back, but she kept quiet, knowing that Miss Perkins was one to dole out a few clouts around the ear, and she didn't feel up to having that happen to her.

The jangling of Miss Perkins' keys set Babs's nerves on edge. When they reached the cell, and the lock clicked open, Babs felt her heart drop with the thought of returning to the confines of the cell. The shove she was given sent her reeling, only to be caught by the lovely Sally. 'There, there, love, don't cry. What happened?'

Between sobs, Babs told them.

'But that's great news, darlin'. You've a good man in Mr Drayford, he really fights for his clients. If there's anything to be done, he'll do it. Have faith, love. It'll all turn out right in the end.'

'But he says it could take months.'

'Yeah, that's right. None of this can be hurried. You're on serious charges, girl. He's got his work cut out. I'm glad that he's going to have you looked at by a doctor too.'

'Yeah, come on, girl.' Dorothy patted her back. 'Buck up. It ain't the end of the world, it's the best news you've had in a while.'

None of it felt like good news. Jasmine and Roman had more than likely moved on. No one knew where Emma was, though Babs was so happy that she hadn't died. But even if found, she didn't see Rita jump. But, yes. She did have hope. Mr Drayford believed her, and she trusted him. Men like him – solicitors and the like – could find out anything, couldn't they?

Beth woke feeling shivery. Her throat rasped when she swallowed. Memory hit her as it had every morning on waking, and the terrible feeling of loss engulfed her. She missed Babs so much. The cold feeling turned to a burning one, and she threw the woollen blanket off.

The darkness of the night cloyed at her and hot tears fell from her eyes. *Babs, Babs, why did you leave me? Where are you?*

Seven weeks had passed, and Jasmine and Roman were talking of moving on. The farmer they'd all been working for was satisfied with their work and would have no more for them until the harvest. They would go to a few gypsy fairs and be travelling most of the summer. How would Babs find them? Yes, she knew about the fairs and what time of year they were, but in between these times they could be camping anywhere, and usually with other gypsies.

Beth enjoyed these times much more than the work they did in the spring as she loved to be with other families. She enjoyed playing with the little ones and teaching them to read, and she liked being with those of their own age, though she hated how the boys thought it their right to molest the girls and treat them as if they were nothing.

In preparation for this new season, their work now would be to gather bunches of heather and make tiny bouquets. And to help Jasmine with the crafts she made, and Roman with the wooden pegs he fashioned. For these, they would gather branches from pine trees – strip the bark from them, and then Roman would sit hours cutting the shapes and shaving them. It had been Beth's and Babs's job to bind the two pieces together with wire.

The heather they would give away, telling folk that it was lucky heather, and this would be an opening for them to sell their wares. Often this would be accompanied by a tale or two from Jasmine of what might happen in the future of those stopping to accept. It would be then that she and Babs would try to sell them pegs, or whatever Jasmine had made, from lavender bags to peg bags, and tablecloths to cushions. Beth always loved all that they had to offer and felt proud of Jasmine's skills.

She was looking forward, too, to learning the skills herself. She and Babs had mastered the basic sewing of hems, and the neat stitching of seams, but this year they were to learn the cutting out of patterns and Jasmine said they could make the pin cushions, which were always a good seller.

She and Babs had planned that this summer they would try to convince someone to help them to get back to

Blackpool, but Babs's impatience had got the better of her and she hadn't waited. Now Beth felt so alone, and so afraid for Babs.

A sudden feeling of sickness swept over her. Getting off the bed, her body swayed. The tickly cough she'd had the day before hacked from her, leaving her feeling as if she would choke.

'What is it, Beth, me little darling?'

The sound of a match being struck was followed by a shadowy light as Jasmine lit a candle. The curtain between their bed and Beth's swished back and light doused the rest of the wagon. 'Are you not well, little one?'

Beth couldn't speak. Her head and body were burning. Her throat was dry, and the hacking cough took what breath she had.

'Get back into bed, Beth. I will get you a potion that will make you better.'

Beth's head swam. Jasmine's voice sounded booming one minute and then faded the next until she could hardly hear her.

'Is it that the wee child is ill, Jasmine?'

'It is. I think it is the shock she has had. She has got low in her spirits. Our lovely Babs has been gone this seven weeks now. Oh, Roman, will she ever come back to us?'

'Now, it isn't that you should lose hope, that will not be for helping Beth.'

Beth lay back. She accepted the potion. It tasted of mint and honey and she felt her throat ease. Jasmine and Roman's hushed voices swirled around her, and she felt a little better as she drifted off to sleep. She dreamt that Babs came back and was sat by her side holding her hand. With this a sense of peace washed over her.

When Beth next woke, it was to a different world. Everything seemed very bright. She blinked against the hurt this light was causing her eyes.

'Oh, Beth, it is that you are back with us. I have been so afraid.'

Turning her head, Beth saw Jasmine. 'Where's Babs?'

'We don't know, little one, it is that she never came back.'

'She needs us. We must find her. Eeh, Jasmine, find her, please find her.'

'I am not for knowing where to look.'

'She's in a dark room. She's afraid, and sommat bad's going to happen to her. You must find her. Go to the police, tell them what she looks like.'

'Please, Beth, you must calm down. You are in the hospital. You've been very ill. You have some terrible infection on your chest.'

Beth tried to sit up, but she couldn't. She looked from side to side but could see nothing but walls.

'You are in isolation. They say you have the pneumonia. They didn't want me to stay with you, but I refused to go.'

'Am I going to die, Mama?'

'No. I won't let you. I have been bringing in my potions, but they do not know. Look, already you are feeling better.'

Beth lay back, but her mind wouldn't rest. Her dream haunted her. She knew that Babs was in a dark place, she could feel it. Babs was hurting and afraid. In the dream, Beth had tried to go to her, but her body wouldn't move. She'd called out to her, but she knew that Babs couldn't hear her. 'Please, Mama, find Babs. Please go to the police and tell them she is missing.'

'I – I cannot. I'm sorry, little one.'

'Why can't you?' But then Beth remembered. 'Because you stole us? That was a wicked thing to do. That's why Babs has gone. She wanted to find our ma. She's going to bring Ma back to me and Ma will take us home.' This last Beth said on a sob. Her chest tightened as the sob came from deep within her and a fit of coughing took her breath.

'No! Please, little one, please don't get upset. Your ma wanted me to take care of you.'

'Naw, I'll . . . never believe that . . . never.'

'What's going on? You mustn't get upset, Beth.'

Beth looked up into the lovely face of a young nurse.

'She has been dreaming.'

Beth looked into Jasmine's frightened face, and then back at the nurse. The nurse smiled and Beth thought she'd never seen anyone lovelier. What she could see of the girl's fair hair was parted in the middle and combed back into a soft curve under her cap and fell in folds down her back. Her eyes were large and a deep blue. They twinkled when she smiled. Beth watched her don a mask before she approached the bed.

'Now, what were you dreaming about?'

'I have a twin sister, and—'

'She is hallucinating. There is no sister.'

Beth gasped in shock. She looked at Jasmine and saw that the fear that had been on her face had now turned to terror and her eyes pleaded with Beth. Beth looked away and caught the pitying look that the nurse gave her. Unable to protest for fear of hurting Jasmine, she lay back as weakness took the little strength she'd had on waking.

A cold damp cloth soothed the ache in her burning head, and the nurse's gentle voice came to her. 'Rest now, Beth. Don't be troubled by your dreams.'

Beth wanted to be like this nurse. She wanted to make people feel better in the way that she did. She'd ask her how she came to be a nurse, but now all she wanted to do was to sleep.

NINE

Tilly stood back and admired her handiwork. The tall, twisting vase made of wicker had posed a challenge to her, but she felt certain that Malcolm would love it. His words kept going through her head: 'If you make a good job of it, there will be other items I will need – a basket chair for the conservatory, and storage baskets with lids. I have a lot of ideas that I know will work in cane, but I need to find someone with the skills to make them.'

She so hoped that she was given the job of making all the other items Malcolm needed. Apart from being lucrative, Tilly loved taking on something different that she hadn't tackled before and the everyday stock for the shop was no longer giving her the feeling of excitement that making this vase had given her.

'Eeh, Tilly, that's grand. Them twists and how you have picked out the edges in a darker cane, I reckon we could do a good number in them.'

'Naw, Liz, I told you. This is an exclusive. The designer said there mustn't be any others like them.'

'Well, I hope you're charging well then. It's never easy to make a profit on a single item.'

'Don't worry, I am, and look.' Tilly turned the vase upside down.

'Your initials! Eeh, Tilly, that tells everyone it was made by you.'

'It does.' Tilly had loved fashioning the letters from light cane into the dark base. Molly had drawn them for her, and she had copied them. Not that she didn't know them, but Molly had a special way of writing and she'd wanted these letters to look special. The 'T' for Tilly was intertwined with the 'O' for O'Flynn, and yet, each letter could be clearly read.

Picking up the vase, Tilly went to take it upstairs to her flat when the shop doorbell rang. Glancing towards it, her heart leapt to her mouth to see a policeman standing there.

'Beg your pardon, ladies, is there a Mrs Henshaw here?'

Liz stopped in her tracks. She'd walked away from Tilly and was making for the counter. She turned and stared at the policeman. 'Aye . . . Aye, I'm Mrs Henshaw.'

The policeman looked around the shop. 'Is there somewhere private we could go? I have some bad news for you.'

'What? What news . . . It ain't me Dan is it? . . . Naw. Is he hurt? What's happened?'

Tilly put the vase down and called out to Molly as she crossed the shop floor. In no time Molly came running from where she'd been making a brew in the back kitchen. 'What's wrong? Your call sounded urgent.' When Molly caught sight of the policeman, her gasp echoed Liz's. 'Oh, what's happened? Not me boys?'

'Naw, its not for you, Molly.' Tilly held the shaking Liz. 'Take care of things, I'll go out the back with the policeman and Liz.'

Molly's face looked full of concern, but she didn't protest, and as they passed through the door to the kitchen, Tilly heard the bell go again, and wished she'd locked the shop while they found out what was amiss.

They went through to the kitchen, a little make-do, painted in a dark green with a sink, an oil burner big enough to fit a kettle on and a small table on which stood a tin of tealeaves and a tin of sugar. Under the table was a bucket of cold water for the milk bottle to stand in. Besides these was the box of biscuits which they always had handy.

Tilly could smell the freshly made tea, something she always welcomed but which now turned her stomach. Liz clung to her hand, her face drained of colour. The policeman removed his helmet. 'I'm sorry, ma'am, but there has been an accident further down the promenade. A horse pulling a trap was suddenly spooked and bolted. He ploughed into your husband's stall and brought it crashing down. Witnesses say that this further terrified the animal and he reared up. His hoof hit your husband's head, just as he was crawling out from under the canvas that had landed on him.'

'Is – is he de – dead?'

'He's hurt badly. They've taken him to the Victoria hospital. I have a cab waiting outside. You have to hurry, ma'am.'

Tilly took the full weight of Liz as her legs gave way. 'Hold yourself together for Dan, Liz. I'll come with you. Come on.'

Grabbing their shawls off the hooks behind the door, they followed the policeman through to the shop. Tilly sighed with relief when she saw there were no customers in. 'Molly, Dan's hurt. A runaway horse. We're going to the hospital. Lock the shop after us and run upstairs to tell Tommy, will you? Ta, love.'

Molly hurried to the door with them. When they reached it, she took hold of Liz's arm. 'Happen he'll be all right, love. Keep your chin and your hope up.'

Liz didn't answer. She clung on to Tilly, hurting her arm, but Tilly didn't mind. She knew the pain Liz was in. After all that Liz had been through losing her whole family – six children and her first husband – it beggared belief that she might lose Dan too. Dan had brought happiness back to Liz when Tilly thought no one ever could. They'd only been married four years.

At the hospital they were told to wait a moment while checks were made with medical staff on Dan's ward, but soon they were running along a corridor behind a lovely young nurse, who'd come to fetch them and informed them they could go straight in when they arrived on the ward.

When they got there, a sister came out. 'Just Mr Henshaw's wife, please. Mr Henshaw must be kept from too much noise.'

'That's me. How is he? Is he . . . ?'

'He is very poorly, as he was kicked in the head. I'm sorry.'

Liz turned to Tilly. 'I – I can't do this, Tilly. I can't.'

'You can, love. Do it for Dan. Let him hear your voice. Give him some hope. Go on, Liz. I promise, you'll be all right.'

As Liz walked away from her, Tilly slumped down on the chair outside the ward and waited. Her thoughts were with the lovely Dan and how he had made Liz so happy, but now this had happened. Tilly felt like screaming at God. *Why? Surely, you've sent enough sorrow to Liz's door?*

When Liz came back into the corridor, Tilly feared the worse. She waited.

'Oh, Tilly, he's bad.'

'Does he knaw as you're with him, love?'

'Naw, I don't think so. His face is covered over with bandages. I can only see his mouth and that looks twisted and swollen, and his breathing . . . well . . . Oh, Tilly . . . I – I think I'm going to lose him. I can't bear it, I can't.'

Tilly couldn't answer, her tears were choking her with the effort she was making to hold them in. The lump in her throat felt like it was constricting her breathing. She swallowed hard. Taking Liz in her arms, she held her to her. Together, they rocked backwards and forwards, locked in grief. Liz with so many to grieve, and now her Dan clinging to a fragile thread of life, and Tilly, remembering her twins, with a heartache that was just as deep and a pain that cut into her.

The ward door opened and the nurse sitting with Dan beckoned Liz in. Tilly followed, hoping she would be allowed to support her friend. The nurse didn't stop her.

As soon as she looked at Dan, Tilly knew he wasn't long for this world. 'Hold his hand, Liz.'

'Yes, and speak to him, he might hear you.' The young nurse didn't sound to Tilly as if she believed this.

'Dan, I'm here. Your Liz is here. I love you, Dan.'

Tilly was surprised to see one of his fingers lift and then drop again. 'Dan, I'm here an' all. It's, me, Tilly, I'm with Liz. I'll take care of her.'

With this, Liz's head shot round and her shocked expression made Tilly realise that she hadn't truly prepared herself for the truth of the situation. Another movement from Dan had her turning back to him. 'Aye, you're not to worry about me, Dan. I'll be just fine till you come out of hospital, you knaws that. And I'll not leave your side, Dan, not for long, I won't. Get better, Dan. Get better, me love.'

There was no movement from Dan at this, nor would there ever be again, as whilst Liz had been talking, he'd let out a deep sigh and hadn't drawn the breath back in.

'I'm sorry, Mrs Henshaw, but I think he's gone. I'll fetch the doctor.'

As the nurse left the ward, Liz repeated one word over and over. 'Naw, naw, naw . . .'

Tilly was at a loss as to what to do. She stood steady, taking the weight of the sagging Liz, and waited. Her eyes rested on Dan, and silently she prayed that his good soul would find the peace he deserved.

The next day, when she and Tommy could least deal with it, they had a message from the solicitor to say that the old farmer was willing to sell and had named his price. Tommy was torn between rejoicing as it was all within his reach, wanting to go to view, and the needs of Tilly and especially Liz.

Tilly understood. 'Tommy, you need to go. I can't view with you but will trust your decision. The important thing is that the land is what you want and you feel you can make a go of it. The house can be fixed, no matter what state it's in.'

'This should be for being a joint decision, Tilly. Can't Molly take care of Liz just for a few hours?'

'Naw, she needs me with her, Tommy. Molly wouldn't cope on her own. Eeh, I'm sorry, lad. Sorry to the heart of me that it's happened, but sorry too that I can't come with you to see what I knaw'll be our future home.'

Tommy held his arms out. 'No, it is me as shouldn't expect it of you, me little Tilly. I'll go, and I'll be for making the right decision, I promise.'

'I knaw that, Tommy.'

'I'll be for taking Ivan with me, if it will help?'

'Naw. Molly said she'd care for him whenever we need her to. He loves Molly, and her lads. Aye, and they love him an' all, so he'll be fine. She'll take him to her home. Will is going to teach him how to work with the leather. Molly says that the flagon was just the start and that Will and the boys are working on making purses now. She'll bring the flagon in soon. I want to show it to that designer I told you of.'

Even though she said all of this, Tilly didn't feel any interest in it; her mind was consumed by thoughts of Dan. His loss had hit her hard. He'd been a real friend to her when she'd most needed one. She couldn't believe that he'd gone.

Liz had stayed on the sofa in the flat with Tilly and Tommy overnight, and looked as though she would for a while yet. The little place was crowded with the three of them and Ivan, as Tilly had bought a few more bits of furniture in readiness for the possible move to the farm, and to help to settle Ivan. She'd wanted it to be homely for him, not like the empty shell it had been when they first arrived.

She thought of how cosy it was now that she'd added chests of drawers and a wardrobe, and another sofa, besides rugs and cushions. The effect of this homemaking had helped her to feel settled. Though she'd tried not to feel too much at home, as she knew it was only temporary.

Pulling herself up, Tilly wondered how her thoughts could run away like that at such a time. It must have been with Tommy reminding them that they would soon leave it all. But what did it matter when the world they had known was now changed forever with losing their dear Dan.

When the hearse pulled up outside Liz's house a few days later, there wasn't a sound to be heard. The street was lined with folk, many of whom had known Dan since he was a boy, as back then he'd visited his aunt, whose house this once was, and had played with them, if they were the same age, or with the children of the older ones. All called on him on his stall whenever they were on the promenade. Their heads were bowed in sorrow for the loss of this lovely man.

Tilly's heart was heavy. She didn't want to go through a funeral. But more than that, she didn't want Liz to have to. She was worried for Liz, who'd shown signs of her mental illness coming back. She'd sit for hours rocking back and forth and wouldn't talk. Not even Ivan could get her to say a word.

Tilly wished that Tommy was here as she needed his love to lean on, but she couldn't ask Molly not to attend and so someone had to take care of Ivan.

Standing in Layton Cemetery after the service, the lovely early June day didn't warm Tilly. *Oh, Dan, I'm going to miss you.* Though she tried not to so as not to invite more pain, Tilly glanced over a few rows of graves to where her first husband, the twins' da, was buried. *I've never stopped loving you, Arthur. You've a special place in me heart, lad. If it's possible for you to do so, go to our Beth and Babs and take care of them, and Arthur, bring them home to me. Please, bring them home.*

Someone nudged her, and her attention came back. The thuds she hadn't properly registered were the mourners throwing handfuls of earth onto the coffin as a final gesture to send Dan on his way. It'd been Molly who had nudged her. She whispered, 'Your turn, Tilly, then help Liz too.'

Tilly bent down and scooped up a handful of dirt. She handed this to Liz. 'Let yours be the last, love.' Liz took the small sod of earth, but her face registered a nothingness, as if she was there, but only as an empty shell.

Tilly threw hers. Inside she cringed as it clunked, and then spread out over the top of the coffin. 'Goodbye, Dan. I'll never forget you.'

When she prompted Liz, Liz's head shook. 'Naw, Tilly, naw. I can't, I'm going with him.' This shocked Tilly, as did the movement of Liz as she made to jump into the grave. Tilly caught her and held her. 'Naw, Liz, naw, me love, you can't. Be strong for Dan, Liz. Give him the send-off he deserves.'

Spittle ran from the corner of Liz's slack mouth as she shook her head. A fear embedded in Tilly. These were the signs she'd seen in Liz in the asylum. 'Liz, Liz, please.'

The priest stepped forward. 'I think you should take Mrs Henshaw home, she's clearly had enough. The burial service is finished now.'

'But, Father, she ain't thrown her soil. I have to get her to do that, or she'll regret not doing so for the rest of her life.'

'Very well. I'll lead the congregation away, so as to give her some dignity.'

'Aye, that'll be kind of you. Me and Molly'll look after Liz. There's naw wake as Liz isn't up to it, but folk understand.'

'I know, so I have got the ladies of the church to make tea in the church hall. I'll tell everyone to follow me there. At least it will be something.'

'That's kind of you, Father. Liz will appreciate it, when she's able to think about it all.'

The weight of Liz was getting too much for Tilly. 'Help me, Molly, lass. I can't hold on much longer.'

'I've got her, Tilly. Now, come on, Liz. Throw your earth and say your goodbyes.'

Liz responded to this. She extended her hand and let her handful of earth trickle gently through her fingers. 'I'll not say goodbye, me darling, Dan. Just see you soon.'

This sent a shiver through Tilly. If it had been said with the emotion of the moment, she probably would have taken it in her stride, but in the way that Liz said this, there was a truth that Tilly cringed against.

She and Molly helped Liz to the waiting carriage, but as they walked away from the grave a remark from the grave digger made her blood boil. She hoped Liz hadn't heard it. 'Eeh, about bloody time. I've to fill him in afore I can go home.'

Tilly turned and gave him a filthy look but said nothing. She had a feeling it would go over his head and felt sorry that in such a sensitive job he didn't care enough to show his respect.

Once back at the flat, she and Molly helped Liz to bed. 'We'll put her in our bed, Tommy. Me and you'll have to be on the sofa tonight.'

Tommy didn't object and Tilly was grateful to him.

Later, once Molly had gone and over a meal of boiled bacon and cabbage with mashed potato, something that Tilly hadn't really put her heart into but had cobbled together, Tommy said, 'A lot's happening. Is it that you are up to discussing it with me?'

Though tired to the bones of her, Tilly said she would be once she'd settled Ivan. She looked at her son, propped up in the highchair that Tommy had adapted for him. His little head was laid on the table and his eyes were closing.

'Ahh, me lad, you've had enough today. Let's get you to your bed.'

As she undressed him and made him comfortable, her heart went out to him, as it had all his life. That he should have this affliction made her so sad. Pulling his nightshirt over his floppy head, she tried to bring a little lightness into his life. 'By, lad, have you been at that good Irish whiskey your Pappy likes?'

She was rewarded with a tired little giggle and something he often did – a mimic of her. 'Naw, Mammy. Eeh, Pappy would skin me.'

'Ha! You're a cheeky monkey, I'll have to tickle your tummy for that.' With this she lowered her head and ruffled her hair in his stomach. More giggles burst from him and he tugged at her hair to stop her. 'Mammy, don't. Me eyes are tired, and I just want to be closing them.'

'Aye, I knaws the feeling, lad. Mine are tired too. Night night. Sleep tight, little one, but call out if you need owt, and Mammy will come running.'

Before she reached the door, Ivan was asleep. To her, he looked like an angel, with his cherub-like face relaxed in slumber. She stood looking at him with pictures in her mind of two little girls looking almost exactly the same as Ivan. A huge sigh came from her. In a few days they would turn fourteen. Her heart constricted. She leant against the door and wept. But it wasn't a deep crying. Not like the tears she truly felt like releasing. She couldn't let herself give in like that; if she did, she would never stop.

Forcing herself to take a deep breath, she controlled the terrible pain dragging at her heart and walked across the hall to her own bedroom. Peeping inside, she found that Liz was fast asleep too. Letting out a sigh of relief at this, she closed the door quietly. Every bone in her body held the weariness that had taken her and the last thing she wanted to do was to talk to Tommy about his plans for their future, especially when Dan didn't have a future to live and her dear friend Liz was facing a future of coping once more with unimaginable pain.

But she listened to Tommy while he outlined how far he'd progressed in the last two or three days and found herself growing in interest. 'So, you reckon you can have us moving in in just a few weeks?'

'I do. The house is huge, Tilly. It is for having four bedrooms, and three rooms and a kitchen downstairs, and an attic that could be for being another flat, it's so big. It all needs attention, but I'm for thinking that we could get two bedrooms and two rooms downstairs looking really nice in no time.'

'One of them being the kitchen? I mean, we have to have a decent kitchen, Tommy.'

'Aye, it has the makings now. It needs a good clean, and a new stove and pot sink, and the rest is just a lick of whitewash.'

'Eeh, Tommy, it sounds so exciting. And you have all you'll need to get the farm up and running?'

'Everything. A strong shire horse with a fair few years left in him; a plough that's rusting, but in good order otherwise. There's for being everything I need, it all just needs attention. I'll hire a couple of lads to help me, and we'll soon be having ourselves a thriving farm.'

'I'm with you all the way, Tommy. You go ahead and call on me whenever you need to. But, me love, I cannot talk about it any longer tonight. My head's falling asleep, as Ivan would say.'

'Now, that's for being a shame, as I had plans for your body.'

'Tommy! By, you just saying them words lights me fire. Well, me head can wait for its slumber.' With this, she let Tommy guide her to the sofa and went willingly into his arms, accepting his kisses and giving her all to him. It was the salve to her pain that she so badly needed.

TEN

The door to the cell opened. 'Cleaning and exercise.' These words barked out by the warden were music to Babs's ears. It had only happened three times in the two months that she'd been here, and always when something was going to happen. The first time, the prison inspector was due to make his rounds, something she'd been told was a rare occurrence. The second time had been because there was to be a move around of all the prisoners, except those on remand, like herself. Now, she hoped this time was because of a doctor's visit, which was long overdue.

'About time.'

'It is, Pixie. I feel as though I'm going mad. Thank goodness the bloody assizes are next week.'

Sally and Pixie had spoken of being released before and each time Babs had selfishly hoped that they wouldn't be. They were what made this experience just bearable. They were like two big sisters to her, caring for her and helping her to cope.

They took being in these poky, uncomfortable conditions in their stride and had even joked with each other that their time inside gave them a rest from the men's demands. Though they did make Babs curious lately by saying they were missing having sex and that they needed to get out. Pixie had said that once she did, she'd grab the first man and rape him. Both she and Sally had laughed at this, but Babs had wondered why they missed something she'd found painful and disgusting.

When she'd said this, Sally had told her that she'd find out differently and that she was to put that behind her. 'From what you've said about that man, he was mentally ill, and so probably went at you in a hungry way, knowing he had the urge, and how to satisfy it, but without having any care for you. Most men are different. Oh yes, even those who pay for it, though we do come across some brutes. I've got a few customers who don't have willing wives and who are superb lovers.'

Both girls came from Maidstone and worked the city. 'But if ever you want to try our line of work, don't,' Sally had added. 'It's not good. We're controlled by our pimp, and have to go with all sorts, no matter if we want to or not. We get beaten up regularly and make very little money. And hauled in here often too.'

Babs knew she would never want to do what they did. She just longed to be set free, and to go to Blackpool.

Outside in the yard, the sun warmed her skin. She walked round and round the enclosed yard. A girl of about nineteen joined her and chatted. She said she was from London. Or *Landon*, as she pronounced it. Her name was Mavis.

Babs learnt from Mavis that the lives of the other prisoners were much different to the one she led. 'Yer see, love, we've been convicted and are doing our time. You're not really a convict yet, just a suspected one. We're put to work; we do all sorts. It ain't bad as it passes the time. I work on a machine sewing mail bags. But some others work in the kitchens and the library. Then there's the gardeners. What yer in for then?'

'Nowt as I did. They say I killed a girl and hurt another in the convent where I was, but I didn't. This beast of a nun did.'

'Blimey, that's a tale and a 'alf. No one's going to believe you over what a nun says.'

'I knaw.'

'Where you from? You don't 'alf talk funny.'

Babs had to smile at this. 'I'm from Blackpool in the North, but you've got nowt to shout home about, you talk funny an' all.'

They both laughed at this, and Babs knew that she liked Mavis, and that life with her by her side, and working instead of sitting around, would be ten times better than it was at the moment. 'Can you choose your jobs, Mavis?'

'No, why? Is there something you fancy?'

'Gardening. I've been doing that. Well, working in fields. I like being in the fresh air.'

'Don't we all, mate. But it is what it is.'

As they talked more, Babs learnt that Mavis was in prison for stealing. She said it was to get money to eat as her mum and sisters and brothers hadn't eaten for days. 'We only had this stew that me mum made and was thinning down every day. Eight of us there are, and we were starving. So, I went to the grocery shop to 'elp meself, but when I got there the delivery bike was outside and it was loaded with orders. There was no one with it, so I jumped on it and rode like 'ell back

’ome. The whole street ate that night and I sold the bike at the pub for five bob into the bargain. I thought I’d got away with it, but the coppers got wind it was me, and ’ere I am. I’m doing three years for it, and I’ve only done eight months so far.’

‘Me solicitor said that I’m looking at a long, long time. Years, even, if I’m convicted. I don’t knaw how I’m going to do that.’ As Babs said this, she felt herself breaking.

‘Don’t worry. You never know what life brings. You’re a mystery, though, saying you’re from Blackpool and being down here.’

‘I can’t tell you everything, Mavis. I don’t knaw where to start. Anyroad, it looks like everyone’s filing back inside, so we’d better go an’ all. I hope I see you again.’

‘No doubt you will. Keep your chin up, Babs.’

When they got back inside, the cleaning began. Not that she, Sally, Pixie, Doreen and Lilly got involved in the general cleaning, but they did sweep and mop out their own cell. Babs felt sorry for Lilly, as the other three set her on cleaning the bucket they used as a lavatory. It was emptied every morning, and swilled, but that didn’t clean it properly. Lilly had to take it to a washroom block and scrub it out, but she didn’t seem to mind.

It was good to have a clean cell, and to be given some clean bedding.

They’d just settled down, all feeling tired after the exertion, when the key sounded in the door again. ‘You, Barbara Smith. You’re to attend the doctor. He was going to do the rounds, but there’s too many to see, so none of you others will get to see him this time.’

'What were the point in all that cleaning then?'

The warden ignored Sally's remark and marched Babs down a long corridor from which many doors led. All were the same as the door to their cell, made of heavy wood and with peepholes and iron hinges and locks.

At the end of the corridor, she went through a door that led to a much wider hall. The doors off this were more like the ones found in houses and each had a plaque on it. The one she was led to gave Babs a shiver down her spine and brought memories to her of the last time she'd been through another door with the same inscription: 'Clinic.'

Once inside she was greeted by a sour-faced nurse and told to strip and then to wash herself all over. 'Go behind that screen. You'll find a bowl of water and a flannel and towel. Pay particular attention to between your legs.'

Babs shivered as she waited for something to happen. There was nowhere to sit behind the screen, and draughts were coming from all directions. She could hear voices – the nurse, instructing and questioning other prisoners – but no one came behind the screen, so there must be a lot of places they could all go.

When eventually the nurse did come behind the curtain, she didn't make any conversation. 'Name?'

With this answered, she went on to ask date of birth, which Babs could only give approximately. She and Beth had worked out long ago that as they were six when Jasmine had taken them, and that was 1895, meaning that they must have been born in 1889. They knew their birthdate was in the summer, and Beth was insistent that it was the twelfth of June, so they went for that.

'So, you're going on fourteen in a few weeks, then?'

'Aye.'

'Right, well, the doctor is going to examine you down below. The notes from your solicitor have asked for you to be checked to see if you are pregnant. He says you were interfered with. Is that right?'

'Aye. Just afore I came here.'

'So, let's see. You were admitted just over eight weeks ago. Have you seen your monthly since?'

'Naw, ma'am.'

'Well, that's not a good sign, but not unexpected in here. Fear and shock can have an effect on you. But either way, the doctor won't know if you are with child. It's too early. He will need to see you when three months have passed, and if by then you haven't had a monthly. Nevertheless, he will check to see if you have caught any disease. Are you generally fit and well?'

'Yes, ma'am, I never ail.'

'Good.'

The doctor was equally stern, but he was at least gentle in his examination and didn't hurt her. 'She could be pregnant. Oh, I know it's very early days, but I've learnt to feel some differences in the entrance to the womb, and her breasts are tender – she flinches when you touch them. There's some darkening of the nipple too.'

'Naw, naw! I don't want a babby.'

'You'll have no choice. And don't speak to the doctor unless he speaks to you. Besides, you should pray that you are, as the sentence passed on a pregnant woman is always lighter than it would be otherwise. And given what you've done, you need any help you can get.'

'I've not done owt.'

'I'm warning you. If you chat back again, you'll find yourself in big trouble. Everyone who comes in here says they haven't done anything. Have you finished with her, Doctor?'

'I have, but if she is still here in six weeks, I want to see her again.'

'Right, Miss Smith, follow me.'

With this the nurse turned and marched out of the doctor's room. 'Get dressed, and then I need to check your hair for lice.'

This done and nothing found, the nurse called for a warden. When the warden came in she looked at Babs. 'You've a busy afternoon. Your solicitor's here and wants to speak with you.'

Babs felt her spirits lift.

'In that case, you'd better wait for her notes. There's something her solicitor should know. I'll see if the doctor has written them up yet.'

'Sit there, Smith.'

Babs sank down onto the chair the warden indicated. Her heart was racing. It was true then? *Naw, a babby? I can't be having a babby!*

'Are you all right, Barbara? You look very pale.'

'It's all in her notes. I had a look coming along. Another one with her belly full.'

'You can leave us now, Warden.'

When the door shut on the warden, Mr Drayford looked at Babs with a pitying look. 'I'm sorry, Babs. I'll just look at your notes and see what the doctor says. After a moment, he looked up. 'Well, nothing is definite. The doctor says that it is too early to say, but that he has seen some very early signs that indicate that you are pregnant.'

'I knaw. He said. Eeh, I don't knaw how I'm to cope. Does they let you have a babby in prison?'

'I have to be honest with you, Barbara, though I am loath to be. But no. Initially, it can help your case, as they don't put pregnant girls in prison – they can't cope with them, they haven't the proper facilities. It is most likely that you will go to a closed convent for unmarried mothers, and then afterwards back to prison.'

'But what about me babby?'

Mr Drayford coughed. 'I'm afraid you will leave it behind and never see it again. But the nuns will find it a good home. So that's important for you to know.'

'I don't trust nuns. Not anymore.'

'I know. But there is very little that I can do about that. Anyway, I do have some news. I know where Emma is, though I haven't been able to contact her. Her parents have moved to the Isle of Wight. That's an island off the Bournemouth coast. Have you heard of it?'

'Naw, but does that mean as she can't be asked the truth of what happened?'

'No, it doesn't. But it will take a while to get a communication to her. I have written to a solicitor friend who practises on the island to ask him to track the family down and to ask if Emma would give him her version of events. But it is like I said before, all of that will take time.'

Babs hadn't dared to ask, even though the question had been on her lips from the moment she entered the room. But taking a deep breath, she found the courage to. 'And what about me ma? Did you find anything owt about me ma?'

'No. I'm sorry. It may be that your mother and father didn't register you. Many parents didn't. It was made compulsory before you were born, but that didn't mean that the parents did it, and keeping records in the early days was a vast task. Did you go to school? Church? Can you remember?'

'Aye, we went to school. And we were baptised. I remember the teacher saying we had to be. It was on our first day, and she asked for a certificate. I was scared, and so was me sister, and I remember everything that happened because Ma said it was such a big event, us going to school. You see, she didn't, and she couldn't read and write. Me and me sister used to teach her what we had learnt each day.'

'Very interesting. That means that you went to a church school. Well, I can soon track those down, there can't be many in Blackpool. They will have kept records of you. But don't get your hopes up. Now, in the meantime, the assizes are on Monday. It's Thursday today, so that's four days from now. I will ask that you're given a clean uniform that day. You do your very best to look neat and tidy, though even if you had a comb, I can't see you getting it through that mob of curls you have.'

'Eeh, I do manage it, but they don't let us have a comb.'

'They will let you wash that morning, so dampen your hair a bit; it might tame it. Now, I have other news, and this is very bad. Sister Brenda was taken ill. She has been moved to a convent where they take care of nuns who have had a breakdown. She is no longer considered sound in her mind and can't be called to testify . . .'

'She'd have only told lies anyroad.'

'That's as it may be, but ... well, she did give a written statement confirming events as she'd said they'd happened just before she was taken ill, and this makes things look even worse for you, as the prosecution will argue that your actions caused this breakdown on top of everything else that you're responsible for.'

'Naw ... but that's wicked, to make a false statement that she knaws will be used in court, and she's meant to be a holy woman.'

'And probably what caused her breakdown, if indeed she truly has had one. And so, unless I can get hold of Emma, we are not in a very good position. I'm going to concentrate on that quest, much more than trying to find out who you are and substantiating your story that you were stolen. I am loath to bring that up as it does sound so untrue. Even to me, and I have given you the benefit of the doubt over everything you have told me. But I won't give up on that because if I don't find Emma, you will have to face a full-blown trial and where you came from will be a big part of that and your story could be used to discredit you further.'

There seemed to Babs to be all doom in what Mr Drayford had just said. She felt she had no hope. Tears prickled her eyes. Her thoughts went to Beth. Her heart longed for her sister. But sometimes she thought she would never see her again.

Beth stared at Jasmine. 'But you will tell the farmer where you're going, won't you? What if Babs comes back? How'll she ever find us?'

'Little one, it is that Roman says that Babs will never come back.'

'Naw! I'll not believe that. If she's made it to Blackpool, she'll bring Ma. I knaw she will.'

'Try not to think like that, it is only for upsetting you. Your ma didn't want you. Try to believe that. I am now your mama, and I will still visit. I will come once a week, and when they let you come home, I will take you to the new place where we are to be staying. It will be by the seaside where the air will make you fully well and where it is that I can sell many of my wares, as many rich people are for making their way to the coast now for the summer months.'

Distraught, Beth begged of Jasmine to leave a note with the farmer. Her head began to throb and her chest tightened. Taking in a gasp of air, she found that it wouldn't fill her lungs. Frightened, she tried harder, but her lungs felt as though they were going to burst, and yet she couldn't get air into them.

'Nurse! Nurse!'

Beth began to sink. Her mind swam into a swirl of cloud that threatened to engulf her. When she next woke, her bed was swathed in netting, and she felt very cold.

'Ahh, you're awake. You gave us a fright there, Beth, but you're going to be all right. You had what we call a crisis, but now that it is passed, you will get well again.'

Beth looked up into the face of the lovely nurse she now knew was called Philippa.

Philippa had hold of her hand, which she squeezed. 'I'll take your temperature, Beth. Then I'll fetch Sister to see you. She will be very happy that you are all right. How do you feel?'

'Cold, and wet, but all right, ta.'

'Well, that will be because we have been packing ice around you and have all the windows open. It's a windy day today, though not cold outside; the sun is shining, as we are nearly in June now. But we will close the windows if your temperature is down, as then we can warm you up bit by bit.'

When the sister came in, she had a lovely, calming smile on her face. 'My, you look much better.' Looking at the chart that Nurse Philippa handed to her, she added, 'Yes, much better. I think we can stop the ice treatment now and get Beth into a chair. Then make her up a nice, ordinary bed. Make sure you support her at all times, Nurse Brown, as she will be very weak.'

As Philippa helped her out of bed, Beth's legs felt wobbly. 'Eeh, I feel like the rag doll that Jasmine made me when I were little. All floppy and as if I've no bones.'

Philippa laughed out loud. 'That's a good description. I have one of those dolls. I still keep her with me. She sits on my bed in the nurses' quarters, and she stares at me, but it's a nice stare, not a frightening one as her lips are stitched into a smile. Sometimes, even though I have sat her straight up, she has flopped to the side. I call her Polly . . . Now, take it easy, Beth. That's it. Small, steady steps. Hold on to me. I'll sit you in the chair near to the window. The sun will warm you up.'

'I call mine Janie. And me sister's is Millie.'

'You've mentioned your sister before, Beth, and yet the woman you call Mama denies you have a sister. Why is that and why, if your sister exists, doesn't she come to see you? I feel that there is something wrong. Why are you with that gypsy woman? You don't look like a gypsy. I mean, you do have tanned skin and dark hair, but . . . Look, it's none of my business, and if you tell me to mind my own, I will, but you seem very unhappy and sometimes it helps to talk to someone.'

Beth put her head back. A tear seeped out of the corner of her eye. She so wanted to tell Philippa everything, but she didn't want to get Jasmine and Roman into trouble. They had been a good mama and papa to her and Babs. And despite everything, she loved them. 'I'm all right. I – I do have a sister, but she ran away, and I don't knaw where she is. We're twins.'

Philippa looked very curious. Beth hoped she wouldn't question further.

'Oh dear, that's sad, Beth. But I'm sure she is all right and will come back. Where are you from? You don't talk like your mama, or even look like her.'

Beth looked out of the window. If she told Philippa the truth, then Jasmine and Roman would suffer. They were already broken-hearted over Babs going. A lie formed in her head. 'Me parents are dead . . . I, me and me sister, were taken in by the gypsies. Jasmine and Roman are our mama and papa and are very good to us. They love us. But Babs, me sister, she, well, she . . .'

'Look, don't get upset. I shouldn't have asked you.' Philippa had stopped her task of making the bed and come over to Beth. Beth felt her arms around her. She leant into the comfort given and rested her head on Philippa's shoulder.

'I'm going to be a nurse, Philippa. I want to be like you and make folk feel better when they're ill.'

'And you'll make a good one too. Mind, it's very hard work, and you don't get to see your family often. The other nurses become your sisters, and the sister and matron become your parents – very strict ones they are too.' Philippa laughed as she said this. 'But we have a lot of fun, me and the other nurses. And we all love making people better when they come to us very ill.'

Beth asked how she could become a nurse.

'Well, you have to apply, and then they assess you. You sit exams and this helps them to decide whether to take you or not. Did you go to school, Beth?'

'I did when I were little, but not for a long time. It didn't stop me and me sister learning, though. We've allus needed to knaw everything we could. So, we badgered Jas . . . Mama and Papa to get us some books. And not just storybooks. We liked books on all subjects – birds, wildlife, other countries. The best was when we were given some money and allowed to go and choose our own. We both loved the smell of the book-shops and the feel of a crisp new book. Then when we had read it, we had to let Mama sell it as there's naw room in the wagon for a lot of books. We did keep some favourites, though. Mine were about Africa, and me sister's were stories about orphans, or poor folk.'

By the time her bed was made and she was back in it, though feeling very tired, Beth felt even more determined to become a nurse. Philippa had promised to bring in some books for her to read to help her to prepare herself. 'You can keep them and take them home when you go. They helped me. And they're not boring. *Practical Nursing* is one, and *Your Guide to Nursing* is another. If you really want to become a nurse, then these will encourage you.'

When Philippa left her, Beth knew where her future lay. Dreaming about it, and seeing herself in the crisp blue frock, with the starched white apron and the flowing hat, she smiled. She'd be the best nurse there ever was.

ELEVEN

Malcolm loved the twisted imitation vase, and commissioned Tilly to make the chair, which he described as being in a Japanese style. He told her stories of a journey he'd made visiting most countries in the East, an area he was fascinated with. Tilly found the stories captivating, but suspected that half of them weren't true. Or if true, they had been elaborated on.

She'd never seen any Japanese people, but Malcolm showed her pictures of them and she was surprised to see how different they looked. She loved the colourful silk clothes they wore, and listened in awe to stories of how there were girls called 'geishas' whose faces looked as though they'd covered them in white paint, and who glided rather than walked. 'They all live together and giggle a lot. Their sole purpose is to look after the men's needs and tend to the many children that are born. They are very happy and though at first you think they are strange to look at, you come to see them as beautiful inside and out.'

Tilly had gazed at the girls, and yes, she could see a peaceful happiness in them that she wondered at with such a lifestyle as they led.

'Well, now, Tilly. Come. I want you to make me that very same chair in the picture.' Malcolm waltzed towards the conservatory. 'I'm going to place it just there. What do you think, darling?'

Tilly giggled. It still felt strange for this man to call her 'darling'. Even Tommy only rarely, if ever, called her that. 'Eeh, Malcolm, I reckon as it will look beautiful.'

'And I want it in the same colours as the vase. And with the same patterns on. Now, how soon can you make that, and that twisted little table?'

Tilly looked at the picture again. Next to the chair was a small table no bigger than a stool. It looked almost like an egg timer. It's top was made of glass which had a delicate painting of a flower stem with the prettiest little pink flowers blooming from it.

'I reckon at least two months.'

'Two months! Oh, Tilly, I'll need them in one. Please, Tilly. My whole Japanese theme needs to be in place by the time the family visit in August, and I have so much to do in the six weeks before then.'

'I'll try, but there's a lot of work involved, and some will be trial and error.'

'You are up to it, darling?'

Tilly wanted more than anything to take on the challenge of making the chair and table. 'Aye, I'm up to it. But you need to give me time. All I can say is that I'll do me best.' Her thoughts were with all that was going on. Liz needed her. In the daytime, she had Molly, though Molly found it difficult running the shop and seeing to Liz, whose mental health was deteriorating. She needed medical help really, but Tilly dreaded what that would mean. She couldn't see Liz put back into an asylum, she couldn't. No, her place was with friends until she got better.

And then there was Tommy and his plans. He was at the farm most days now and for long hours, overseeing the repairs to the house and trying to get the farm straight and up and running. She should be by his side. And little Ivan too. He needed her more and more as his body seemed to want to do less and less. He spent a lot of time with his pappy, but that made Tilly feel guilty. He needed her.

'Tilly?'

'Aye, I can do it. But it's the time you're giving me. Let me see how it pans out, eh? If they're not finished—'

'They have to be, darling. The Smythes cannot come and the conservatory – my *pièce de résistance* – not be finished!'

Tilly smiled. Malcolm always made her smile. 'Aye, well, whatever that was that you said, I can only say as I'll do me best.'

'Thank you, Tilly, I know you won't let me down. If you did, it would break my heart.'

Tilly laughed. She had an idea that it would too. Malcolm was a fragile soul. *Eeh, if he had a slice of real life, of how we folk have to cope with all that is thrown at us, he'd just crumble, that's for sure.*

As she made her way home, Tilly wondered at herself for taking this work on. But she *needed* to do so. Her basket work kept her from going mad from all she had to contend with. When weaving away, she lost herself. Her mind went to another world, a world of baskets, and different canes and wicker. A world that smelt of the different scents that came from the materials she worked with. And a world that engrossed her. Especially when making items such as the twisted vase, and now this beautiful chair and table. She couldn't wait to get started. A sense of excitement built in her. But when she passed by where Dan's stall used to be, that died and was replaced by a deep sadness.

'Eeh, Tilly, am I glad to see you back.'

Molly met her at the shop door. 'Liz is bad. I reckon as we've got to call for a doctor. She needs help. She came down with naw clothes on, and I had the devil's own job to get her to go back upstairs. She didn't seem to knaw as she were naked, she just wanted to go to Dan. She could hardly walk. By, she were a handful. Once I got her through the door to the stairs, I had to lock it. Eeh, Tilly, it's sad, so sad. Our lovely Liz, brought to this.'

'I've never told you, Molly . . . There were no need to and me and Liz wanted to forget it all, but well, we lost touch for a long while over a misunderstanding, and when we found each other . . . well, it were in an asylum.'

'What? By, Tilly, you? How? I mean, why? I can see it with Liz, though if you'd have told me afore Dan died, I wouldn't have thought it possible of her either. Even though she has told me over the years about the loss of her family. Poor, poor, Liz.'

'Let me see to Liz, and then we'll have a cuppa and I'll tell you. You knaw some of it. You knaw as I took to the drink and it got hold of me. Well, that were the path that took me to the asylum. Me and Liz had only just got out when we met you, only we were ashamed, and we didn't want anyone to knaw.'

'I can understand that, Tilly. By, you've been through sommat, lass.' Molly's lovely hazel eyes filled with tears. She brushed them away. A strong character, Molly always saw the better side of situations. 'Well, you're all right now. We just need to get Liz better again.'

As she went up the stairs, Tilly could hear a soft moaning. She followed the sound into her bedroom where Liz lay, still naked, on hers and Tommy's bed. The noise she was making was pitiful. 'Liz, Liz, me dear friend. I'm here. Come on, Liz. Try to hold on, lass.'

'I've nowt to hold on to, Tilly. Nowt. It's all gone.'

'You've got me and Molly, and Tommy and Ivan. Aye, and one day you'll have the twins again. Remember, we allus said as we'd find me girls one day.'

'But we won't, Tilly. We never do owt that'll help us find them.'

Tilly sat down heavily on the bed. Liz was right. But then, what could they do? 'You knaw what we allus said, don't you? That one day, when they're old enough, they'll find us. We're here in Blackpool, and they could never forget Blackpool. They loved it. The crowds, seeing the funfair being built, the tower, the sea and the sand, they loved it all, Liz.' Tilly didn't register that she was crying, but Liz had hurt her by saying she never did anything to find Beth and Babs. What could she do? Gypsies were like ghosts in the night. She knew that better than most. Here one day, gone the next. Her only consolation was that though she hadn't known Jasmine and Roman, Jeremiah had, and he'd told her that they would love and take care of her girls.

'Eeh, Tilly. Help me, help me. I'm falling.'

'You're not, Liz. I won't let you.' Taking Liz in her arms, she held her close. 'Please try to get strong, Liz. Dan wouldn't want to see you like this.'

'I knaw. Me lovely Dan. I just want to go to him, Tilly.'

'You will one day. Nowt's as sure as that. But in the meantime, you have to live your life, Liz. You have to stay in the real world. Don't descend into that terrible place where you were when we were in the asylum. Please, Liz.'

But even as she pleaded, Tilly could see that Liz was travelling far away from her. Her eyes held no life. Her lips hung loose, and spittle dribbled from her mouth. Liz had gone. The lovely Liz she knew was no longer there, and Tilly didn't know what to do for her.

A little snore told her that Liz had dropped off to sleep. Lying her down, she covered her with the eiderdown that Molly had made. A beautiful patchwork quilt. Into it, Molly had stitched pieces of the past. There was a square of the gingham tablecloth that she and Liz had on their table back in their little cottage. And another of the bridesmaid's dress that she'd worn for Liz and Dan's wedding, and some squares she'd cut from some old material she'd found at a jumble sale that had little baskets on it.

As Tilly gazed at the quilt, she thought of how Molly's talent was wasted now, and how her own talent for basket making had taken over all of their lives, although Molly still stitched the linings with little pockets in, for the baskets that were to become sewing baskets, and baskets for the nursery, to hold all a nanny would need for the baby she cared for. They had a lot of nannies coming into the shop for them in the summertime. It seemed that these women were a breed of their own and word went around them all when one found something new. That line had been very popular.

It began to dawn on Tilly how they could expand their range, as quilts such as this one would sell well too. A plan formed in her mind. This flat could be turned into a work room. It was like one now with her bits and bobs about, though a lot of the baskets were made by Liz and Molly in the shop during quiet times – the plain, easy-to-make ones that was. But they could turn this place into a proper factory. Molly could have a room for her sewing. She could make all sorts of things that would sit nicely alongside the baskets and would sell well. Cushions, and tablecloths . . . well, no, perhaps not those sort of lines as they wouldn't want to rival Pauline. But cushions, yes. And maybe curtains to order. Hadn't Malcolm said that he'd had to go back and forth to London to get such items?

Excitement built in Tilly as her ideas crowded her mind – they could employ staff to serve in the shop . . . Yes, it all made sense. It would help, as it would lessen their workload, as currently they all had to tend to the customers as well as try to make the stock.

Seeing that Liz was now sound asleep, Tilly hurried back downstairs. She couldn't wait to tell Molly what had occurred to her.

When she opened the door that led to the shop, she had a surprise waiting for her.

'Look who's here, Tilly.'

'Florrie! Oh, Florrie, lass, it's good to see you. We were just going to make a brew.'

Before she knew it, she was in a hug with Florrie, the young woman, who, when she was a maid in one of the big houses in St Anne's, had helped Tilly by buying a basket from her, and just by being friendly when she most needed a friend.

Florrie had fallen on hard times herself, and it had been Tilly's turn to help her. Now Florrie was married to Reggie and they lived in a cottage on a large estate in Lytham, where her Reggie was the gardener and Florrie the housekeeper.

'So, what brings you into Blackpool then, Florrie? Mind, it's good to see you, and by, you're blooming. You look really well. How's Reggie?'

'He's blooming too, we both are. I'm to have a babby, Tilly.'

'Eeh, lass, that's good news, though you took your time, didn't you?'

'Aye, we had to practise a lot.'

They laughed at this, as did Molly as she greeted Florrie. 'You're looking wonderful, lass, and I'm happy to hear your news. By, you've come a long way since the days when you were yet another waif and stray that this one helped. Did you knaw as Tilly got the nickname of Angel? Well, she's still at it. Tell Florrie about Liz, Tilly.'

'Oh, I knaw what happened, and I wanted to come. I read about it in the *Gazette*, but I was so poorly, and I didn't knaw what ailed me. Well, I do now. How is Liz?'

Over a cup of tea, they told Florrie about Liz and caught her up with other news too.

'Oh dear. Poor Liz. Happen after a bit of time has gone by she'll get better. You say as you're moving out to the country, Tilly? Maybe it'd be good for Liz if she could go with you for a bit? Look at how me and Reggie have got better. The country air is a great healer, as is being close to the land. And on top of that, it sounds as though your Tommy will have farm animals too. He'll need a hand with all of that.'

'Ha! I don't see Liz as a farmhand, but come to think of it, you and Reggie were in a poor way when I found you. So, maybe the farm work would help Liz. I'll see what I can do. The house is coming along just fine now, so it shouldn't be too long afore we move. And Tommy is on with finding me a horse and trap so that I can bring meself into the shop.'

'Eeh, Tilly, fancy you being that posh. A horse and trap indeed. You were a ragged-arsed down-and-out when you came knocking on the door of the kitchen where I worked!'

'By, you've got a cheek. I were never ragged-arsed! But I were a down-and-out, and you and Cook helped me when not many would.'

'Aye, but you paid back tenfold with what you did for me and Reggie. Eeh, I miss Cook. But she writes now and then. She's loving her retirement in Wales. And she and her sister seem to have a wonderful time together. Well, I can't stop long. I have to get back or Reggie will be sending out a search party.'

They hugged once more. Florrie never mentioned the twins, but then nobody did these days. Tilly knew they hadn't forgotten them but were treading carefully so as not to hurt her. But just sometimes she'd like them mentioned so that she still felt they were part of the family. As that was what she, Liz and Molly were, and Florrie, though they didn't see her often; she was soon back in the fold when they did.

Seeing her off now, with her happiness shining from her, Tilly felt confident that nothing would now go wrong for Florrie. And how exciting to soon be welcoming a new baby.

As she thought this a sudden feeling of sickness came over her. She rushed past a gaping Molly and only just made it out the back where they had a shared lav. Thankfully, no one was in it. Tilly emptied her stomach into the pan.

'Eeh, Tilly, what's to do? Are you ill?'

'Naw. I've a confession to make. I think I'm pregnant an' all.'

'Eeh, Tilly, that's wonderful news.'

'Naw, it's not. Eeh, Molly, what if me babby's like me poor Ivan?'

'You mustn't think like that, Tilly. It won't happen again, I'm sure of it. And if it does, well, it will be a blessing, as I haven't met a more wonderful little lad than your Ivan. He's a gift from God and brightens all our lives. Me lads and Will love him to bits.'

They walked back into the makeshift kitchen. 'I knaw what you're saying, Molly, but what will Ivan's future be like? How can he fend for himself? And when me and his da have gone, what then?'

'Don't meet trouble when it might not be travelling your way, lass. Ivan has a clever brain. We haven't told you yet as he wants to surprise you, but after the very few lessons I've given him, he can already write his name. Just you wait and see.'

'Really? By, that's cheered me.'

'So it should. There's plenty of desk jobs that he could do. But anyroad, he's a long way from that, he's only just going on five, and you're a young 'un an all. What are you now? Thirty-three? That's nowt. I'm knocking forty on the door. You've years and years to be here for your Ivan.'

'Aye, and to still hope to see me girls an' all.'

'Aye, and that. It will happen. I can feel it in me bones. Now, when you came down them stairs you had that look about you. What's been going through your head, lass?'

'What look?'

'The look you have when you're planning sommat.'

Tilly told Molly what it was that had come to her while she was settling Liz.

'Eeh, that sounds grand. I'd love that, Tilly. I've wanted to contribute more to the business for a long time. I can do it an' all.'

'Well, let's make a start. Go down to that stall that sells the materials and pick sommat really striking that'd make a cushion for a special chair. It has to have some purples in it.' Tilly told Molly about her new commission from Malcolm. 'Look, I have the drawings in me basket, and you'll be able to see some of the rich colours that the Japanese use. There'll be sommat similar on the stall, as Gracie gets some of her cloth off the boats that come in to Liverpool from exotic countries. She tells me that the show folk who perform in the theatre buy a lot from her for their costumes.'

'I'd love to go to the theatre sometime, Tilly. We should do it one of these days. The menfolk wouldn't be interested, but would you?'

'I would. When I see the billboards, I feel drawn to it, but like you say, it's not owt you can suggest to the men. Yes, let's do it. I'll check out what's coming this season. But now, get yourself off, as Liz might wake soon and need me.'

Left alone in the quiet shop, Tilly thought about her condition. She'd suspected for a few weeks now but hadn't let the thought of it really take root. Now she had to as the little one was letting its presence be known. She patted her stomach. 'Now, naw giving me trouble. I've a lot on me plate and can't be throwing up all over the place, or putting up with swollen ankles or owt like that. You're in there now, so settle down for the few months before you make your appearance, and you and I will get along just fine.'

'Who are you talking to, Tilly?'

'Liz! Oh, Liz, you've had a wash and dressed yourself. Are you feeling better, lass?'

'Naw, I'll never feel that again, but eeh, I did have a moment when I just wanted to try.'

'That's what it's all about, Liz. Trying. Keeping on, keeping on. That's all any of us can do. Sit down and I'll put the kettle on.'

When the tea was brewed, Tilly took it through. 'By, the shop's quiet today. I don't reckon as we've had a customer all day.'

'The calm afore the storm. The seasonal visitors are already arriving. We'll soon be rushed off our feet.'

Tilly thought about what Florrie had suggested, but then decided not to say anything yet. Maybe Liz was on the mend and would be better keeping involved with the shop. She was used to the hustle and bustle of the prom and was at home here.

But this thought was proved to be wrong almost as soon as it had occurred, as in answer to Liz's simple question of where Molly was, she broke down once more. Her body bent double as if in terrible pain and a moan came from her.

'Liz? Liz?'

Liz didn't answer. Tears tumbled down her face.

'Eeh, Liz, lass, what's to do?'

Through rasping sobs, Liz told her it was the mention of one of the stalls. 'Wh – what will happen to Dan's stall, Tilly? Where is it? Why has it gone?'

These questions were asked between gasping sobs. Going to her, Tilly held her close. 'Everything's been taken away, lass. You've nowt to worry over, it's all been seen to. The stock is in storage – that as survived the accident. We thought you'd want to sell it as a job lot, when you're up to it.'

'Dan's gone, ain't he, Tilly? Gone. Gone! Gone!'

The shop bell rang at that moment and as the door opened. Tilly was never so glad as to see Molly. 'Eeh, what's to do? Liz, lass. Come on. You'll be all right.'

Liz didn't answer Molly. Her mouth had gone slack again and her eyes drooped.

Molly looked over her head at Tilly. 'You have to get her some help, lass. I knaw as you have a tale to tell about an asylum and the bad time you both had, but Liz can't go on like this. Maybe sommat to make her sleep? Oh, I don't knaw, there must be sommat the doctors can do.'

'Aye, they'll do sommat. They'll lock her away, and that ain't going to happen. Not while I have breath in me body it ain't. I'll help her, Molly. I'll try Florrie's idea. In the meantime, close the shop and let's get her upstairs, eh? We can do this, Molly. We can get Liz through this.'

But as Tilly said this, she wondered if they could. Could anyone get through such a terrible second blow as Liz was having to contend with? *Poor Liz. Of all people, she doesn't deserve this.*

TWELVE

As they stood waiting their turn to climb into what looked like no more than a cart, and which was already crowded with women – some frightened, sitting hugging themselves and others, calling out obscenities to the harassed wardens who were checking that every prisoner bound for the assizes was present – Sally spoke softly to Babs. 'You'll contact us if you need us, now, won't you, love? You only have to walk round Maidstone centre at night, and you'll find one of us or both on a street corner. We'll always help you, won't we, Pixie?'

'We will, love. And if you get convicted, we'll find out where you are and come and see you. We promise.'

Sally held her shoulders then and looked deep into her eyes, 'And you're to be a brave girl. Snivelling in the court room never did anyone any good. Look remorseful. That'll get you everywhere with some of them holy types that sit in judgement of us.'

With this they both hugged her tightly and Babs saw tears glisten in their eyes as they released her.

Her heart was heavy and her own tears weren't far from spilling over, but she swallowed hard as she knew if she let them tumble, she would never stop crying. Such was her fear of what today held for her.

Doreen didn't speak as she hugged her, but the gesture showed the love she had for Babs. But Lilly compounded Babs's fear as she passed them and mumbled: 'Trouble will follow you, girl.'

All went as Mr Drayford had said it would. She was called to the stand, asked to swear on the Holy Bible and give her plea. In a determined and loud voice, she said, 'Not guilty.' And so, the formality of referring her case to a higher court was dealt with.

'The date will be set by the court secretary, and you will be informed through your solicitor,' the magistrate told her, and then, turning to Mr Drayford, he said that any petition for a particular date will be made through the proper channels. He seemed to finish speaking abruptly and this was signified by him banging his gavel on the table in front of him, which made Babs jump. This was followed by a voice bellowing out, 'All rise.'

With this, it was all over.

Babs didn't see any of the others she'd shared the cell with again and didn't know what had happened in their cases. On the way back to the prison, she had new companions: a sour-faced girl not much older than herself and an older woman, who spent the time crying.

Back in her cell, she was all alone. 'Don't worry yourself, girl, they'll soon arrest more who have fallen by the wayside, and then you'll have company.'

This warden was much friendlier that the one on the late shift, and Babs always liked it better when she was on duty.

Meals were given to her at a regular time and were even still hot sometimes. The quality of the food didn't improve, but Babs was always too hungry to care.

As she went to lock the cell door, the warden said, 'It's a sorry world when we have to lock up youngsters like you. No matter what you've done, it seems harsh. How are you feeling? Have you been sick in the mornings?'

'Naw. I've not had owt like that. I'm tired and allus hungry. Does you reckon that I am having a babby? I don't feel like I am.'

'More than likely. And I'm sorry for you. But I haven't seen a report of you having your monthlies and needing rags. Is this the second one you've missed?'

'Aye, I think so. I can't keep track of the days.'

'Well, you're down to see the doctor in a few days, so you'll find out then. And there will be a cleaning and exercise morning too.'

Babs's heart lifted at this, and she really hoped that she would see Mavis again. Mavis had a way of making you feel that you could cope and at this moment, in an empty cell, feeling as though there was no one else in the world, Babs didn't feel as though she could cope.

She slept for long hours and dreamt. Sometimes good, happy dreams where she was in this lovely, kind lady's house eating meat pie. She was with Beth and Ma was coming to fetch them later. And sometimes her dreams were frightening. There was something wrong with Beth and she couldn't get to her to help her.

After these dreams, Babs broke her heart. Ma had always said that she was to look out for Beth, and she wasn't doing that. If Beth was in trouble, she would need her. It was at these times that she would berate herself for ever leaving, but then turn her anger on Beth for not coming with her. With two of them, that Cecil would have had a fight on his hands, and they would have escaped.

None of these thoughts helped her. Each day went into the next, marked only by the meals they brought to her. On the third day the lock resounded around the room as the key turned. The nasty warden stood there. 'Cleaning and exercise. Get your lazy body up and out of here.'

Babs almost ran out. In the yard she craned her neck to see if Mavis was among the women and girls circling the yard. And then she spotted her. 'Mavis! Mavis! Over here.'

Mavis came running over. 'You're still here then?'

'Aye, I am. Eeh, it's good to see you.'

'What's 'appening to you, Tilly? You look fatter.'

Tilly looked down to the ground.

'You're not! Oh, Tilly, that's good news.'

'Good? By, I feel like killing meself with the shame of it. Where I come from, girls getting pregnant are frowned on.'

'No, I mean, not good news in one sense, but good news for your trial. Me only concern is where you'll land up.'

'I knaw, me solicitor has said it'll be a convent. But that's the last thing I want to happen. Awe, Mavis, if I hadn't been taken to that convent, I wouldn't be in here now.'

They were quiet for a few moments as they walked behind others, all going in the same direction.

'Are you still working on that machine, Mavis?'

'I am. I can operate it with me eyes shut now. They say as I'm the fastest machinist they've ever 'ad, and the neatest too.'

'Don't you get bored?'

'No. I just think me thoughts and work 'ard and count off the days.'

'I'm bored. What I wouldn't give to have a book to read or sommat.'

'You should ask. There's plenty, and it wouldn't 'urt for you to 'ave something to keep your mind occupied.'

'Will they let me?'

'You can only try. You get nothing if you don't ask, love. If they say no, start wailing. That'll sort it. They can't put you on punishment, not if you're 'aving a baby. Are you down to see the doctor later?'

'Aye.'

'So am I.'

For the first time, Babs registered that Mavis looked peaky. Then she realised that Mavis had a bandage on her finger. 'Have you hurt yourself on the machine, lass?'

'Lass? That's a funny thing to call me. I've not 'eard you say that before. *Lass*. I like it. Is that what you all say up in Blackpool?' Mavis giggled and Babs joined her. 'I love 'earing you talk, Babs. I wish we could be together. But I might see you at the doctor's. I cut me finger badly, and it's infected now. It don't 'alf throb.'

'You didn't have your eyes closed, did you? Eeh, and you're meant to be good an' all.'

They giggled together again, and Babs could feel her cares lifting off her shoulders. Their laughter was interrupted by the bell.

'Grab yourselves a mop and bucket. And you, Miss Smith, make sure you clean that bucket in your cell, it stinks.'

Babs blushed at this.

'Well, get to it, girl. I'll see you in the clinic.'

Mavis was gone then, leaving Babs feeling bereft and alone. She looked around her. There were all kinds of women in here; some looked as though they would kill you rather than look at you. Big, chunky women, who looked more like men. Some looked as though they didn't belong in here. Even in their prison garb, they carried themselves like ladies. And others looked like everyday women that you would see in the street, doing their shopping and coping with young 'uns. All spoke like Mavis, if not quite so broad. There were no Northerners amongst them, and this made Babs feel even lonelier.

'Ah, you're back, are you? Well, same routine: strip off and wash thoroughly.' The same nurse as last time barked this out. Babs wanted to tell her that it would be a pleasure for she felt dirty and longed for a proper wash instead of rubbing her face and hands on the damp flannel that was passed through to her every day.

The water left out for her was warmer than last time, and Babs really enjoyed sluicing herself down and rubbing her elbows and knees with the flannel.

When the curtain swished back, the nurse stood there. 'Good. You've done a proper job.'

Naked as the day she was born, Babs waited in a line of other naked women. She kept her eyes to the front until a sharp nudge from the woman next to her made her jump. 'You got more than your fair share, didn't you, love' The woman laughed a cackling laugh that sounded as rude as what she'd said. ''Ere, look at this one. Hardly left her mum's knee and she's got the biggest pair of breasts that I've ever seen.'

Babs felt her colour rise. 'Don't. Leave me alone.'

'Ha, don't tell me you ain't had them gawped at before, love. They're standing prouder than a chapel steeple. I'd like a bit of them.'

This shocked Babs. Did the woman mean that she'd like to have some the same size, or that she wanted to . . .

'Leave it out, Jo. She's only a young girl.'

'I'd say she knows what it's all about. Look at them dark brown nipples, a sure sign.'

Babs felt sick. She tried to cover her breasts.

'Barbara Smith.'

'Ooh, let's watch them wobble as she walks, girls.' Laughter rippled through the line of women.

'What's all this noise out here? Barbara, go in to the doctor at once, and the rest of you, stop your stupid giggling.'

Babs scurried into the room. The same doctor was sat at the desk. 'Ahh, and how have you been? Has nature proved me to be right? Let me look at you.'

The examination was done in a gentle way once more, not causing any pain to Babs.

'Yes. I was right. I would say you're at least four months now. Does that fit in with when you last had your monthly?'

'I don't knaw, Doctor. I can't keep track. But it was back in February that I were raped.'

The nurse sighed. 'They all say that, don't they, Doctor?' In a mocking voice the nurse said, '*I was raped!* Ha, if I had a farthing for every time that I've heard that one!'

'Nurse, I think with the innocence of this child, I'm inclined to believe her.'

'None of them are innocent, Doctor, I thought you'd learnt that by now.'

'I have learnt not to be as judgemental as you are, Nurse.'

The nurse looked furious and stormed out of the room.

'You can sit up now, Miss Smith. So, if it was February, then it is now almost July, which means that I am not far off the mark. Make sure that you eat well and take exercise.'

'I'm locked in all day, Doctor. I only have a walk on the day that you come to visit.'

The nurse shot back into the room. 'Liar! They walk every day, Doctor.'

'Naw, we don't. I ain't been out in the yard, or outside me cell, since the last time the doctor was here. I've only been to the courthouse and back in a cart and that's it.'

'Oh, and what happened at the court?'

Babs told him how she was remanded for trial. 'I cry every night, Doctor, 'cause, I didn't do owt. I didn't.'

Another 'humph' from the nurse.

'Don't upset yourself, Miss Smith. I'm sure if you're innocent, the truth will come out.'

'Come on. Get out of here. You've taken up enough of the doctor's time.'

The doctor sighed but didn't say anything to the nurse on this occasion. Outside, the nurse shoved Babs. 'Get behind there and get dressed and be quick about it. We don't like mouthy cows in here. You'll soon learn to keep it shut.'

Babs shivered. The revengeful tone made her afraid of what might happen to her. Sally and Pixie had warned her not to say anything to the doctor or any other person visiting, but the doctor had been so nice to her that she'd forgotten.

Outside in the corridor she bumped into Mavis. Just seeing the lovely Mavis brought tears swimming to her eyes.

'I take it you've got it confirmed that there's a bun in the oven then?'

'Aye. I'm four months gone.'

'Well, there's no use crying about it, love. Chin up and think of the good it'll do you.'

That evening no food was delivered to Babs and only a mug of cold water the next day. No words were spoken to her. The door was unlocked, the drink shoved in and the door banged closed.

When nothing came at midday, Babs felt a deep sense of loneliness settle in her. She lay on her bunk for a while – a hard wooden structure with a thin, horse-hair mattress and one blanket – then got up and paced up and down, but nothing settled her. No one came that night to collect her bucket, or to feed her. The night hours dragged as her rumbling stomach gave her no peace. Nor did her mind as it churned with thoughts of what it would be like to have a baby, but nothing in her imagination gave her answers.

It was when she let herself think of Beth that the floodgates opened, and a deluge of tears cascaded from her. Deep, lonely sobs wracked her body, leaving her feeling that the world had abandoned her and that she would be left here to die.

Beth tentatively put her feet into the slipper-type shoes. It felt strange after so many weeks to be wearing shoes again. Her undergarments restricted her, and her clothes felt heavy and cumbersome after weeks and weeks of just wearing a nightshirt. The long skirt was grey in colour, but wasn't dull looking as Jasmine had crocheted rows of daisies onto it, with white petals and yellow centres that made them look so real, and she had stitched three rows of these around the hem. The crisp white blouse she wore had pretty lace stitched to the cuffs. The same lace edged the high collar that buttoned under her chin.

'You look lovely, though I haven't been able to do much with your hair – it just curls no matter what I try. It looks pretty, though, with that ribbon holding it back off your face.

Beth smiled. She wished she felt lovely, but she didn't. Her body was weak and sweat trickled down her face. The weakness made her tears spill over.

'Hey, don't cry. You're going home, Beth. You should be very happy. Your mama is waiting in the corridor for you. You have no signs of the infection that lingered for so long. I told the doctor about you wanting to be a nurse, so he wrote, "Suspected, but not confirmed lung damage" as he knows that medical history is considered when a girl applies to be trained as a nurse.'

'Ta, Philippa. I – I'm going to miss you.'

Philippa enclosed her in her arms. 'And I'm going to miss you too. You're a lovely girl, Beth. I will worry about you. I hope your sister comes back, as I do believe you have one, and you're mama denying it will always be a mystery to me. I really hope you do become a nurse. I know you're going on your travels now, but if ever you're back in this area, drop in to see me and let me know how you're faring, eh?'

'I will.'

'Come on then, let's take you to your mama.'

It came to Beth to shout that Jasmine wasn't the woman that she'd told Philippa of, but a wicked gypsy who'd taken her from her ma, but she just nodded and followed the nurse out of the room that had been her home for weeks and weeks.

In her bag, she had the precious books that Philippa had given her, the pages of which she'd turned many times over the last few days, discovering fascinating and sometimes funny facts about the inside of the human body. None of the make-up of the male body surprised her as many boys and men in the gypsy camps would swim in the rivers without a stitch on and the little ones would run around naked on a hot day. But what happened to them during what the book called the 'reproductive process', which she knew meant making babies, did surprise her. She wondered what it would be like for a man to do that to her, and this had given her a funny feeling in her tummy.

'Beth! My darling girl. Mama is for being so happy that you are coming home. Papa is waiting outside with the trap as we have a long way to go to our new encampment. There's a lot of gypsies waiting to greet you.'

As Jasmine took Beth into her arms, the familiar smell of violets from the perfume that Jasmine made for herself helped, as it gave Beth a sense that yes, she was going home. Once outside, however, a sudden attack of shyness took her as her newfound knowledge of men made her see Roman in a different way. The noises she'd heard during the night hours in the wagon suddenly became very vivid to her. For some reason, Babs had always seemed to know what was happening and had giggled about it the next day, but it had all passed over Beth's head. Now she wondered if she could bear to hear it again.

When they reached the encampment, Beth was so tired that all thoughts of these fears left her, and she went willingly into their wagon and lay on the bed, which usually wasn't assembled until the night time but which Jasmine had thoughtfully made up for her.

She hadn't done more than acknowledge the group of familiar faces that waited to greet her. 'It is that Beth needs to rest. She will be seeing you all later,' Jasmine had told them before leading her into the wagon.

'Do you want to remove your clothing, Beth?' With this from Jasmine, Beth looked over at Roman, who'd followed them in and was sat on the edge of his and Jasmine's bed. Never before had she felt shy of him. 'Naw, I'll stay in me clothes, ta. I only need a nap.'

'Well, it is that I have a potion ready for you. Drink it up. You will soon feel your energy filling your body once more.'

Beth took the potion. She never questioned what was in these concoctions of Jasmine's but knew the power of them.

'You should make lots and lots of this stuff, Mama. There are many sick people who would benefit from them.'

Jasmine smiled her lovely warm smile. 'Thank you, darling, I will teach you the secret of them when you are well. Everything is provided by nature. Mother Nature holds the power of healing, but it is that people have forgotten this and look to the chemist and the doctors to heal them with artificial substances.'

'I'm going to be a nurse, Mama. I want to heal folk.'

'Oh? But you can do that with the potions, darling. Being a nurse is not something that we gypsies do.'

'Mama, I'm naw gypsy.'

At this, Jasmine sighed heavily. 'Get your rest now, little one.'

As Beth closed her eyes, she felt the effect of the potion relax her body and with her newfound enthusiasm for such things, wondered what was in this particular one that could relax you in this way. And how Jasmine had this knowledge.

She made up her mind that yes, she would learn the skills, and maybe use the knowledge when she was a nurse. But she must stay determined, or she would never make it to being one, as she knew that she could be swayed to do what others wanted her to. Babs had done that to her all her life. Maybe now, being on her own, she could grow a stronger will.

This thought shocked her as she never thought she would feel a benefit from not being with her beloved twin. Guilt crowded her, as did the pain of her loss. *Oh, Babs, Babs, I didn't mean it. I'll never be whole without you by my side.*

THIRTEEN

The rain pelted Tilly as she manoeuvred her cart pulled by Foxy, her horse, through the throng of other horses and carts, and the crowds of people. Not even the prospect of a soaking deterred the folk determined to travel or walk along the prom. But she felt no irritation at the inconvenience they posed and knew that if she lived to be a hundred, she would always love the excitement of Blackpool.

The sight before her was of many colours billowing in the wind, as the gusts played with the ladies' skirts and the plumes of the fancily dressed horses, whose owners ran a business giving pleasure trips from one end of the promenade to the other, now known as the Golden Mile.

Traders didn't mind the rain. Many had extended their canvas awnings so that folk could shelter under them, as while there, they would examine and buy their goods, often meaning that a little wet stuff from heaven was a welcome sight rather than a hindrance.

Tilly loved and admired these traders. Their resilience and ingenuity never ceased to amaze her. She called out to them as she rode by every morning on her way to her shop. Today, she felt a little guilty that she had a nice dry place to work from, but like them, she didn't mind the rain. The holiday-makers were turned out of their boarding houses after breakfast and not allowed back until teatime, so they had no choice but to brave the weather. Everyone selling anything did better on wet days than on sunny days as then the visitors would stake out their pitch on the beach and stay put for the day. Today, her shop would be busy all day, and this pleased her.

All her plans were beginning to take shape. They had a woman called Gertie working in the shop, who lived on the same street as Molly. A widow with a grown-up family, Gertie had no ties and was a gem. Her way with the customers endeared them to her, and many dropped in for a chat with her and ended up leaving with some knick-knack or other, as now they had a corner of the shop given over to some of the stock that had been salvaged from Dan's stall and from the stock he'd kept in his shed. It wasn't what Tilly wanted, but it had alleviated one of Liz's worries. For now, she felt that she was still contributing to the business, even though she spent her time at the farm, sometimes helping Tommy, but mostly watching over Ivan and doing small jobs around the house – the best of these being having a meal ready for Tilly and Tommy to enjoy in the evening, when Liz would take herself off with Ivan to the nursery and get him ready for bed. This gave Tilly valuable time with Tommy.

Life was definitely better as they welcomed early September, although it was getting harder for Tilly as she coped with what she called her 'bulk', as she was now five months pregnant and expanding faster than she liked. She hadn't been like this when carrying Ivan but had when carrying the twins.

Dear God, don't let me be having twins again. But please send me lovely Babs and Beth home to me.

The latter part of this prayer was never far from her lips, but sometimes she despaired at it ever happening. Like always, she didn't dwell on it. Life had to be lived. There were people who depended on her and that was that.

As she passed the house where Malcolm had worked, she felt a sense of pride. The work she had done had been so well accepted by the owners that they had given her orders from their friends in London who had been on visits. Her business was booming. And so was Molly's, as now they had decided to share the premises and the expense of it, but to run their businesses separately, albeit complementing each other's. It was a really good arrangement and them becoming proper partners had further cemented their friendship, instead of Molly and Liz deferring to her. Not that Liz took much of an active part, but with Dan's goods on sale, the income from those was hers and gave her a financial independence.

Liz's house was closed down, with dust sheets covering everything. She didn't want to sell it, but for some reason had insisted on seeing Mr Fellows and making a will, leaving the main bulk of her estate to Tilly with a legacy going to the traders' benevolent fund.

Tilly had been shocked when Liz had told her this. Not only because it had frightened her, as Liz was still very delicate, if much better than she was, but because she didn't feel deserving of it. She tried to persuade Liz to leave something to Dan's relations, but no, she just said that they hadn't cared about her after Dan had died, not even to ask after her or to invite them to their houses, and she'd always felt inferior to them. She felt she owed them nothing.

When she reached the shop she was met by Molly. 'Eeh, Tilly, you look like a drowned rat.'

'Ha, ta very much, Molly. Actually, I feel like one. Put the kettle on, lass, while I go and change.'

Tilly went through to what was once her and Tommy's bedroom. Here she kept a change of clothing for just such events as getting a soaking on her drive in to work. Peeling off her wet coat, she found, but for the hem of her skirt and petticoats, the rest of her clothing was dry. Reaching for another skirt of the same dark brown colour, she stepped into it, only to find that it wouldn't fasten. 'Damn! Damn being pregnant! Tommy may be happy, but I'm not!'

Try as she might, Tilly had never been glad to be in this state. She knew it was bad of her, but the pregnancy only served as a nuisance and a reminder of times she didn't want to visit, besides making her scared that she may birth another crippled child.

Slumping down on a chair they'd left in this room, she felt tears prickling her eyes. A sudden jerking movement in her stomach had her tapping it. 'You can shut up as well, you little pest!' The lump inside her kicked harder. 'You cheeky thing. Well, I'll soon get that out of you when you get here.' Another jerk, but a much gentler one, more of a ripple, and Tilly looked down and told her bump, 'I knaw as you're sorry, it ain't your fault, little one, it's your grumpy old ma.' With this the lump became a child in her mind. Her child. And with a rush of emotion, she knew she loved it.

Gently stroking her hand over her stomach, she spoke in a much kinder voice. 'We'll be all right, you and me, little one.

I'm your ma, and I'll take care of you. I'm sorry, I knaw as I haven't welcomed you. But I knaw as I love you with all me heart now, so things'll get better between us. Ma'll see to that.'

'Who're you talking to, lass? Are you going around the bend or sommat?'

'Naw. I'm chatting to me young 'un. And it's a cheeky one, Molly, answering me back like a good 'un.'

'Eeh, that's good to see. I've been worried about your rejection of this babby. But it sounds like you're going to meet your match with this one.'

'Aye, just like I did with my Babs . . . Awe, Molly . . . Molly.'

In Molly's arms the floodgates opened, making Tilly feel weak and suddenly very fragile.

'By, love, I've never met anyone like you and Liz. Such wonderful lasses, and yet, you have the world's troubles thrown at you. Look at how you do all you can to help others. It just ain't fair.'

Thinking of Liz calmed Tilly. Yes, she did have troubles, but nothing like poor Liz. 'I'm just tired, Molly. This one is taking it out of me. I often feel very unwell.'

'Aye, it can happen like that. They're all different. You can sail through carrying one, and then have a hell of a time carrying another. Why don't you take a couple of days off? It's been all go for you with moving and taking care of Liz. How is she?'

'She seems fine on the surface, but I often hear her crying, which is only natural. It definitely suits her out in the country. Tommy says she spends a lot of time with him in the fields. She takes Ivan up at snap time, with a billycan for Tommy, and he says she seems at her happiest then and really mucks in, so that's good.'

'Aye, it was kindness itself, you taking her up to the farm with you. Your first proper home in England with Tommy and you have to share it.'

'It's working out very well. She's a help and doesn't intrude a lot. She soon takes herself to her bedroom when I come home . . . Mind, that's uncomfortable sometimes as I feel as though I'm pushing her out and I wish she'd stay and spend the evening with us.'

'Best to let her do her own thing. Have you owt pressing at the mo?'

'I've to finish that table that's ordered. It needs to be on the train by Saturday. The folk who've ordered it want it delivered by Tuesday at the latest.'

'That's going to London, ain't it?'

'Aye.'

'Well, I'll have them cushions ready by then and they're going to an address in London an' all, so we can dispatch them together.'

'We'd better get on then. I've nearly done, only a bit of tidying at the edges.'

'Right, when that's done, Tilly, you're to go home and not return till Monday. I'll see to getting the shipment ready and picked up for transporting on Saturday. And I'll take care of opening and closing the shop and be on hand if Gertie needs me.'

'Happen I will. Aye, I'm warming to the idea. I'll take a couple of days and get body and soul together. And catch up with Liz as she can't avoid me all day. I might go up to the field with her an' all. I can't do the heavy work, but I can sit on the grass if it's nice and I can play with Ivan. I'd love that.'

'Done then! Come on, let's get cracking.'

As they worked, Tilly remembered something she'd forgotten to tell Molly. 'Eeh, Molly, you'll never guess what. Our Ivan can crawl.'

'What? Awe, that's wonderful news. How did that come about?'

'Liz and Tommy did it. Tommy made a joke that I mother him too much and don't let him try things, which is true to a certain extent. Anyroad, it appears they had him on the lawn and encouraged him to try to get from one to the other of them. And he did. He moves in a sort of wriggly way, but not in the way he was used to by dragging his legs behind him, but using his legs by bending them and pushing himself with them. By he can shift himself an' all. He's in seventh heaven to have this independence as it means he can get from room to room, or even take himself outside. But, eeh, I feel awful about holding him back, but not anymore. From now on the sky's the limit. Whatever he wants to try, he can.'

'What about his lessons, lass? I enjoy teaching him and he loves to learn. He should have them on a regular basis, you knaw.'

'Aye, we have to sort sommat out for him, and you of course, it has to suit you.'

'What about, once you've had this break you bring him into work with you every Wednesday? I'll try to have a clear bench by the afternoon and take him home and give him his lessons and his tea. Will and the lads would love that.'

'Aye, that's a great idea. We'll do that. Right, that's that. All finished.'

'Eeh, you really did just have a bit to do. That's wonderful. I'm not doing so well, I've to unpick this last bit. That's with chin-wagging to you.'

'You concentrate while I tidy up my bench and check there's nowt that I can't leave till next week.'

As Tilly tidied her bench, she thought how well their new arrangement was working out. What used to be the living room now contained two long workbenches, one for Molly and one for her. Molly's had her sewing machine on the end, a cutting area, and all her tools, scissors and the like. Her stock of materials, buttons, press studs and what she needed in that line were stacked on a set of strong shelves built into the chimney breast on her half of the room.

Tilly had her own set of shelves for her tools and some bigger ones for her cane and wicker. Her tubs for soaking the cane and wicker were out in the backyard. There was a tap out there, so it was easy for her to fill the tubs using a small bucket.

The kitchen was as it was, and very useful for the umpteen cups of tea they brewed and for keeping a stock of bread and cold meats which were stored on the cold slab in the pantry. This meant they could always feed themselves, though they were both partial to hot chips from the chippy along the prom and often sent out for these.

'Well, that's me done. I'll go and tether Foxy to the cart and get off home. Give me a hug, Molly, lass, and I'll see you in a few days.'

Coming out of the hug, Tilly donned her outdoor clothes, gave a last wave to Molly and headed downstairs. 'I'm off early, Gertie, are you managing?'

'Aye, it's been steady. Take care now, the prom's busy today.'

Waving goodbye, Tilly was glad to get outside. The rain had stopped, and the air smelt of the salty sea, which vied with all the usual Blackpool Prom aromas – various food cooking and, of course, fish.

Tilly enjoyed the drive home. Foxy set a good pace, trotting along, and she began to feel exhilarated and couldn't wait to get home to Tommy and Ivan, and Liz. She hoped that Liz was having a good day. Tommy had said that he hadn't so much work in the fields now as his ploughing and sowing were all done, so he was going to work in the barns that surrounded the house. They all needed putting in order, especially the milking parlour as he was going to market soon to buy some cattle. She hoped it wouldn't be in the next couple of days as suddenly, she really wanted to spend time with him. They could leave Ivan with Liz and come back to Blackpool and buy fish and chips and walk along the prom eating them out of newspaper and have fun on the stalls that stay open late. The idea took root and Tilly could feel a quickening of her heart. She loved her Tommy, he was her world, and that was completed by their precious Ivan and the new child they had made. She couldn't wait to tell Tommy how at last she loved the little one he had planted inside her.

When she reached the farm there was no one about. Untethering Foxy, she led him to the meadow and let him loose, laughing as he galloped away in a playful manner. He loved the grass and was ready to feel the softness of it under his hooves after being in the stable behind the shop all morning.

Going up to the house, she nearly called out, but then thought she would surprise Ivan, so crept inside. No one was in the huge kitchen. She loved this room. Bigger than any kitchen she'd ever seen, it had a huge range on one wall, flanked by two pine dressers. On the opposite wall there was a deep pot sink and draining board. This was skirted by a lovely gingham curtain that Molly had made. And the tablecloth and curtains at the two windows were of the same material.

In the centre of the room was a huge scrubbed table surrounded by six matching chairs. And hanging from the beams of the ceiling were bunches of onions and lovely copper pans. Two wooden rocking chairs, one each side of the range, completed the furnishings. They had cushions on them, again made by Molly, in a lovely daffodil yellow. Smiling, Tilly felt better already. She just needed to find her menfolk and her friend.

She didn't find them in the living room, which still needed a few touches to make it homely. Tilly had ordered cushions from Molly, but as she'd been snowed under, they were still waiting. This room was dominated by a huge brown leather sofa and two armchairs. They'd been left by the previous owner and had all seen better days, but they were so comfortable that they'd decided to clean them up and keep them. The room needed everything from a lick of paint to some nice fabrics to brighten it. Its best feature was a grand fireplace that took up almost one wall. Built from red bricks, it was a real feature and Tilly had days when she couldn't wait for autumn so that they could see it with a fire roaring up its chimney.

The stairs led off this room, and Tilly, thinking that it was likely that Tommy had changed his mind and that they were all in the fields after all, ran up to get changed. When she came to her and Tommy's bedroom door, she stopped. Voices were coming from inside. Holding her breath, Tilly listened.

It was Tommy . . . and Liz! Tilly stared at the heavy door, which didn't allow much sound through, trying to understand why they would be in her bedroom. Putting her ear to the door, she heard Liz giggle. Shock held her rigid. Bursting into the room she stood stock still as she saw them dart apart. 'Naw, naw . . . Tommy, Liz . . . why?'

Turning, she ran back down the stairs. Tommy chased after her. 'Tilly, me little darling, it's not for being what you're thinking. Tilly, stop, let me be for explaining. Tilly!'

Tilly couldn't stop running. She had to get as far away from this betrayal as she could. Her heart was splitting in two. That her Tommy and her best friend . . . Oh God!

Outside she ran towards the gate, with no idea where she was going. She was nearly there when she tripped and fell. Her head banged on a cobble.

The world spun around her. A pain shot through her. She couldn't see. All sound was muffled. She was floating. The feeling was good. There was no hurt now. No pain, no broken heart, just a whooshing sound like the wind blowing through the trees. Through the wind she could hear her name, 'Tilly! Tilly!' She knew it was Tommy but didn't want to leave this place to go to him, because then she would have to face something that she didn't want to face, so instead she relaxed and went with the wind deeper and deeper into the peace it offered.

When she came to, she was in Tommy's arms being carried towards the house. His voice droned in her ear, but she didn't know what he was talking about. 'Tilly, it is that nothing was happening! Oh, me little darling, I wouldn't be for betraying you.'

Drifting back into unconsciousness, Tommy faded away and Tilly knew that was how she wanted everything; she wanted the oblivion, but didn't know why.

The next time she woke, she knew she was in hospital. Familiar sounds and smells assailed her, bringing her memories of the last time she had lain in a ward, and the terrible wrenching pain of being told the twins had been taken. This time the pain of Tommy's betrayal hit her.

'Tilly?'

Turning her head, she looked into Tommy's haggard face. 'Naw . . . naw, why?'

Pain clenched her heart.

'I didn't, Tilly. It was that I went up to be changing me clothes. I was scrubbing the floor of the barn when I slipped, me foot kicked the bucket and spilled its filthy contents over me trousers. I was soaked to the skin of me and I stunk to high heaven. So, I doused meself with a couple of clean buckets of water, so as not to drag the filth into the house. When it was that I went up the stairs I could hear Liz crying and moaning; she was making a terrible sound. I thought to leave her to calm. I looked for Ivan and found him in his room asleep. So, I went to our room.' Tommy hung his head and shook it from side to side as if in despair.

Tilly's head throbbed. She wanted to hear what he said. Wanted to believe him but didn't know if she could. What she'd heard, Liz giggling, and what she'd seen, her Tommy holding Liz to him, shouted at her that he was lying. That he'd had time to think up a tale and was now struggling to lie to her.

'Me little Tilly, how is it that I'm to convince you of the truth of what happened?'

Tommy was once more looking at her. Tears ran down his cheeks. She waited.

'I changed me trousers, whistling a tune as I did, thinking it best to let Liz hear that I was near, so that she might try to calm herself. When I reached for a shirt from the cupboard and turned back towards the bed, I was shocked to see Liz standing just inside the door . . . I – I . . . Oh, me Tilly, it is that I don't know how to tell you, for what happened will hurt you so much, and I'm not wanting to do that.'

'You mean . . . Tommy, tell me. Did – did you . . .'

'No. I need you to believe me that I was only for offering comfort. I – I . . . Oh, Tilly, there's no easy way for me to be telling the truth of it, but I have to. I cannot lose you, me Tilly, but it is that I might do that whichever path I take in the telling of what happened.'

'I have to knaw, Tommy.'

'In me telling it is that you must remember that Liz isn't herself. But before I could be asking her what she wanted, she ran around the bed and flung herself at me. The shock of this happening left me unable to think what to do. She was begging me to . . . well, to love her. To make her feel like a woman again. She was saying that it is that you would never know. With the force of her I found meself pushed to the bed, but there I recovered and held her at bay. I was for wanting to be kind to her, Tilly. I talked to her, telling her that I could never be doing that to her, that me only woman was you, Tilly . . .'

'Naw . . . not Liz! I – I can't believe it, Tommy, Liz wouldn't . . .'

'So, is it that you'd rather be for believing that I would then?'

'Naw, but . . . Oh, Tommy you were holding her, you – you had naw shirt on, and you were both giggling . . . Oh, what am I to believe?'

'I had calmed her and then she was for being mortified. She begged of me to forget it ever happened, said it was the comfort of a man loving her that she was needing, but she was so sorry that it was me she'd turned to. I tried to make light of it. I thought to get us back to normal and that it was that you would never know it happened. We had just agreed on that and she asked me for a hug. I'm for promising you that it was no more than that, but then I said something that made her giggle. I can't even remember what it was as at that moment you opened the door. Please be for believing me, Tilly.'

It all sounded plausible but if it was, then Tilly knew that she still had the hurt of Liz's betrayal to contend with. Would Liz ever betray her in that way? Would Tommy? At this moment and with what she had seen crowding her mind, she didn't know the answers. She closed her eyes. Whichever one, what did it matter? Both of them she would have trusted with her life and for that to be gone, she found the pain too immense to deal with at this moment.

FOURTEEN

Eight weeks after seeing the doctor, a drawn and tired Babs stood in a different court from the assizes. Void of hope, she stared ahead. The jury had taken their seats after the formality of swearing them in and the judge now sat behind a huge counter-like desk. A few people sat in what the solicitor told her was called the public gallery – a place that looked like a balcony and was set higher than the courtroom. On glancing up there was no one that she knew.

To the side of her was a witness box that was much the same as the one in the magistrate's court, but this one was fancier as it had a pattern similar to picture frames around its base. Her first impression of being brought into this room was one of polish as the smell of it was very strong and everything from the benches to the floor gleamed.

The next two days were harrowing. Part of her held hope as Mr Drayford had said that his friend had made contact with Emma, but that was the last he'd heard. 'Don't give up hope, Barbara,' he'd said. 'My friend knows the urgency of Emma's testimony, and if there is a problem with it, we will get an adjournment, but at the moment, I have lodged with the judge that I am waiting for a crucial witness to your innocence and indicated that though we will allow the trial to proceed, I may be asking for more time if the witness doesn't turn up. In view of where she lives, the judge indicated that he would be favourable to my request.'

Every movement at the back of the court had her and Mr Drayford looking back with eagerness, but Emma didn't appear.

Now all looked gloomy to Babs as she'd listened to evidence given against her, the most damning being from Sister Anne, who could only relate what she was told. Despite Mr Drayford calling out that this was all circumstantial, the judge allowed it, saying that as they had little else, and the account of events was given by one nun to another – women in his opinion who could be trusted to relate the truth – he saw little to discredit the evidence offered.

Sister Anne did help a little by answering Mr Drayford's questions loud and clear. 'Yes, I have seen Sister Brenda in a temper many times.' And to another, 'Yes, that is true, I have never approved of her methods of cleansing the girls.' When she'd tried to elaborate on this Mr Drayford had said, 'That's all, Sister.' The Judge had asked her to carry on with what she wanted to say: 'I was going to say that Sister Brenda is the most holy of women and believes that cleanliness goes with Godliness. She believes that she can help to bring that about by scrubbing the body to cleanse the soul.'

With the judge saying, 'I understand,' Mr Drayford looked furious. 'Sister Anne, isn't it true that you didn't agree with the practice as it wasn't just a scrubbing as one might imagine – a vigorous rubbing down with soap and a flannel – but a vicious assault with a scrubbing brush that would normally be used on floors?'

Sister Anne looked to the judge. Babs had the feeling that she was afraid. Her eyes went from the judge to the gallery. Babs followed her look and there, sat as stiff as a rod and glaring down, was the Reverend Mother.

'Please do not continue with this line of questioning. The witness has said that she does not agree with the scrubbing of the girls and has given the reasons that Sister Brenda did it. How is it relevant considering that we have heard nothing of that nature actually happened to your client? And this we know was because carnage broke out before it could. What is the purpose of you following this through? Surely you don't want to prove that your client was afraid of this happening to her, as that would implicate her guilt in taking measures for it not to happen?'

When Babs was taken back down the stairs that she'd climbed to get to the courthouse, she was once more locked in a cell in the cellar of the building. This room was a big improvement on the one she had occupied in the prison. The walls were painted white, and the bed looked clean. A barred window let in a lot of light.

When Mr Drayford came to see her, he looked worried. 'That hasn't helped us, Barbara. The sister came across as someone to love and trust and the judge allowing her to explain her reasoning, and then his words to me, put a motive into the jury's heads.'

'Am I going to be convicted?'

'We still have the hope of Emma turning up. Keep your chin up.'

On the third day, evidence was heard about Rita. Her father stood tall and confident as he answered questions about his daughter, telling the court that she was a good girl who'd been taken in by a young man who had no intention of marrying her. Yes, she had been suicidal when it all happened, but was looking forward to getting it all behind her and restarting her life.

Babs had thought about Rita and the fear she'd displayed. Her heart went out to her da. Even more so when Mr Drayford questioned him as she thought some of the inferences were very cruel. 'Knowing she was suicidal, wouldn't it have been better to keep her in what you have described as a loving home with you and her mother? The records at the convent show that you and her mother never visited, or enquired after your daughter, so how do you know that she was looking forward to getting all of this behind her?' And on and on until Rita's father agreed that his daughter could still have been suicidal, and admitted that he didn't know if he was or not. When he left the stand, he was crying. Babs couldn't help crying for him. Mr Drayford reprimanded her for this. 'It could be misconstrued as if you are admitting your guilt and are now feeling remorse.'

When the prosecution said they had no more witnesses, the judge invited the defence to begin calling any witnesses they may have. Mr Drayford rose. Babs held her breath. There were no witnesses to stand for her. And though she knew there would be an adjournment granted, it wasn't what she wanted. She wanted an end to it. She wanted to face whatever conclusion the jury brought in and to get on with what was going to happen to her. She couldn't bear going back to that prison and had long wanted to be sent to a convent, no matter what that might entail.

'My Lord, as previously spoken about, I do have a key witness, Miss Emma Reading.'

'No!' The gasp stopped Mr Drayford from continuing. He looked towards the gallery, as Babs did. The Reverend Mother looked shocked and had her hand over her mouth.

The gavel banged. 'Silence in court!'

Mr Drayford took a deep breath.

'My learned friend, you may continue.'

'Thank you, m'lord. I am in contact with Miss Reading, through a learned friend. He has said that he is doing his best to persuade her family to allow her to travel to give evidence, but I haven't heard, and so wanted to apply to have her summoned to court, and if this is refused, then arrested and brought here.'

This shocked Babs. She hated the thought of Emma being arrested. But the judge agreed. 'The court will adjourn for—'

'M'lord!'

A shout from the gallery echoed around the room. Murmurings rippled and the collective sound of people fidgeting filled the courtroom.

'Forgive me, m'lord, for this intrusion into the court proceeding's, but I have just arrived and have travelled all the way from the Isle of Wight. I have a crucial witness to this case with me. Miss Emma Reading.'

The judge gave an audible sigh. 'Very well, the witness will be allowed. The court will adjourn for one hour to allow Miss Smith's legal team to speak with their witness.'

The objection of the prosecution wasn't allowed.

When Emma stood in the witness box, tears ran freely down Babs's face and relief flooded her as the truth of what happened was related. Emma didn't waver under cross-examination. And even though she didn't see Rita's suicide, she told the court that she had stopped Rita from cutting her wrists on one occasion and from swallowing some cleaning fluid on another. 'She told me that she didn't want to live, that she couldn't take the cruelty of the sisters, or the thought of having to give her baby away.'

When the prosecution cross-examined Emma, she stuck to her story. It was when the prosecuting lawyer turned to the judge and asked, 'M'lord, are we to take the word of these wayward girls? I mean, they were in the convent because they had sinned. We have had an upstanding nun stand in this witness box and tell us the truth.'

A hush descended on the court. Babs waited, holding her breath. They had to believe Emma, they had to.

A sob resounded in the silence, then a voice echoed around the court. 'Emma is not lying. It is I who didn't tell the truth and may God forgive me.'

'Sit down at once, Sister Anne.'

The voice of the Reverend Mother trembled through Babs. Still after all these months she remembered the fear she felt when this formidable woman spoke.

'No, Reverend Mother, I will not.'

What followed held Babs in suspense as the judge ruled that the court would adjourn and summoned Mr Drayford, the prosecution lawyer and Sister Anne to attend his chambers.

The time they were gone stretched interminably for Babs.

When at last they emerged, Mr Drayford smiled over at Babs. She willed him to come over to her to tell her what was happening, but he took his place.

The usual formalities of 'All rise' were gone through. However, the judge didn't sit down, but picked up his gavel and addressed the court. 'This case is dismissed. Barbara Smith, you are free to go.' Babs didn't know whether to rejoice, or break her heart.

Outside in the corridor, Mr Drayford put his arm around her. 'Everything's going to be all right now, but I must speak to you about your future and the future of your unborn child.'

'What will happen to Sister Anne? And can I see Emma to thank her?'

'What happens to the sisters will be up to the prosecution. They are in contempt of court and did pervert the course of justice. But I don't know if that will be pursued or not. And no, I'm sorry, but you cannot see Emma. Her father was with her and he said he wanted to take her away from this the moment her evidence was heard. Emma didn't object, but then, from what you say, you weren't friends and what she did was an act of her own defiance – one very brave girl standing up to those harming others.'

'Can I write her a letter for your friend to give to her?'

'Yes. If it will make you feel better. Now, follow me into the office over there, I have the use of it today.'

Once in the small, wood-panelled room that contained just a desk and two chairs, one behind the desk which Mr Drayford sat in and one in front that Babs was told to sit on, Mr Drayford leant forward with elbows on the desk and rested his head on his two fists. 'I cannot let you just walk out of here, Barbara. I want to make sure you are safe and cared for. To that end, I have already contacted a convent run by nuns . . . Now, before you protest, hear me out.'

Babs listened as he told her that he'd carefully selected the convent. That it was in a place called Sevenoaks and was not far from where he lived. 'I have been to see them and told them what you have been through and what I believed happened at the other convent. They were mortified and said they would welcome you. Please give it a try, Babs. At least until you have had your baby. I promise you that I will visit every month and ask for a private meeting with you, so that if things are not good, you can tell me, and I will do something about it.'

'But I want to go to me ma.'

'I know. And I will keep trying to locate her. You keep trying to remember your surname, but Barbara, it isn't going to be easy, especially if your mother has remarried. So, you may have to wait a few years until you can visit Blackpool and physically search for her. Try to settle down with the nuns. They take unmarried mothers in. They find homes for the babies and make sure the mothers either get back home or, for those who haven't a home, which they tell me is very few, they either allow them to stay to help out with the other mums or they try to find them a position in service.'

Not sure of all this, but feeling that she had no other choice, Babs agreed.

The nun who greeted Babs introduced herself as Sister Bernadette. Her Irish lilt sent Babs reeling back to Beth and the wagon home she missed more than she thought possible, though Sister Bernadette's accent was softer than Roman's and the rest of the gypsies'.

The kindness shown to her overwhelmed Babs, as she was handed over by Mr Drayford and told that she was welcome. After a hot mug of cocoa and answering questions about herself she was taken into a room where there was a bathtub. A young girl not much older than herself was filling it from a large kettle, toing and froing from the stove that stood in the corner of the room. Next to the stove there was a tall stand of shelves holding dozens of white towels.

'Hello, Sister. I've nearly done. That's two kettle-fulls. I'm only to put some cold in it and then it'll be ready.'

'Thank you, Daisy. This here is Barbara. It is that I am for asking you to watch over her. Take good care of her and be showing her the routines we follow here.'

As the sister closed the door behind her, Daisy said, 'Well, get yourself undressed. There's a screen over there, you can go behind it.' Then, looking Babs up and down, she asked, 'What's that you're wearing? It ain't very becoming. Is it a uniform or something?'

'Aye, it is, and one that I hate and can't wait to get rid of.' Not that she could forget the prison, Babs thought. Not ever, and this girl would remind her of it every day because she spoke just like Mavis, and she thought then how she would miss Mavis, even though they had only met on a couple of occasions.

Daisy's voice wasn't as brash-sounding as Mavis's had been. She had a nice face, and her eyes were a lovely blue colour with the longest lashes Babs had ever seen. She wore her straight fair hair pulled back into a bun at the nape of her neck.

'Well, not to worry, love, you'll be able to now as I'll soon kit you out in the uniform we wear. It ain't bad. It's made so that as your baby grows inside you, it will still fit you, so those who've had their kids use a belt with it, but I can see that you'd be more comfortable without. I'll go and get you all you'll need. You get yourself in the tub.'

'Ta, Daisy.'

Daisy just smiled.

Sinking into the hot tub, Babs felt that she'd landed in heaven. Even the smell of the carbolic soap didn't put her off thinking this as she relaxed back and let the water soothe her.

When Daisy returned, she asked, 'Are you nearly asleep then? It ain't bed time, but I can see you're exhausted. Have you eaten? We have our tea in an hour and then supper just before we go to bed.'

'I'm not hungry. Me solicitor got a bun for me to eat on the way.'

'Solicitor? Bloody 'ell, you're posh, ain't yer?'

'Naw. I were in trouble – I didn't do owt and that were proved, but some rotten folk said that I did, and I've been in prison for a long time waiting me trial.'

'Prison! Crikey, mate. And you were innocent? That must 'ave been tough. Well, you're 'ere now, and you'll be all right. The sisters are good to us. Mind, there's a lot of rules, but once you grasp them, and if you go along with them, you'll have no trouble.

Once she was dressed in a long blue frock which, as Daisy had said, didn't have any shape to it, and grey woollen stockings that felt itchy but she was told she'd get used to, Daisy took her on a tour of the building. Wherever she went there was the lovely scent of flowers. Vases were filled with them and stood on stands in the corridors. Their aroma mingled with the expected wax polish smell as everywhere wooden surfaces shone, including the floors that edged the rugs.

The feel of the place was of warmth and calmness, and yes, happiness too. Daisy quoted the rules to her as they went around – 'Going through that door is out of bounds, unless yer put on cleaning duties as it leads to the nuns' bedrooms and bathroom. That door leads to their sitting room, so again, yer not allowed in there under any circumstances. And that one leads to the chapel. You'll see plenty of the inside of that one. Every morning starts with prayers, and then there's mass on Sunday. Some don't like that, but I find I get some peace from the quiet and from going through the rituals of the mass. I even say me prayers now.'

After having the ward where the babies were born pointed out to her, they arrived at a door that led to the outside. The garden was enclosed by buildings on both sides but still the sun managed to bathe it in light and make it look beautiful. Here a few girls worked – some in the vegetable patch to the right of them, and a couple on their knees weeding the flower beds that surrounded a lovely lush green lawn with a fountain at its centre. The gentle tinkle of the water was a soothing background to what Babs thought of as a haven.

'This is Babs, everyone.'

The girls all waved, and Babs smiled and waved back. She could see that some of them were in various stages of pregnancy.

'You'll get to know them all as time goes on. Now, follow me.'

'Are we allowed in the garden when we want, Daisy?'

'Yes, as long as your work's done, and any lessons, as we all have to attend the lessons.'

This pleased Babs. 'And how do you get to work in the garden?'

'You can choose what work you do according to 'ow far gone you are, but I wouldn't choose gardening – it's bloody cold out there some days, and there's always something to be done, even if it's raining cats and dogs.'

This made Babs laugh; she'd never heard that saying before. 'I don't mind working in all weathers, I'm used to it.'

'Oh? Do you live in the country then?'

Not wanting to explain, Babs told a half-truth. 'Aye, I live on a farm.'

'Well, you're the first to say that. So 'ow did you get to 'ave a bun in the oven?'

'I – I were raped.'

'What, by a farmhand or something?'

'Naw, not anyone I knew. A – a bloke at the barn dance.' How this occurred to Babs to say, she didn't know. She knew of barn dances as they were held on all the farms they worked on, especially at harvest time, but they had never been invited. She and Beth would dance around their camp fire to the music they heard coming from the barn and would follow the instructions of the voice they heard calling 'Take your partners and swing them round,' though didn't know what a do-si-do was.

'I've never heard of them dances. I'm sorry for yer, though. I were attacked an' all. I didn't know the bloke. I were in an orphanage and he was hanging around outside. He called me over when I was returning from school, and said he had some toffees that I could 'ave if I went in the bushes with 'im. I said no, but 'e grabbed me. It were 'orrible and hurt a lot. When I were found to be 'aving a baby, I was sent into 'ere, but I lost me baby. The orphanage didn't 'ave a place for me then and so I stayed on 'ere. The sisters are waiting for a place in service for me, but I 'ope they never find one as I don't want to leave. I feel safe 'ere.'

As she said this, Daisy opened a door to a huge kitchen. Steam rose up from large pans on a stove that seemed to run the length of one wall. The smell of delicious stew cooking gave Babs an awareness of a hunger that she hadn't realised she felt. Mixed with this smell was that of warm baked bread. The kitchen was a hive of activity as girls, again in various stages of pregnancy, worked away in an atmosphere that seemed full of jolliness as they chatted and giggled. There was one nun supervising them, and she was a happy-looking soul, with bright red cheeks and a rounded body. 'And who do we have here, Daisy?'

'This is Barbara Smith, but she likes to be called Babs.'

'Hello, Babs. My, you look as though you need feeding up. Would you like to work in the kitchen, dear? There's always titbits to feast on.'

'Naw, but ta, Sister, I ain't one as likes to be inside. I'd like to work in the garden.'

'Oh, well, it's your loss, dear. Where are you from? That accent's very different to any I've heard.'

'I were born in Blackpool.'

'Well, you are a long way from home. Not that I've time to chat. I must get on. Tea will have to be served soon.'

'I'll take you to the dining hall, and then the dormitories, Babs.'

Babs just nodded. She had a feeling that she'd landed in heaven. It was strange how that made her want to cry. She'd had very little kindness shown her for a long time now and it was overwhelming.

The dining room was noisy with the clatter of cutlery and the chatter of the three girls setting up the tables. It looked lovely with its high ceiling criss-crossed with beams, and its walls lined with big windows which let in the sunlight. The rows of tables had white cloths covering them, and the knives, forks and spoons gleamed like silver. Babs wondered at such a place existing and even more so at having landed here. She wished Beth could see all this, and know that she was safe, but these thoughts of her sister didn't mar the sense of happiness she felt.

The dormitory held rows of beds on one side and had the same long windows on the other. Some of these were open and the net curtains were gently billowing into the room.

'That's your bed at the end there. Next to that door which leads to the toilets. I'll get you a change of clothes, and you can keep them in the locker beside your bed. And I'll bring a pinny too, as you need to wear that when having your meals. Your first job will be to stitch your name on everything. Can you sew?'

'Aye, I can, Jasmine taught me.'

'Who's Jasmine then?'

'Oh ... er, just someone who worked for me ma.' Again, the lie tripped easily off her tongue and she realised that in her quest to hide the truth, she'd have to remember a lot of these lies so as not to trip up in the future.

'Well, if you are given a gardening job, then you'll put a grey pinny on like you saw the girls wearing. They'll show you where everything is kept for you. You can sit on your bed if you like, while I'm gone.'

Babs found that the bed gave under her weight as if it was filled with feathers, it was that soft, though she wondered if it felt so because she'd been used to the hard bed of the prison and before that, the one in the wagon had been very firm. As she lay back, she thought she would give the world to snuggle up to Beth as she always had in the wagon, and not for the first time, she wondered at herself for taking such a decision as to try to get to Blackpool. But she wouldn't give up on that dream. She'd never give up on finding her ma.

FIFTEEN

'Eeh, Tilly. I can't believe what's happened. Come in, lass.' Turning to look at Tommy, who'd brought Tilly to Molly's house from the hospital, Molly told him, 'You're best to leave her with me, lad, as that's what she wants.'

'No. I can't go home without me Tilly, Molly. It is that I've been staying in a boarding house since I collected Ivan and brought him to you. But that was strange so it was.'

'What was?'

'Well, when I got to the farm, Ivan was on his own in the kitchen, sat in his chair with a bag packed. Liz was nowhere to be found and Ivan didn't know where she was, only that she'd said goodbye to him. I think she was hiding, unable to be for facing me.'

Tilly hadn't spoken to Tommy on the journey here, but with hearing him say this, she felt an immediate pang of jealousy. 'So, you looked for her then?'

'I did, Tilly. Of course I did. She had charge of Ivan. And I wanted to ask her to tell you the truth. It is breaking me heart that you're not for believing me.'

Molly led Tilly inside. 'Come on, love, sit yourself down. I was shocked to the core of me when Tommy came and told me. We'll have a talk when you've rested a while.'

'Mammy!'

Ivan crawled across the floor and made it to Tilly's knee. She ruffled his hair. 'Good to see you, me lad. I've missed you.'

'Are you for being better now, Mammy? Are we going home to the farm?'

'Naw, lad. We're staying with Molly a while. And then we'll fix up the bedroom in the flat above the shop. We'll be fine, lad.'

'No, Tilly. No.'

'Now, we'll have none of this in front of the lad. I knaw how you feel, Tommy, but you've got to leave things for now.'

For a moment, Tilly didn't think Tommy would heed Molly's words, but then Ivan's fear-filled plea of: 'Pappy?' made him hesitate. He looked over at Ivan. 'Everything'll be just as it was, son. Mammy needs to get well. You stay with her and look after her for me. I'll be seeing you in a couple of days, so I will.'

Just before he left, he said to Tilly, 'I thought it was as you loved me, Tilly. Well, to me it is that trust goes along with love.'

With this he was gone.

Tilly slumped back on the sofa. 'Eeh, Molly, help me.'

'I will, lass. Don't take on. Hold on a mo. Gerry, Gerry, lad.'

The door that led to the kitchen opened and Gerry, one of Molly's two sons – a strapping lad of almost fifteen – stood there. He looked so like his father, with the same sandy-coloured hair and hazel eyes. Molly's second son, Brian, now fourteen, had inherited his ma's bright red hair and looked much more like her.

'What is it, Ma? Oh, hello, Aunt Tilly. Are you feeling better?'

'Aye, I am, ta, lad.'

'Take Ivan for a walk, Gerry, lad. His chair's out back. You've an hour till you have to go to the theatre.'

'How's your job going there, Gerry?'

'By, it's grand, Aunt Tilly. I love working with the men who make all the sets for the stage. I enjoy painting the scenes and being in the wings when the show is on as we have to make scene changes every time the curtain goes down.'

'Aye, you're a good lad, Gerry, and an artistic one,' Molly said, pride beaming from her. 'He designs a lot of stuff for his da to make at weekends.'

'I love doing that an' all, and working with the leather, but I couldn't have gone in to the saddlery to take up an apprenticeship as Brian has.'

Though the lad was full of enthusiasm, Tilly couldn't completely engage and was glad when Molly lifted Ivan and took him to Gerry. 'Take him to the beach for a while. Take your da's pocket watch so you knaw what time to head for home. Good lad.'

Gerry took Ivan and immediately had him giggling as he pretended to drop him. Tilly didn't want her lad to go from her when she'd only just seen him after three days of being apart, but she so wanted to talk to Molly.

'Now, lass. What's to do? I've only heard Tommy's version, and to me, it seems true, but why is it that you doubt him, lass?'

'I saw them, Molly. They were sitting on mine and Tommy's bed.' Tilly explained what she heard and saw. As she did, a tear plopped onto her cheek. She felt so desolate.

'Look, Tilly, that seems to fit with what Tommy said, but saying that, I can't see Liz making a play for your Tommy. It'd be a despicable thing to do when you've been so good to her and given your close friendship.'

'But what if she ain't well in her mind, Molly? She seemed to be getting so that she could cope, but suppose she ain't and she didn't really knaw what she were doing?'

'If that was the case, then she's sicker than you can cope with, Tilly, and it ain't fair to ask Tommy to an' all. You never did tell me what happened in that asylum you were in.'

As tired as she was, Tilly told Molly all that she could about the asylum.

'Eeh, Tilly, I've never heard the like, but it does sound as though you changed everything there, and aye, it sounds as though Liz had a proper breakdown and is probably having another now. Which makes me wonder where she is, Tilly. Did she not realise what she was doing? Was she looking for anything, or anyone to make her feel well again? To comfort her raw emotions? But at the time, she saw nothing wrong in turning to Tommy?'

Fear ran through Tilly at this. Tommy had said that Liz was nowhere to be found at the farm. 'Oh, Molly, what if she's done sommat daft?'

'Naw, Tilly, she wouldn't, would she?'

'I don't knaw, but . . . Oh God, she has said that she wants to go to Dan.'

'We'd all say that. She might not have meant it. Look, Will is due home in an hour, I'll get him to go over.'

'We'll go with him, Molly. Liz may need us. Get Will to go and get Tommy. He has Foxy and the cart, he'll take us. Will Brian watch Ivan?'

'Aye, and he'll be glad to. But are you strong enough, Tilly?'

'I am, I can't not go. Naw matter what she's done or ain't done, I've got to help Liz, Molly, I've got to.'

'I knaw, lass. But prepare yourself, for I'm feeling right scared all of a sudden.'

'Oh, Molly, naw. How will I ever forgive meself?'

'Now, none of that. You have done all you can for Liz, and no doubt if we find her safe and well, you'll carry on doing so, naw matter what's she's done, so you've nowt to feel guilty for if she's reached the end of what she can endure.'

'But what of Tommy? I don't knaw why, but I can suddenly see how it could have happened how he said and I knaw as he were telling the truth now. Oh, Molly, why didn't I believe him?'

'You'd had a massive shock, love. What you saw looked bad on him. I'll get Will to make him see that. He's a good mediator is Will. But for now, let me get you a cuppa while we wait for Will to come back.'

An hour later they were on the road. The evening was warm and balmy, but Tilly felt icy-cold fingers clutching at her heart. Will sat on the bench seat next to Tommy. Tommy had hardly looked at Tilly, even though he'd helped her and Molly to get settled on the hay bales that were in the back of the cart.

Tilly didn't care, she felt dead inside her where Tommy was concerned. She just wanted to get to Liz.

Part of her was hoping that Liz would confirm Tommy's story, but then, could she? Even if it was true, how could Liz admit to her best friend that she'd made a pass at her husband?

I have to try to think of Liz as sick. I have to blame that sickness for her actions. Oh, Tommy, I love you, but feel so cold towards you. And I don't feel that ever lifting.

And this frightened Tilly. How could she feel like this? And why did she know she would continue to feel like this even if Tommy's story proved true? But then, she knew the reason. *It's 'cause I don't want him to have even been polite with Liz. He should have ordered her out of the bedroom, naw matter what state she was in. He shouldn't have sat on our bed with her in his arms!*

She wanted her Tommy to have dealt with Liz away from their bedroom. *Will I ever get the image of them holding each other and giggling out of me mind? Oh God, please help me to.*

'Tilly. Tilly, lass, are you all right?'

'Aye, I'm just scared, Molly. I'm on with praying that Liz is all right.' She couldn't find it in her to admit her innermost thoughts; they were private.

'Keep hoping, lass. Happen it's as Tommy thought and she hid when Tommy went back to the farm, eh? She'll be feeling her shame on top of everything else she has to contend with.'

'Poor Liz. Oh, Molly, I should have helped her more.'

'You couldn't do any more than you did. I thought you went above and beyond as it was, lass.'

When they neared the farm, Tilly's heart thumped heavily in her chest. Her fear was such that she could hardly breathe.

There was something eerie about the farm. A door to one of the barns banged as the breeze that had whipped up swung it open and closed.

'That was closed when I left last time.'

Tommy's voice shook. He turned and looked at Tilly and it was as if he suddenly believed what Molly had told him she feared Liz would do.

As they went to climb off the cart, Tommy took hold of her. 'Tilly, lass, don't you go in. Leave this to me and Will.'

'Naw, Tommy, she may need me.'

Will came over to them. 'Tilly, do as Tommy says. Stay with her, Molly.'

Tilly stood still while Tommy and Will went into the barn. She knew in her heart that Liz was in there. She prayed to God to let her be all right. The sound of Tommy gasping, 'Be Jesus!' had Tilly breaking away from Molly and dashing inside.

'Naw, naw, Liz!'

Tommy grabbed her and turned her away from the swinging body of Liz, but not before she saw the blueness of Liz's face, and the bulging eyes. A horror she knew she would never forget as long as she lived.

Clinging to Tommy, Tilly allowed him to steer her towards the house. Inside the kitchen, she saw a note propped up on the table.

Fourgiv me Tilly. I love you and dont naw ow I come to be in your bedroom, but Tommy was kind to me. He dint do owt, he just elped me and made me see that I dint reely want to do wat I was askin of him, and that it was me mind playing triks with me because I wernt well. He sed he wood get a doctor to me to elp me. He promised that dint mean I'd go away. He sed we wood tell you wat apened and you wood naw ow it was and mite do your work at ome so you were allus with me to elp me. Then he made me gigle to make me feel beter. But tho it went wrong I want you to naw that I am not goin because of that. I ave to go Tilly. I cant face me life now. I want to be with Dan and me young uns, pleese try to see that. I will wach over you Tilly, and allus be by your side, my lovely frend. I love you. Liz x

Into the silence a whispered voice said, 'I never could teach her to spell, now I never will.' A pain-filled moan followed this, and Tilly looked up to see Will take a sobbing Molly into his arms.

Tilly felt as if she had shut down. An arm came around her; she knew it was Tommy, but she couldn't react. Her mind kept going around in circles. If he had taken hold of Liz and steered her out of the bedroom and downstairs, he could have talked to her there and all of this wouldn't have happened. *And Liz . . . was she really so out of her mind that she didn't know that she was making a pass at my husband? Mine – her best friend who has done nothing but help her!*

As she rose the chair scraped on the floor, grating on her nerves, but she needed to get out of here, away from these mourning for the so-called friend who had broken her heart. Pulling away from Tommy, she made for the door. Once outside, she ran for all her bulk would allow her. As she reached the barn, she stopped but didn't go in. 'Why, Liz?

Why? What did I ever do to you, eh? Tell me that! What did I ever do!'

Her screams reached fever pitch; her body trembled till her stomach retched uncontrollably. Then a splitting pain made her crumble to the ground.

'Tilly! Tilly, lass!'

'Help me, Molly. Help me.' With this another pain shot through her, making her gasp.

'What's to do, Tilly? What's wrong?'

'Me babby! Me babby!'

Molly turned and ran back to the house, shouting for the men. Tilly saw them come running towards her and heard Tommy calling her name in an anguished voice that spoke of his love for her.

Between them they lifted her and carried her inside and lay her on the sofa. Tommy knelt down beside her. 'Tilly, me little lass.' His head came down onto her breast, 'Forgive me. I've been for thinking for many a day that I should have been for making Liz leave our bedroom and looked after her downstairs. Why didn't I? Oh God, why didn't I? All of this is me doing. It's all on me head. I've been for contributing to Liz's death and for breaking your heart, when you are the world to me.'

His sobs were pitiful.

'Tommy, lad, let Molly tend to Tilly. We should go and fetch the police and the doctor. Come on, lad.'

Tommy rose. 'Tilly, me little Tilly . . . please . . . please . . .'

But Tilly's heart was like a stone at this moment.

Molly touched Tommy's arm. 'Go with Will, lad. Go on. Will can't drive the horse and cart, and the doctor has to be fetched. Tilly needs help.'

Standing tall and wiping his eyes with the back of his hand, Tommy's voice shook as he told them, 'I'll be for going, Will. I'll take me other horse. Finchly can set a good pace. Foxy is only a cart horse.'

Will didn't object. Tommy gave Tilly another pleading look, but she looked away. A pain seared through her once more and she doubled up, letting out a terrible moan. Tommy turned and ran out of the room.

Sweat poured from Tilly. Her stomach cramped every few minutes. In between crying out with the agony of it, she asked Molly, 'Did you tell Tommy that I said as he should've taken Liz out of the bedroom, Molly?'

'Naw, I didn't. I didn't even say owt to Will about that. He's come to realise it himself, Tilly, lass. But you knaw, we don't allus do what's right when faced with a situation we can't handle. Try to imagine how Tommy felt. Liz was in a very bad state. He could see she didn't knaw what she were doing – and she didn't, Tilly. I believe her when she says that she doesn't knaw how she found herself in your bedroom. This was a woman who was going mad, and I mean really mad, losing her mind. This wasn't our Liz. Our Liz would never in a million years do owt like that.'

'She did in the workhouse. I told you. She were with the governor when the fire broke out.'

'Stop! Stop that now! That was another life and you told me that Liz was a desperate mother at the time. You're just soothing your pain with piling everything onto Liz. Well, she suffered enough of her own. I hope to God that she is at peace now, but will she be? Will she forever be without your understanding, eh? I'll not say forgiveness, as in my mind, the lass has nowt to ask forgiveness for – her sick mind made her do what she did. Not Liz. Not our Liz that we knew afore Dan died.'

This outburst shocked Tilly. 'Molly, I – I don't knaw what to say. Oh ... Oh, Molly!' Tilly sat up. She couldn't breathe; she gasped as her anguish and desperation enclosed her. Molly sat down beside her and took hold of her. Together, they sobbed as they rocked backwards and forwards.

When the bout passed, Tilly found herself in a calm place. Her body still convulsed with rebound sobs, but her mind had cleared, and all physical pain had stopped. 'Ta, Molly. I needed that said to me. It ... It's as if everything is clear to me now. Aye, me Tommy didn't do the right thing, but like you say, how often do we ... Eeh, Molly, I've done a terrible injustice to me Tommy.'

'Well, he had it coming to him. We women have to make them toe the line. Men think with two things only; their logic ain't like ours, what they have in their trousers usually dictates to them, but in situations such as your Tommy found himself in, it was his soft heart that let him down. I can see my Will doing exactly the same, as he can see no wrong in what Tommy did. He thinks he showed great restraint, as he could have enjoyed what was offered and no one might ever have known. But he loves you, lass, and he had respect for Liz.'

'Oh, Molly, I never thought of it like that. What have I done? Oh God, Molly, what have I done?'

'Nowt more than any of us would have done. And don't now take this on your own shoulders. All of this was caused by love. Liz's mind telling her that to seek love would help to ease the pain of her loss. Her not being able to reason that the way that she sought it would devastate you. Tommy, for the love of you, doing what he thought was the best he could in the situation. And you hurt so badly because of your love for Tommy and Liz. Eeh, and they say as love brings happiness an' all.'

Despite herself, Tilly smiled at this. Everything seemed clear to her now and she found that she could accept that Liz truly didn't know what she was doing.

'But I didn't want Liz to die . . . Eeh, Molly, the pain of that hurts so much.'

'I knaw, lass. I'm suffering from that meself, but it helps to think of her at peace and if there is any justice, not being punished for taking her own life but given the eternal happiness she deserves.'

'Do you ever pray, Molly?'

'Aye, I do. Praying ain't just for them moneyed folk who go to church, you knaw.'

'I pray a lot and it brings me comfort, if not all I ask for – rarely that. But maybe if we prayed together, we might influence Him up above to welcome our lovely Liz into heaven, eh?'

As they joined hands, Tilly heard the sound of the door opening and looked up to see Will quietly leaving the room.

'Please, God, me and Molly, who's me mate, ask that you let our friend Liz into heaven. She's a good lass and has suffered enough.'

'Aye, and we knaw as she took her own life,' Molly added, 'and only you have the right to take life, but she were sick in her head and didn't knaw what she was doing, so we ask that you overlook that and give her the happiness of being with them as you took from her.'

Together, they said, 'Amen.'

As they hugged each other, they cried, but Tilly felt that they were better tears than before as they didn't hold despair and anger, only sadness and a little healing.

SIXTEEN

Beth had studied hard over the last months. Her pleas to be allowed to go to school had fallen on stubborn ears. Her days while they were camped near to Margate were spent helping Jasmine make and sell her wares and it had been there that she had found a second-hand bookshop and what to her was a treasure: four volumes of *A Weekly Journal of Medicine and Surgery*. Each had fascinated her.

Now, they were back on the land. Apple picking was over and they were preparing to leave the county of Somerset, but first there was the traditional gypsy autumn fair.

Beth loved these fairs now that all the hustle and bustle didn't frighten her. She wore a traditional gypsy gown in bright red. The layers of the skirt were edged with black lace, and the laced bodice showed her shape. Being almost a replica of the ones that Jasmine had dressed her and Babs in on the night she and Roman stole them from their Ma; painful memories were evoked. But she brushed them away, knowing she couldn't cope and that if she didn't think about her ma, she'd feel much more settled in the life she had.

As the fair got into full swing, the excitement gripped Beth. And when the sun went down and the bonfires were lit, the sound of violins and mouth organs filled the air with music. It was then that the dancing began, and now, at fourteen years of age, Beth was encouraged to join in. She swirled to the rhythm. Her hair broke free from the ribbons that had held it and cascaded down to her waist. She loved the feel of it as it swished around her.

When the music stopped, so did her heart, as she saw that the gypsy tradition of grabbing had begun, the one thing that Roman and Jasmine had always said they wouldn't allow to happen to her. Memories of this barbaric way of the boys bagging themselves a wife made her shudder with fear. She looked around for Jasmine and Roman. Always before they had protected her, but they were nowhere to be seen.

In sheer panic she turned and ran towards their wagon, screaming for them at the top of her voice. Glancing back, she saw a gypsy boy bearing down on her. She had to make it back to safety as the boys could not touch a girl if she was in her home, but then she tripped and fell to the ground. Before she could scramble up, the boy landed on top of her. Her skirt restricted her movements as she tried to kick out at him. She could feel his breath on her cheek and smell the sour stench of alcohol on it, tinged with the crude tobacco the gypsies chewed. Getting her hand free, she clawed at him. 'Naw, naw, leave me alone!'

In the light that the bonfire threw in their direction she saw his fist rise up and cringed away from the blow she knew would come, but then Roman's voice came to her. 'No! Get yourself off her, or you will have me to contend with! This is for being my daughter and she is not for grabbing.'

The boy, his fist suspended in the air, looked up. Shock and disbelief registered on his face.

'Roman, it is that you promised.'

The sound of this plea from Jasmine surprised and confused Beth. What did Roman promise?

'I cannot lose her, Roman. I have already lost my Babs. If it is that Beth marries, she will stay as she will be a gypsy wife.'

'No, Jasmine. Not like this. Our daughters are for being above this. They are different. We have been for protecting them from this barbaric practice, that is not in the traditions of me clan. Did I be for grabbing you?' As Roman said this, he took hold of the boy's collar and pulled him off Beth. 'Get yourself away. Be for never touching my daughter again. She is not for betrothing in this way.'

The boy stood in defiance. 'It is for being me right to have her.'

'Not if her father is refusing you, and I'm doing just that. Now go, afore me temper is for getting the better of me.'

The boy turned and walked away.

'Oh, Papa, why did you leave me?'

'Come, my child, it is that I will not withdraw my protection again.' Lifting her up, Roman carried her to the wagon. A sobbing Jasmine sat on the steps to the entrance. 'Move yourself, Jasmine. It is tonight that you brought shame on us and fear to Beth. I should not have listened to you when you said that your friend's husband was protecting Beth along with his own daughter!'

'But, Roman, despite all our love and care, Babs has gone and now Beth prepares to go when she is old enough. I cannot bear it, I can't.'

'And so it is that you would sacrifice her to the likes of that scum? I will not be for allowing it. There are gypsies of our own class that will do right by her. Love her and cherish her. Build her a wagon she can be proud of owning. And keep her near to us. You tricked me. I am for being ashamed of you.'

Beth clung to Roman's neck. Her body racked with sobs. That Jasmine should have done this to her filled her with disbelief and fear, for would she ever feel safe again? At this moment, she wished that she had gone with Babs.

Laying her down on her bed, Roman brushed her hair from her face. 'Little one, is it true that you plan to leave us?'

'Naw, Papa. I want to be a nurse when I'm old enough, and Philippa who took care of me told me that nurses do have to live in the nurses' quarters, but they go home on leave. I'd come back to wherever you are. I have to be a nurse, Papa. But is it a long time in the future. I cannot begin to train until I am eighteen, and then I have to be sponsored.'

'What is it you are meaning by sponsored?'

'I have to have someone who will pay me fees and all of me expenses and buy me uniform. And I have to be educated so that I pass exams.'

'That is for being a lot that you are asking of me, but if it is that you will be happy, I will think about it. And what is it that these girls do about going to a husband?'

'Philippa told me that one day she will meet someone and fall in love, and that the man will love her too, as she says there is someone for everyone and it is their destiny to meet. Then they will go courting, which means they will meet and enjoy time together. When they are sure of each other's love, the man will ask her father's permission to marry his daughter.

They will become engaged, and the man will buy Philippa a ring that she will wear on her left hand, and that will proclaim to the world that she is betrothed. Then will come the wedding, which sounds just like our weddings, with family and friends gathering to celebrate.'

'And it is that they do not do this when they are fifteen?'

'Naw. Philippa is twenty and she has not yet met the man of her dreams.'

Roman looked mystified. 'It is a strange way, but it is the way of your people and I can see it is what you want. As your papa, I will see it is done. But it is that you must promise to come home to us, and not abandon us, as that will be for breaking Jasmine's heart. Already, she pines for Babs.'

'I do an' all, Papa. I miss Babs so much. Do you think that she made it to Blackpool?'

'I don't know, but I fear that it is for being unlikely. Blackpool is many miles away. I worry every day, how it is that she is feeding herself, and finding shelter, but there is nothing that I can do.'

At this he held her to him. 'We did wrong by you both. I am sorry, so sorry. It is that I wanted to make me Jasmine happy, and I could see that your mama couldn't take care of you. She tried, but her people didn't care for her as they should have. She turned to us, but she was for driving the menfolk wild with the beauty of her. They were for betraying their wives and their betrothed, for a chance of sampling the nectar they thought she could give to them. And she sought love wherever she could find it, as she was bereaved, and lost. She turned to the gypsies for protection, and it wasn't given to her.'

'Do you think she found happiness, Papa?'

Roman released her and knelt down in front of her as he told her, 'There was a Romany gypsy, an honourable man called Jeremiah, who loved her and I heard that when she was taken to the hospital the night that Jasmine and I were for taking you to look after you, he stayed behind when the rest of the clan moved away. He was thinking to marry her when she was well. The tale is that they did live together and were for doing well, and that your mama was happy, but Jeremiah wasn't long for this world. What happened after he went to his rest I am for not knowing.'

'Oh, Papa, do you think me ma is all right?'

'I am sure that she is.'

'And do you think that she misses us, me and Babs?'

Roman hung his head. 'To my shame, I know it is that she must do, for she loved you both very much.'

Beth's tears turned to sobs.

'Don't, little one. Mama and I are for always being here for you. We love you as if you were our own. I'll make your dreams come true, I promise. When we go to the farm near to Maidstone, I will take you to the town hall where you can enquire about having the lessons that you are wanting to have. I think the children of the English people leave school at thirteen or fourteen, but it is that some go on to what they call college. Perhaps you can attend one of these. We only want for you to be happy.'

'Philippa told me that there are people who give private lessons, Papa. They are called tutors, and they would be able to help me to catch up on what I have missed, especially as I can read. And I have learnt such a lot from the books you bought for me and Babs, and from what Philippa gave me. And I bought those journals, as she said a nurse needs to know something she called biology. But she also needs to show that she is intelligent and has learnt all her lessons, her maths, English and history.'

'My, that is a lot to know. And can you learn all of that from this tutor?'

'Philippa said that if I worked hard, then I will.'

'Then I promise you that we will look into this for you. There, is it that you will now be happy with us?'

'I am happy, Papa, it is just that I miss Babs so much and . . . well, me ma an' all. I remember her dancing as I was tonight, and how beautiful she was, and how loved I felt when she cuddled us . . . Will I ever see her again, Papa?'

In the background, what had been intermittent sobs from Jasmine as they'd talked, now increased to deep, agonising cries. Roman turned from Beth and went to his wife. Taking her in his arms, he tried to soothe her. 'Didn't we always prepare for when the little ones would want to go back to their mama, Jasmine? It may be that one day we will have to let go.'

'No, no! I can't, don't make me.'

This cry gave Beth a pain in her heart. She loved Jasmine and didn't like to see her hurt. Sliding off the bed, she went to their bed where Jasmine sat. 'Mama, I'll never leave you, I promise. I love you and Papa. I'll allus come back to you, to visit, even if I find me ma.'

Jasmine reached out to her and held her close, stroking her hair as she whispered, 'Forgive me for tonight, little one. I – I . . . well, it is that I thought to have you marry a gypsy would keep you near to me.'

'I knaw, Mama. It's all right. He didn't kiss me, Papa stopped him.'

'I'll never do that again. I promise. Oh, Beth, I love you.'

The hug comforted Beth, but still, though her heart warmed and felt safe again, Beth knew there was something missing and she wondered if she would ever again be held like this by her real ma.

Babs eased her bulk by supporting her stomach with her hands. The ache in the bottom of her belly had worsened today, and yet she didn't think that she was in labour as it was too early; she had another three to four weeks to go as her baby was due in November.

She dreaded the time coming. This was due to the work she now did in the convent. At first, she'd worked in the garden, but as time went on, she became interested in what happened in the clinic and asked to be allowed to help out in there a couple of times a week.

And though she hated the pain she saw the girls go through when they gave birth, she loved the feeling of being a help to them, and to others who were in the ward suffering from various ailments.

She loved too how they were all encouraged to learn their lessons in many subjects and had been proud when the tutor, Sister Theresa, had said that she was like a sponge, soaking up knowledge.

Sister Theresa had helped her a lot, giving her books to read and setting her extra lessons. And then she'd received praise from Sister Ruth too. Sister Ruth ran the clinic and was a trained nurse. 'You could become a nurse, Barbara,' she'd said. 'You have a natural empathy and bring healing with how you care and encourage.'

This had stuck in her head, and a few days later she'd asked Sister Ruth what she would have to do to become a nurse. The answer had been daunting, as she didn't know anyone who would sponsor her. But then, the sister had said that there were organisations such as the Red Cross that would train her without her having to pay.

The idea took root, and already Sister Theresa was steering her learning towards useful subjects such as anatomy, though the sister seemed very embarrassed about this, and so she had obtained books for her to study and had asked Sister Ruth to help Babs if she had any questions.

The pain in her lower stomach suddenly worsened, and Babs bent over to ease it. In doing so, she dropped one of the kidney-shaped bowls that she was sterilising by boiling them in a large pan.

The door to what was called the 'sluice' opened and Sister Ruth stood there. 'Are you all right, Barbara? I heard a clatter. Oh, my dear, what is wrong? Are you in pain?'

'Aye, I've a cramp and it's hurting.'

'Oh dear. I expect it is your baby turning. They do that sometimes, and a foot gets stuck. Let me help you to a bed where I can examine you. Maybe if I massage the painful area, I can get the baby to move.'

Babs didn't think that this was the cause of her pain as her baby hadn't moved for over a week now. It seemed funny to think of a baby in her tummy, and she never ceased to marvel at them coming out from between a girl's legs. The babies seemed so huge to pass through such a small hole. She knew it was small as she had investigated her own after she'd been near to the first birth she'd witnessed. But then she'd learnt that it grew wider for the purpose and that's why there was so much pain.

The thought of having her baby was something she tried not to give much attention to. She wouldn't let herself love it, as some of the girls did. She'd seen their pain when their baby was taken away, held them as they'd cried pitifully for their child, and had decided that if she ignored hers, then she wouldn't feel that agony.

'Now, then, let me see. Where does it hurt?'

'It's here, Sister. It's like a dragging feeling, and then it gets very sharp.'

'Oh, my dear, you are bleeding!'

'Eeh, naw! It's too early for me babby to come.'

'I know. I'll have to examine you. Has the baby been moving a lot?'

'Naw, not at all for a while yet.'

'Hmm, that's not good, Barbara. I think we might have to call a doctor. Get undressed, and I'll fetch you a gown. I think bed rest for now is the best action, and I'll elevate your feet to try to stop the bleeding getting worse.'

'But I'll stain the bed, Sister.'

'Don't worry about that. As you know, most girls do at some stage. That can be sorted. We must find out what is happening and take care of you.'

Sister was soon back and helped Babs to undress and get into the gown, a big cotton robe that tied at the back, which she knew was usually worn during the birth of the baby.

Her fears began to deepen as she wondered what was wrong. She hadn't known this to happen to any of the other girls. She counted the months from mid-February, and this being early October, she knew that if she was having the baby it wouldn't survive. A pain shot through her heart at this thought. Her hand went to her bulge. *I knaw as I haven't paid you much attention, and have tried not to love you, but I didn't mean you any harm. I didn't.*

With this, Babs realised that she did love her baby, and tears fell onto her cheeks as the desperation of her situation sank in. If her baby died, she would be heartbroken, but then, if it lived, it would be taken from her. Her mind called out for her ma, but she knew that her ma wouldn't come. How could she?

Two hours later, the doctor produced a long steel instrument, telling her that he was sorry but he had to help her baby to come into the world. As the doctor inserted it inside her, Babs felt a terrible searing pain, before falling into a deep faint.

When they brought her round, Sister Ruth held her in her arms. Tears were flowing down the sister's face. 'My dear Barbara, I am so sorry, but your baby has gone to heaven.'

'Dead? Me babby? But – but how can it go to heaven? It weren't baptised! You – you said all babbies must be baptised to go to heaven.'

'He was. I took him straight to the chapel the moment he died, and if a baby is baptised in less than twenty-four hours after they pass, then the soul hasn't left them and that baptism stands, sending them straight to heaven.'

'He?'

Sister Theresa had joined Sister Ruth and now told Babs, 'Yes. You had a little boy. We named him Mario, as October is our Mother Mary's month and Mario is a similar name to Hers.'

'And – and he lived? He was alive! I – I want to see him.'

'He has already been buried, my dear. He . . . well, he wasn't properly formed, and only managed one breath, which means that he lived. Be thankful for that, Barbara, as that means he was a person. If born dead, a baby isn't classed as a human being and is not dealt with in the same way. Now, your little Mario, who couldn't live on this earth, is living with our loving father.'

At this moment, Babs couldn't think of God as a loving father if he took tiny babies from their mother, but she felt too weary to argue.

Sister Theresa took her hand. 'Barbara, you can stay here for as long as you like. You can continue with your studies and to help Sister Ruth with her mothers. She finds your help invaluable, and you bring special strength to the girls.'

'You do, Babs, and as Sister Theresa says, I would love to have you working by my side.'

Babs looked up at these two dear nuns and couldn't imagine being anywhere else now. Yes, she wanted to be in Blackpool, but she had no way of getting there. Neither did she know if she would find her ma if she did. Some of the fear she had felt for so long lifted with this offer, as many times over the past months she'd thought about whether the nuns would let her stay after the baby was born. 'Ta, Sister.'

'Well, get some rest now. And Barbara, try to think of little Mario as always being yours. No other woman has taken him to be theirs. He is living in extreme happiness and can be by your side whenever you want him to be. Oh, and he looked like you. He had your hair, and lots of it, and your face shape. His eyes were closed, but I can't tell you any more. Just think of him as a precious angel that nothing on this earth can hurt, or spoil. God's little soldier.'

With these gentle words, Babs found herself drifting off to sleep. Her mind was at peace. She didn't ask why Sister Theresa couldn't tell her any more about Mario's looks. It didn't matter. Her baby was safe. She knew where he was and knew too that he would always be there. And she was safe too. One day, she would be a nurse like Sister Ruth, and then she would find her ma. Because then, she would be a grown-up and would know how to travel and find people. *I will find you one day, Ma.*

As she walked away from Liz's graveside, Tilly felt the pity of Liz not being buried in the same grave as her beloved Dan. They had implored the priest to give his permission, but to no avail. 'If someone takes their own life, they cannot be allowed to be buried in consecrated ground. We have a section in the churchyard for suicides and for babies and adults that haven't been baptised. I am sorry, but that is the ruling of the Church and I do not have any authority to change it.'

'I knaw what you're thinking, love, but it don't matter where the body lies, it's the soul that counts and that's with Dan's and her young 'uns, I'm sure of that.'

'Eeh, Molly, there's some cruel rules in this world. They don't take into account that someone like Liz couldn't reason that it was wrong to take her own life. And imagine little babbies being cast to one side. How can they help not living long enough to be baptised, eh?'

'Maybe one day folk will think differently, but there's nowt we can do about it all now. You're exhausted, lass. Let's get you home and get your feet up.'

'Tilly?'

Tilly turned to see Tommy standing a little way away. She hadn't seen much of him in the last few days. She knew he'd stayed on at the farm but hadn't cared one way or the other. Nothing had mattered to her. Not whose door any fault could be laid at, or what Tommy was doing, but now as she saw the tilt of his head and his appealing expression, she did care.

'Can I talk to you, Tilly?'

A sudden shyness took her. Could he forgive her accusations? Could she forgive him? Because it didn't seem to matter how much it was all reasoned out, she still felt pain from witnessing the scene between Tommy and Liz.

Tommy walked towards her. 'How are you, Tilly? Oh, it is that I know as your heart is breaking for Liz at this moment, but how is it you are in yourself?'

'I'm all right, Tommy.'

'Are you up to talking to me? Can we try to straighten out what is between us?'

Tilly looked around. Molly had walked on a little way, but she stood now looking back at Tilly. Her head nodded towards Tilly and Tilly knew Molly meant for her to go ahead and chat to Tommy and that she would go back home and see that Ivan was all right with Gerry and take care of him till Tilly came. Turning back to Tommy, she said, 'Aye, we need to talk, Tommy.'

'Oh, me little Tilly. Come here.' His arms were extended to her, and in that moment, she knew she needed the comfort of them. They met halfway as once she moved, Tommy did too.

When his arms enclosed her, Tilly felt as though the split in her world was beginning to heal. She clung to Tommy. Their bodies swayed, Tommy's tears wetting her hair, hers wetting the collar of his Sunday-best jacket. When finally they parted enough to look into each other's eyes, there was no need for them to talk. Their love had spoken for them.

'Tilly, I'm so—'

Her finger went to his lips. 'Naw, Tommy. Naw more apologies. Let it just be sommat that happened, that we never talk of again. We've done all the talking about it that we can. Whatever hurt we inflicted on each other must now be healed. We have to go forward without it casting a shadow over us. Liz deserves that. She paid the ultimate price for the tricks that her mind played on her.'

'She did.'

With this, Tommy led her back to Liz's graveside. They stood looking down on her coffin, their bodies close together as if they would never part again. 'Rest easy, lass. We understand. We don't hold nowt against you. And I'll allus look on you as me very best friend in all the world. If me babby is a girl, I'll give her your name. I allus loved the name Eliza.'

'Eliza? That was for being me granny's name. I thought Liz was short for Elizabeth?'

'Naw. Eeh, Tommy. Elizabeth were the name of one of me twins. We shortened it to Beth and Babs was short for Barbara.'

Tommy pulled her to him. 'If ever it is that you want to talk about them, Tilly, I'm here for you.'

'I knaw. Awe, but I cannot visit that part of me life at the moment. It would break me.'

'My poor little Tilly. Let us be fetching Ivan and be getting back to our own home, eh?'

'I'd like that, Tommy. I'm so tired. So very tired.'

'Lean on me, me little darlin'.'

As Tilly leant on her Tommy, some of the weight of her grief lifted and she knew that with him by her side, she could get through anything.

PART TWO

THE PATH HOME

1914–1916

SEVENTEEN

Babs adjusted her hat.

'Have you got everything, my dear?'

'I have, Sister Theresa. How do I look?'

'You look lovely, my dear. Do your coat up, there's a biting cold wind which could bring snow.'

'Eeh, Sister, we're not properly into winter yet.' She hadn't wanted to say it was still October, as this was the month that she hated the most, being the anniversary month of her son's birth and death. Always she felt the pain of his loss more acutely at this time of year.

'Ha, when you've lived as long as I have, you expect the unexpected. Now, that's better. Oh, Barbara, we're all so proud of you going off to France to look after our poor wounded soldiers, but we're so going to miss you.'

'And I'm going to miss you, Sister Theresa. I owe everything to you.'

'No, you owe it all to yourself, and your hard work. Look at you. A qualified nurse, and now working for the Red Cross. Now, run along and say your goodbyes to the Reverend Mother and the other sisters, and I'll get Mr Robbins to bring his cart around to the front to take you to the station. I'll take your bag.'

Babs found saying goodbye very difficult. She felt more like a young girl leaving home than a twenty-five-year-old woman setting out to take up the career she had chosen. But then, this convent had been her home since she came out of prison and even when away doing her nursing training, living in the nurses' quarters of the Queen Mary hospital at Roehampton, she had always spent her leave days here.

Before her acceptance into training as a nurse, she'd helped in the clinic and had seen umpteen young unmarried mothers through their pregnancies, and comforted them when their children were taken from them – something that she never got used to and hated with a vengeance. But she had long accepted that it was necessary, as many families wouldn't take the girls back if they kept their baby. They thought the child would bring shame on them.

For the most part, this was a happy place for the girls to be and it had been Babs's salvation. She could not recognise herself from the girl that she had been before she arrived here. Nearly everything about her had changed.

Everything, that is, except the real core of her, she thought as she skipped from one part of the convent to another, saying her goodbyes. For inside, she still harboured a longing to be reunited with her twin sister, Beth, and her ma.

Sister Theresa had tried a few times to trace her ma but hadn't had any success. Babs knew that one day it would happen, but for now there was a war on, and she was needed.

When she came to the office where all the administration of the convent was done, she called out to Daisy.

'Are you off then, Babs?'

'Aye, I'm to go to the station to catch me train back up to London.'

'Take care, love. And write often.'

'I will. You're a good friend, Daisy. Make sure you write to me an' all. I'll need to hear from home. Sister Theresa said she would, but she won't give me any of the nitty-gritty of what's happening.'

'I've me pen poised as we speak.'

They both laughed and then held each other in a tearful hug. 'Eeh, you've spoilt me resolve, I weren't going to cry. You just make sure that you get out a bit more. You never knaw, you might meet someone who'll sweep you off your feet.'

'Fat chance, they're all at war, or preparing to go. Anyway. I've something to tell you. I'm thinking of becoming a nun.'

'What! You, Daisy, don't be daft ... Oh, I mean, well, by 'eck, you surprised me there, and just as I've got to go and have naw time to talk to you about it ... But look, if it's what you want, good luck, lass. I'll be rooting for you.'

'Ta, Babs. Like I say, I'll write and let you know all that happens around here. Bye, love.' They hugged once more, and Babs turned away to make her way to the front door. This news had shocked her, and yet, she didn't know why. She'd noticed that when she'd come home, Daisy had been a little different each time, spending a lot of time in the chapel. *Well, good luck to her, but it wouldn't do for me.*

'Ah, here you are. Hop onto the cart.'

As Babs climbed up onto the cart, it suddenly hit her how different her life was going to be. The extra preparations she'd been involved in recently at the Red Cross HQ in London, and her elevation from nurse to sister, had all been changes that had excited her. And now, she was really going, and she couldn't imagine what it would be like in another country, let alone working on a train that transported wounded soldiers from various clearing stations from the border of Belgium to Paris.

Everything was hustle and bustle once she arrived at Victoria station but luckily, being of rank, she was found a seat, while some had to make do with sitting on their haversacks in the corridors.

The travelling to another country posed no problems as everywhere there was someone waiting to meet the contingent of Red Cross nurses and send them to their next port of call. For Babs that was the Red Cross HQ in Paris, a journey that gave her wonderment as she enjoyed seeing so many different sights. The sea seemed to snarl at the intrusion of the boat in its waters and to do its best to capsize them as it lashed the boat with waves. This caused sickness to many, but for her – brought up with this same motion as she'd travelled around the country in a gypsy caravan – the swell wasn't a problem. Then the train journey through countryside that gave her glimpses of shuttered houses, so different to those in England, less inviting as they were closed to the world, though some were adorned with lovely window boxes that contained flowers and this transformed them. And then experiencing the different dishes they were offered – no pie and peas here, but lots of fish dishes and seafood, and all presented as if they were a work of art, instead of dinner.

When she finally arrived in Paris she was met by another nursing sister, who immediately made her feel at home.

'Good to meet you, Sister Smith. I'm Sister Catherine Warden – Cathy for short. We're going together to the station tomorrow to join our ambulance train – though mostly we call it a hospital train as that is what it is really. I've done a stint on it already so know the ropes. I'm to take you under my wing.'

'Ta, Cathy. I'm Barbara, but I'm known as Babs. Eeh, what's it like, then? I can't imagine a hospital on a train.'

'You're from the North of England, I take it?'

'Aye, I am, but don't ask me owt about it as me accent is all I have left of it. I were brought up in the county of Kent from the age of six.'

'Me too, though I were born in the country, not any of the towns. My dad's a hop grower.'

'I was brought up by nuns in Maidstone.' Babs didn't want to tell of her early life.

'An orphan?'

Why does everyone want to knaw everything about me? 'Naw, but it's a long story.' At this she told the lie she'd often told, because it was easier. 'Me ma couldn't look after me and me sister after me da died. Me sister was adopted but I wasn't. Now, if you don't mind, Cathy, I don't like talking about it, so can you keep it to yourself?'

'I will. But I do feel curious. I'm a nosy parker at the best of times. It's just that I can't imagine not being brought up with my sister, though there was many a time I wished she'd disappear.' Cathy laughed, a loud laugh that didn't seem to suit her. She was a small girl, with fair hair and delicate features, a combination that gave the impression of someone who would need looking after, but she oozed confidence and seemed to have a strong character and a ready sense of humour. Her manner was open and friendly. Babs liked her immediately.

'They'll only be three of us sisters on board, and we're not allowed to all go off the train together. So, what mostly happens is that we draw lots at the first long stop we have, and then take it in turns on a rota to go exploring. Mind, you have to be aware that when you leave the train, you might be told you have two hours only to find it's left without you. Don't panic if you find yourself in that situation. You'll always know where the next port of call is, so grab a taxi and catch up with the train. It happens all the time and is due to the schedule being suddenly changed if there is an emergency.'

Babs's excitement mounted. The idea of travelling from place to place and being allowed off every now and again to explore really appealed to her.

'Sorry I can't show you anything of Paris, but we're to join our train straight away, as the dispatch says we are needed to help clean up before we get underway for our trip towards the Belgium border.'

Cleaning up sounded innocent enough but that assumption was far from what it entailed. It seemed that the whole train was splattered in blood. Beds were covered in it, and all had to be stripped, scrubbed and changed. The shortage of nurses meant that the sisters had to get stuck in to this work too. To Babs it was a revelation and gave her the first indication of what she was in for. It didn't daunt her, though. She rolled up her sleeves and scrubbed for all she was worth, getting to know the third sister in the process.

Belinda was a much posher version of Cathy, but just as

nice. She was older and had already had plenty of war experience in the second Boer War.

By the time the work was done, and the nurses dispatched to rest before dinner, Babs felt that she knew the train from the engine through to the officers' quarters – which were at the very back of the train and reserved for the doctors. The sisters' quarters were along the corridor from those, and although small, they consisted of a sitting room and a shared bedroom and washroom. Then the nurses' and voluntary aid workers' rooms were next to the wards, which were long rows of bunks each side of three of the carriages. These were followed by two operating theatres, and finally the stores and the kitchens were nearest to the engine.

'Eeh, it's all amazing. I never thought in a million years that you could fit a hospital onto a train.'

'It'll get cramped when we start to pick up the wounded, I can tell you.' Belinda waved a clipboard as she said this. 'Now, let's have a cuppa and go over what duties we are all going to take on. I've them all listed.'

With this, Babs felt a little nervous, but told herself that she would cope. She knew her stuff, and though she was new to the position of Sister and hadn't yet taken charge of others, she wouldn't baulk at doing so. She couldn't wait to get started.

Beth was in her second week of duty in the small clearing station in Passchendaele, where it seemed to her that it never stopped raining.

When she'd first arrived, she'd helped to set up the equipment in the newly erected tents near to the raging battle in Ypres. A job that had to be done quickly and efficiently as they moved frequently in order to keep near to the ever-changing position of the frontline. Their mission was to receive all of those wounded and to ensure the best course of action is taken in order to save lives.

Once assessed, the minor wounded were tended to and sent back out to the front line. Those that needed surgery or were more seriously injured were dispatched by ambulance to field hospitals in Brittany, or to be picked up by the hospital train to be taken to more specialised hospitals in Paris.

The crashing of explosions around her made her legs tremble and her stomach churn, but she couldn't show this fear as she tied a tourniquet around the thigh of a man whose leg had been blown off.

Sweat soaked his brow and his eyes stared out from hollow sockets. 'You're going to be all right, don't worry. They'll get you on the train and the surgeon on board will sort you.'

'Am I for Blighty, Nurse?'

This was the question on most of the lips of the injured British. 'Yes, you'll be shipped home, your war is over. You've done us proud.'

The face that had looked at death's door lit up.

'That's the spirit. You can do a lot towards your own healing if you focus on something good.'

Moving on to the next soldier, Beth gasped. Somehow this lad hadn't been prioritised when he should have been. His arm had gone from the elbow down; his stump hung off the side of the stretcher. Blood poured from it. His ashen face showed that he was almost bled out and would die at any moment. 'I need blood, and now!' Beth shouted.

Cissy, a voluntary aid worker, came running over. 'We're low on stocks, I don't think we have enough to go around.'

'Get Matron's permission to take blood from the staff, or the patients who are only slightly hurt. Hurry, Ciss.'

Trying to stem the bleeding, Beth applied pressure to the main artery, but she knew it was too late. She looked into the face of the lad and saw to her horror that he could be no more than sixteen or seventeen. His eyes flickered. 'You're all right, I've got you. We'll make you better. What's your name?'

'Mi – Mickie.'

'I'm Beth, Mickie.'

She would never know if Mickie knew her name as his last breath left him on a deep sigh. Tears ran down Beth's face. They were of sorrow mixed with sheer exhaustion. She closed the young man's eyes, said a silent goodbye and covered his face.

Turning away, she took a deep breath. This latest influx were some of the worst cases she'd seen. The ten she'd been assigned to assess and do all she could for had injuries that had turned her stomach – one with his guts spilling out, several with smashed limbs and deep gashes. Mickie was her last and, so far, the only one she'd lost. In the chaos around her she spotted the ambulance crew with an empty stretcher and shouted above the din, 'Patients ready for ambulance here!'

But her cry disappeared in a crashing explosion. Her body catapulted across the room and something pierced her leg. As she fell to the ground with a thump that jolted her back and had her biting her tongue, she saw the canvas roof of the tent collapse and its central thick, heavy pole falling towards her.

* * *

'Beth, Beth. Eeh, Beth.'

As the swirl of whooshing clouds circled her brain, Beth felt her body floating. Somewhere in the distance she could hear Babs calling her. She wanted to go to the voice, open her eyes and see her beloved sister, but the swirling was too powerful for her and she couldn't surmount the fog that oppressed her.

'Eeh, lass, me lovely sister. I've found you. Don't leave me, Beth. Fight, lass. I'm here. Babs is here.'

The voice sounded clearer, telling her that it really was Babs. She tried to call her name, but the only sound that would come from her was a moan.

'You're going to be all right, me lovely Beth. You've injuries to your leg and your back, but they'll mend. I'll take care of you, lass.'

Babs's voice sounded tearful and desperate. Beth wanted to tell her not to worry. She wanted to beat this fog that had trapped her and open her eyes and look at Babs. Take her in her arms and hug her to her, but she couldn't move.

Another voice came to her. 'Well, Babs, who'd have thought. And you say that you two haven't seen each other for some twelve years or more?'

'Naw, Belinda. But by, to find her like this.'

'Hold yourself together, Babs. Matron's on the prowl, she'll expect all the cases that are on board to be ready for the next clearing station.'

'Eeh, I must speak with her. I need to stay with Beth.'

'I understand, old thing, but you've your nurses to think of. They need your help and encouragement, and your skills to help them to cope and to save lives. Let's work through them all, doing what we can for each and tagging them to where we consider they should go. I've set my lot on the less serious cases as they are all new to nursing.'

Beth couldn't sort out what this had all been about. Babs must be a nurse. *Am I in a hospital?* The strain of the effort to sort out the reality from her dreams was too much. It was easier to let the swirling take her and to relax into the peace it offered.

When Beth next came to, all seemed calm around her. She could hear murmurings but couldn't understand the softly spoken words. Opening her eyes, she knew at once that she was in a hospital as familiar sounds and smells assailed her – carbolic and iodine, and the squeak of rubber-soled shoes on polished linoleum, besides the moans of someone in pain. 'Nurse?'

'Ah, you are awake.'

The voice sounded foreign. 'Where am I?'

'You are in a hospital in Paris. You were injured. Your hospital was hit by a shell.'

'Where's Babs?'

'Sorry?'

'Babs, me sister. She was here.'

'You are confused, *mon petite.* There is no Babs in this hospital.'

'But . . . she spoke to me.'

'You have been unconscious for three weeks and have concussion. Now, don't exert yourself. You are badly injured, but you're going to be all right. In one week, you will be shipped home. The British Red Cross are to take care of you. I will fetch someone to you.'

As the nurse left her side Beth tried desperately to bring Babs's voice back to her. She knew it had been real. It couldn't have happened in her imagination, or be a trick of her unconscious state, could it? But then, all she'd heard was a nurse with a Northern accent trying to calm her and discussing with another what they could do for her. Maybe, in her confused state, she'd convinced herself it was Babs.

'So, Nurse Petrilona – a lovely name. How are you? I'm Doctor Murray. I also work with the British Red Cross. I'm stationed here in Paris and I'm sorry to hear what befell you and our fellow workers.'

'Thank you, Doctor. I– I'm afraid, I'm not feeling too good. I can't sort my thoughts out. Do you know if there is a Red Cross nurse called Babs working here?'

'No, I don't think so, why?'

'I thought . . . well, my sister's called Babs, and I thought she was by my side.'

'Your mind can play tricks when you've had a head injury, as you probably know, but if it makes you feel better, then I'm sure she was. Now, we are taking you on the next train to the port at Le Havre where a hospital ship will dock tomorrow. They will take you aboard and get you home to England. The Red Cross there have been notified and they will contact your next of kin. You'll soon be safely home. Although, home will be a hospital for the foreseeable future as you're not fit by any means.'

When asked for her next of kin, Beth had said that her father was a casual farm labourer who travelled according to the season. To this end she had given the addresses of the farms Roman and Jasmine would be working at and when.

'What happened to me and what are my injuries?'

'Your right leg was pierced by a steel table leg, such was the force with which you were thrown. This splintered bones in your thigh. Now, that may take a while, but it will heal. You had a nasty head injury and had to undergo surgery – a cracked skull, which resulted in a clot on the brain. And there is a back injury too. They are not sure of the severity of this as you are still badly bruised. But we'll strap you up well so that no further damage can be done.'

This was a lot for Beth to take in. 'Will – will I walk again?'

'I can't answer that, I'm sorry. You're young and could heal completely. Time will tell.'

'How did everyone else fair? Did they all get out?'

'No. I'm sorry, but a voluntary aid worker was killed . . .'

'Oh, no! Ciss, poor Ciss.'

'Try not to upset yourself, you need to keep calm.'

'I'm all right. Was it just Ciss?'

'I'm afraid not. Most of those already badly injured in battle lost their lives. I haven't any names for you, I'm sorry. And sadly, the matron died too. Everyone else had injuries, some minor, some severe, but all are being taken care of.'

The crossing was very rough, and many patients became sicker as the boat made its way slowly over the Channel. Beth did well; she'd always been able to travel without becoming ill but was frustrated in not to being able to help as the staff were rushed off their feet.

A sense of fear for her future visited her as she lay quietly in the semi-darkness of the ship's ward. She'd put all her efforts into becoming a nurse. Roman had kept his promise and engaged a tutor for her whenever he could, and she and Jasmine had visited every bookshop when in a town to buy her books on medical subjects. She'd sat the school certificate at age fifteen and had passed with very high marks. There'd been a lull then as she'd waited to reach the age of eighteen so that she could apply for nurse training. During that time, she had taught the gypsy children to read and write, something their parents were both fascinated by and afraid of.

When she applied to train to be a nurse, she again passed all the exams, but getting a reference had posed her a problem. In the end, Roman had approached both priests of the churches in the areas that they worked, as all of the family were regular churchgoers, along with the whole gypsy community.

Luckily, the priests had helped her. From that moment, life became how it always should have been for Beth as she lived in the nurses' quarters in the manner that she knew she should live and had loved it. For her, there was no going back. Never again would she sleep in a gypsy wagon. And from that moment on, she reverted to calling Jasmine and Roman by their names. They were hurt at first and she tried to explain that though she loved them, in her heart she wasn't their daughter and never could be.

Her thoughts turned to Babs, and how real it had seemed when she'd heard her voice. Thinking about it hurt and she wondered if they would ever be reunited again. *Oh, Babs. I miss you every day of my life. I love you, my sister, and wherever you are, I hope you know that.*

EIGHTEEN

'Eeh, Molly, lass. Both lads?'

'Aye, both going. They went out yesterday together and never said a word, then when they came back, they told us that they'd both volunteered.'

'I'm sorry. By, it's a frightening world we live in.' Tilly took Molly into her arms. They were in the work room of their shop. Nothing much had changed over the last twelve years. The orders from London had dried up, but the season in Blackpool kept them going and they used the winter months when trade was slower to replenish their stock.

Coming out of the hug, Molly said, 'The upshot is that they both want to marry before they go! So, not only did they sign up, they'd made all the arrangements for their weddings. With the help of Vera and Mary, of course. And they presented me and their da with all the arrangements.'

'By, they move fast, them lads of yours.'

'I wish that it was that I could go. I'd be there like a shot.'

This from Ivan gave Tilly mixed feelings. It was always hard for Ivan as whatever was happening in life, his limitations often barred him, or meant he had to compromise. Tilly looked over at him and watched for a moment as his deft fingers wove an intricate basket. His skill matched her own and his love of basket making had been his salvation.

Ivan sat in a specially adapted bath chair – one that he'd designed and made himself. It allowed him movement around the room as the wheels were large enough for him to turn them with his hand, and it also gave him height enough to reach the workbench.

He was a genius at invention this lad of hers. Determined that he would join her in her work, he'd devised a sort of pully system for getting himself up the stairs. It took great strength to achieve, but then, over the years, he had developed a strong upper body with the way that he moved himself along the floor with his arms.

There were bath chairs kept where he would need them, all made by himself using the chassis and wheels from old prams. Tommy had said they should do a line in them, but they hadn't done that so far.

Ivan's health often gave Tilly fears and as she gazed at him, now a lad of fifteen, she tried not to worry about how his chest was lopsided, and how he struggled with taking in air and wheezed when he breathed out.

'Well, I'm glad that you can't. I would worry meself sick. Eeh, Molly, lass, how're you going to cope?'

'I don't knaw. I never slept a wink last night, neither did Will. Anyroad, the wedding's next Wednesday. It's a double wedding, and the girls have asked me to make a frock each for them. I don't knaw, the young 'uns think everything can be done at their whim.'

Though said lightly, Tilly noticed a tear trickle down Molly's cheek. 'Well, lass, at least that'll give you sommat to focus your mind on, eh? Forget making cushions and stuff, get yourself to your suppliers and get the material for the lasses' frocks and make them here.'

'I were going to say that to you, Tilly. I'm well in front with what we need for the shop. I'm glad you suggested it, though. I'll get me coat on. I knaw what the lasses want. By, I feel for them. No doubt they're in for a few years of heartache.'

'Aye, I feel for them too. They're lovely lasses. It'll be fun having them here for their fittings. Their ma's stall's so near, they'll not be long getting here, and she'll not miss their help at this time of year.'

'Naw, Iva's a good 'un. I love it when she drops in for a cuppa. She came around to ours last night and were a great comfort. She said that I were to look on it as gaining two daughters, and she'd take me sons as hers. Its sommat as we do anyroad, but it were nice of her to say it. And she said she'd support me if ever I needed someone.'

'That's grand. And you allus have me and Tommy.'

'I knaws that. But, eeh, it's hard, lass. Me fear's making me feel sick.'

Tilly held Molly once more. She was no stranger to the fear of the possibility of losing a precious son, and she knew the agony of losing any child. Beth and Babs would be twenty-five now and there wasn't a day went by that she didn't hope that they would bring themselves to Blackpool and come back to her. Her mind raced around possibilities – had anything happened to them? Had they forgotten her?

As Molly came out of her arms she sighed heavily. 'When you think of all the young lads it breaks your heart. How old is Florrie's lad now?'

'He's just a bit older than our Eliza. He's twelve turned, so naw, he's safe. He's a nice lad is Phil. Takes after his da, as he loves working on the land, and Tommy loves having him working with him.' Tilly glanced over at Ivan, but he didn't seem affected by what she'd said. She knew he loved to work with his da too and did in the harvest months as he would drive the big cart horse along the field while Tommy loaded the bales of hay onto it, and in spring Tommy would hitch the plough to the horse and Ivan would happily plough a huge field, strapped safely to an improvised seat.

'Well, let's hope the war don't last long enough for Phil to have to go. By, the young 'uns are heading off in their droves.'

'I knaw. Their heads are filled with all this glory stuff of fighting for your country. None of them take notice of the casualty figures that are reported in the papers and we're only four months into the war.'

'Aye, it's going to be a bleak Christmas for a lot of families this year.'

'By, there's a gloomy atmosphere in here! What's up?' They hadn't heard Eliza coming up the stairs and jumped as she burst into the room. 'Eeh, our Ma, I've had a day and a half.'

The tension broke and both Tilly and Molly burst out laughing. 'You have? Well, come on, tell us about it, lass.'

This daughter of hers brought sunshine to any gloom. She took after Tommy in looks, but had Tilly's raven-coloured hair, which was a mop of curls as Tilly's was. And looking at her, Tilly thought she was going to have her figure too, as already she was well developed.

'Well, it started with that lad I told you about – that Richie Hardcastle. He followed me all the way to school. He didn't say owt . . . well, not until I got to the gates, then he said, "I'm going to war, you knaws." Him! Spotted dick!'

'Eliza . . .' The name was said on a laugh as Tilly doubled over. 'You can't call him that, it's rude!'

'Naw it's not. Dick's short for Richard and he has got a lot of spots. Anyroad, I told him good riddance, and then when I got into school, they said that all of us that are almost twelve could leave school if they had brothers who had gone to war and their parents needed them. Well, all them whose dads are farmers said they wanted to go as they were needed on the farm. Then there were the stallholders' kids, they all put their hand up. All me mates! You don't need me do you, Ma?'

'Naw, lass . . . Well, me little love, that was a hard morning for you.' Tilly winked at Molly, then looked back at Eliza. 'I tell you what, lass, nip to the chippy, eh? It's Friday, and we like a few chips on a Friday.'

Eliza grinned. 'Aye. I'll do that.' As she said this, she made her way to Ivan's side. Flinging her arms around him, she hugged him to her.

Ivan's smile lit up his face. 'You've for being in the thick of troubles then, our sis?'

Eliza kissed the top of his head. 'Aye, but I'll cope. D'yer want fish or pie, Ivan?'

With their orders all gathered, Eliza left them.

'She's a one that girl, Tilly. I think she's afraid of leaving school. But she'll have to go in a few weeks. She leaves this Christmas, don't she?'

'Aye, but she's such a clever lass that me and Tommy have been talking about getting her a tutor. She could make sommat of herself.'

'She could, Ma. You should do that. It is that she's a very clever lass. She could turn her hand to owt.'

Ivan's way of speaking always amused Tilly. His Irish lilt that he'd had as a very young lad was now mixed with the Northern accent of those he'd been brought up amongst.

'Aye, I've thought of that, but there's a lot that our class of folk wouldn't be considered for. And she'd be ridiculed for trying to better herself.'

'Well, you could get her lessons in talking like the posh folk, Tilly.'

'Mmm, that's a thought. I might talk to her about that, Molly. But I can't see it. Eliza is so down to earth that her attitude is one of "you love me as I am or not at all". Anyroad, it shouldn't be that them as are posh have all the opportunities. Who knaws, maybe this war'll change that as posh or working class, you're all the same when the Germans . . . Eeh, I'm sorry, Molly, lass. Me tongue wagged away without me thinking.'

'Don't be. I knaw, and what you say is true. Come on, let's not get all gloomy again. I'll put the kettle on. I like a pot of tea with me fish 'n chips.'

The chatter went on as they savoured the delicious hot food. Eliza was excited to hear about the wedding. 'Can I take the day off from school, Ma? I can't miss the wedding. And I'll help with the frocks, Aunt Molly, I'll stitch the hems. I'll start as soon as I get home on Monday, if you get one of them ready by then.'

'Oh, that'll be grand. I don't knaw a neater stitcher than you, Eliza. And aye, I'll have at least one ready, if not two by then, as I'm going to get the material after this and get started on them.'

A voice called out, 'Can we come up? It's us, Vera and Mary.'

Tilly went to the top of the stairs. 'Come up, girls, the more the merrier. What're you doing here then? Oh, and congratulations . . . I think. I don't knaw whether to be happy for you, or sad as your lads are leaving you.'

'Be happy, Tilly. We're just thinking till Wednesday, and then the few days after when we'll have our honeymoon. Owt else is on the back burner at the moment.'

Tilly loved these sisters. The same age as her twins, she often used them as a benchmark for what her girls would be like. Now she saw two lovely young women and knew that Beth and Babs were that too. Swallowing hard, she showed the girls in.

After greeting everyone, especially Molly, who they both hugged and kissed, Mary set down her bag. 'I've brought a couple of samples of the material we like, but neither of us can decide on a style for our dresses. We think we should dress the same, but though we're sisters, we don't like the same styles.'

'Then have your own styles, me lasses. I knaw as you have to wed on the same day, but you're to look on it as your own wedding day, not each other's.'

'Ta, Molly, but d'yer reckon as folk might think it odd that we have chosen to look different?'

'Naw. They'll just be glad for you. Aye and glad of the free butties and a swig of ale an' all.'

They all laughed at this from Molly, but Tilly realised just how much there was to arrange and the work that was entailed. 'Let's see what you have in mind, girls, and don't worry about owt. We'll all put everything aside and get your wedding sorted between us.'

'Ta, Tilly. Me ma'd love to be involved, but she daren't shut the stall, she'll have to shut it on Wednesday as it is.'

'I could be taking care of it for a day for her. I'd only need do an hour with her and I'd knaw all I have to knaw. I often work in our shop, so knaw how to go on.'

'Would you, Ivan? Eeh, that'd be grand. But it's cold, you knaw. We freeze our lugs off some days.'

'I'll be all right. Is it this afternoon that you're wanting to go shopping?'

'Aye, well, we thought that best as Molly needs the material.'

'I'll help an' all. We don't do owt much at school on a Friday afternoon. Ooh, let me, Ma. You knaw as I'm up to me eyes with what's going on.'

Tilly laughed as she ruffled the hair of her beloved daughter. 'All right, then, lass. I'll feel better if you're with Ivan, then you can get him a hot drink if he needs one. Get your coat on and your bonnet. I'll get your coat, Ivan, and your warm scarf.'

The wedding was lovely. The girls looked a picture in their frocks. Mary's was a straight style that hugged her figure, in an ivory colour, with a lace bodice – graceful, Tilly would call it – while Vera had chosen a more glamourous look in the same material, but her straight skirt had a swatch of netting encircling her hips which gathered in a bow at her waist. The sleeves were puffed out too. They both wore huge hats of the same style and were wrapped in fur stoles to keep them warm. But it was the lads that warmed Tilly's heart.

Gerry and Brian stood at the altar, tall and handsome in their army uniforms, Gerry waiting for his Mary and Brian for his Vera.

Tilly's mind went back over the years as she looked at them. She thought of how when they were lads, they would gather vines from the hedgerows for her, and of how they'd always been so lovely and polite and were hard-working lads with good jobs – Gerry had made his name as a respected head of stage set production and travelled to many theatres to plan, advise and be involved in the making of sets for plays and shows, and Brian's skill in saddlery rivalled that of his dad's. And they were willing to leave all that behind to fight for their country. *Please God, take care of them. Bring them back safely to us, and while I'm at praying, can you see as me twins are safe an' all . . . Eeh, the times I've asked you, but please listen to me and bring me girls to me, please!*

Tommy squeezed her hand. He always knew when she was having a sad moment. She looked up at him, uncomfortable in his suit, as he was more used to his farmer's togs, but still looking so handsome for his forty-five years. Where had all of those years gone? And all they held? But despite it all, she was happy. Tommy loved her and still made her feel beautiful in her middle age.

She was proud to have kept her figure despite four births. She smoothed her blue skirt that she'd chosen to wear; the woollen material felt soft. The slight flare of the skirt which billowed at the hip due to her stiffened underskirt gave some balance to her figure. With this, she wore a grey silk blouse and a cape that matched the skirt. Her hat was a small, quirky affair with a feather attached. A couple of times Tommy had sneezed as she'd caught him with it and they'd both laughed.

With the formal proceedings over, the bells rang out as the two married couples left the church. Even the early December weather was being kind, as a wintery sun shone down giving a little warmth as it played with the remaining white frost that still clung to the hedges and trees.

The reception was held in the Fox Inn on the promenade, a place that held more memories for Tilly, as it was here that she'd brought the bottles of gin on the fateful night they'd carted her off to the asylum. But she blotted them out. For many years now, she'd had her drinking under control and didn't worry about going into such places, though she wouldn't take a beer even when it began to flow freely, as she still feared the demon inside her.

But she laughed as Ivan took his first sip of beer and pulled a face. 'Ugh! It's horrible.'

'It's the Guinness that you should be drinking, lad, for aren't you a born Irishman?'

'Naw, Tommy, that'll be too strong for the lad.'

'Get away with you, Tilly, it's purer than this muck that the English serve.' With this, Tommy asked for a glass of the house's finest Guinness. Ivan took a sip and coughed. They all laughed, but Tilly felt a little concerned and took the glass.

'I'm not for being man enough yet, Pappy, but one day, I'll join you in a pint.'

'That you will, son, that you will.'

Tommy put his arm around his son and hugged him. They were sitting side by side, Ivan in his chair and Tommy on the end of the wooden bench. Laughter rang out all around them. And Tilly smiled at the companionship that Tommy and Ivan had always had. Tommy never saw his son's disabilities; he only saw his beloved first born.

At that moment, Eliza came up to them and Tommy pulled her down next to him and enclosed her with his free arm. Tilly felt a tear prickle her eye as she looked at her lovely family. She knew she should be grateful she had them, and keep her twins safely tucked in her heart. But she couldn't help this longing for them that had lately begun to overwhelm her again.

'Haven't we the loveliest of children, me Tilly?'

'Aye, we have. We're blessed, Tommy.'

By two o'clock they were seeing the happy couples off on the train. They were going to spend two days in Liverpool. A funny choice, Tilly thought, but it appeared that Gerry had been working in the theatre there and had become fascinated with the city and its docks and wanted to see one last production that he'd been involved in, and so the others had humoured him, the girls not caring where they went as long as it was to spend precious time with their lads.

It was as the train pulled out of the station that Tilly turned and saw Ivan struggling to breathe. Ever since Friday, when he'd sat out in the cold working the stall, he'd had a sniffle. 'Eeh, lad, what's to do?' Rushing over to him, Tilly's fears for him heightened. 'Tommy! Ivan, he . . .' Ivan's face turned blue. 'Ivan, Ivan, lad! Eeh, me lad!'

Ivan slumped forward. Tilly clung to him. 'Move away a minute, Tilly, I need to be getting near to him and he needs air.'

Tilly did as Tommy bid, and heard him ask everyone to stand back, but her world had closed and frozen her so that she couldn't react to what was happening. She watched as Tommy shook Ivan. 'Ivan, me darling son, it's your pappy. Talk to me Ivan, talk to me.'

But Ivan didn't open his eyes or take another breath. Beside Tilly, Eliza whimpered. Tilly put her arm around her and tried to gain strength by supporting her daughter, but still she felt detached.

'Ivan, me lovely lad.'

The despair in Tommy's voice confirmed Tilly's fears. She stared at the unmoving, bent form of her beloved son. Pain ripped through her heart as she registered the gasps from everyone around her. Eliza broke free and ran to her brother. Tilly still stood as if carved out of ice as she watched her daughter and son, the one crying and calling out the name of the other, who could not respond.

'Naw, naw . . .' The words weren't shouted but came in an anguished whisper. Molly was by her side in an instant. 'Help me, Molly, I'm falling.'

'Eeh, me lass, you'll not fall. I've got you.'

Molly's words went into a terrible wailing sound. Tilly looked over at Tommy and knew it was him making the sound. Several people crowded around him. Tilly couldn't see him, or Eliza. 'Tommy, Tommy!'

The crown parted and her Tommy came towards her. His face was flooded with tears. 'The day I was for dreading is on us, me little Tilly. Oh God . . .'

His arms came around her and his body slumped as he leant his weight on her.

'Pappy, naw . . . Pappy.' The cry seemed to give Tommy strength. He stood and reached for Eliza and huddled her and Tilly to him.

Tilly clung to what was left of her family. Their sobs gave her the strength she never thought to feel again. 'It'll be all right, Ivan's at peace now. Come on, we'll see him on his final journey. You push his chair, Tommy, and me and Eliza will walk each side of him. Let's get him home.'

Everyone parted to let the little group pass through. The men took off their caps, the women sobbed, but no one stopped their progress.

'We're going home, son. Home, where your spirit will allus be looking down on us.'

NINETEEN

Babs's hand burnt with pain as the writhing soldier clung to her hand and squeezed so hard that she wanted to cry out. His moans were terrible grunts from his throat as he bit onto the strap that the doctor had placed in his mouth.

The last two trips had been back to back, and the casualties high. They hadn't had time to restock before they'd had to go back to Dieppe clearing station on an urgent call. Now they had run out of anaesthetics.

'Nearly done.' Dr Benjamin Carter's face glowed a deep red with the effort he was making to pull the lad's leg back into line. Fractured badly, they were afraid his supply of blood would be cut off.

One last wrench and the lad screamed, dislodging the strap. Saliva ran from his mouth and his bloodshot eyes stared out.

'It's all over, lad. There, the pain will ease now.'

'Nurse, splinter his leg as quickly as you can, we don't want it coming out of place again.'

This done, the lad was much calmer. 'How's it feel now, lad?'

'Better. But by, I could do with a drink.'

Babs laughed. 'Eeh, you're from the North! Well, if by that you meant a beer, you're out of luck. It's water for you, me lad.'

The lad gave a half-smile. 'Where you from, Nurse?'

'Blackpool, but not since I were a nipper.'

'Bolton. But we goes to Blackpool for our holidays. We stay in a boarding house. It's like staying in a prison, there's that many rules.'

'Rules?'

'Aye, naw making any noise in your rooms, naw returning to the house from after breakfast till dinner. Meals are on the table even if you're not there, and aye, cleared away and no more offered if you're more than five minutes late.' The lad laughed. Tilly did too, but hers was a painful strangled sound. No one but she and Beth had ever talked much about Blackpool.

Fighting the longing in her, she looked at the soldier properly for the first time. He had a lovely round face that was splattered with blood, and a dimple formed in his cheek when he smiled. She couldn't discern the colour of his hair as what little the army had left him with was caked in mud. She thought him near to her age and felt akin to him in some strange way. 'I'll get you a drink, then once we've everyone seen to, we'll be back to clean you up. What's your name?

'Ronald, but I'm called Ron. What's yours?'

'I'm Sister Smith.'

'Naw, your first name.'

'Barbara, but I'm called Babs. But you must call me Sister Smith here.'

'Awe, that's a pity as I like the name Babs.'

Babs felt herself blush, but not in an unpleasant way. She walked away, but when she went back with the water, she was shocked to see that Ron was writhing in pain again. Sweat rolled from his face.

'What is it? Is it your leg?'

'Naw, me stomach! Aaaggh!'

'Doctor, over here!' but even as she called out, she saw Ron's face drain of colour and his eyes close. 'Doctor!' With this desperate cry Babs ripped Ron's shirt from him. It was then that she saw the terrible bruising and knew that his injuries were much more extensive than the leg that his cries had pulled their attention to.

'Give him oxygen, Sister, hurry, he's turning blue. This looks like internal bleeding. Did you check for further injuries?'

With a sinking heart, Babs realised that she hadn't, that she'd taken the assessment of the nurse who had the task of rating the urgency of the patients. The tag on Ron's toe had said 'broken leg' and nothing more.

'We're going to lose him. I can't stem the flow without cutting him open and I haven't the anaesthetic to put him to sleep – the shock of the pain will be too much.'

Something in Babs's memory clicked then – a trick she'd seen the gypsies use many times to put someone in an unconscious state. Roman had described it to her when she'd asked about it.

'I knaw a method, Doctor.' Calling for a nurse to bring oxygen, Babs applied pressure to Ron's neck. 'There, he's out like a light.'

'What? How did you do that? My God, I've never seen anything like that.' Pulling the nearest trolley to him, Dr

Carter began the delicate task of opening Ron up. The nurse had the oxygen in place and Babs prayed that Ron's life could be saved.

But it wasn't to be. The blood flow couldn't be stemmed, and Ron drew his last breath. 'Naw! Awe, naw. Poor lad.' With this her tears flowed.

'We did our best, Sister Smith. Try to hold yourself together. If we give in, everyone will.'

Swallowing hard, Babs controlled her emotions.

'Whatever it was that you did to enable me to go in, I don't know, but I don't think we should use it again. It unnerved me.'

When Babs explained, the doctor was impressed and knew how it worked, but still felt that it was too dangerous as a practice to use. 'Not that I think that you contributed in any way to his death, Sister, it's just that it's not a recognised medical practice. What we need to learn from this is that our nurses are taught to make a thorough assessment and not to take the cries of the patient as an indication of what to examine. Every patient must receive a thorough check-over.'

'Yes, Doctor.' Babs was glad that he wasn't blaming her, and neither was she blaming her nurses. They all did what they could under the extreme circumstances.

When they reached Paris for the second time in a fortnight, but a month after she'd seen Beth, Babs asked Belinda and Cathy if she could take leave. 'I knaw as it ain't me turn, but I have to find out if me sister is still in the hospital. There was no time when we were here before as we had to turn around straight away.'

* * *

When she entered the hospital, Babs had a sinking feeling. She hadn't been able to make anyone understand her. But from what she understood she was to wait and someone who could speak English would be brought to her.

The nurse that came looked taken aback for a moment. 'But how is this possible? I – I put you on the ambulance to be taken to England!'

Babs's heart sank. 'It wasn't me, it was me twin. Beth's me sister.'

'Oh, I see. Well, you are how they say, iden – very much the same. But wait, are you called Babs?'

'Identical. And aye, I am Babs. Did Beth ask for me?'

'She did. She said that she'd heard your voice, but we all thought she was hallucinating.'

'Has she gone?'

'She has. I'm sorry. I'm afraid she was badly injured. I can see that you are a nursing sister, so I will tell you the truth. Your sister may never walk again. She had a spinal injury, and we think her spinal cord may be damaged as she had no feeling in her legs. I'm very sorry.'

Babs gasped against this knowledge. 'Oh naw! Oh, poor Babs. Did she see me note?'

'What note?'

'I pinned a note to her. I only had the tickets that we tie on the injured when assessing them, but I wrote on it that I loved her and where to contact me.'

'There was no note. I received her and all the injured that day, as I do most of the English, and there was no note. By the time I got to her, she was stripped and prepared for surgery.'

Babs stared at the girl. 'Naw. Eeh, how is she ever to find me again?'

'Find you? Does she not know where you are?'

'Naw.' Not wanting to tell their story, Babs thanked the girl and left. Outside in the grounds of the hospital, she saw a bench. Making for it, she slumped down and cried. She cried for all the lost years with Beth, for her ma, and for all those young soldiers who had lost their lives, especially Ron. She'd never forget him.

Wearily, she made her way back to the train. The sights of Paris held no magic for her now. The glittering Christmas trees were like an insult as they spoke of a promise, but there was no promise on the horizon for her. She'd had a brief moment with Beth, and it was gone. Beth had gone. It was then that she thought for the first time that Beth had been wearing the remnants of a nurse's uniform, and that it was the colours of the Red Cross. She wondered how it came about that Beth was a nurse, and at them choosing the same profession as each other; they'd never spoken of it as children.

An excitement built in her. All hope wasn't lost. She could enquire at the Red Cross HQ when she got back to England. She could ask for Beth Petrilona, as that was the name that they had used as children, and she was sure that Beth would have stayed with Jasmine and Roman and still be using that name. Or she could go to the farms where Jasmine and Roman frequently worked.

With these thoughts, she cheered up. But then wondered at herself never going to find Beth before. It had all been tied up with her not wanting to be taken back to Jasmine and Roman as she'd thought that if she was, she would never escape again.

★ ★ ★

She only just made it back onto the train. 'We have been called to travel back to Dieppe.'

'Oh, but we were meant to be here for three days, Cathy. What about supplies and the cleaning of the train?'

'Supplies were waiting at the station for us and have been loaded. The poor, tired nurses are on with scrubbing the beds. But I think we are needed, so we'll have to muck in and help.'

The work occupied Babs's mind, keeping her from thinking too much about her sorrow at missing Beth. She felt tired to the bones of her but knew that that was the case for everyone. So, she renewed her effort helping a young VAD to scrub a bedstead down. A sob alerted her to the girl's anguish. Some of these girls had only had a few weeks' training and had never seen any blood in their lives. All were from wealthy families, as they were the only ones who could afford to pay their own way. Well educated, they were a big help with languages and were able to comfort the French soldiers as well as the British.

Babs knew there was nothing she could say to alleviate the girl's weariness or the nightmare she found herself in, so sought to cheer her up by singing. She only knew hymns and carols, so decided on a carol as it was only three days until Christmas. '*Oh, Little Town of Bethlehem . . .*'

Before she'd completed the first line the voices of all the girls rang out as they joined in with her. The atmosphere lightened. And Babs felt a sense of joy enter her, though it was tinged with sadness. Her joy held her hope that she now had the means of finding Beth, but her sorrow was deep for Beth's plight. *I'll take care of you, Beth. Once I find you, I'll never leave your side. I'll nurse you for the rest of me life if that's what it takes.*

The girls went on to sing 'Silent Night' next. And this time some male voices joined them. One was particularly lovely, and Babs looked up to see Dr Carter singing his heart out. A man in his mid-thirties, he never interacted much with them other than for his work, so it was good to see him relaxed in this way.

With the work done, Belinda called for a drop of sherry to be served. 'Sherry?' Dr Carter looked up in surprise, 'Have you sisters got a secret stash?'

'We have, Doctor Carter. We had a plan to get a couple of bottles every time we were allowed off the train. As that's only happened once and two of us went, we have four bottles. We were keeping it for Christmas night, but as we none of us know where we will be then, and we have a few hours now, I think this Christmas carol service – as that's what it has been – can be nicely rounded off with a drop of sherry. Then everyone can wash and go to bed.'

'Hear, hear, Sister. A jolly good idea.'

The sherry tasted much the same as the wine that was kept in the chapel at the convent. The priest magically turned it into the blood of Christ and then drank almost a chalice full. His words would slur after that.

One night, she and Daisy had crept to the chapel and sampled it. They'd liked it too much and had both been sick, pretending the next day that they had an upset tummy.

The memory made Babs smile, as did thinking about Daisy, who'd been like a sister to her during her years at the convent. And yet, she'd missed any real clues that Daisy would become a nun.

'Here you are, Babs. You need this more than most. Take another and down the hatch. Cheers!'

Babs laughed and sipped her second drink, feeling light-headed as she did. It was a nice feeling, as if all her cares were lifting off her shoulders. She laughed, but didn't know why. 'You've a lovely laugh, Sister. It doesn't seem to belong to you.'

She looked up into Dr Carter's grey eyes. 'Oh? And why's that?'

'Well, it sounds, sort of, well ... gentile.'

'Ta very much! Are you saying as I should have a coarse laugh then? We ain't given our laughs according to class, Doctor.'

'Oh, I'm sorry, I didn't mean ... I mean ... Oh bugger ... I've wanted to find something to say to you other than asking you to hand me something medical, and I've mucked it up on my first attempt.'

Babs felt her cheeks redden at this. She'd never thought of the doctor in this way and felt confused at him suggesting that he had wanted to approach her. 'Don't worry about it, many have judged me by me standing, you're naw different.'

'I'm not judging you, honestly. I just wanted to get to know you better. Would you walk along the train with me to the back carriage? We doctors often stand on the balcony at the back of the train having a cigarette.'

'Aye, I could do with some fresh air. Ta.'

Babs took no notice of the looks she was given by Belinda and Cathy. Cathy's was a cheeky wink, but Belinda's was one of complete surprise.

When they reached the balcony, the night looked beautiful as it travelled in the opposite direction to them. The moon shone and the stars looked like a twinkling carpet. The shadowy trees came and went, and the occasional peep of the landscape showed a flat surface, broken by a few hills dotted here and there. The air was chilly, which spoilt it a little as after the warmth her work and the sherry had generated, it made Babs shiver.

'Here, put my jacket around you. I take it that's all dry blood on your uniform?'

His arms came around her as he swished his jacket over her shoulders. It was a funny sensation, as was the maleness of him – that certain smell that only men have, of fresh sweat which now mingled with the aroma of the tobacco.

His arm lingered around her, making her feel uncomfortable. She tried to move away, but she was already against the bars of the balcony. 'Barbara, don't be afraid. I won't hurt you. May I kiss you?'

'Naw. I want to go inside. I thought you just wanted to chat.'

He barred her way as she went to skirt around him. 'Please move, Doctor Carter.'

'Adrian. And don't be unfriendly. You're used to men, surely. I just want to relax with you, that's all, and well, if that leads to more, it can't be new to you to do that.'

Anger shot through Babs. 'How dare you! Move out of me way or I'll scream.'

'Do you think anyone will hear you? I don't think so. And neither will they disturb us; they know what we've come out here for.'

Shocked, Babs couldn't take this in. Shoving him hard, she managed to get around him and run for all she was worth through the store carriage. But a hand grabbed her before she reached the door. His vice-like grip held her so that she couldn't move. 'Don't play games with me. You know why we came here. Now, stop fighting and let's get on with it. This is a good place, actually, as you can lie on that pile of sheets.'

'I'll not! Now let go of me. You're a doctor and should knaw to behave better than this.'

When his grip tightened, a fear shot through Babs. Memories assailed her of the hateful Cecil and the pain he caused her. A scream came from her that went into the noise of the train as if she'd only whispered. Then a pain shot through her head as he grabbed her hair. 'Shut up, you slut!'

Lifting her foot, she kicked out. His grip released as he doubled over. 'You bitch!'

Taking her chance, Babs ran through the door and didn't stop until she reached the sisters' quarters. There she flung herself on her bed and wept.

'Babs, what's to do? Babs, are you all right?'

'Doctor Carter, he attacked me!'

'Oh, you didn't want to go with him, then?'

'Want to? What're you saying, Belinda? I just thought it would be nice to get some air! I never dreamt . . .'

'That's a funny thing to say to Babs, Belinda. It sounds as though you are asking if she wanted him to take advantage of her.'

'Well, everyone knows what he's like.'

'Well, I don't. What is he like?'

Babs was astonished at this conversation and what Belinda said next. 'Oh, he's known for being one after the ladies. Not for rape, though, I can't see him taking advantage like that. He must have thought you wanted him to, Babs.'

'Well, why should he? I've never given him any reason to think that of me. And I didn't knaw as he were a ladies' man, I've never seen the signs. I thought he was a gentleman.'

'He is. I cannot believe he would go this far. Are you sure you're not mistaken? Maybe he thought you wanted to.'

With Belinda saying this a deeper fear entered Babs. *Is that how it will look? Did they all think I knew what I was in for when I went with Carter?*

'Look, get your bath, Babs, and forget about it. It's the best way. Let's all try to get a good night's sleep, eh?'

'Thanks, Cathy.'

'I'll help Cathy to fill the bath while you get your night clothes sorted, Babs.'

Babs didn't know what to think of Belinda. On the one hand she was almost accusing her of making a play for Carter, but on the other, she was helping her in this way.

The bath was soothing, though the solitude now that the others had left her gave her mind free reign. She thought about the horror of being held and raped by Cecil, about Mario, the son that she lost, and then let her thoughts drift to her ma. It was getting harder and harder to conjure up her ma's image; it seemed to mingle with that of Beth's.

Tears of longing stung her eyes, but she didn't dare let them spill over for fear of never being able to stop them. Climbing out of the bath, she dried herself and donned her nightshirt. Tomorrow was another day. She decided she would get on with things and not dwell on the past so much.

When Matron summoned her the next day, Babs's heart beat heavily in her chest.

'Sister Smith, come in.'

Babs stood in front of Matron's desk. The atmosphere prickled with tension. When Matron lifted her head, she sighed. 'It has come to my notice, Sister Smith, that you behaved unbecomingly last night. And besides that, you were instrumental in causing a soldier's death. What do you have to say for yourself?'

'Naw, I didn't, Matron. I – I . . . the soldier was assessed in the normal way and tagged; we treated him according to that information. And as for afterwards, the doctor attacked me, he was going to rape me!'

'What? Good Lord, Sister, control yourself! You cannot tell such lies about a trusted member of our staff. What do you think you were doing, enticing Doctor Carter to go with you, and then propositioning him?'

'But it didn't happen like that! He asked me to go for a walk with him to get some air. I didn't think owt of it, but when we reached the balcony, well, he . . .'

'Sister! Stop this now. That isn't how Doctor Carter reported the incident to me.'

Babs hung her head.

'Now, I want you to apologise, both to me for your outburst and to Doctor Carter for putting him in such a compromising position. He seems to me to have shown the utmost constraint in his dealing with you.'

'But, Matron—'

'Be quiet! I have always admired you, coming from the class that you do, having acquired the skills and qualifications that you have, but breeding will out, and your true colours showed last night, as did the lack of true nursing insight with your overlooking of the soldier's life-threatening injuries. I have never had anyone like you to deal with before. Now, you stay out of trouble or I will ask for you to be removed from my staff.'

Babs fell silent. This was so unfair but at this moment it felt as though the world was stacked against her.

'Your apology, please.'

'I can't apologise for sommat I ain't done.'

'Very well, leave my sight. Carry on with your work until I hear from HQ. But mark my words, you will not remain on this train long.'

Babs walked out of the office with her head held high, but her heart full of hate. For the matron, but most of all for the spiteful Dr Carter. She'd be glad to leave the train. She didn't want to work with that lying letch of a man.

Rubbing her tears away with her sleeve, she took a deep breath and walked towards the ward carriage.

TWENTY

'You have a visitor, Beth.'

Beth opened her eyes. She seemed to spend the most part of her time asleep. Not only because she was tired, but because when asleep the truth of her reality didn't haunt her.

Since coming to this hospital in Margate, she'd not only realised that she couldn't move her legs, but that she may never do so again, which meant relying on others for everything and never being able to nurse again.

'Beth, oh my Beth! It is me, Mama.'

Beth turned her head. Jasmine looked beautiful as always with her black hair sleeked back, her large eyes outlined in black and her clear-cut features. Two large earrings dangled from her ears. She'd called herself Mama, but Beth had long since dropped that address. 'Jasmine. Oh, it's good to see you. How did you find out I was here? Did the Red Cross contact you?'

'It is that they did. We arrived at Farmer Belver's farm as soon as Christmas passed, and he had a message for me. Oh, my Beth. That this should be happening to you ...'

'Don't get upset, Jasmine. I have cried so many tears that I am exhausted from them.'

'What of your future? Will you come home, my little one? It is that we will look after you.'

'I don't know, I have to think about it all. But how is Roman?'

'Oh, he is waiting to see if they will let him in as he is anxious to see you.'

To Beth's shame, she didn't want Roman to come in to see her and felt embarrassed having Jasmine here. Brushing these thoughts away, she put out her hand in a gesture of amends. 'Don't worry about me, Jasmine. I will come to terms with it all. I – I'm just finding it hard at the moment.'

'Are you in any pain? I will leave you one of my potions.'

'No, I'm not in pain. Everything's numb and the bruises to the rest of my body are healing. I can't remember much about it. I was tending . . . Oh, Jasmine, they all died . . . the soldiers.'

'My poor darling.'

Jasmine just held her hand while the tears flowed down her cheeks. Once Beth was in control again, Jasmine said, 'No matter what it is that you decide to do, we will be always on hand for you. Papa has been keeping his eyes open and he has a surprise for you.'

'Oh?' Beth couldn't think what it could be.

'It's a bath chair! He saw it in a second-hand shop and bought it, so when you are able to come out of here, we are all ready for you.'

This shocked Beth. Of course she'd thought that she would need such a thing, but actually having one made her situation suddenly real.

'I'll go, Beth, darling, you look tired. I'll send in Roman, and then we will come again tomorrow. We'll come every day that you are here.' With this, Jasmine leant forward and kissed Beth. There was something strangely comforting in the familiar smell of her perfume and the soft touch of her hand on Beth's cheek. She smiled a teary smile. 'Thank you, I'd like that.'

When Roman came in, his face looked very serious.

'I'm all right, Roman, you mustn't look so worried.'

'It is that I can see that you are very weak, little one. You have to get stronger. And you're not to think of this as everything coming to an end. It is for being a new beginning. I promise. You will walk again, but if it isn't for a long time, then there is a lot that you can do once you are for being well in yourself. You can assist a doctor who has a surgery, you can learn to drive one of those motor cars . . . Oh, I know that it is that they have pedals to help them to go, but I'm for thinking that I can adapt one for you until you can use your feet again. And—'

'Oh, Roman! You alway have such faith in me. Thank you for that. But we'll see, eh? Firstly, I have to come to terms with it all. But I promise that I won't give up, not with your determination and faith in me I won't.'

'That's good, because your brains are in your head, and are not for being in your legs. So, even if it is that you never walk again – which will not be for happening, then there's a lot of things that need you to be clever to do and that you don't need legs for. It is that you can still have an enriched life doing them.'

Catching hold of his hand, she told him, 'I'd have never become a nurse without your help, Roman. You made it possible, and I'm so grateful.'

'Well, it is that I can make a lot of things possible, and I will. Now rest, little one, and look forward to your future with hope.'

When he'd gone, Beth did lay her head back. Roman was right, there were a lot of things that she could do, if her paralysis turned out to be permanent, but at the moment she was too tired and afraid to even think about them.

'Miss Petrilona?'

Beth jumped out of the doze she'd gone into. Opening her sleepy eyes, she looked into what looked like pools of blue. When her focus adjusted, she saw that they were the eyes of the handsomest man she'd ever seen. If ever she'd dreamt of the man that would appear that to her, it hadn't been a man with chestnut-coloured hair, olive skin and a few freckles over his nose. But this man had these and made her heart flip over.

'I'm sorry to make you jump, but I need to talk to you. I'm Doctor Freeman. I've just been briefed on your case, and I'd like to examine you. Is that all right?'

'Aye.' Though she said this, Beth was overcome by shyness. She didn't want this man to be a doctor and have to look at her in this state. She wanted to be a young woman he took a shine to and was asking out to dinner ... *What am I thinking?*

'Just lie still. I'm—'

'I've naw choice on that, Doctor. I can't move.' With this, for some unexplained reason, Beth burst into tears.

'Cry as much as you want to, Miss Petrilona, I know that I would. But don't give up hope. There's always hope and, as you know, medicine is making advances all the time.'

'Me name's Beth. And ta. But even though I knaw all of that, it don't help. Not when your friends come in and say they've bought you a bath chair.'

'But that's an excellent idea. Do you think they will bring it into the hospital? I think it would help your recovery to get out of this bed and see different things. We have a balcony that looks out over the sea. I'm sure it could be arranged for you to be wrapped up warmly and taken out there.'

'I'd love that, Doctor.'

His smile warmed Beth, and it might have been her imagination, but she thought she saw something more in his eyes than kindness. She managed a smile back.

'That's the spirit. Now, I need to check a few things, so I'll take a pillow away and lay you flat.'

Nothing he did – lifting her legs, scraping the cap of his pen along them or sticking little pins into her – had any effect. She felt nothing.

Sighing, he pulled the covers back over her, then leant across and lifted her. She was so near to him as he manoeuvred her pillows back into position that she had the notion to plant a kiss on his cheek, but forced herself not to, shocked that such an idea should enter her head.

'There, are you comfortable now?'

'Aye, I am, thank you.'

'Well, I'll see you later. I'm going to confer with someone and will let you know what we think.'

As he left her, she felt bereft and wanted to call him back. She resisted doing so, but instead closed her eyes and tried to imagine what it would have felt like to kiss him. And even more, what it would feel like to have him kiss her.

'Miss Petrilona?'

Opening her eyes, Beth knew she'd slept again as she could see that it was dark outside. To the left of her were two long windows out of which she could only see the sky. 'I hope you don't mind, but I thought you might be bored just lying here, and too much sleep isn't good for us.'

Yawning, Beth said, 'I do it because I can forget.'

'I know. And that's why I've brought you something.'

Suddenly, she realised that Dr Freeman wasn't here in his capacity as a doctor but was wearing casual clothes – brown corduroy trousers and an open-neck collarless shirt that was topped by a grey cardigan. He looked beautiful.

'A book. It's a Jane Austen novel, *Pride and Prejudice*. I think you will enjoy it. My sister loved it, so I borrowed it from her. She said that you can keep it for as long as you like.'

'Thank you. That's very kind. I've always wanted to read it.'

'I think it will keep you amused. And it is better to stimulate the brain rather than let it lie idle.'

'I know. But I had nothing to help me to do that. I have now.'

'Are you from the North? Only earlier, you were speaking with a slight accent. I found it rather endearing.'

'Yes, originally. But . . . well, something happened, and I was brought up in and around Kent. I learnt to speak properly for my studies, only for some reason, I lapse back when nervous or in shock, as I still am after the accident.'

'Were you with the gypsies?'

'How did you know that?'

'Sister told me that you had a visitor today, a gypsy lady, and she said you seemed very fond of her.'

'Yes. They did bring me up.'

'May I sit down? I'm fascinated by you and would love to hear your story.'

Beth wanted so much to tell him, but she was afraid for Jasmine and Roman. 'I – I don't feel up to telling it. Not yet.'

'Oh, I'm sorry. I've intruded. Sister will be cross with me as she said that I could have five minutes to deliver the book and that was it.'

'Oh no, don't go. I . . . well, the nights are long in here, Doctor.'

'All right, I'll stay, but only if you call me Henry. I'm off duty and this is a friendship call, not a professional one.'

'I'm Beth and thank you. I really have felt very lonely. I know I've had visitors, but . . . well, I have so much time on my own.'

'We can put you in a ward with others if you like? You're in a side ward at the moment.'

'No. I don't want a lot of people around me. I can't face all the questions, and yet . . . well, it's daft, but I do want to talk to someone.'

'Try me. Tell me what your fears are for your future.'

She found Henry so easy to talk to that she blurted out all the deep fears she held. 'How am I going to take care of myself? Oh, the couple who brought me up are saying that I can go back there, but I don't want to. I've left that behind me now. But how am I going to earn a living? I'm so scared.'

'Don't be, please don't be scared, Beth. I . . . well, I came back tonight because I couldn't get you out of my mind. I – I would very much like to be your friend. It's okay, I'm not your regular doctor, I was only brought in to assess you so I'm not proposing anything improper.'

'I'd like that. Thank you.'

They were quiet for a moment and held each other's gaze. Beth's mind was full of what a mess she must look; she'd only been given a quick swill with a flannel each morning and no attention had been paid to her hair, which felt like a tangled wire brush when she touched it. But above these thoughts was the one thing that mattered most to her. 'When you did your assessment, what did you find, Henry?'

'Well, it isn't easy to tell what the long-term outcome will be, because it is clear that there is a lot of swelling, and this can be applying extra pressure to your spinal cord, but there is a spinal injury and they are always serious and could mean long-term, maybe even permanent paralysis. I'm sorry. I wish I had better news for you.'

Hearing this, even though it had been something she knew in her heart, devastated her and though she fought against it, tears rolled down her cheeks. Once more Henry allowed her to cry, only this time she felt his hand take hers and that was a comfort to her, and also gave her feelings she'd never experienced before.

Confused, Beth couldn't say why there was a sense of joy now mixed in with the sadness she was feeling because they were merely holding hands, and yet it seemed that in that moment her life changed. She no longer felt alone, and it was as if Henry's hand was a lifeline to her.

Her eyes found his again, and she smiled through her tears.

'Everything will turn out for you, Beth. Have you no family that will help you?'

'I do have family. A sister and a ma, but I don't know where they are. Well, at least I think my ma is in Blackpool, but my sister – my twin – ran away when we were thirteen, and I haven't heard from her since.'

'So, how did you come to be with the gypsies? Oh, I'm sorry, I'm doing what you didn't want, asking questions. Forgive me. And don't answer if you don't want to.'

'If I tell you, and I do want to talk about it all, will you promise me that you will take no action?'

'What kind of action? Oh, you mean ... Did the gypsies steal you? My God, you read about such things in children's books, but did that really happen to you?'

Beth nodded. 'But I don't want anything to happen to them. I don't want them punished, please, Henry. It was a long time ago, and they thought they were rescuing us.' She told him what she could remember, which was most of what happened as she'd thought about it almost every day since.

'Oh, Beth, that's terrible. I've never heard anything like it. What your mother must have been through, and is still going through, doesn't bear thinking about. We'll get you back to her, Beth. I promise. There must be a way of finding her. I've never been to Blackpool, but I've heard of it. I don't think that it's a big place, so it may be easier than you think to find her, if she is still there. But your sister ... well, that might be a little more difficult as you haven't got a starting point, unless she made it back to Blackpool, then you may find them both.'

'I don't think she did as she promised me that she would bring our ma to me, and that never happened. Babs always kept her promises if she could. She used to look out for me. I've missed her so much, so very much.'

'Try not to break down again, Beth. Not that it is a bad thing to cry, but you need to keep a positive outlook.'

'I know. Being a nurse, you do learn that a lot of healing is done with the state of people's mind. Someone who is positive and works towards getting better usually does, but something happened that I can't get out of my mind and it's set me back a bit, made me feel all the old heartache much more acutely, whereas I had come to terms with my situation.' She told him about hearing Babs's voice and of how certain she felt that the incident really happened, but before he had time to answer the cross voice of the ward sister interrupted them. 'Doctor! I think you should leave!'

'Sorry, Beth, I have to go, but I'll come back, I promise, and we'll talk some more.'

As he went, he turned to wave, but soon turned back again as the sister berated him. 'Did I see you holding the patient's hand? What do you think you are doing? You could get struck off for this!'

'I'm not her doctor, Sister, and was visiting as a friend.'

'Technically, today you *are* her doctor! You were brought here for the purpose of assessing her. Now, I suggest you go and do not come back!'

'I'm sorry, Sister, but I will be back. I am certain that I haven't done anything improper, nor would I, but I am now a friend of Beth's and intend to come back to see her as often as I can.'

'Well! I've never heard the like. We will see about that, young man. In the meantime, you think about your actions, and about your future, as one affects the other in the medical profession!'

'I will. Goodnight, Sister.'

Beth was glad to hear a note of determination in Henry's voice. He sounded like he was a strong character, capable of standing up to the likes of the sister. And that gave her hope as Henry seemed the type of man that would keep to his word no matter what obstacles were put in his way. Maybe he really would help her get to Blackpool to find her ma.

Sister bristled into the room. 'Well, Miss Petrilona, I must apologise for the doctor's actions, I—'

'Please don't stop him coming, Sister, please. I need a friend more than anything in the world.'

'But it isn't proper behaviour on his behalf. He knows that he must not build a personal relationship with his patients.'

'I know that, but as he says, he isn't really my doctor, he isn't assigned my case. He came as an independent to give his expert opinion. Please, Sister, I beg you. I know we haven't known each other long, but Henry is special to me, and I have so little to look forward to in my life.'

'Henry, is it? Good Lord, what is the profession coming to . . . Very well, I will overlook what I see as an indiscretion, but it pains me to do so. Now, is there anything you need, Miss Petrilona?'

'Please call me Beth. I may be here a long time and it will help me to feel like one of you. We do have the same profession and are colleagues really.'

'Of course. What can I do for you, Beth?'

'I do need the bedpan for starters!' Beth laughed as she said this, and to her relief the sister laughed too.

'I'll send a nurse to you, Nurse.' This address was said with a wry smile. 'Anything else? Are you hungry, perhaps?'

'Yes, I am. I am suddenly very hungry.'

'Good, you need building up. Well, it seems our doctor has done some good for you. I'll see about getting you some toast and a mug of cocoa, how does that sound?'

'Delicious, and a nurse's staple. Oh, and Sister, do you think that someone could get me to the bath and help me to wash my hair?'

'Not tonight, but yes, it can be done. I'll put it in my notes and in my handover that you are now ready to be bathed. And, Beth, I'm so glad to hear you taking charge of your own destiny. Only you can in the circumstances you find yourself in. You're a very courageous young woman. Many had the chance to go to France but didn't. You took up the challenge and have paid a heavy price for your bravery.'

'Thank you, Sister. The conditions were horrendous, and we should keep our colleagues who are still out there in our thoughts and prayers. They are going through a living hell.'

The sister nodded her head, and then bid Beth goodnight. As she left, Beth wondered what it was that made sisters so judgemental, as most of them were, and critical too. She could have been a sister but had chosen not to be. She didn't see herself taking charge of others and trying to keep them on their toes; she was much more a follower than a leader and had always been so. Even as a youngster, she'd always followed Babs's lead. *Oh, Babs, was that truly you that spoke to me, or did I dream it? One day, I will find you. One day . . .*

TWENTY-ONE

Since Ivan's funeral, Tilly had sunk into a deep depression. Nothing seemed to hold any meaning anymore. She had children and they had been taken away and she had been left with a broken heart – a broken life.

She clung on to Eliza. It was as if she let go of her, she too would disappear.

'Ma, you're hurting me, Ma!'

'Eeh, I'm sorry, me lass. I just feel that I might lose you an' all.'

'I knaw, Ma. By, I miss our lovely Ivan. And you knaw, I do have a part of me that longs for me half-sisters an' all. But you haven't talked about them much lately.'

They were sat together on the bench outside in the farmyard, wrapped up warm against the bitter January wind. Christmas had come and gone without it being marked in any way, and they'd all gone through the motions of the burial of their beloved Ivan as if in a daze. And now they were lost. Tommy tried to carry on – he had to as he had the farm animals to see to, and in this Phil was a big help, despite his own sadness as Ivan and Phil had become very close over the years.

'Naw, it's too painful to. Talking about the twins slices me heart with more pain than I can bear at the moment, lass.'

Florrie's voice came to them. 'I've made tea, you two. Come in out of that bitter cold. By, you'll make yourselves ill.'

Florrie and Molly had taken it in turns to stay with them these past two weeks and had lightened the load for Tilly as she didn't seem able to function properly.

'That's it, take them coats off and come and sit around the fire. Eeh, Tilly, you've to take care of yourself and the young lass here, we don't want owt happening to either of you. Me and Molly are doing our best for you, lass, but it's going to take you to bring yourself to take the reins again.'

'I knaw, I'm sorry to put on you both, Florrie.'

'Naw! That's not what I'm meaning. We'd both go to the end of the world for you, Tilly, love, but you need to get strong again. Awe, I knaw as it's not easy. I cannot imagine what pain you are in. Come here, let me give you a hug. I'm tying meself in knots here.'

Going into Florrie's arms, Tilly did feel some comfort. How could she not, as the love that Florrie had for her shone through her hug. 'I will, Florrie, I promise. I'm just finding it so difficult to lift meself. It seems that all me young 'uns are taken from me.'

'Aye. It does. And me heart goes out to you. I'm afraid, Tilly. Afraid for you. Try to get stronger, lass. Don't do owt, well, like Liz did, will you?'

'Naw! Is that what's driven this? I promise you, I've had naw thoughts of ending me life. Despite everything, I still have a lot to live for. Me little Eliza, me Tommy, you and Molly, and well, the hope I hold in me that me twins will one day walk through that door and say, "Hello, Ma."' With this a sob shook Tilly's body. Florrie held her tightly to her and allowed her to cry.

A hand came into hers, and Tilly looked into Eliza's tear-filled eyes. Extending her arm, she drew her daughter into the hug and together they formed a circle of love. Florrie broke it. 'By, that tea will get cold, like umpteen other pots I've made these last days. Let's sit and try to enjoy a hot cuppa for a change, shall we?'

As they sat down, Tilly asked, 'How's Reggie holding up? Is he managing without you, love?'

'Not very well, you knaw what men are like, but he understands. He's devastated to lose Ivan too, they got on so well together.'

'I knaw. Me Ivan were like a beacon of light, everyone loved him. And, you knaw, I did knaw I couldn't keep him forever, and did keep him for a lot longer than any of us expected, but it still hurts so much that he's gone. I knaw he had his difficulties, but he lived life to the full, joining in its daily grind as well as enjoying all the good times.'

'He did. He was so happy at the wedding. We had a right laugh together at Tommy dancing the Irish jig, and Will and Reggie trying to copy him. It was so funny, I thought Ivan would split his sides. He tried to get Phil to join in, and then said how being as he was let him off from having to make a fool of himself. He said, "I knaw I have me limitations, Aunt Florrie, but I have me compensations an' all."'

'Eeh, did he say that? Well, you knaw, he did have, didn't he? He got to spend time with everyone, whereas most young lads are stuck in a job for most of the week and then disgruntled at the weekend as it's not as exciting as it should be, but Ivan got to do all the jobs he loved and to allus be around them as he loved at the same time.'

'Aye, and he never grumbled about not being able to do owt. He was happy with his lot. Sometimes I wonder what it will be like if me Phil has to go to war. Oh, I knaw as they say it won't last long, but I'm not so sure.'

They were quiet for a moment, and Tilly began to see the blessings she had. She would never have to see Ivan off to war, like Molly had done with her two, and like Florrie may have to if it went on for a long time. No, her Ivan was safe now . . . Safe? Aye, naw one could hurt him, and he'd never feel pain again, as sometimes the poor lad had been in agony. She wouldn't wish him back to go through that again.

Suddenly, she wanted to be with Tommy. She wanted him to be reassured as she was. 'Is there still some tea in that pot, Florrie? I think I'll fill a billycan and take it to Tommy. He must be freezing out there. I'll send Phil in for a brew and a warm an' all.'

She found Tommy leaning against the back of the cowshed. As she'd passed Phil, she'd sent him indoors. Flurries of snow were beginning to fall and were large enough to settle. She'd seen that they had all the cattle inside and felt glad at this as there would be nothing pressing that had to be seen to.

'Tommy!'

Tommy poked his head around the shed wall. Tilly didn't miss seeing him wipe his face on his arm. 'By, Tommy, you must be frozen. Come inside the barn, lad. I've brought you a sup of tea.'

Tommy walked towards her and to her, he looked like a broken man. 'Awe, Tommy, me love, I've come to talk to you. I've found some good to think on.'

Inside the barn they were sheltered from the wind and the now driving snow. They huddled together, not speaking, but trying to be as close to each other as they could. 'So, what is this good that you are for thinking can help us, eh?'

'Here, cup your hands around this warm billycan, and take a sup to warm your insides, Tommy.'

She watched as he unscrewed the cap and poured some of the still steaming liquid into the lid that doubled as a shallow mug. 'It's not a lot, but the thought gave me some comfort, love.' She told him how she'd been thinking about the good things in Ivan's life and the fact that he was now at peace. 'And you knaw, they do say that them as have passed can't rest unless we let them.'

'And how do we do that when every waking hour is for having us longing to have him back?'

'By stopping doing that, and instead rejoicing over the time that we did have him, which was a lot longer than we thought. And by being thankful for the life that he did have, and the joy he brought to so many, and by thinking on what I have just told you – the blessings of what he won't have to go through. Our lad touched everyone's heart and will live on in their memory and ours. Awe, I'm not saying as we shouldn't feel sad or shouldn't cry for him, but I am saying that we shouldn't let ourselves plunge deeper into this pit of misery. We have Eliza to think of, and our lovely friends, whose lives we're disrupting.'

'Me lovely Tilly, you're right, I know you are, but, oh, it's hard.'

'It is, but we can do this together, Tommy, we can. We gave Ivan life, we cared for him through all the things that he had to put up with and loved him beyond words, but now, we have to let him go in peace and not hold him back. We'll be with him again one day.'

With this Tommy put down the billycan and held Tilly to him. She found comfort in the love he was giving and taking. 'Tilly, I love you, me little darling. I love you more than life itself. We will get through this, as you say. It will take us pulling together and thinking different thoughts, but we will get there, we must, for our little Eliza.'

'Aye, who isn't so little anymore as, bless her, she started her monthlies yesterday.'

'No! But it is that she is just a child.'

'Ha, she's twelve now! And that's for being about the right age for turning into a young woman. But the point is that she needs our support as it's a frightening time for her. And she needs us to help her to take the next step in life. She's finished school now and wants to carry on her education.'

'She does, does she? But isn't that for being a waste for a girl? I mean, what does she need an education for?'

Tilly playfully hit out at Tommy. 'Don't you dare go down that road, Tommy. Lasses should be valued as much as lads, and not looked on as only good enough to cook, clean and have babbies!'

'I'm for knowing that being married to you, Tilly, but is it that the rest of the world knows it? Any careers that there are for women are reserved for the posh ones – teachers and the like.'

'I knaw, but at least we can give her the tools she needs in the hope. She's a clever lass, and that shouldn't be wasted. Anyroad, it's good that we're even having this conversation as it shows we've taken a step towards the future and aren't holding so much on to the past. Eliza is our future, Tommy, and we have to do all we can to help her in whatever path she wants to take. Now, let's go in, I'm freezing. And let's send Florrie and Phil home afore this weather gets so bad they can't get home.'

'Aye, and now we're just for being us. Me, you and our little Eliza, our family.'

They walked arm in arm, heads down to combat the snow that was coming down thick and fast now.

Once Florrie and Phil were on their way, taking the horse and trap which Phil was adept at driving, Tilly set about cooking the first meal that she'd attempted to make since Ivan's passing. Eliza helped her, looking much happier now after a hug from her pappy.

'I've the spuds done, Ma. What's next?'

'Roll this pastry out to fit that dish there. Florrie has already cooked off the beef and I've added some onions, so we'll soon have a lovely pie. I'll tell you what, I'll put some of that stout that we have in the pantry in with the meat. It's a trick that me old aunt as brought me up taught me. It gives a meat pie a rich flavour.'

'I like cooking, Ma. It's got a feeling about it that you're achieving sommat. Can I make the pudding? When I went to me mate's, we had a delicious pudding called Queen of Puddings, and I asked how it was made. I can make that for our tea. It's a bit like a bread pudding topping with snow on the top.'

'Snow? Eeh, that's all right then as it looks like we've plenty outside.'

'Haha! Naw, not real snow. It's made out of whisking egg whites and mixing sugar in with them. It's grand, all crunchy and sweet.'

'Eeh, it does sound grand. Aye, get on with it then. By, I never knew you had this liking for baking. When did that start?' A pang of guilt nestled in Tilly at her even having to ask this question of her daughter. It made her realise how wrapped up she'd been in Ivan and making his life easier and happy, and that she'd neglected her daughter. And it made her realise what a lovely, unselfish girl her daughter was as she'd never complained about the lack of attention but had given all of hers to Ivan as well.

'When I was with me mate Maxine's family. As you knaw, they're Italian and they're allus baking. The dad makes ice cream and sells it down the prom. He's so funny, as he's allus trying to invent ways of stopping it from melting. His latest is a generator that works by the pedals of his bike.' As if someone had switched her on like a light, Eliza was full now of this family and how she and her friend dreamt of one day owning a little cake shop. 'Maxine makes lovely cakes, and she's on with teaching me.'

'Eeh, come here, lass. I need to give you a hug. You've surprised me today. I never knew. You're special, you knaw that. Very special. Well, me and your pappy have been talking about your future, and if you'd like to follow that path, then there must be cookery classes that we can pay for for you. We'll look into it.'

'Really, Ma? I thought you were set on me carrying on me education.'

'I was, 'cause I thought that's what you wanted to do, lass. Eeh, I'm sorry. I've not given you the time that I should have.'

'Naw, Ma, don't be sorry. Our Ivan had to come first, he had to . . . You knaw, he knew of me hopes and he'd promised to talk to you and Pappy about it after the wedding.'

'He did? Awe, you two were allus in a huddle chatting about sommat or other.'

'Aye, and he told me as he wouldn't allus be there for me. Not in person, but that when it happened that he had to go, I wasn't to be sad for him as he'd had the best life he could have had for someone afflicted as he was and that he'd never really leave me, not really, as he'd allus watch over me.'

Tilly couldn't speak. She had a strange feeling of peace descend over her. Nothing had helped her more than what Eliza had just told her. An idea came to her. 'That's lovely, me lass, and me and your pappy are blessed to have such wonderful children. Now listen, I've had an idea. Ma Ridley's Bakery on the prom had a sign up not long ago for an assistant. She's a mean old cuss, but by, she can bake the finest bread and cakes and you couldn't learn from anyone better. How about we ask her if she'll take you on? Not as a skivvy, but as a sort of apprentice? Me and your pappy would pay her a fee for her tuition, and she'd be getting a helper an' all.'

'Eeh, Ma, that'd be grand. I've stood many a time gazing in her window, and often nipped in to buy a tart, just so as I can enjoy the smell of the bread and cakes coming from her oven.'

Tilly gazed in wonderment at her daughter, who almost seemed like a stranger to her, she knew so little about her. She watched her as she deftly whisked the eggs. Oh, she knew she was loving and funny without trying to be, and had always been caring of her brother, but this side to her was part of her she didn't know, and it saddened her to realise it.

The meal was delicious and the happiest one they had enjoyed since one place had stood empty at the table. And this was the first one that there wasn't that empty place to remind them and to prod at their sorrow, for Tilly had determinedly removed Ivan's special chair and asked Tommy to put it in the loft. He'd not wanted to, saying he felt as though they were outing their son, but though he'd taken his time and come back red-eyed, he'd seemed a lot more relaxed during tea than he had been since Ivan's passing.

Eliza made them laugh with her tales of her friend's family. 'They seem allus to be arguing, but I've learnt that they're not. They just express themselves, and don't hold anything in. They talk with their hands an' all, and half in English and half in Italian, unless the mama of the family gets really angry, then it's all in Italian and everyone ducks as she throws things. The other day, she threw the flat iron across the room, shouting, "Mama Mia!" and a lot of words that Maxine told me meant that she would kill the lot of them if she had to set eyes on them again! But five minutes later, she's cuddling them all and telling them that they are the love of her life. She even does it to me!'

Tilly laughed, but inside felt a little wary of this woman who sounded mad. 'What if she'd hit anyone?'

'Awe, that wouldn't happen. She never throws it where anyone is. They needn't duck really, but everything's a drama in their house. Naw, she allus throws it at a picture, the one of her ma-in-law, and then we have to take it to be mended before the da comes home. The man at the picture frame shop has a stock of frames exactly like the one it's in so the da never knaws that it's happened. He thinks his wife is caring of his ma's memory and that she's allus sending the picture to be cleaned, but she hates her ma-in-law's memory with a passion that I've never seen.'

They all laughed again. Eliza had a talent for relating a story like none Tilly knew. She brought scenes alive so that you felt that you were there.

With this thought and with Eliza proudly presenting the beautiful pudding she'd made, Tilly brought the subject around to the new revelation about Eliza's hopes for her future. Tommy couldn't be more pleased, and Tilly half suspected that he felt he'd won a victory over her, as domestic work was just what his daughter was choosing over what she'd suggested. But she didn't mind. To her now, the most important thing was Eliza's happiness. But she'd seen something else in her daughter this evening and now broached that too.

'Have you ever wanted to be in the theatre, Eliza? You'd make a terrific comic actor, like them as Aunt Molly told us about. You knaw, what's her name? Oh, I can't remember, but Gerry took Aunt Molly to see her as she was so funny. Ask your Aunt Molly about her sometime, as you're a natural.'

'Eeh, Ma, do you reckon as I could?'

'I don't knaw. I tell you what, we'll go together one day. I've said as I'll go before to the theatre but never made it. Well, this year I will. There. A bit late, but that and getting you settled on your chosen path is me New Year's resolution.'

'And where do I come in all of this? You're not to forget that you are for having a husband.'

'Eeh, time I went to bed, Pappy has that look in his eyes.'

Tilly blushed, and Tommy's face was a picture as his jaw dropped. Brushing it over, Tilly laughed and said, 'By, any excuse to get out of washing the pots. Come on, naw look in your pappy's eyes, there or not, is going to get you out of helping me with this lot, lass.'

They all laughed, and the moment passed, but Tilly was left wondering just what her children knew about their ma and pappy, and how they had chatted about things she'd never known about, like Eliza telling Ivan of her future hopes and dreams and Ivan sharing that he knew he wouldn't be here long and preparing Eliza. *By, I've said it many times, but though I've been through the mill, on the whole, I've been blessed. Truly blessed with having Eliza and Ivan.*

When Eliza finally went to bed, Tilly snuggled down on the sofa with Tommy. They were in semi-darkness as one of the oil lamps had flickered and died, but the fire roared up the chimney and shadows danced in every corner of the room, lighting up their little world. 'So, what's this look you had in your eyes, Tommy?'

'I'm not for knowing. Huh, these young 'uns.'

'Oh? 'Cause I thought I saw sommat an' all, but I didn't knaw as our young 'uns knew of it.'

'Don't. I could have been for crawling under the rug.'

'I knaw. It's embarrassing when you knaw as your young 'uns are aware what you get up to and when it's about to happen.'

'Is it?'

Tommy's voice held that gruff tone that thrilled Tilly and told her that he wanted her. Tonight, it was special that he did, because it marked another milestone for them both. Neither had felt like making love for over three weeks now, they'd been so consumed with their grief. 'I might let you, if you're very good, and give me nice feelings.'

'I can be doing that, me little Tilly.' With this, he drew her closer and turned his body so that he was looking directly at her. His lips came down onto hers and his tongue gently opened her mouth and played with hers, leaving her wanting to beg him to take her. But this was a night for gentle loving, not a frenzied giving and taking. They needed to be careful with each other's fragile emotions, and so Tilly allowed Tommy to go at his own pace, savouring each step he took, until at last she had him fully inside her and her world began to knit together again, piece by piece.

TWENTY-TWO

Babs had tried to carry on as normal, ignoring the snide remarks that Dr Carter made to her about her being a tease, and that one day he would have her. Cathy had counselled her to be this way, saying that it was unjust what had happened to her, but that women didn't have a say in these things and had to accept that the man would always be believed. She'd thought that was the end of it, but now, she was on her way to Matron's office, having been summoned.

Apart from her irritation at having to put up with the doctor's manner towards her, life had carried on much the same as before over these last few weeks. Many hundreds of dying and injured soldiers had been helped on whichever journey they were taking, and though it was gruelling, unrelenting work with many horrors to face, Babs was enjoying the sense of achievement it gave her and the satisfying feeling that she was making a difference. Now, she feared it was all to end in disgrace.

At least she hadn't had to face Dr Carter these past few days. Rumour had it that he was confined to his room with some sickness or other. Well, Babs hoped that it was a very painful one, that rotted his privates so that he could never hurt another woman in the way he had tried to hurt her. This thought made her smile, but that went from her face as she knocked on Matron's office door.

'Come in, Sister Smith.'

The tone wasn't one that Babs was expecting. Matron sounded friendly, not triumphant as she'd expected her to.

'Sit down. Babs, isn't it? Well, I think we can be informal on this occasion, as I have an apology to make to you. Forgive me for not believing you, but you can see the position that I was in. On the one hand I had what I thought was a respected member of the upper classes, with an impeccable reputation, and on the other a working-class girl – well, not even that, an orphan – made good. Anyone in my position wouldn't think twice who they should believe.'

Babs was fuming at the insinuations in this statement, but knew she must keep calm. Whatever had happened was in her favour and she didn't want to spoil that.

'I have received a communication. It was waiting for me in Dieppe. It turns out that HQ have had more than one complaint in the past from female patients about Doctor Carter's behaviour and, worse than that, he was only sent here because he had been on the verge of being struck off for improper behaviour towards a nurse when he worked in a hospital in London. It appears that his father is an eminent surgeon and very influential and it was that which saved him. He will be leaving this train when we reach Paris and will be sent home. He will find himself struck off.' Matron sighed. 'The pity is that he will be a great loss to the medical profession as his skills cannot be denied.'

'I'm glad to hear this, Matron. It's grand news as it has taken a load off me. But I too respect Doctor Carter's skills. There should be help for people like him – he obviously needs it. He's made my life hell these last weeks, threatening me and sniping at me, but you gave him the upper hand by not taking any notice of my account. It's them things that need looking at an' all – the attitudes of folk in authority towards them as are born less fortunate than others. It don't make us all dishonest.'

Matron looked astounded at this outburst, but then coughed and said, 'Quite. Well, I haven't time to put the world to rights, I have my rounds to do. I take it that everything is in order with all those we have on board?'

'Aye, it is. All are being cared for to the best of our ability, as they allus are.'

'Well then, get back to your post, Sister Smith. And don't worry about or talk about what has happened. It is all sorted to our satisfaction now.'

As she left the office, Babs wanted to scream out, 'What about my satisfaction?' But then, she did have some feeling of being gratified by how it had all turned out.

When they pulled into Paris, she couldn't help but make sure she was on the station platform very quickly and opted to be the one to supervise the taking of all the injured off the train. It was a busy time as each was allocated either an onward journey home or transportation to a local specialised unit. Her eyes constantly went to the door of the carriage from which Dr Carter would alight. When he did, she stood and went towards him. The spittle had gathered in her mouth and her intentions put a spring into her tired legs.

'No, Babs.' An arm grasped hers.

'I have to, Cathy. If I never do owt else in me life, I have to spit in that man's face.'

'No, you don't, and I won't let you. You'll have to fight me off, as I'm not letting go. Despite what punishment he seems to be having, he'll get away with this. His kind do. But he can drag you down with him by just clicking his fingers. He belongs to a set of people who rule our country and will get him out of anything as half of them behave in the same way that he does and think it is perfectly fine to do so. You cannot beat the system, Babs. Let it go. Please, Babs, let it go.'

Though shaking with anger, Babs listened to this plea from Cathy, and turned back towards where she was sorely needed. 'I'm sorry, lass. It just got to me for a moment. I've been brought up to think an eye for an eye but I can see as that ain't allus the best way.'

'Well done, Babs. We can beat the likes of Carter in other ways. With our dignity for one. That will show him that he hasn't beaten you, that you still have your pride and your job and that he hasn't blotted any of that, because that would have been his intention. Those of his class despise the lower classes, and he sought to demean you and bring you to your knees.'

At this Babs lifted her head high, turned and caught the eye of the amused-looking Dr Carter. Turning her head away as if he was nothing, she directed a nurse what to do about labelling the patients who were to be taken home to Britain. When she next looked, Carter was gone.

With a sigh of relief, Babs knew that she had learnt a valuable lesson. Now, all she wanted to do was to help as many people as she could by using her skills and to get through this war. Then she would concentrate on putting the rest of her life right.

When they reached the next pick-up another doctor joined the train, and took up the position of surgeon. On first sight of him, Babs was instantly transported back in time and felt the same flutter she'd experienced when she'd met him as a boy. Her heart flipped in her chest. Taller by at least four inches than he had been then, his sandy-coloured hair and hazel eyes were the same as they were in her memory. And he hadn't lost his endearing cheeky look or his ready grin that made him look like he'd been up to something and got away with it.

She didn't say anything about them having encountered each other in the past when he was introduced to her as Dr Rupert Bartram – embarrassment at the situation she'd been in held her back. And not only that, but all that had happened to her since, not only immediately after they met, but more especially with his predecessor as that incident had travelled and seemed to have given everyone in every clearing station an opinion. Some accepted that she'd been wronged and gave her sympathy, while others made remarks that indicated that they thought she'd asked for it. These two schools of thought seemed to be divided between those of the upper classes who thought her cheap and believed that they had the right to let her know this, and those of the middle and lower, who championed her. Rupert was definitely of the upper classes and Babs felt sure that he would look on her as a slut. She remembered him saying his father had many tenanted farms on his estate, and news of him joining them had been full of him being the son of an earl.

Rupert didn't seem to recognise her, but then, she had just clambered out of a ditch when they met. And with his standing in life being far above her own Babs didn't hold out any hope of him ever taking notice of her, so she threw herself into her work, praying that all the gossip about her would quieten down and the same would happen for the thumping of her heart.

It was six weeks after Rupert joined them that Babs had her first encounter with him. In this time worshipping him from afar had been becoming very painful, as he didn't seem to notice her at all.

'We're coming into Dieppe, Babs. Stand by your bed.'

Babs laughed. Belinda said this or similar every time they approached a station.

Springtime was showing its clothes everywhere as buds burst open and birds busied themselves, twittering and arguing over scraps as they did so. The sun had more warmth in it, but still it vied with heavy clouds that seemed to wait until they were over the battlefields before shedding their load. Almost every station assessment was done in pouring rain. Being cold and wet seemed to be part and parcel of the job.

Cathy calling out brought Babs to the immediacy of the moment. 'Right, I'll take the red tags, and get the stretcher bearers to get them onto the train first.'

'Aye, and I'll take the yellows, Cathy, and get them settled in minors. That's if the staff on the station haven't already dealt with them.'

'I know, SBG – stitch, bandage and put their gun back in their hand. Poor buggers.'

'Eeh, Cathy, you swore.'

'I feel like using worse words than that. All of this seems senseless. All the bodies – dead, or broken – and the toll on the mind, what's it all for? One lad said to me on the last trip that all his mates had been killed in one battle and yet the officers drank a toast to them gaining a field. It's beginning to sicken me.'

'You're right, Cathy, I knaws that, but ours is not to ask questions, just to try to mend the casualties.'

'That's how I see it too, Sister Smith. And I cannot believe what's asked of you girls, but you always rise to the challenge.'

Rupert stood behind her as he said this. Babs felt her legs going. *For goodness' sake, I'm acting like a young 'un, and I'm going on twenty-six!*

When the train slowed and then stopped, Rupert gently moved her and then jumped down onto the platform. As he landed, he turned and put out his hand. 'Let me help you down, ladies. We seem to have stopped on the slope and it's a good jump. Give me your hand, Sister Smith.'

When he touched her Babs felt herself light up. For a moment, his eyes held hers, and she felt sure she saw a glimmer of appreciation in his, and a look as if he'd suddenly been taken aback crossed his face.

'Move along, Babs, let someone else get off the train.'

Feeling silly, Babs snatched her hand away and hurried to where the casualties were laid out. Their cries went through her as they begged for help, and for someone to relieve the pain.

* * *

When the train set off again, there was no time to do anything but what Babs called 'process' the patients. Always now she double-checked anyone's assessment. Often, she had to add to what needed attention, and in some cases found more life-threatening wounds than had been flagged.

'Sister, over here. I need help with this one.'

Babs dashed over to Rupert's side. 'Prepare him for an operation. I'll go and scrub up – he needs an urgent amputation.'

The young man stared up at her, his eyes wide with fear. 'Don't worry, lad. Doctor Bartram is first class, he knaws his stuff, you'll be all right. What's your name?'

'Gerry.'

'Right, lad, I'm going to scrub you down and put you in a gown, one that you'd not want your mates to see you in.'

Gerry gave a small smile. 'You sound like me ma.'

'Cheeky, I'm only the same age as you by the looks of you. Where you from?'

'Blackpool.'

Hearing the name of her hometown gave Babs a jolt. 'Eeh, lad, I were born there an' all.' Babs wanted so much to ask if he knew anyone called Tilly. But she was afraid of the answer so busied herself washing him down, treating him in a special way as if he was one of her own.

Between cries of pain, Gerry told her he had a brother, and that he worried every day about him. 'Naw one'll survive this lot, naw one.'

Babs wiped a tear from the lad's eye. 'Don't say that, lad. Don't even think it. You're going home and can be of some comfort to your ma.'

'I have a wife an' all. We wed just before we came out here, both of us did. Me and me brother.'

'Congratulations. Now, I'm going to get you stretchered and into the operating theatre. Good luck, lad.'

Gerry caught hold of her arm as she went to walk away. 'Can I ask you sommat?'

'Aye, but let me call for a stretcher first.'

With this done she held Gerry's hand. 'What is it, lad?'

'This may sound daft, but have you any relations in Blackpool, only you look like me Aunt Tilly.'

Babs felt her legs give way. She clung to the bed that Gerry lay on. Somehow, she got the words out. 'She's me ma. She—'

'Babs, Doctor Barnham's ready. Have you got the patient sorted?'

'Aye, Cathy, he's ready. I'll go in with him.'

'Are you all right? Do you want me to assist the operation?'

'Naw, this is a Blackpudlian, and we stick together. Don't worry, Gerry, I'll be by your side all through it.' Babs didn't know how she was managing to think straight after what Gerry just said, but she went before him and hurriedly scrubbed up. By the time she went into the theatre, Gerry was sedated.

Everything went like clockwork with the operation, though Babs knew it was the aftermath that was worse for the patient and her heart went out to Gerry, facing life restricted in such a way. But for all that, her heart ached for him to come round as she was desperate to ask him more about his Aunt Tilly.

'Good job, Sister, thank you. How about a cup of tea?'

Babs felt strangely elated at this praise and the lovely grin she received. 'I'll organise it, and get the theatre cleaned up ready for the next one. There are about five ops needing to be done.'

'And have one yourself. We can take five minutes, there are no more urgent cases as I understand it.'

Stripping off her blood-soaked gown, Babs called through to the kitchen to bring tea into the corridor outside the theatre where the theatre staff took their breaks. For this purpose, there was a bench against the carriage wall.

'Help me with this, will you, Sister? Look, can I call you Babs? I hate all this formal stuff. We're all in this together, and it's better if we can be friends.'

'Aye, you can.'

'Well, call me Rupert, not Doctor.' He turned around as he spoke and Babs undid his gown. As she did Rupert pulled the gown off, and then discarded his wet-with-sweat shirt to reveal his chest: tanned, honed and only slightly hairy. Babs thought she'd never seen a man so beautiful.

Rupert coughed, bringing her eyes to his. The colour crept over her cheeks at the look of amusement on his face and the realisation that she had been staring. Turning away, Babs went to the sink and scrubbed her hands.

'Tea's up.'

'Ah, just what the doctor ordered.' With this he laughed. 'Come on. We've just got time before the next one is wheeled in.'

They sat sipping their tea, chatting about this and that, mostly work, and Babs began to feel herself relax – until he mentioned the incident. 'I was sorry to hear what happened to you, Babs. I know Carter. He has no respect for women and thinks they are there for his taking. If scorned, he can be very nasty. Try not to let it affect you. You're like a nervous rabbit around me, and you have no need to be. I don't bite.'

Babs smiled. 'Eeh, I'm glad to hear that.'

Rupert laughed. 'I love the way you speak. My old nanny speaks just like you. Listening to you brings her to my side. We had so much fun together, but Mother sacked her after I ran to her one day and said, "Eeh, Ma, it ain't a right nice day today, is it?"'

Rupert put his head back and laughed out loud. Babs joined him, imagining the scene as she did.

'You look lovely when you laugh. You should do so more often.'

'I used to.'

'And you should be proud of your heritage. Nanny was; she refused to take elocution lessons, or she could have stayed on. But I keep in touch with her and write often. She doesn't live far from our estate and gets all the gossip from the staff who visit her. Her letters are so funny. She was, and is, the loveliest and funniest nanny I ever had.'

'Aye, well, we're often judged by how we speak. It's as if folk look down on us. You're different. As you were the first time we met many years ago.' Babs cringed. She hadn't meant to mention it. What would he think?

'What? When?'

'I was the girl in the ditch.'

'My God! I would never have known you, but then, you were . . . well, I thought of you as a ragamuffin! What happened to you? I often wondered, but I went back to school the next day and didn't come home for a whole year as it was my exam year. Well, fancy that! I hope I wasn't rude to you. I could be in those days, boyish chip on my shoulder and all that.'

'Naw, you weren't, you didn't even comment on me accent.' Babs left it at this, not wanting to be drawn further.

'No, well, as I say, I was used to my nanny. But I know what you mean about Northerners. Being looked down on – well, those ... I mean ... those who speak with an accent – but I don't go along with that thinking, and people who do are just ignorant. But having said that, wouldn't life be easier for you if you did learn to speak without your accent?'

'I daresay, but I never want to lose who I am. I've strived all me life to hold on to that.'

'Oh? Want to talk about it?'

'Naw. But ta. Anyroad, we'd better get ready. Tea break over.'

'Ha, it's uncanny. I can see Nanny now and hear her. "Come on, sup your milk, young Rupert. We've to get you ready for bed, lad."'

They laughed together at this, and Babs felt that at last she was beginning to feel at ease in Rupert's company. But still he didn't seem to notice her in the way she wanted him to.

Once the last operation was finished, Babs hurried along the corridor to the intensive care ward to see how Gerry was. He was nowhere to be seen.

'Nurse, where's the soldier who had to have his leg amputated?'

'We lost him, Sister. He never came round. He just faded away.'

'Naw! Naw! Please God, naw.'

'Did you know him, Sister? Here, let me help you to a chair.'

'I'm all right. Sorry. Naw, I didn't knaw him, but he came from Blackpool.'

The nurse stared at her with an expression of bewilderment on her face.

'I . . . well, I'm from Blackpool and we were going to chat when he came to. It was just such a shock to hear that he didn't, poor lad. You knaw, you never get used to losing any of them, but when someone comes from your own town, it's like you've lost one of your own.'

'Yes, I understand that. There've been a couple of lads from Reading, my home town, and I wanted to write to their mothers and tell them that a Reading girl took care of them.'

'We should do that. Our letters would go to the war office with the deceased's belongings and would eventually land back with their families I think I will for Gerry's ma. Do we have any of his effects?'

A twinge of hope entered Babs as she realised that there was still a chance that she could contact her ma. She would put a second letter with the one for his ma and address it to his Aunt Tilly.

'Yes, I put his cap and his badge on his body, and he had a photo of a lovely girl in his pocket, poor chap, so I left that where it was. I thought he'd want to take her with him to his grave.'

'Thanks, Nurse. It's a shame their bodies can't be taken home, but at least his things go to his family. I'm sorry I didn't get me chat with him, though, but I will do that note for his ma.'

As she left the ward, Babs felt more than sorry; she wanted to sob her heart out, for the lad, for his ma, his new young wife. But as sad as she felt, she couldn't suppress the hope that had been planted in her. *Please let me contact details reach me ma.*

Once her notes were written she went along to the make-shift morgue. Standing looking down at Gerry, she brushed his hair from his forehead. 'Eeh, lad, we did our best for you. I'm so sorry. You were me hope, you knaw. Me link to me ma as I'm sure she loved you and I knaw as she loves me and would never forget me. But now, you still might be the one to help me to find her. If I do, and I meet your ma and wife, I'll tell them how brave you were. I've put it all in this note anyroad. It'll get to them, with your things and the letter you wrote, the one all of you lads wrote in case you didn't make it back. I've told them in mine how you worried about your brother and that you said how you loved them all as I knaw as you would have. And I've told them that they can be very proud of the man they waved off to war.'

With this the tears flooded, and she bent her head and kissed Gerry's cold cheek.

'Did you know him, Babs?'

Babs jumped. She turned around to see Rupert standing in the doorway.

'I'm sorry, I didn't mean to intrude. I've come to certify his death. It was a shock as I thought we did a good job for him, and everything looked all right when we sent him to the ward. Did we miss something?'

Babs could see how upset Rupert was. 'You did a grand job, Rupert. You couldn't have done more. Maybe there was sommat as we didn't knaw about. But you gave him the best chance you could. It just wasn't to be. And naw, I didn't knaw him, but he was a link to me past. He came from Blackpool.'

'Oh, I see. I've heard about the strong sense of community amongst you Northerners. He was one of yours, and so you felt akin to him. I find that rather endearing . . . Look, I have some brandy in my hip flask. I always find somewhere quiet and have a sip and think of home and the after-dinner chats with my father and friends.'

They were quiet for a moment, each remembering different times, each trying to compose themselves. For Babs the memory of the last time she had a drink with a doctor came to her mind and the fear of what happened visited her now. 'I – I . . . well, I'm sorry, but I won't have a drink, ta. I vowed never to do that again.'

'Oh? Oh God, I forgot, I'm so sorry. That cad Carter lured you in just the same way. But I wasn't doing that. I would never do that. I promise, you're safe with me. I just thought we could toast this young man and all the young men who have lost their lives and all the wounded and hope that we can save more than we lose.'

'All right, I will.'

With Rupert's job finished, and both saying a little prayer together for Gerry, they stepped out into the corridor.

'I'll tell you what, we'll have that toast right here, then you can feel safe as anybody can come along at any time and it isn't secluded as the back balcony is.'

Babs took the lid that Rupert had unscrewed from the flask, and held it while he filled it with brandy. It wasn't much bigger than a thimble, but when Rupert made his toast and she knocked it back, it made her cough. Rupert patted her back, but as soon as she had control, he laughed at her. 'Not a drinker then? Though I must admit, it's not the good stuff. I finished that a while back and this is all I could get hold of – or afford!'

His eyes twinkled as they looked down into hers. She smiled up at him. Something passed between them and they remained looking into each other's eyes for a moment. Babs looked away first. 'Naw, I'm not a drinker, but now that it's down its warming the cockles of me heart.'

Rupert laughed out loud, and Babs felt their friendship was sealed, and maybe, just maybe, something a bit more than friendship was developing between them. She hoped so.

TWENTY-THREE

An excitement built in Beth. Today, Henry was going to take her for a walk in the bath chair that Roman had brought in. It had been stored for her but now stood waiting by her bed. When she looked at it, she thought of her ma. Woven in cane, it looked really comfortable with the cushions that Jasmine had made for it.

Henry had a day off and had said he would rather spend it with her than anyone. Beth struggled to know why. What use was she?

Today was the first time she'd worn clothes. A nurse who was the same size as her went shopping for her and bought a warm woollen frock in a lovely royal blue and a fitted coat in navy with a matching felt tea-cosy hat. The frock had a white lace collar and cuffs and fell to her ankles.

She loved the clothes and the pretty undergarments and silk stockings she was given too, but having to have someone dress her had put her back into a frustrated and sad state of mind. Somehow, she'd lifted herself out of this, but it hadn't been easy.

Henry had kept his word and visited her often, and now they were so relaxed in each other's company that Beth felt she'd known him for a lifetime. When she heard footsteps coming towards her room, her heart raced. Henry's head popped around the door. 'Are you ready, madam?' He came fully into the room and his face changed as he stared at her. 'You look beautiful, Beth.'

Beth felt her colour rise. 'Thank you, kind sir.'

'Ah, I'm not Mr Darcy!'

Beth wanted to say that he was her Mr Darcy, but she just laughed.

When he came up to her he said, 'So, this is the chair? Looks good. Look at the work that's gone into it.'

'My mother does that work. At least, she makes baskets.'

'Oh? You never said.'

'I know, I remember things at different times.'

'Well, let's get you into it. I'll turn it so that it's wedged against the wall and can't go anywhere. Now, your legs will take your weight, even though you cannot feel them doing so. I'll take your arm and you lean on me as we slide you off the bed. Then we will turn you and sit you down. You're going to have to trust me, Beth, and then it will work much better.'

In no time she was sat in the chair and as she thought it would, it felt very comfortable. The feel of the wicker sent her reeling back and she could see her ma working away. And then she found herself in a field with her ma cutting lengths from the hedgerow while she and Babs played in the long grass.

'Beth? Are you hurt? Oh, Beth, you're crying.'

'I'm all right. I – I just had a memory, that's all.'

'Beth, I promise you, once you are well, I will take you to Blackpool. Now, let's get out in the fresh air. And believe me, it is fresh. The sun is out, but the wind is a bit blustery.'

Once outside, Beth thought she had landed in heaven. Seagulls ducked and dived as they called out in sometimes deafening squawks. Daffodils were doing as it said in Wordsworth's poem: '*tossing their heads in a sprightly dance.*' And the sea when they reached the quayside gently lapped the sand. Holding on to her hat, Beth shouted above the noise, 'It's beautiful, but hardly peaceful.' Suddenly she felt the urge to cry out, *Take me to Blackpool now! Please, take me this minute!* But she bit the words back.

When they reached a bench, Henry sat down and manoeuvred her to face him. 'Oh, Beth, did I say you looked beautiful? That's nothing to what you look now with red rosy cheeks ... Beth, I – I ... well, I think you know how I feel about you. Is there a chance that you feel the same?'

Beth nodded, unable to speak. She'd dreamt of this moment and couldn't have wished for it to come in a more lovely setting. She held Henry's gaze as he leant forward and took her hands in his. 'I love you, Beth. I love you so much.'

Beth caught her breath with the joy of hearing those words. When she breathed out, she said, 'I love you, Henry. With all my heart, I love you. But—'

'No buts. Love is all we need, everything else will come. Don't think of all the obstacles we have to surmount. Let's just tackle them when they present themselves and do the best we can at the time.'

Beth nodded. Was Henry asking her to marry him? He hadn't said as much. Just a sort of 'let's wait and see'.

'Are you all right, darling? May I kiss you?'

Again, she could only nod. Henry stood and leant over her. When his lips touched hers, the feeling was so wonderful that she put her arms around him and held him to her. When he came out of the kiss he laughed. 'Well, that's our second obstacle achieved, how to kiss. Getting you this far was the first.'

Beth giggled. 'And both very well done too.'

They both laughed. 'And easy, so I don't see that we have a problem, which only leaves me to ask, will you do me the honour of becoming my wife, Beth?'

'Oh, Henry, yes, yes, I will! Thank you! But are you sure? We haven't known each other long and, well, what if I'm useless? What if I can't . . . well, be a proper wife?'

'Surmount when it occurs, right? That can be our motto, so no what if's. We always will surmount everything, but in our own way. And if I knew you for a lifetime, it wouldn't make any difference. I fell for you the moment I saw you and knew then I was going to ask you to be my wife – and no one could be a better wife to me because I don't love anyone else, I love you, Beth, and I want to spend the rest of my days with you.'

Beth felt as though she would burst with happiness and wanted so much to hold Henry in a hug. 'Henry, will you help me to stand? There's something I want to do.'

With a bit of a struggle they managed it. Beth was already clinging on to Henry, but she gained confidence as he held her in a strong grip and moved her arms until they were around him. 'I wanted to hug you.'

They stood in more of a huddle than a hug as Beth leant on Henry, but it felt like a hug and filled Beth with happiness. 'My fiancé, I love you.'

As Henry lowered her back into the chair, she saw a tear glisten on his cheek.

'That was the loveliest hug I've ever had, Beth. Let's marry soon and then we can lie together and I can hold you properly and make love to you.'

Once more a blush swept over her face, but she determined to broach the subject. 'Will – will I be able to make love?'

'You will, darling, I promise. We will be wonderful together. It's only your legs that are affected, the rest of you is intact. And I don't see why we can't have children. We will live a normal life, Beth, a very happy normal life.'

Beth was quiet for a moment, wondering if she should say anything, but then Henry, as a doctor, would understand. 'That may not be possible. I . . . well, I haven't seen any monthlies since my accident. I know that's normal when the body has suffered a trauma, but I wonder if there's been any damage done?'

'I don't think so, Beth. It is rare for a back injury to affect the workings of the body – well, of that nature. Other organs can suffer through bruising for a while. But let's not worry about it, let's wait and see. I don't know much in the field of gynaecology, but most things are touched on in my own subject, and there is evidence that temporary seizure of normal functions occurs. Oh dear, I'm sounding like your doctor now, and I don't want to. Darling, children or no children, I love you so much and know that we will be very happy together.'

A smile seemed to start deep within her and burst onto her face. Henry looked in wonderment at her before once more taking her in his arms and kissing her. Beth felt as though her world had come together at that moment when she had thought it shattered forever.

As they walked back towards the hospital, a different way to the route that they'd come, they came across a tea shop. 'I could do with a hot drink, darling. Shall we see if we can get inside?'

Beth nodded, but didn't think the door wide enough. *Is everything going to be a struggle for us? Will Henry not get fed up in the end?*

But she needn't have worried as Henry didn't attempt to get the chair inside but lifted her out of it and carried her in his arms. The lady serving ran to help, lifting a chair out for her. 'There you are, love. Park yourself there. Now, what can I get for you?'

They both ordered tea and scones and Beth began to feel quite normal, as if nothing had happened to her and she was the girl that she always had been. She looked around her. Another couple sat at a table in the corner holding hands; he wore a soldier's uniform and for a moment the horror she'd left, and he was going into, crowded Beth. Henry's hand came over hers. 'Was it really bad, Beth? You've never spoken of it.'

'It was like visiting hell. I can't describe it other than to call it carnage . . . You won't have to go, will you, Henry? Oh! I never thought . . . Please say that you won't have to go.'

'I don't know, darling. I haven't volunteered yet, as I am in my third year of my specialist training in spinal damage, and in the middle of writing a paper that investigates advancements and current research all over the world. Not an easy task as it entails writing to different hospitals in all countries and with communication how it is, I'm not getting many answers. There are plenty of books, though, so I think I'm fairly up to date. That work is eagerly awaited by the medical council; it's considered vital and is what brought me to you. But when it's completed, and if the war is still raging, there is a possibility. And if the conscription that is being bandied about by parliament comes into force, then I'll have no choice.'

'Oh no. Oh, Henry, I couldn't bear it.'

'You can, darling, we both can. It will be dreadful if it happens, but like that young woman over there, you will be brave and send me off with a smile, I know you will.'

They held hands for a moment, not speaking. Their tea was served, and though the scones looked delicious and far superior to anything she'd been served in the hospital these past weeks, Beth no longer fancied them.

'Beth, let's enjoy every moment we have, darling. This is our celebration of our engagement; these scones will taste the best we've ever tasted.'

Beth knew Henry was right. He had a way of looking at everything from a positive angle, and she knew that she must too. Taking a scone, she cut into it. Its light texture crumbled a little and she knew then she was in for a treat.

'Let's talk about our wedding. Shall we marry quietly, or do you want to find your family first and have both of our families celebrate with us?'

Beth thought for a moment. She marvelled at how natural it all was to sit here with Henry and talk about their wedding. Part of her longed to have her ma there, but suddenly, with the revelation that Henry might have to go to war, she didn't want to waste a moment. She said all of this to him, going for the quiet wedding suggestion. He understood, but she thought that he looked a little sad so changed her mind. 'Quietly, that is, with your mum and sister there of course. I would love that.'

'Really? Oh, darling, thank you. My mum has been so sad since my father died last year that I would hate to hurt her further by not including her in my special day. And my sister has always said that she will be a bridesmaid and her fiancé – one of my very best friends – my best man.'

'That would be lovely. But will I get to meet them first? And what will they all think of me, and my background, and . . . well, I'm not the best of catches, am I?'

'Don't ever say that, or even think it, none of it. My family are not snobbish in any way, darling. They will love you and, if anything, want to smother you.'

Beth hadn't meant to infer that they were snobbish, and for a moment was mortified that Henry thought that she did, but then, his reply didn't indicate that he was offended, but was honest and reassuring, so she let it go and relaxed as Henry changed the subject.

'Now, where will we live? I know where we will honeymoon – Blackpool! Without a doubt.'

'Oh, Henry, that would be wonderful.'

'That's settled then. The honeymoon will be a find Ma quest, but where to live? That's not an easy one to solve. I want it to be here, in Margate, near to my work so that I can get home quickly and maybe even at lunchtimes, but that isn't near to my family, who live in Maidstone and would be a help to you.'

'I'll learn to manage when you're not there. Don't forget our motto – surmount when it occurs. That's what I'll do.'

Rupert smiled at her. 'And I know you will. It just takes having the willpower to find a solution rather than thinking that it can't be done. I'll start looking to see what's available.'

They chatted on and Beth felt that she'd never been happier than she was at this moment.

That feeling was shattered when the couple got up and walked towards them. The man had a grim expression. He looked straight at Henry and in an aggressive voice asked. 'Don't you know that there's a war on? Haven't you heard that your country needs you, eh?'

Shocked, Beth seethed. 'How dare you? I served as a nurse in Ypres, and lost the use of my legs, and my fiancé is carrying out vital work that will help those injured like me. Not only that, once that's complete he is intending to serve as a doctor in France, so don't make assumptions about us, soldier!'

'Oh, I – I'm sorry, I . . .'

His girlfriend pulled him away.

'Good Lord, darling, I see you have a temper hidden under that gentle exterior. I'd better watch myself!'

Before she could answer, the girl came back in. 'I want to apologise for my Bert. He's mortified now, especially seeing your bath chair outside. And between me and you, he's scared and isn't acting in character.'

'That's all right. Thank you. I'm sorry for you both. I'm dreading when Henry goes.'

'Is it bad out there, love? The reports frighten the life out of everyone. My Bert ain't no fighter, but, well, everyone's volunteering so he felt he had to. I am meself in a way, as I'm going to be working for the railway, doing the job he usually does as a porter.'

Beth didn't know what to say, but then thought that the truth was best. 'It isn't easy. But your Bert will receive training, and remember, for every casualty there are a hundred or so soldiers that don't get hurt, so the odds are in his favour, not against him. That's what I'll hold on to if Henry has to go, as the medical staff are in the thick of it as much as the armed forces. Our tent hospitals are very near to the front line, and it was a shell that injured me and killed some of my colleagues.'

'I'm sorry to hear that, love. I suppose we just have to be brave. I know I will be. Here, if you need anything, you will always find me on the platform. I'm Amy.'

'Thank you, Amy, I'm Beth. I'm still a hospital patient for now but hoping to be out soon. It'll be good to have a friend that I can call on.'

'I'm your girl. Anytime, love. See you. And good luck.'

Henry stood and offered his hand. 'Nice to meet you, Amy.'

Amy giggled, but took his hand, then waved as she left. 'I like her, Henry. Down to earth. The sort who really would be there for you if you needed her.'

'There, you're making friends already. I'll have no worries about you if I have to leave you.'

He didn't say this convincingly, and Beth didn't want to talk about it anymore, so changed the subject back to the wedding. They decided that Henry would apply to the hospital to be able to take Beth out for the whole of the next weekend and he would arrange with his mother for them to go and stay. Though a little nervous about this, Beth was excited too. It would be so nice to be out of the hospital environment for even longer than she had been today and though a little nervous, she was looking forward to meeting Henry's mother and sister.

With everything that she had to look forward to, Beth could feel herself making much more progress than she had up to now. She felt well in herself, and everything pointed to her being well too. There were good results on tests done, though still no movement in her legs; the sensation of knowing when she wanted to empty her bladder had come back, something she hadn't had up to now, and she had suffered a few accidents, though the hospital had managed it well by sitting her on a bedpan at regular intervals.

Now, they kept her bath chair by her bed and wheeled her to the toilet when she knew she needed to go. This was a massive step forward for Beth and had been what worried her most about visiting others, and even about her marriage. She'd had nightmares of wetting the bed, something that had happened in hospital and left her feeling so ashamed.

Then, towards the end of the week, joy of joys, her monthly bleeding suddenly restarted, something she couldn't stop grinning about, for now she knew she was once more a fully functioning woman.

By the time Saturday came her stomach pains had lessened, as Jasmine had brought in one of her potions which Beth had found helpful in the past. Telling her and Roman about her forthcoming wedding, she was shocked at how upset they were.

'But Jasmine, you must have known that one day I would marry, and you will love Henry.'

'But is it that we will never see you again? I have your wedding planned in my head and have made a frock, but a doctor won't want to know us.'

'He will, and yes, we will have a gypsy wedding too, I promise. But no cutting of the wrists – I don't like that practice, and I know that Henry won't. The bonfire and the dancing will be wonderful, he will love that. I'll talk to him and we'll arrange it for when we get back from Blackpool.'

'It is that you will come back?'

'Of course. I will be living near to here.'

A little pang of guilt set up inside her as she realised that it might be embarrassing to have them visit her at her home, so she added, 'We'll visit you often, I promise.' But then felt ashamed of her thoughts and banished them. 'And you can visit me, or if you're not comfortable in a house, you can come and pick me up in the cart. My chair will fit well into it.'

'I can be for making a ramp to wheel you up into it, little one. And lay down some planks of wood to wheel you over the rough ground to our caravan.'

'Yes, that all sounds wonderful.' She was rewarded with happy, relieved smiles from both Jasmine and Roman and wondered at her earlier thoughts, but then, it wasn't easy marrying her gypsy life with what she now thought of as her normal life. She just had to do what her and Henry's motto said: surmount when it occurs.

Henry's mum, Philomena, his sister, Janine, and her fiancé, Gareth, made Beth feel so welcome and loved. They couldn't do enough for her, and Gareth, who was a much bigger man than Henry, insisted on lifting Beth whenever she wanted transporting, making her giggle with his funny sense of humour, calling her a sack of spuds, and saying that he might drop her.

Henry seemed a bit put out at times, but there was nothing Beth could do except insist it was he who took her to the bathroom, where she assured him that he was the more gentle of the two and that she was only humouring Gareth.

He laughed at this and admitted to feeling a little jealous.

'I like that. I think that kind of jealousy shows your feelings for me. I would be the same – if you need anything, I want to be the one who does it for you.'

This had saved the day and Henry had taken it in his stride after that.

Beth had found the house to be beautiful. Next to a park, it had a reasonably sized garden for a city house. All the rooms were big and furnished with antique furniture that looked elegant on the rose-patterned carpets that were edged with highly polished flooring. In the main living room, the colours were blues and creams, giving it a restful appearance. But Beth loved the kitchen – it was so big, and she was able to be pushed into it and up to the table where she sat helping to cut the spring cabbage for dinner and chop the onions for the casserole that the cabbage would accompany. This was when she really got to know Philomena and Janine.

Talk was of her forthcoming wedding, and Janine being a bridesmaid. Janine had really warmed to the idea: 'I'm so looking forward to it all. What colours do you want me to wear?'

'I love blues, Janine. But oh, I just don't know how I'm going to shop for my frock, or for the number of clothes I need.'

'I'll take you! Henry can bring you here and we can take a cab into town. I can push you around the shops,' Janine's excitement gave Beth the reality of it all.

'Thank you, I would love that.'

Philomena smiled at them. 'There's nothing like a wedding to cheer us all up, but whilst a shopping trip is a good idea for purchasing some general, everyday clothes, wouldn't it be better if you had a dressmaker to make your wedding gown, dear?'

'It would. Of course it would, Philomena. And I know just the person. She's the most wonderful seamstress. She has already made me a wedding dress, but that's for my gypsy wedding . . . Oh, I mean . . .'

'It's all right, dear, we know all about you. Henry has told us. We think it wicked what the gypsies did, but as you are prepared to forgive them, then we are too. Gypsy wedding, you say? Henry hasn't said anything about that, but how exciting.'

Inwardly, Beth felt relieved at this reaction from Philomena but somehow it had brought into focus the very different upbringing that she'd had, and yes, they were right. What Jasmine and Roman did was wicked, and she had long forgiven them. 'I haven't told Henry yet, but I know he won't mind. I'll tell him as soon as I get the chance, only . . .' She went on to tell them how upset Jasmine had been. 'So, I just had to say that we would have a wedding with them too.'

'Of course you did, and having Jasmine make you your main wedding dress is another compliment to her that I'm sure will help her to come to terms with everything even more.'

'Mum's right. No matter how they came by having you and your sister, they must have been good to you for you to love them so much, so that's all that matters. But I hope that you find your own mother and sister. I think your story is so sad.' With this, Janine put her hand out and held Beth's. 'I'm going to love having a sister, and I can get a train to see you once a month, then we'll have a girl's day. Go shopping and have lunch out. Oh, it's going to be so good.'

Beth put her other hand over Janine's. 'It is. Thank you for welcoming me. I know I come as an oddball package, not at all what you're used to, and yet, you accept me as if I am one of your own. That has meant so much to me.'

'You're more than one of our own, Beth, you're my sister!'

'And my daughter. I just hope you're not as much trouble as this one!'

'Mum! I'm a model daughter . . . well, a little untidy sometimes, I admit. That's why I'm marrying Gareth. He's rich and I will have a maid.'

Beth giggled at this. She was aware that Gareth belonged to a family that owned a brewery and were very rich, but she knew that Janine was joking. It was obvious they were very much in love.

And she was glad that the 'sister' conversation had passed without her having to make a comment as she couldn't quite bring herself to say that Janine was like a sister to her. It would be disloyal to Babs. *Oh, Babs, Babs.*

TWENTY-FOUR

Tilly looked out of their workshop window at the early May sunshine glistening on the sea. Today was one of those rare occasions when what was normally a churning mass of water looked like a lake: still, and a lovely blue.

The whirring of Molly's machine droned in the background, a normal sound of a normal day, and yet Tilly felt uneasy for some reason. She looked towards Ivan's empty chair and the pain in her heart that was always there, but now dulled, became a sharp stabbing sensation. Somehow, she'd never been able to have his chairs removed from the shop, and yet it hurt to look at them. One had gone, though, to a lad who'd come home injured and couldn't walk. Ivan would have liked that, and the idea was that that's how they would all go, as and when they were needed by someone.

The sight of Mary and Vera coming along the promenade towards the shop made Tilly gasp in fear. Vera was holding an obviously distressed Mary. Tilly looked towards Molly, her head down, grey streaks in her once dark hair, and wanted to run to her to shield her. *Gerry, naw, don't let him be gone, please!*

But she knew her prayer was useless. There was nothing else that would cause this distress, and that seemed confirmed when she caught sight of Ida, the girl's ma, a few steps behind them, her distress clear to see.

Turning, Tilly hurried towards the stairs. 'Be back in a mo, Molly, nature calls.'

She ran down in seconds and greeted them as they came through the door. 'What is it, me lasses? Not . . .'

'Eeh, Tilly.' Ida shook her head, 'It's Gerry. He's—'

'Don't say it, Ma. Don't!'

'Follow me up. Molly's upstairs.' This came out on a shocked whisper. Tilly daren't ask injured or dead, she didn't want to know the worst.

'Molly, love. Eeh, lass.'

Molly jumped up and turned towards them. As she stared at the little party behind Tilly her head shook from side to side.

'Oh, Molly . . . Ma!' With this, Mary flung herself at Molly. 'He's . . . gone. Me Gerry, he's gone.'

A wail came from Molly. 'Naw . . . naw . . . naw!' It sliced through Tilly, laying bare the sore wounds in her own heart.

'Molly, eeh, Molly, lass.' As she said this, Tilly went over to Molly, who was still holding the sobbing Mary and put her arms around them both.

The pain of loss can do different things to different people. Six weeks later, Tilly was witnessing how for Molly, her grief made her work like a madwoman, hardly lifting her head and not wanting to go home at night.

Will was lost and lonely, coming to the shop at all hours saying that he couldn't settle at work and wanted to be with

Molly. But she ignored him and hardly even acknowledged that he was there. Tilly found this so sad and hard to understand. For she'd wanted to be with her Tommy all the time during the first throes of her loss.

'Molly, lass, I've made a pot of tea. Are you going to have a break and enjoy yours with me and Will?'

'Naw. Put it on me bench, I'll drink it as I work.'

'But, Molly, lass, you've naw need to. I don't knaw where we're going to stockpile all the stuff you're churning out as it is. You need a break, lass. Please, Molly, a few minutes drinking tea and having a chat would do you good.'

'Tilly's right, love, you're driving yourself into the ground. Gerry wouldn't want that.'

'You don't knaw what Gerry would want! He's not here to tell you. And he never will be again! So shut up . . . Shut up!'

The scream grew in momentum as it went on, seeming to echo off the walls and hold all the agony of a mother bereft.

Tilly knew the feeling, but hadn't let it in. Now she felt her own armour crack and wanted to scream that neither would her Ivan, but she didn't. She just slumped into the chair next to her and sobbed huge, loud, wailing sobs.

Through the tears that were weakening her, Tilly saw Molly's face drop into a shocked expression. She saw her look over at Will, and then back towards her before crossing the room. 'Tilly, Tilly, lass. Eeh, I'm sorry. I – I'm sorry . . .' The words disappeared in a deluge of tears as she knelt in front of Tilly. Tilly reached out her arm and gathered her to her. Molly's head rested on Tilly's knee. Tilly stroked her hair as both women's bodies shook with their grief.

A sound had Tilly lifting her head. Will had sat down and had his head resting on his arms, his body trembling with his sobs. 'Oh, Will, Will.'

Molly lifted her head and looked over at her husband and, as if a miracle had woken her, she went to his side and willingly into the hug he offered her.

Calming herself, Tilly felt the gladness of the scene, for at last Molly had opened up to Will and was comforting him and allowing their sorrow to be shared.

'Go home, you two. Go home and be together.' Tilly wiped her eyes and blew her nose loudly as she said this. 'Take a week off together. I'm sure your boss will allow that, Will, as you're naw good to him how you are. Find each other again and share how you're feeling.'

'Ta, Tilly. And I'm so sorry to have opened up your pain, lass.'

'Aye, I knaw. I needed me release, and so do you. Go with Will and be together in this. Don't let it tear you apart. And take care of Mary. The poor lass is your responsibility as well as her ma's now. She needs you all.'

'You're right, so right, Tilly. And to top it all, we've just found out she's expecting a babby.'

'Oh, but that's wonderful news as Gerry will live on through his child. But Molly, Mary will need you more than ever now and so will the child. Instead of sewing cushions and the like, you should be making clothes for this first grandchild of yours.'

'Eeh, I hadn't thought of that, nor of you, Will. I'm sorry. I now knaw that in helping you all, I'll help meself an' all.'

'You will, love. Off you go now. I'll see you in a couple of days. I'll call in and see how you're doing.'

As the door closed on them and the sound of their steps on the stairs faded, Tilly sat quietly thinking of all the sadness in the world. For Molly, there'd been no closure, no body to bury, and none of his things to sort out as they had all been moved to the little house he and Mary had rented. And nothing had come to her, it had all gone to Mary, as it rightfully should, but Molly hadn't had time to adjust to that. Maybe, when Mary felt up to it, she would give Molly something that had belonged to Gerry to put back into her house. And maybe, when the time was right, she would suggest to Mary that a memorial service would be nice so that everyone could come together in his name.

With these thoughts, Tilly began to feel a little better. Grabbing her coat, she determined to go to the churchyard and have a moment with Ivan and Liz and Dan, and even her old Aunt Mildred as all of them were up in Layton Cemetery. Whenever she did this, she found comfort.

Then she would go home and be with Tommy.

Eliza cheered her up when she came in from the bakery later that day. 'Eeh, Ma, that Ma Ridley's a one. She moans about everything and makes me feel that I'm in her way half the time, then sits in the backyard smoking her pipe while I scrub everything down, but by, she can bake. She made what she called Bakewell tarts today, and do you knaw, she iced the tops and then stuck half a cherry on each and turned to me, and said, "Enjoy yours while they look like that, lass, as it ain't long afore all they see is the ground!"

'What? Oh . . . You mean . . .'

A giggle started in Tilly's stomach and came out of her mouth like a crude belly laugh.

'Ma!'

'Eeh, I'm sorry, lass. It's the way you tell your stories, you're so expressive. But naw, the old girl shouldn't be talking to you like that.'

This didn't match how Tilly felt as she found the incident so funny that she had a job to keep her face straight.

'Fancy Ma Ridley saying owt like that!'

'Well, I told her as that's rude, and she said, "Rude is as rude may, but it's the truth, girl."'

Tilly giggled again but covered it with a cough. 'So, you can make these Bakewell tarts now then? You should make some for me and Da for our tea.'

'I don't think you've got any almonds, but I'll get some one day and make them. Though I'll make the one that looks like a loaf, as she made some that shape an' all. They looked more decent.'

'Oh dear, you're not going to be a prude are you, Eliza? I mean, it was only a bit of fun, and if you do get involved in comic acting one of these days, a lot of what you'll be doing will be using innuendos that are near the mark.'

'Well, I ain't made me mind up on that yet. I like the idea, but I'm tired out when I come in from working at the bakery. I'm like a slave to Ma Ridley.'

'Eeh, that's just what I didn't want to happen. We pay her to teach you how to bake bread and cakes so that you can go on and realise your dream of having your own little shop one day.'

'Well, Ma Ridley says that the way to learn a trade is from the bottom up, and the bottom allus seems to need to be scrubbed as I see it . . . Eeh, I didn't mean that . . .'

This time, Eliza bent over in a fit of giggles, and Tilly joined her, thinking how Eliza was such a tonic.

'There, I told you, you're a master at the one liners, lass. Come here.' Holding her daughter to her gave Tilly a feeling that warmed the cold places that her heart had been to earlier. She looked up and she could almost hear Ivan laughing too. *Aye, lad, this sister of yours doesn't alter. She keeps me going.* And with this thought, Tilly felt the strength that had deserted her earlier seep back into her and she knew she could cope once more.

Tilly always took notice of everyone in a bath chair. It always gave her a jolt, but instead of looking away to minimise her painful memories, she would make an effort to talk to the person sitting in the chair, remembering how Ivan would say that folk seemed to avoid talking to him as if he was some alien being, and how that hurt him. So as the young couple came towards her along the prom as she returned from the chippy two weeks later, she made a beeline for them. Her mouth opened to say 'hello' but instead a cry that was a mixture of joy and anguish came from her.

'Ma? Ma! Ma! Oh, Ma, is it really you?'

Shock rendered Tilly silent. She could only nod as she looked into the beloved face of Beth. Why she knew instantly which daughter this was she'd never know, she just did. 'How? I mean, oh, my darling, darling, Beth.' Then, not thinking, she said, 'Here, hold me chips, lad, while I give me daughter a hug.'

The hug went into a fusion of tears and joyful exclamations. 'Me Beth! Me Beth! Eeh, lass, lass.'

'You're crushing me, Ma, I can't breathe!' The tinkling laugh took Tilly back years.

'I'm sorry, lass. But, oh, it's me dream come true. Every day of me life I've thought of this moment. Where's Babs?'

'I don't knaw, Ma. I – I . . . she ran away to find you. Oh, Ma . . .'

'Darling, don't upset yourself, you've waited so long for this moment.' The young man pushing Beth's bath chair put his hand gently on Beth's hair and stroked it. 'I'm Henry, Beth's husband. Well, new husband, as we've only been married for three weeks. We came here yesterday, to look for you, Ma, and to have our honeymoon, and now here you are just walking along the street towards us! I'm so pleased to meet you and so happy for my darling Beth.'

'And I'm pleased to meet you, lad. By, this is a lot to take in, but ta, ta for bringing me daughter back to me. Come on, both of you. I've a shop just back up the prom a bit. You might have passed it. We'll go there and talk.'

As they came up to the shop, Beth said they hadn't passed it, but had come onto the prom just before they'd bumped into Tilly. She and Beth held hands on their walk back. Tilly's heart raced with joy, but part of her worried as to where Babs was, and she felt a niggle of concern as to her safety.

'Oh, Ma, if I'd have passed this, I would have known it was your shop without seeing the name of it. Just look at all the lovely baskets! Oh, Henry, I told you that Ma made baskets.'

'Well, I never imagined them on this scale, or so beautiful. You're very talented, Ma.'

Tilly loved how he called her Ma; it made him seem like family, for all his posh look and voice. For that matter, she'd noticed how posh Beth sounded too, but it didn't matter. 'Eeh, I've so much to tell you. So much has happened. Some joyful, some sad, but eeh, none of it seems to matter at this moment.'

Gertie, the assistant, looked astonished at the little party coming through the shop door. 'By, Gertie, I've had the surprise of me life. This is me daughter, Beth!'

'What? One of your twins? How did that happen?'

'I've yet to find out, lass. Let us through into the back. It's a lovely day so we can sit out and have our chips. Give Molly a shout, will you? But don't tell her owt. And then shut the shop and go and have your chips in the chippy. I'm giving your share to me daughter and me new son-in-law.'

Henry and Beth were laughing out loud at this. 'Oh, Ma, you don't change. You're exactly how you were. It's like the years have never happened. I love you, Ma, so much.'

'And I love you, me lass. I want to hug and hug you.'

A sob came from Beth. 'And I need to hug you, Ma. Help me, Henry, help me.'

Henry had tears in his own eyes as he lifted Beth. 'She can't stand on her own, Ma, but if you put your arms around her, and take her weight . . .'

When her daughter was in her arms, Tilly felt most of her world come right. They clung to each other, crying tears of sadness and joy. Sadness for the lost years, and for not having Babs here, but joy for being together at last.

Molly jumped for joy too when she found what all the excitement was about, and she and Beth and Henry got on so well, Tilly felt that this was how it had always been.

'You're so like your ma! If I'd have seen you in the street, I'd have known you. What a wicked pair those who took you were, and you say as your sister ran away? Oh dear, where has she landed? The mind boggles, poor lass.'

'Don't, Molly, I'm so worried for her. Have you naw clues to her whereabouts, Beth, love?'

'Well . . . there's a slight, but only very slight possibility that she is nursing somewhere in France on an ambulance, or hospital train.'

'Eeh, what makes you think that, love?'

They listened as Beth explained how she thought she'd hallucinated about Babs, but how she and Henry had analysed it as Beth felt more and more certain the voice she'd heard was real, and they came to the conclusion that it could have been during her journey from Ypres to Paris, and that would have been on an ambulance train. 'But we've made enquiries and there's no one of the name of Barbara Petrilona working for the Red Cross.'

'Petrilona? But that's not your name!'

'I knaw, Ma, but by the time we needed a surname, neither of us could remember what it was. We only knew it when we first started school, and so much had happened to us since then.'

'It was Ramsbottom, love. Awe, I knaw as it's a long one to remember, but that was the name your da gave you, God rest his soul.'

'Should we try asking for a Barbara Ramsbottom, darling?'

'Yes, Henry, it might work, but only if Babs has since remembered that. I don't think she would somehow.'

They fell silent, but Tilly wouldn't let them stay down for long. 'Look, we will find her, we will. If you're right, it can't be too difficult as we have a starting point. We can get a photo of you, Beth, and take that along to the Red Cross.'

'That's a very good idea, Ma. I'll see to that as it's better to take it into the HQ in London, and I am often there on different courses.'

This from Henry got them started on talking about what he did. Tilly was in awe of his work and his standing. That her daughter should become a nurse had filled her with pride, but to marry a doctor! Well, that really puffed out her chest. 'Right, it's time to bring you up to date. And I've some surprises for you. Oh, and I want to hear about your wedding, lass. Eeh, I can't believe me daughter got married without me.' Tilly had to dab at a tear at this realisation.

Henry stepped over to her and put his arm around her. 'You haven't missed out. We were married in a registry office as we couldn't wait. It was a lovely day, but only a formal joining of us by law. We planned on having a much bigger wedding in church with both our families once we found you, and now we have, we can begin our planning.'

Beth was astonished at this, but pleased too. She smiled up at Henry as a way of thanking him for having this idea and for the smile he brought to her ma's face.

'Eeh, that'd be grand. Grand, son.' Calling Henry that brought Ivan to Tilly. Kneeling in front of Beth, she took her hands in hers. 'Me little lass, I have to tell you that I had other children with me husband as I have now.'

Everyone fell silent. Tilly waited, feeling afraid. She saw Henry move to Beth's side. 'It's been nineteen years, Beth. I never forgot you. But I was powerless, I couldn't look for you. I was told you were taken abroad. There wasn't a day that I didn't mourn your loss, or beg of God to bring you to me, but during that time, I fell in love, twice. Me second husband was killed, but me husband, me lovely Tommy, and me ... we had ... we had two young 'uns. We – we lost your darling brother, just a short while ago. He – he was born a cripple. He was so lovely ...' A sob took Tilly and she couldn't go on. She put her head in Beth's lap.

After a moment, she felt Beth's hand stroking her head. 'Oh, Ma, no. What was his name?'

'Ivan. Oh, Beth, me heart's breaking.'

Eliza's voice broke into the sorrow. 'Ma, Aunt Molly, what's wrong? Eeh, and who's this ... Oh! You're ... me sister! Eeh, that's wonderful! Are you Beth or Babs? Awe, I've waited so long to meet you. I'm Eliza. I'm training to be a baker, as you can see. I'm allus covered in flour.'

Eliza looked from one to the other. 'Everything's all right, ain't it? I've not said owt wrong, have I?'

'No, no. Oh, Eliza, you're a shock, but oh, such a nice one. I'm Beth, and if our ma will move, I'll give you a cuddle.'

'Eeh, I can put me arms around your neck with Ma where she is, as she looks like she's enjoying a good cry.'

As Eliza put her arms around Beth, Tilly heard her say, 'I don't think Ma's enjoying crying, Eliza, as she was telling me about Ivan.'

'Awe. I wish you could've known him. But I'll tell you all about him. Me and him used to pray together that God would bring you and Babs to us, as we so wanted to knaw you ... Where's Babs, anyroad? Ain't she come with you?'

'No, she—'

'Look, I think we should perhaps go to your home, Ma? There's so much for Beth to take in and she isn't fully fit yet. I'm Henry, Eliza, I'm your brother-in-law, and I'm very pleased to meet you.'

'Oh? You're married, Beth!'

'Yes, dear, but there's a lot to tell, as Henry says, and I do feel tired. Perhaps you can comfort Ma and Molly? And then we can arrange to do as Henry says.'

'Aunt Molly and Ma are sad most of the time. Ma with losing Ivan, and allus longing for you and Babs, and poor Aunt Molly 'cause she lost Gerry, her son, in the war. You would've loved him. I miss him and Brian, his brother, who's still fighting in France.'

'I'm so sorry, Molly. That's terrible and, Ma, I'm so sorry about my brother.'

Dabbing her eyes, Tilly told herself to stop all this sadness. She'd tried once and made a hack of it, but she knew she must take charge now. This should be the happiest day of her life. 'Right, when Gertie gets back from having her chips at the chippy, she can take care of the shop and I'll drive everyone home. I've only got a cart, but you'll fit in in your chair. Ivan . . . well, Ivan used to, easily. And Henry can sit on the bench in the back with you, and you, Eliza, can sit on the front bench with me.' Turning to Molly, she took her in her arms. 'Eeh, lass. We cry when we're sad and we cry when we're happy. We're a right pair. Do you want me to drop you off at home, or do you want to come with us, and Tommy'll bring you home later? He'll have to bring Beth and Henry back to where they're staying, though I hope that'll be with us from tomorrow.' Turning to Beth she said, 'We've a downstairs bedroom and bathroom, Beth.'

'I'd love that. Thanks, Ma. What do you think, Henry?'

'Whatever makes you happy, darling. Our "find Ma" mission is accomplished, so now we can do what takes our fancy.'

Tilly noticed a lovely blush creep up Beth's cheeks and she smiled. A wide, happy smile as she could see that Beth and Henry were very much in love. They reminded her of her and her Tommy. And she couldn't wish better than that for them.

TWENTY-FIVE

Babs stood by the window waiting for Cathy as the train pulled into the Paris station. They'd arranged to go on a trip together as Cathy knew Paris, having spent some of her school days there.

'Are you getting off the train, Babs?'

Rupert had come up to her, looking wonderful in his civvy clothes. A brown baggy suit, a straw boater and brown and white two-tone shoes.

'Aye, me and Cathy are going to see the sights.'

'You can join us if you like, Rupert.'

'Thank you, Cathy, I would love that. I can speak the language so may be of help to you.'

'*Mais oui, monsieur, ce serait très gentil de votre part.*'

'Oh, you speak it too?'

Cathy laughed up at him. 'No. I only know very little. I used to nod off in my French classes. I'm sorry now as it would be good to be able to converse with the French patients.'

Babs felt left out, and strangely fearful as the two had such an easy way with each other, and she felt so gawky and uneducated. Cathy was far nearer Rupert's class than she was, and very pretty too. He was bound to prefer her.

'Let's do this then. The train's stopping, and we haven't much time.'

When it did stop, Rupert jumped off and helped them down. *Did his hand linger longer in Cathy's than it did in mine? Eeh, stop this, you're being daft!*

Once out of the station, Rupert made a crook of each of his arms. 'Link in, girls, I think a delicious cup of coffee first.'

Babs had never tasted coffee. On her trip out on her own, she'd wanted to try it but hadn't known how to ask for it. She had no idea what to expect and wished she dared ask for a cup of tea but didn't want to show herself up.

They sat outside a café – something she'd seen people doing but never done herself – as crowds bustled past. The ladies all looked so fashionable and sophisticated, and the gentlemen very handsome. They called out to one another in greeting and sometimes stopped in little groups. Babs loved the sound of their language and felt she could sit and listen all day.

She sat back in the intricately patterned iron chair, feeling herself relax as the sun warmed her face. Next to her, flowers bloomed in a tub that looked like half of a barrel. She didn't know what the flowers were called but the perfume coming from them was heady and filled the air.

'*Café, madame.*' Rupert put one of the three cups of steaming black coffee in front of her. She smiled at him and waited to see what he and Cathy did, but found it was no different to how they drank their tea, except they didn't put sugar in the coffee and there was no sugar on the table. She wondered if she dared ask.

After they took a sip and both made appreciative noises, Babs thought, *Here goes*, and lifted her cup to her lips. The smell put her off, but she braved it, trying to look as if this was old hat. Taking a very small sip, she creased her face up. 'Ugh!' Her body shuddered with the vile, strong taste and then the coughing started.

'Oh dear, has it gone down the wrong way, Babs?'

As tears streamed down her face, Babs couldn't answer Cathy, but then, to add to her embarrassment, a waiter began fussing over her, flapping her with a napkin that kept catching her face. She didn't seem able to get away from him. Losing her temper, she stood up and as her voice came back, she snapped, 'Go away! Eeh, you're like a troublesome wasp.'

The waiter looked astonished. 'Wasp? Wasp?'

'Yes, with your striped waistcoat and buzzing around!'

The waiter shrugged his shoulders, picked up his tray, tweaked his moustache and turned with a flourish which told of his disapproval.

Rupert burst out laughing, and suddenly Babs saw the funny side and collapsed in a heap. All three ended up with tears streaming down their faces.

'Oh dear, Babs, I've never seen anything so entertaining as that. And you were right, he was like a wasp, though the poor fellow will wonder for the rest of his days what on earth you called him.'

Composing herself, Babs apologised. 'But don't give me any of that muck again,' she added. 'Give me a pot of tea anytime.'

'Actually, you're right. What do you think, Cathy? Did you just drink it because it's fashionable?'

'I did. Ugh, it's bloody disgusting! But I don't think we'll find anywhere serving tea. How about we walk a while and then stop again for some beer or lemonade?'

An hour later, having seen what Babs thought was a copy of the Blackpool tower that still stuck in her memory, which she didn't want to leave, and an archway that meant nothing to her but the other two were enraptured with, Babs's feet were killing her.

'We've just time for an art gallery. I've always wanted to visit a Rembrandt collection. I'll hail a cab and ask the driver to take us where we might see them.'

Babs felt totally out of her depth at this suggestion from Cathy, but when they entered the beautiful building the driver had brought them too, she marvelled at the columns at the doorway, and the figures carved out of stone that adorned the walls. Inside there was a faint musty smell, and she didn't know what to expect. But the last thing she expected was to have the feeling of being taken back to another age. An age of such beauty and grace that she almost wanted to dress up like Flora, with flowers in her hair and a beautiful flowing gown of gold.

The other two were deep in conversation, but Babs couldn't speak as she stared at one painting after the other, her favourite being *The Jewish Bride*, though she thought the gentleman a bit forward with where he'd placed his hand, touching the lady's breast.

A memory zinged through her – one that she'd tried to forget, and had almost succeeded in doing so, but now the clawing hands of Cecil came to her mind and she cowered away from the feeling it gave her. Turning, she ran out of the room and stood against the wall outside, panting, trying to get her breath and to dispel the disgusting memory.

'Babs? Are you all right?'

Swallowing hard, she nodded at Rupert. Cathy came up to her, her face full of concern. 'What's wrong, Babs, are you ill?'

Shaking her head, Babs at last found her voice. 'Naw. It was stuffy in there. Sorry, I didn't mean to give you a scare, but I felt as though I were going to faint. I just needed some air. The paintings were lovely, though, and if I hadn't felt ill, I could have gazed at them all day.'

'Phew, you had me worried there, but your colour's coming back now. Let's get you to a café and get you some water to drink.'

'Ta, Rupert.'

Cathy held her hand and she linked in with Rupert as they made their way to a café where even the water tasted different to what she was used to, although it was still welcome.

When Cathy went to find the lav around the back of the building, Rupert leant forward over the table. 'You've been through a lot in your lifetime, Babs. I know I shouldn't have done, but I have asked and been told snippets. If ever you want an understanding ear, you can come to me. I know about your sister. That must be terrible.'

'I don't see how you can understand, Rupert. I mean, I don't mean to be rude, but, well, our lives are so different. You'd not be able to understand how mine's been for me.'

'Don't judge me, Babs. I may have had material things, but love was in very short supply. From my mother, anyway. The one person I craved it from. She didn't sack my nanny for any other reason than Nanny made me happy. That was a crime to

Mother. She even tried to stop Father making a fuss of me. She's never written to me once since I left home to go to university, and always makes an excuse so that she's rarely there when I visit.'

A tear glistened in Rupert's eye.

'Eeh. Why? That's awful.'

'I don't know why. She never had any more children. She's a cold fish. I've never seen her make a fuss of my father, and she won't talk to him unless she has to. I think that she has a mental illness of some kind, but don't know enough about it. But whatever the cause, I have been hurt by her attitude and complete lack of love for me, so emotionally, I'm probably just as hurt as you are.'

'Aye, I never knew what it was like not to be loved. Me ma loved me, and Jasmine, the gypsy who stole me, and the nuns who cared for me. They all loved me.'

'Gypsy? A gypsy stole you?'

'Aye. It's a long story. Too long for now, and I don't knaw about you, but I'm so tired I could sleep here and now.'

Rupert put out his hand and rested it on hers. A feeling shot through Babs, leaving her short of breath.

'You feel it too, don't you?'

Babs lowered her eyes, unable to hold his gaze. A sudden intrusion by Cathy took the moment as she joked. 'Oh, I turn my back and you too get up close and comfy!'

Babs snatched her hand away, but Rupert just laughed. 'Me and Babs are very good friends. We often hold hands.'

'We don't!'

Rupert looked amused. 'I'm only teasing. Cathy knows that. Sometimes we all need to hold the hand of another.'

Babs felt awkward again, but Cathy saved the day. 'I know I do. I often feel like reaching for Babs's hand. You can do that with her as she's all homely, but Belinda, eek! She'd think you'd gone mad. You've kept me going many a time, Babs.'

Babs felt the tears prick her eyes. She bent her head over.

'Hey, come on, let's make our way back to normality. It's all been too much.' With this, Rupert offered his hand to Babs. When she took it, he smiled down at her. 'We should bare our souls more often, Babs.'

Cathy hadn't heard this; she was already down the steps of the café and looking this way and that for a cab, shouting back that she wasn't going to walk another step.

Cathy and Babs sat in the back of the horse-drawn carriage while Rupert sat on the top with the driver. Once they were moving Cathy asked, 'Are you really all right, Babs? You had me worried in that art gallery. You went really pale.'

'Aye, memories knocked me off me feet for a mo.'

'Why don't you tell me about it? You'll feel better. Is it your sister? Did something remind you of her?'

Thinking that Cathy would never understand about being held against your will and repeatedly abused, and worst of all losing a child, Babs nodded. 'Aye, I miss her every day, and I were so close to her when she was bought in injured. I've no idea what happened to her after she left the hospital. It's like I had one brief moment and then it was all gone again. And then that lad who died, the one who came from Blackpool. That upset me all over again.'

'Poor Babs. I can't imagine your pain. I've been loved and looked after all of my life. When at boarding school I had such close friends and Mother and Father used to visit on a Sunday.

This is the longest I've been away from them, but I still get regular letters. I always feel so sorry for you when the mail is passed to us and you very often have nothing, and never from family.'

'I'm used to it, don't worry, and I have me letters from Daisy to look forward to. I knaw as she can't write often, but she allus makes me laugh for someone as wants to be a nun.'

'I'm glad. I love it when those come for you. It's good to have a friend. But lately, you stand there as the names are called out as if you are expecting something.'

'Well, I popped that note on Beth, and even though the nurse at the hospital said she didn't see it, I still keep hoping that Beth found it and will write. And I put a note in with Gerry's – the Blackpool lad's – things in the hope that me ma would get it. I've nowt back so far, but I never give up hope.'

Cathy put her arm around Babs's shoulder. 'No, never give up hope. I'll tell you what, my father works in a government department. I'll write to him to see if he can help in any way.'

'Ta, Cathy. I've not got much for him to go on, but I could give you as much detail as I can. There's naw harm in trying. And I'll write to the convent to Sister Theresa, as took care of me. She probably thinks that I have enough with Daisy's letters, but'll write back once she knaws as doing so would be a comfort to me.'

'There, things look better already, and Babs, don't be afraid to be Rupert's friend. He's very different to Carter, and I think he likes you. In fact, I know he does.'

'Eeh, Cathy, I'm not in his class. He's more likely to ask you out than me. Never me. Not in a million years.'

'Don't you be so sure. And he doesn't like me other than as a friend, which is how I like him. He isn't my type at all. I like tall, dark and handsome.'

'Don't we all.'

They both laughed at this. Their giggles carried on as they changed the subject and laughed about incidents that had happened in their work. 'Eeh, do you remember when I asked that VAD to clean that poor soldier who'd messed himself? Poor girl couldn't stop vomiting for a week.'

'Ha! She didn't last long. Bless them, coming from rich families, they think it's all going to be heroics. Wiping a man's bottom doesn't come into it at all. But you have to admire most of them; taken from all they know and thrown into an alien world of poo, blood and vomit, they cope very well really.'

They giggled like schoolgirls at this and Babs began to feel better. Changing the subject, she said, 'You knaw, I loved the art gallery. Eeh, I knaw as I felt unwell in there, but up to that point, I thought the paintings were beautiful.'

'We can go again if you like. Next time we have a day off in Paris, we can see if we can find more galleries. Paris has many, and all lovely and filled with the work of renowned artists.'

'I'd love that.'

When they arrived back at the train, Belinda was busily ordering everyone around preparing for another trip.

'But I thought we weren't going until tomorrow?'

'That's par for the course. When do we ever go when they say we will? A communication came in; we're needed back sooner. Did you both have a good day?'

As Babs donned an apron ready to muck in, she told Belinda all they'd seen, and what she'd enjoyed and the sights she hadn't thought much of.

'Well, whatever suits you. We can't all be the same. You appreciate art with your eye. If your eye likes what it sees, then you enjoy the experience. You appreciate old historical buildings by knowing of their history. I've some books that you might enjoy. I love history. These are on French history and you can learn why the Arc de Triomphe is there and what all the names on it are – well, who they were. And who commissioned it, how long it took to build and at what enormous cost. These facts might bring it from being just an archway to something of interest.'

'Ta, Belinda. I'll take a look during my rest period. I'd like to understand why it was so fascinating to the others.'

At their first port of call, there was the usual hustle and bustle. But even though it was something Babs was becoming used to, she made sure she never became immune to it all. Still the suffering of the soldiers hurt. And she made it her mission to do her best to make them comfy and pain-free, as well as offering them hope.

She stood holding a young boy's hand, once they were aboard and travelling. She'd bandaged his eye and he'd asked her if he was 'for Blighty'.

'Aye, lad, you're for Blighty. You'll soon be home. And they'll patch that eye up good and proper.'

'Will I be able to see again, Nurse?'

'I can't say, I'm sorry. Most likely you've got dust eye – what we call it when your eyes get blasted by a lot of dust and debris. We've washed out what we could, but some will be embedded. But at the eye hospital in London, they'll sort that for you.'

'Thanks. You're like me big sister. She 'ad a good answer to everything.'

'Well, that's what big sisters do. And it won't be long before you see her again.'

'No, that'll never happen, nor me mam. I won't see any of them. They were killed by a runaway horse.'

'Eeh, lad, I'm sorry. When did that happen?'

'Just before the war. The soldiers were parading as they made their way to the station and a gun was fired in the air, like a salute. There was a gentleman on a horse and the crack frightened it and that was that. It threw his rider and careered into the crowd. Twelve died that day.'

'That's a sorry tale, lad. How old are you, you don't look knee-high to a donkey?'

'Ha, you talk funny. You make me laugh. I'm sixteen, but I told them I was eighteen because I wanted to get away. I wanted to get as far away as I could from Stepney, where it happened.'

'Aye, I can understand that, lad. Well, now I should think you can't wait to get back.'

Instead of answering the lad crunched up in pain and then vomited in a way that made him look as though he was one of those gargoyles on a fountain with water pouring from its mouth.

Babs called out for someone to fetch the doctor before examining his stomach. The next vomit was full of blood.

'What's wrong, Babs? I thought this one had been fixed up?'

'I'm not sure, he had no signs of internal bleeding. Maybe his appendix, it could have ruptured, but he hasn't complained of a stomach pain. It just came on suddenly.'

Assisting in the theatre, Babs had a sinking heart. The young lad wasn't responding well, and he was weakening by the minute. When he took his last breath, Rupert bent his head. 'God! I hate this job. He was chatting away while I fixed his eye. There was no indication that he had anything else wrong with him.'

Though she felt like weeping, Babs took charge. 'Stitch him up, Rupert. I'll get a nurse to come and wash him and lay him out and a couple of orderlies to scrub the theatre down. Have you some of that brandy left?'

Rupert let out a sigh. 'I have. I'll have a wash and meet you in the corridor.'

'Naw, let's go to the balcony. I need some air.'

Once outside, with the world rushing by them to the rhythm of the train, Rupert poured the brandy. 'Now, don't choke on it this time.'

'I might, lad, but by, I'll enjoy it once it hits me—'

'Cockles? Haha, I've still no idea what your cockles are.'

Babs laughed with him. 'Naw, neither do I.'

They laughed easily together. When they became serious, Babs told him about the lad's family.

'Well, let's hope that he's with his ma and sister now, poor fellow.'

They were silent for a moment. Babs didn't know how it happened, but she became aware that Rupert was standing closer to her than he had been. She looked up at him and held his gaze. Lit only by the moonlight, she thought him so beautiful.

'Babs. I – I . . .'

He said no more. His lips were on hers. His free arm came around her and held her close. Babs was transported to a world of light and love, and yes, desire as his kiss deepened and his tongue probed her mouth. When he pulled away, he stared at her with an intent look. 'Babs, I'm falling in love with you.'

Happiness exploded inside Babs. 'And I love you, Rupert.'

'Oh, Babs, really? You love me? Me? I can't believe it.'

Taking the cap to the flask from her, he put that and the flask down on the floor. When he stood he held her to him. Babs thought she'd landed in heaven. All past hurts dissolved and became meaningless in this moment.

His whispering of her name over and over enraptured her.

'I can't believe that you love me, Babs. I'm so happy. We'll be together always.'

But at this a doubt crept into Babs. How could it be possible? They were worlds apart.

'Are you all right, Babs? Am I going too fast for you? You stiffened.'

'Naw, it's just that our lives are so different. Naw one of my class ever married one of yours.'

'I know. What usually happens is the woman who a man of my class truly loves becomes his lifelong mistress and—'

Babs pulled away from him. 'Naw. I'm naw one's mistress, and never will be. I thought . . . I have to get away from you. I feel a like a fool now.'

'Babs, no. Babs, it'll work, we'll make it work. I'm going to be an earl. I can't . . . I mean, well, my father has a mistress. She's lovely, and he spoils her because he truly loves her.'

'Naw wonder your ma's like she is then. He's a bastard! Your poor ma. Let go of me, Rupert. Let go of me!'

'Please, Babs, let's at least talk about it. Let me explain how it works.'

'I don't want to knaw. Now, let go of my arm or I'll scream!'

Rupert let go. His cries of his love for her made no difference to her as she ran from him. Making her way to the stores, where she could be alone and come to terms with what just happened, she stood and stamped her feet in anger and frustration. *How could I have been such a fool as to fall in love with the son of an earl? It was never going to work. Never.*

Crumbling to the floor, Babs wept her heart out. She so wanted her ma and Beth. Would she ever be with them? She wanted to be held by people who really loved her and would care for her. *I'm so tired. So very tired.*

TWENTY-SIX

Everything was ready, and Beth looked beautiful. It was so wonderful to have Beth back with her, as Tilly had missed her so much when she and Henry had gone back to Kent. But now they were here, and it was their wedding day. The one they had promised they would have in the church in Blackpool. Looking down at her daughter, Tilly told her, 'Eeh, love, this is going to be the wedding of all weddings.'

'Shift yourself, Tilly, I'm trying to fix Beth's veil.'

'Sorry, Molly. Eeh, you've done a grand job on Beth's frock. That silk organza is such a lovely material. And you look like a princess, Beth. Henry will fall in love with you all over again.'

'We can't love each other more than we do, Ma. And we'll eventually be wedded to our eyeballs we have our . . . I mean, well, this is our second already. But it is the loveliest. I feel so happy.'

Tilly wondered what Beth was going to say. A couple of times on this second visit, she'd almost told her something. Letting it pass, she went to see how Eliza was getting on. She found her in her bedroom with Janine. They were laughing together. Tilly marvelled at how lovely this posh family of

Henry's were. None of them made you feel as though you were below them in anyway. 'You two look lovely. That blue is such a nice colour.'

'Ta, Ma. And Janine fixed my hair an' all. She's made it all neat and pinned these flowers into it.'

'It looks lovely, me little lass. Now, I wonder where Molly's daughters-in-law are. Mind, I wonder if Mary feels like coming. Bless her, she's trying to cope with so much – not only losing Gerry but finding that she is pregnant an' all. Me heart goes out to her.'

'They'll probably meet us at the church, Ma, it might be best for them.'

'I suggested that, but they said they'd feel better coming here to the farm with their ma, Ida, and all going together with us and Molly. They thought it would be easier for Molly an' all. Though she's keeping herself busy, which is her way of coping.'

A noise in the yard had Eliza jumping up and looking through the window. 'They're here, Ma. Eeh, but Ma, there's only Vera and Ida, so you may be right about Mary.'

'Oh naw. I did hope the lass would be all right. Anyroad, you two come down and be ready to go with your uncle Will. Phil's driving you. I'll go and greet them and get them organised.'

When she got to the bottom of the stairs, Tommy met her. 'I was just coming to get you, me darling. My, it's bonny as you look. That yellow really suits you.'

Tilly smiled. She felt good in the yellow outfit. Its long skirt in a satin material gave the effect of swirling around her as it was gathered at the back and fell in folds at the front. The matching jacket was cut into her waist and had black braiding around the collar and down the front. She'd finished the outfit with a quirky black hat that dipped on one side, and black gloves and shoes.

'Ta, love. I see Mary didn't make it.'

'No. There's been ... well, let's just say as something has happened. Something that is for being wonderful news for you and Beth and will be making this day even more special than it is. But it is that though the news is good for you, me darling, the means of it coming to us has been for rendering Mary unable to attend. She has a friend staying with her, and she may come later.'

'What is it? Tommy?'

'I'm going to fetch Beth down first and Molly. Especially Molly. I've asked Ida not to be sharing until I have you all here. Molly is going to need us all. Will knows and it has upset him, but it is that he is ready to support Molly.'

When they all gathered together, Tilly could wait no longer. 'Eeh, Ida, what's happened that can make me and Beth happy and yet sadden poor Mary, Molly and Will?'

Ida handed Tilly a letter.

'Read it out loud, me little Tilly.'

Tilly felt her hand shake. She smiled at Tommy as she opened the letter. The paper the words were written on looked as though it had been torn out of a notebook.

Dear Gerry's ma,

Tilly dropped her hands by her side. 'It's to you, Molly. Oh, Molly lass.'

Will stood by Molly's side and held her to him.

'Shall I go on?'
Molly nodded.

My name is Babs . . .

'Oh, dear God! Eeh, Tommy, Beth, it's from Babs!'
'Oh, Ma, at last, at last! What does she say? Where is she?'
With a shaking voice, Tilly read on:

You don't know me, but I was born in Blackpool. I am a nurse on a hospital train that runs from the north-east of France to Paris, tending the wounded.

I nursed your son. Gerry was the bravest young man I have ever met. Before he died, he said how much he loved his wife and his mother, father and brother. And he said that he had an Aunt Tilly that he loved and that I reminded him of her. My ma's name is Tilly.

'Eeh, me Babs! It's me Babs!'
Everyone was silent. Tilly read on:

I want to tell you how sorry I am, and how it helped Gerry to be with a fellow Blackpudlian. We had a laugh together and he was very peaceful and calm. He held a lovely picture of his wife in his hands and we left it with him so that they will always be together.

If you could find it in your heart to find out if Gerry's Aunt Tilly is my ma, I would be so grateful. You see, me and my twin sister Beth were taken from her, but we never stopped wanting to be with her.

Tell her that Beth and I were separated, but that I have met Beth. She too was a nurse, but sadly, she was injured and was brought to my train and didn't regain consciousness before she was removed and taken to a hospital in Paris.

I left a note on her clothes for her to contact me, but when I enquired, the hospital didn't know anything about it and by that time, Beth was on her way home to England. They did tell me that she was all right, though, and would recover.

If Ma contacts the Red Cross, she will find Beth. She goes under the name of Petrilona, which is the name Jasmine and Roman gave to us. But I am known as Smith, Sister Barbara Smith.

I know that this is such a lot to ask of you when you are grieving for your son, but I beg of you to try to find Tilly for me, if the Tilly you do know isn't my ma. When you do, please tell her that I love her very much and will one day be with her and ask her to contact the Red Cross, who will forward a letter to me.

Yours sincerely

Sister Barbara Smith

Tilly backed into a chair. She wanted to go to Molly, and to Beth, but her strength had gone. 'How? Where did it come from, Ida?'

'It was with Gerry's personal effects, sent to Mary. There's not much, but Mary said to tell you, Molly, that you and Will can have what you like. There's a letter for you, written by Gerry, and one for Mary an' all. And his cap and badge, and that's it. Oh, it came with a letter from the King too. Mary were right proud of that.'

At last feeling able to go to Molly, Tilly squatted by the chair that Molly sat in. 'By, Molly, love.'

'I knaw. It were lovely to hear that he were peaceful and that he had a photo of Mary with him. Poor lass. But, Tilly, you've found your twins at last. Eeh, I'm so happy for you. And that happiness is lessening me sadness. Beth, Beth, lass, what a lovely gift on your wedding day. Now, naw tears, only happy ones today. Come on, everyone, we've a double celebration to get underway.'

'Eeh, Molly, lass, I love you. I love your strength. You have allus propped me up.'

'And I love you, Tilly. And despite me sadness, to knaw as you've at last got your twins is making me happy inside.'

'And me, Tilly. That our Gerry should bring Babs back to you. That's a lovely thing to happen out of a bad thing.'

'Ta, Will. I couldn't have enjoyed this moment if I thought as it would bring you and Molly more sorrow.'

'Well, it didn't, it brought comfort to us, didn't it, Will? Now, where were we, Beth, lass? Let's get you finished. You look so beautiful.'

The wedding was wonderful. A full nuptial mass, held in St John's church in the centre of Blackpool, the service brought tears to everyone's eyes.

When they came out of the church, the sun was shining and the bells peeling, which added to the feeling of happiness Tilly was encased in. As she looked at Beth sitting in the bath chair that Ivan had designed and used, she felt a tinge of sadness and yet pride too, as Ivan's invention had allowed Beth the independence to get herself up the aisle wheeling its large wheels with her hands.

And Tommy had been so proud to give her away. How Ivan would have loved it. *You never did get to meet your half-sisters, me little love, but I knaw as you're happy for me now I am at last reunited with them.*

An arm came around her and she looked up into Tommy's face. 'Are you all right, me little Tilly?'

Then a hand took hers and as she looked down at Beth, who'd wheeled over to her, she nodded. 'Aye, I'm doing fine.'

'Ma, Tommy, before the reception, can we go to the cemetery? I'd like to put my bouquet on my brother's grave and introduce myself to him and thank him for this wonderful chair.'

'Eeh, that'd be grand, lass. I knaw he's with us, but that will include him, and'll make me feel at peace.'

'Me and Will will see all the guests are looked after. I popped in to the church hall before we went into church and the ladies of the church committee have done us proud. There's a mountain of butties and the wedding cake that you made, Eliza, looks grand.'

At the churchyard, Tommy and Tilly led the little party – Eliza, Beth and Henry – to the graveside. Tilly held her emotions in check as the new headstone came into view.

Here lies one of God's Angels, lent to us to give us happiness and hope. And then Ivan's name and the date of his birth and death.

'Awe, that's a lovely inscription, Ma. Ivan, my little brother, I'm sorry that I didn't meet you, but I know that you loved me. I've brought my wedding flowers for you as a token of my love for you.'

As Henry lay the huge bouquet on the grave, Beth put her arms out to Eliza. Eliza went into them and the two hugged. 'I'm so glad to have you, Eliza. Thank you, you and Ivan kept Ma happy despite her sadness at not being with me and Babs.'

Hearing a sob from Eliza, Tilly couldn't control her own tears. She looked at Tommy and saw that his eyes were streaming.

'I'm sorry, both, I didn't mean to upset you. But I suppose, it was always going to be a sad moment for us all.' Tilly dried her eyes as she said this. 'Eeh, our Ivan. Look at us all. And we have such a lovely day to finish yet. But we miss you, lad, and wanted you included.'

Ivan's smile came to her, and the little wink he always gave her when she was being daft. She smiled back. When she looked at Tommy, he was smiling a watery smile too. 'Eeh, it's as if he's here, ain't it?'

'It is, me little Tilly. Come on, Eliza, Pappy knows that Ivan is happy and that he's going to be with us all day. We've shenanigans to get underway.'

'Ma, shall I put my flowers with Beth's or shall I just leave Beth's there as they look so beautiful?'

'I tell you what, Beth, do you remember Liz, me mate as you used to call Aunt Liz?'

'Vaguely ... Didn't she move away? I seem to remember playing with her children and that there were so many of them.'

'Aye, well, there's a long story to tell, and a sad one, but like all the catching up that we have to do, we've to put it on hold for now to just enjoy being together, but your Aunt Liz is buried over there. I'd love to put your flowers on her grave, Eliza, and I knaw as Ivan would like that an' all. He loved Aunt Liz, and you're named after her.'

'Oh? That makes her special then. What do you think, Beth? Is that all right with you?'

'It is. But will I get my chair over there? There's no path. Why is she buried away from everyone, Ma?'

'Well, that's part of all I have to tell you, lass. But me and Eliza and Tommy can take the flowers over.'

'I'll carry you to where Liz is resting.'

'Thanks, Henry. I wouldn't let you, but it isn't far.'

When they arrived at the graveside, Tilly looked down at Liz's unmarked grave and felt the sadness of yesteryear visit her. Eliza lay her flowers down and stepped back. Tilly bent down. 'I tell you what, I'll take a couple of the blooms and lay them on Liz's husband's grave. His name was Dan and he's buried just by the path, then for today, they will be united as if in the same grave.'

Whether questions were going to be asked by Eliza, Beth and Henry, who she knew must be intrigued, she didn't know, but she suspected that Tommy would have cautioned them by some gesture or other, as no one objected or asked to know why Liz and Dan weren't together.

The vibrant colours of the freesias fluttered in the light breeze as Tilly tugged a couple free from the ribbon that bound them, and to her it felt as though Liz was saying, 'Ta, love.'

* * *

There were no more tears, only happiness and joy as the wedding party swigged Guinness, courtesy of Tommy, and sherry supplied by Henry's mother. A friend of Molly's played the piano, and Tommy did his usual Irish jig, accompanied by Eliza who had learnt the dance so well that Tommy bowed out and left her to dance solo. Everyone clapped and eventually joined in, with Beth being swung around in her wheelchair, laughing her head off.

Waving the bridal couple and Henry's family off on the train afterwards saddened Tilly. She never wanted to say goodbye to any of her girls again, but Beth and Henry had to get back to Kent for Henry's job and so she was to content herself with waiting for their next visit.

'By, that were grand, Tommy. Just to think, I'm a ma-in-law.'

'You were before today, lass.'

'I knaw, but only by law. Now I am in the eyes of God. Eeh, I'm getting to be an old biddy.'

'What? You? Isn't it that you are in your prime, me little Tilly, and when it is that I get you home, I'll be after showing you that you are, so I will.'

'Ha, Tommy, you're drunk, and I'm guessing when your head hits the pillow, you'll be dead to the world.'

Tommy slapped her bottom. 'We'll be seeing about that.'

The familiar feelings tickled Tilly's stomach. She tried to quieten them being used to Tommy's bravado when he'd had a few and knowing that the drink had its own say in these matters.

Hugging and kissing everyone goodbye, they eventually set out for home. By the time they reached there, Eliza was asleep on the sacks in the back of the cart. Tommy lifted her inside the house and to her bed, where even as Tilly undressed her, she didn't wake.

Downstairs, Tommy was sat on the sofa. As she came down, he stood up and looked at her. 'Will you do me the honour of strolling in the moonlight, me lovely Tilly?'

He crooked his arm and Tilly giggled as she took it.

Outside, it was a warm night, and the moon lit the yard, bigger now as the barn that Liz had killed herself in had long been pulled down. The cobbles that had formed the floor of the barn remained and Tommy had dug out a couple of flower beds. In these they had rose bushes, and the heady scent of these now drifted to them. To their right was the new barn, almost empty of hay now, as most of last year's harvest had been used. It would fill up again when harvest came around in the autumn.

'I think it is that I will build a garden seat between those rose beds. It will be a nice place to sit on a night such as this as I'm for loving being outside in the summer months. All the animals are roaming free in the fields, and the peace is wonderful.'

As if to deny him, one of his cows mooed. They both laughed. 'It's thankful that I am for the help of Phil. He did the milking on his own tonight.'

'He's a good lad.'

'Well, the cows are for settling down again, so, me Tilly, it is that I feel like dancing.'

Tilly laughed. 'Here?'

'Yes, here in the moonlight.'

'All right, you daft apeth, but naw Irish jig. Just a waltz or sommat.'

As Tommy took her in his arms he began to sing 'When Irish Eyes are Smiling' as he waltzed her around the yard. Tilly was lost in a world of love and didn't resist as she was danced into the new barn.

The feelings she had earlier returned as Tommy lowered her gently onto the remaining hay that lay in heaps on the floor.

His kiss heightened the clenching sensations that were making it hard for her to breathe. When he came out of the kiss, she begged him to make love to her.

'Me Tilly, me little Tilly, I love you with all of me.'

When he entered her, her world exploded in a cascade of sensations that she could hardly bear. 'Tommy, my Tommy.'

Tommy's cry joined hers as he hollered out his release, then both sank into sobs that shook their bodies.

They clung to each other, rocking back and forth. They didn't have to voice the pain that was draining them. Their letting go had left them fragile.

When the bout passed, they hugged as peace enclosed them. Then lay back in the hay holding hands.

'So many good things overshadowed.'

'Aye, Tommy. But it's time for us to look to the good.'

'We will, me little Tilly. I couldn't be for being happier that you have Beth. I love her like me own, and was honoured to take her down the aisle today.'

'And now I knaw where me Babs is an' all, Tommy. I just want this war to end and for her to come home to us.'

Tommy rolled over and pulled her to him. 'Well, me little Tilly, I'm feeling hungry now. Let's go in and have some of that ham that you cooked off yesterday. I nearly attacked it while you were upstairs with Eliza. God love her, she did a great job today.'

'Aye, she did.'

As Tilly sliced two thick slices of ham off the bone, she felt weary. Putting it on plates with some home-made pickles and doorstep wedges cut from the loaf she'd cooked off earlier, she went through to the sitting room. While they ate, they both came to terms with what had happened to them in the barn.

'You knaw, Tommy, it was as if them tears were stuck on me chest and you, and the happiness of today, released them. As if all we did today, visiting Ivan and Liz and Dan, and with Beth and the wedding, helped me to let go.'

'I know. I feel better for it, me little Tilly, as me grief had been choking me and making me unable to function properly. I'll never stop grieving for our lovely Ivan, but now I think I will cope with it, and be at helping you to do so too – it is that I'm for feeling stronger.'

Tilly smiled. Maybe they would have many a moment like tonight, but they'd get through them. Together, they'd find a way to cope.

TWENTY-SEVEN

'Babs, won't you forgive me? I . . . well, I didn't know any different to what I proposed. This is hell, working with you and not being able to get out of my head how much I hurt you. And wanting you so much. I love you, Babs, and cannot think of living my life without you, but I also know that you could never be happy leading the life I will have to live.'

After Babs had assisted Rupert in the theatre, something she had tried to wriggle out of, he'd followed her out to the corridor and barred her way. Since the incident three weeks ago, he hadn't pestered her, and they had both carried on in a professional manner, not referring to it, and yet for Babs it had been a time of heartache that had left her feeling unworthy of being loved. Now, her resolve was weakening, and to hear him say again that he loved her rocked her world. She looked up into his lovely eyes. 'Oh, Rupert. I love you, I do, but I can't live how you want me to. It's best as we go our separate ways. I – I've written to HQ and asked them to let me go home.'

'No! Please don't, I couldn't bear it.'

Rupert put an arm on the window and leant his head on it. 'I'll leave my family, Babs. I'll renounce my entitlement and my cousin will become the next earl. Then we'll marry and live somewhere where we can make new friends and be happy and have a family.'

'Rupert, I need to tell you sommat about me, about how I've been brought up, and what has happened to me. I . . . well, I haven't had an ordinary life.'

As her story unfolded, Rupert didn't interrupt other than to occasionally gasp, 'No, no!' or 'Oh God!' At the end of her telling, Rupert stared at her for a long moment. 'Good Lord! Oh, my darling, that's dreadful. Babs, please may I hold you?'

That he wanted to after hearing all that had happened to her broke the cocoon she'd shielded herself with. Her tears fell and turned to sobs as she went into his arms. Tears for her lovely lost son, Mario. And for her ma and Beth. Tears at the way she'd been taken from her ma, and how her da didn't come home ever again, and tears for the terrible memory she'd let in about the despicable Cecil who did those rotten things to her.

As her sorrow subsided, she became aware of Rupert kissing her hair and holding her now as a lover would. She put her arms around him. 'Oh, Rupert, how can you still want me?'

'I love you even more now, my Babs, because I understand. Knowing all you've been through is breaking my heart. My God, what that beast did to you, and . . . prison! And, losing your child. How brave you are. My love has extended to admiration of how you have come through all of that and still made something of your life. You are a wonderful person and a caring and loving nurse who has brightened the last moments of many poor chaps' lives. I hope with all my heart that the letter you put with the Blackpool soldier's belongings finds your mother for you, but if not, I promise you, Babs, that I will find her. Oh, my darling.'

The door of the surgery sliding open made them jump apart. The two VADs that had been cleaning down the theatre looked astonished for a moment, and then went into a fit of nervous giggling.

Babs drew herself up, trying to regain her dignity, even though she knew that her face would show how she had been crying. 'Carry on, nurses, I'm sure you've done a good job. You allus do.'

The older of the two, a nice girl even though she spoke with a plum in her mouth, asked, 'Are you all right, Sister? I'm sorry that I giggled, it was rude of me, but it was the shock of seeing ... well, anyway, I can see now that something has upset you.'

'I'm fine now. Ta. Go about what you have to do, and please, say naw more about this. Doctor Bartram was just comforting me, that's all. We all need that sometimes.'

The other girl tried to control her nervous giggling but couldn't. Babs let it go, thinking that to make too much fuss would just make things worse. When they had left, Rupert pulled her to him again. 'I'm sorry about that, I should have been more careful. Oh, Babs, I'm still very shocked at what you have just told me. Those gypsies should be strung up as most of what happened to you can be put at their door.'

'Naw. I've long forgiven them and realised that they thought they were doing right by me and Beth. They have allus been wonderful parents to us, even though I was disruptive all my life, as I wasn't accepting in the way that Beth was. Sometimes it's difficult to knaw how twins can be so different. We are identical, and yet have such different personalities. I've allus been the strong one. Beth followed everything I did and did as I told her to. I looked after her. I'm only glad as she didn't follow me for once in her life when I ran away. I'm glad as she remained safe. But how she came to be a nurse I can't imagine, as the gypsies didn't go in for learning. They live close to the earth and knaw all its secrets; they have naw need to be educated, and don't see why anyone needs to be.'

'But surely they need doctors?'

'Naw. They heal themselves, and don't seem to ail in the way others do. Their potions are made from natural substances, and they work. And they have this method of making someone unconscious.' She told him how she had used it once when they had run out of anaesthetics.

'Really? That's amazing. And using this method, the gypsies set broken limbs and stitch up wounds? But what of other ailments – appendicitis, for instance?'

'Huh, the doctor's coming out in you, Rupert. You're forgetting our predicament now that you have interesting medical facts to pursue. Well, I'm exhausted, and ain't up for a long discussion on gypsies, ta very much.'

Rupert laughed. 'I'm sorry. It is fascinating, though. But . . . well, not as fascinating as you, my darling. May I kiss you, Babs?'

Even though her head told her that she shouldn't – not least because if they were caught, they would be disciplined – her heart won, and she went willingly into his arms. His kiss awakened her world, brought her alive, and made her feel that her heart would burst with the joy that surged through her. As they came out of it, they clung together. Rupert spoke of his love, and how he would take care of her forever and never let her be hurt again. 'Let's wrangle a day off together. One of the other doctors would cover for me. How about you? Is it your turn to leave the train when we reach Paris?'

'Aye, it is as it happens. And it's also Belinda's, which is good as she has taken to going off on her own. If it was Cathy, then we'd have a job to get out of taking her with us.'

'Well, we'll get off the train separately, as we don't want to arouse suspicion. We could be in trouble if caught. I'm already worried about those two nurses gossiping.'

'Awe, you've naw need to. They'll have a giggle about it and make their own minds up, I'm sure, but they're not the vindictive type, and I don't think they'd want to do me harm. I treat them decent, and with respect, and they love me for it. They wouldn't want to cause me any trouble.'

'Good, as I have been worrying about them and we do have to be careful, so how about we meet in that café we went to with Cathy? Can you find your way to that all right?'

'Aye, I can. I went back to it the last time I had a leave day. I had a mind to apologise to waspy, but he weren't there.'

'Ha, I should think that after that day he left and never returned! But that's settled then, and if anyone sees us, we can pretend we just bumped into each other and decided to have a drink together.'

They held hands for a moment, without talking, but then the moment passed as Rupert said, 'Well, as much as I don't want to, I need to do my rounds and check on those we have operated on. I can't wait for our leave day, but in the meantime, I'll have to carry on as usual and go into professional mode when around you. I won't want to, my darling, but you know that I must.'

'Aye, and I will an' all. But you will knaw what is happening to me heart even though I may not even glance your way.'

He kissed her lightly then, and Babs wanted to take hold of him and never let him go, but she knew how they had to behave, and prepared herself for that by moving away from him. After he'd left, she stood a moment in wonderment at what had just happened between them. How easily she'd told him of her life and how he'd said that he would leave his family and the life he knew just to be with her. Could she let him do that? Wouldn't it be cruel to do so? But could she follow the alternative and be his mistress while he married a woman of his own standing and had a family with her? *Naw, naw, I could never live like that, me heart would break.*

When her rest period finally came around, Babs walked towards her quarters, knowing in her heart that their love could only be fleeting because she couldn't make that sacrifice for Rupert, and she wasn't going to keep him to his promise – she could never take him from his family. She knew the pain of that. *But,* she asked herself, *how will everything pan out*? She didn't know the answer, she only knew that until they parted she would enjoy every moment she had with him.

When they reached Paris, Babs could hardly contain herself, to the point that Cathy was a little peeved. 'Well, I wish you were this excited when I was going with you, Babs . . . You're planning something, I can tell. Come on, what are you going to be doing all day that has you in this stew? It's Rupert, isn't it? You dark horse. Well, have a lovely time, but be careful, both of you. I know how you feel, but, well . . . Look, Babs, it's never going to work . . .'

Babs sighed and paused in pulling up the silk stocking she'd been carefully putting on. 'I knaw, we're just friends.'

'Oh, Babs. I feel for you, I do, but you can only end up with a broken heart.'

'I knaw as that will happen an' all. But I'm grasping at the happy moments that I can have. You don't blame me, do you, Cathy?'

'No, I don't, just as long as you know what you're doing, that's all.'

Giving Cathy a hug, Babs escaped as quickly as she could, not wanting her resolve to weaken. She would have today – just today – and then she would tell Rupert that it was over. She would post the letter she'd written to the Red Cross and hope against hope that the powers that be would consider posting her to a hospital in England. She'd told them about Beth and had said that she couldn't function properly knowing that her sister might need her and asked them to locate Beth for her. Now, she could only hope they would grant her request.

The post bag waiting for them had a letter from Sister Theresa that also contained one from Daisy, but not the hoped for one from her ma. But then, as Rupert had since told her, it took a while for the government to send the belongings to the family, and the letters they received were sometimes written three weeks or so previous to them arriving.

Putting the letters in her bag to read later, Babs hurried to the café, her heart pounding her excitement around her whole body – even her toes tingled with it.

She was there before Rupert. He looked lovely in the same corduroy trousers, shirt and pullover that he'd worn before, and complimented her on her long dark blue cotton dress topped with a hip-length navy blue cardigan and he loved the straw boater hat that she'd bought on one of her trips into Paris. Natural coloured, it had a long silk ribbon around the brim, and this hung down her back. Her wrist-length lace gloves and low-heeled white shoes completed her outfit. But it was her hair that Rupert was most complimentary over. 'It's beautiful, I never knew it was so long. The sun is picking up red lights in it.'

'That's why they call it "raven". It's like the colour of the birds. Me ma and me sister have the same.'

'I want to run my hands through it.'

Babs trembled at the tone of his voice and smiled shyly as he took her hand and looked into her eyes. 'Babs, if I was careful of you, would you . . . I mean . . .' He looked down for a moment. When he looked up again, he said, 'I'm so sorry, Babs, I should never have asked, I – I'm a cad. It was just that my feelings are so deep for you and the thought of stroking your hair, I'm sorry.'

But Babs didn't want him to be. She wanted him as much as he wanted her, and could see no wrong in expressing that. 'Don't be, I knaws how you're feeling, I'm feeling just the same.'

He held her eyes with his own. The trembling in her stomach increased. Wild thoughts entered her mind, of Rupert touching her, not just her hair, but her breasts and her . . . *Naw, I mustn't think like that. It were the most repulsive and painful thing when Cecil . . .*

'Darling, are you all right? I'm so sorry. I'll never mention it again until we are wed, I promise.'

But we never will be wed, and I'll be leaving, and then, I'll never knaw ...

'Babs? Babs, believe me, I shouldn't have spoken like that. It was, well, the moment. Forgive me. Let's carry on as if it never happened. Please.'

'I've nowt to forgive, I want you to. I want to be with you proper. Is it possible?'

'You mean ... you mean, you would? Oh, Babs. I don't know now. I feel terrible, I don't think we should, though I want to, more than anything in the world, I want to.'

Babs knew for certain that it was what she wanted too. 'I do mean it, Rupert, me love. We're adults, we can do as we like, we don't have to follow convention, but how? How can we be alone together, let alone ... well, you knaw?'

Suddenly, Babs felt as if she was behaving very improperly, and not at all how one of the ladies that Rupert knew would behave, but she felt compelled to do this, to take with her a memory of having been truly Rupert's, just once in her life.

'We could go to a hotel. This is Paris, they thrive on such things. It is the normal way of things to them. There's no having to wear a wedding band and call ourselves Mr and Mrs Smith ... Oh, I've just realised, that's your name!' Rupert burst out laughing. The sound eased the tension between them and made Babs giggle. She hadn't told him that it wasn't her name, but what did that matter?

When they'd stopped laughing, Rupert looked at her with a boyish expression. 'Are you sure?'

'Aye, I've never been more sure about owt.'

* * *

They left the café and walked along the street to where a line of cabs was parked. The streets, compared to last year during the shut-down of Paris, were almost back to normal, with only the remaining damage of the bomb, dropped not many weeks ago, a stark reminder that there was a war on. The people of Paris had adapted to wartime existence and were very resilient; even the theatres had reopened. As they walked, Rupert told her that they hadn't yet brought their most treasured art collection back to Le Louvre from Toulouse.

The cabs were all red with bright yellow wheels, and again, Rupert told her a fact of how the war had impacted on Paris. 'During last year, these and hundreds of other cabs ferried soldiers to the front, as there wasn't a train connection for them to use at the time. They drove tail to nose all the way. It was a marvellous spectacle to see them arrive, as I was in the area at the time. It did the trick too as along with our lads the French soldiers drove the Germans back.'

'By, that must have been sommat to see.'

Rupert spoke in French to the cab driver, then got into the leather seat next to Babs and found her hand. He held it tightly in his as if sensing her fear. Putting his head next to hers, he whispered, 'It doesn't matter if you change your mind, honestly.'

She shook her head. The nearness of him had confirmed for her that this is what she wanted. And the feeling that this would be the only time in her life that she would truly love and be loved by her Rupert made her determined not to let fear spoil it for her, though her guilt hit her when they passed the Grand Palais, which was now a military hospital and where Beth had been taken to. *Eeh, Beth, I don't knaw what you'd think of me, lass.* Beth was such a prude and so innocent in all the ways of the world that she couldn't imagine her ever doing such a thing as making love.

The hotel was grander than she'd expected. She'd imagined being taken to a seedy back-street place, and feeling like a lady of the street, but instead a porter met the cab and opened the door, bowing to them as he did. Rupert spoke to him and gave him some money, which she assumed he would pay the cab with and perhaps there would be a tip for him too.

When he opened the gleaming glass hotel doors, which were inscribed in gold with the name of the hotel, Vendim, he ushered them inside. The interior made Babs catch her breath, as the reception had a magnificent arched ceiling with golden carvings. The floor was a multi-coloured marble, and everywhere were huge Roman-looking golden urns.

Without Rupert seeming to arrange it, as he only spoke briefly to the receptionist, they were shown to a room that was so beautiful Babs audibly gasped. It was decorated in reds and golds and there was no bed, but she could see that other rooms led off from it.

The deep red sofas were edged in gold; the carpet was gold with a pattern of huge red swirls woven into it. The curtains were gold, edged with the same red, and there were occasional tables everywhere, all gold enamelled, with carved legs. Babs stood and stared in wonderment.

'Darling, I have a confession to make. I couldn't tell you before, because it would have seemed that this was something I always do – although I promise you, you are the first lady guest I have ever brought here – but this apartment is permanently let to my family and only to us.'

'What? Oh, Rupert! I don't knaw what to say. I knew that you were rich, but I didn't really knaw what rich meant. I can't believe it.'

'And you're not cross? You believe me when I say this is something that I've never done before?'

'Aye, I knaw you are an honourable man. You gave me a choice and I chose to come with you. I love you, Rupert.'

Rupert crossed over to her and held her in his arms. Together they rocked gently in a comforting, loving motion. 'Darling, I want us to take our time, to relax together and let everything take its course. We have all day and part of tomorrow.'

'You mean, we're going to sleep here?'

'If you want to. I know that I want to. I want to experience having you in bed with me all night and waking up in the morning with you. None of us know how long we have with this bloody war. The fighting is getting towards the Somme area now, and we visit that every day. How long before we are attacked?'

'You think that can happen? Eeh, I never thought.'

'Don't be afraid, darling, but yes, it could. Anyway, don't let's spoil our time talking about the war and what might happen. Sit down for a while. I have put an order in for us to have some champagne delivered and for a hot bath to be prepared for us. The bath's big enough for two.'

Babs had never heard of such a thing as getting in a bath with a man, but the idea appealed.

When it happened, Rupert helped her to undress and step into the bath. The water felt like silk and the perfume that came from it transported her to the heart of Kent when the blossom is out. She lay back and closed her eyes, letting the experience take her whole self, body and spirit, into the depth of its pleasure.

When Rupert climbed in, she caught a glimpse of his beautiful body. Slim and yet strong, he was everything she knew he would be.

Her first sip of champagne gave her a heady feeling. All of her last inhibitions left her and she gave herself up to the wonder of the love she felt as they sponged each other down. Rupert lingered on her breasts and between her thighs, taking her out of herself as the strange, but wonderful sensations rippled through her body, and then she found pleasure in exploring the contours of Rupert's body, and feeling the joy of his obvious pleasure.

When they dried, they almost ran through the door that led to the bedroom, a haven of beauty in golds and creams, with a lace canopy over the huge bed.

Not stopping to get into the bed, their lovemaking continued with kisses so deep and passionate they left them both gasping, until the moment came when Rupert rolled on top of her and entered her. This was when she was made whole. When all the bits that had been dragged through hell mended, and came together in a fusion of love, desire and completeness.

Clinging to Rupert, she begged of him to stop as a feeling vibrated through her that she could hardly bear. She called out her love for him, unaware that he was trying to disengage from her. His cry of 'Babs, oh, Babs, I have to get . . .' went into a moan of pleasure as she felt him pulsating inside her.

They held each other, trembling from the intensity of what had passed between them. When at last they parted and lay side by side, Rupert was full of apologies. 'I wanted to stop the possibility of pregnancy, darling, but I couldn't leave you. I promise I won't abandon you if this results in you having a baby. I'll always be by your side.'

This shocked her. What had she been thinking? The feelings that had stuck with her now left her as the possibilities screamed at her. But Rupert's words and his tenderness soothed her.

By the time they boarded the train again, they'd made love with abandon so many times that Babs no longer felt concerned. She was the happiest she'd ever been in her life.

She was going to be married. Yes, married.

Rupert had been appalled at her plan when they had talked after the first time that they'd made love. He wouldn't hear of them parting and making this the one and only time they would be together. He'd asked her to marry him, telling her again that he would give up his right to the title. And he was so adamant that his plan was the best that he convinced her and even sat and wrote there and then to his parents.

He'd read the letter to her. It was full of his love for her, and of how he was going to make her his wife and if that meant denouncing his title and it going to Hubert, his cousin, then so be it. 'I am going to marry you. We will go out in the morning and get a licence. And I'll engage a solicitor to make it legal in England, then when all of this is over and we are home, we will marry in a church.'

Just one week later they were in the solicitor's office ready to get married. How it was managed, Babs didn't know, only that it seemed to her that when you are rich you can accomplish anything, but the solicitor had all the papers drawn up that made their union, later that day, legal and binding. Once signed, a copy was sent to Rupert's parents – something that for some reason worried Babs. Whether it was the idea of presenting them with something that they could do nothing about, or her concern that her future would be so different to what she'd expected it to be, she didn't know, but by the time they had said 'I do' to the registrar, with Cathy and Belinda witnessing, her happiness vied with the feeling of trepidation she had. Matron had covered for them – she'd been surprisingly pleasant about it all, if more than a little shocked, saying that she would have to report to HQ and revoke Babs's request to leave and then await their decision as to whether Babs, or either of them, would be allowed to stay on. She also told them that they must follow the rules and remain strictly in their own quarters during rest times and night hours whilst on the train.

Putting it out of her mind, Babs had relaxed and allowed her happiness to take precedence and her concerns and her nerves to leave her as she enjoyed the meal that they all went for after the service. Rupert had said she looked beautiful in the cream-coloured outfit that Cathy had lent her. Why she'd brought it on such a trip as nursing on an ambulance train Babs couldn't imagine, but she was glad that she had, as it was the perfect thing to wear. The dress was straight but pinched in at the waist with a silk cummerbund. It reached her ankles so a little of the white silk stockings that one of the posh VADs had given her showed. Another VAD had some white sandals that she borrowed, and to top it all, Matron of all people came up with a little hat that was veiled from the top brim.

Back in the hotel for a honeymoon night, though she didn't think it possible, their lovemaking surpassed what they had experienced the first time.

It wasn't until she woke the next morning that the reality of what had happened really hit her. *Eeh, I'm a married woman. I wonder what Ma and Beth'll make of that!*

They'd left the train the day before without waiting for the post bag to be delivered. When they arrived back, there was a welcome that touched Babs and yet made her laugh. The nurses had made a row of bunting out of the brown paper that they had an abundance of as everything they needed came wrapped in plain brown paper. The flag-like shapes fluttered in the breeze as they hung from window to window. Each had a letter on, spelling 'Congratulations and best wishes from us all.' It was a wonderful moment that was only surpassed by the distributing of post and finding that at last there were letters for her from her ma and Beth, both in the same envelope. She was enthralled and felt her happiness to be complete.

But as she read them, Babs's joy began to be overtaken by feelings of hurt. Her ma, married again? And given birth to two children! She was sorry to read that one had died, she knew that agony, but still it felt as though these children had been given the love that should have been hers and Beth's. And to read that Beth and Ma were together! And Beth married with Ma there and this new sister as a bridesmaid! It all began to simmer inside Babs and leave her unable to enjoy at last finding her ma. *Did they ever think of me, or care about me in all of this?* She suddenly felt the urge to scream and cry, but she made an extreme effort to control herself as she changed into her cleaning-down uniform. There was a lot of work to do before the train got to the Somme.

TWENTY-EIGHT

Tilly worried constantly about not receiving any letters from Babs. Christmas had come and gone, and been one of their best yet, as despite shortages, they were almost self-sufficient on the farm and the table had been laden with food. They'd been joined on the day by Molly and Will and Florrie and Reggie, and all of their families, but best of all was having Beth and Henry there.

Now, here they were in July 1916 and still no reply to any of the chatty letters she and Beth had sent to the Red Cross. And more worrying than anything was that the Red Cross told them that their letters, though delayed as the fighting intensified, were getting through to Babs. However, they cautioned, life on the ambulance trains was extremely busy now, and left no time for doing anything other than work and sleep, and they explained that very little time was given to rest periods. They had assured them that their daughter and sister was well and had advised them that they should be patient.

The reports coming from the Somme were horrendous, and Tilly couldn't sleep at night for thinking of what might happen to Babs.

It was Tilly's day at home today as she and Molly took turns in going to the shop now. There wasn't the business there used to be and Molly had her hands full helping Mary with baby Gerry, named after his da.

Tilly paced up and down, hoping against hope that the postman would at last bring a letter from Babs.

He brought two letters, one from Beth and an official-looking one with a government stamp on it for Tommy.

Tommy shuffled his in his hands. 'So, it is that there is still no word from Babs? I'm for being sorry, love, but what is it that Beth has to say?'

'Oh no. Henry has been called up.'

'But he's a doctor, he's for being needed by the lads returning. His research is invaluable.'

'Beth sounds distraught. She says that he finished his research paper and had applied for a position as a neuroglial surgeon, which would have made him able to stay with Beth but his call-up came before that was finalised. He's asked to be posted to a military-field-based hospital. Ah, but wait a minute … Eeh, Tommy, Beth wants to live with us while he's away! By, that'd be wonderful, and sommat as I tried to talk to her about before. Well, it seems she must have taken it in. Like we said, she can have Ivan's room, it's perfect for her, and she can come with me to the shop. There's lots that she can do to keep her mind off things.'

'So, it is good news for you then.'

'Naw. Well, half and half.'

'Aye. Now, let's see what it is that is being asked of me.' Tommy's face dropped when he read his letter. 'Be Jesus!'

'Eeh, Tommy, whatever's happened to make you curse like that?'

'They're coming to pick up the horses on Monday! How is it that we are to manage?'

'What? All of them? Why? And how will I get into Blackpool?'

'It says that they are needed for war work, in particular the cart horses and shires, as they will be used to move heavy artillery from place to place, but they will be inspecting the rest of our horse stock, and if deemed suitable to carry officers into battle, they will be taken too.'

'Oh, no, Tommy. What will we do?'

Tommy read on. 'It's for saying that we will take delivery of a tractor, supplied by the government, and there is also another note here telling us that most of our land is to be given over to food production . . . Well, it is that I don't know what to say. It will be sorry I am to see me old faithful horses going into danger, but well, a part of me feels excited about having a tractor.'

Tilly had seen a picture of a tractor in Tommy's farming paper and he'd said then how he'd love one and that they were the farming of the future, but he'd also said that he couldn't see a day coming when he would own one. Now the thought of doing so had taken the sting out of losing the horses.

'Don't you be worrying your head about how you're to get to Blackpool, me little Tilly. I'll buy a donkey and a small cart. They're smashing little runners when they get a trot on.'

'Tommy! And what am I to do if it stops and refuses to go any further? Eeh, if that's on the prom, I'll look an idiot, and be a laughing stock.'

Tommy laughed. Tilly couldn't help but join in with him as a picture of such a disaster formed in her mind.

'Well, Tilly, me little lass, if I'm to go mechanical, so can you. I'm for thinking it's one of those motors as we should be buying.'

'Eeh, Tommy, they look dangerous things. By, we might get ourselves killed driving one of them. I haven't a clue.'

'We can learn. I was for hearing at the farmers' meeting that the garage selling them gives you lessons. One or two of the folk around here have them now – there was for being a few parked at the market. Very useful they are too, especially if we were to have a van.'

Tilly wasn't sure, and yet she felt a little excitement nudge her trepidation at the thought of these contraptions. Noisy and smelly as they were, her resistance to them taking over from horses had lessened recently. 'Eeh, Tommy, with a van we can put Beth's wheelchair in for her, just as we did with the cart, and you can take your produce to market. Aye, I'm for it, Tommy. I'm sure if I can drive a horse and cart, I can drive one of them motors.'

It was sad to see the horses go. They were only left with the old mare that they'd put out to grass months ago. 'Old Lilly is going to be lonely. She loved to chat with the others after they were for going to the paddock after their day's work.'

'Eeh, you daft apeth, Tommy.'

'You will be for seeing that what I'm saying is the truth. I don't see her lasting long.'

Tilly knew that Tommy was talking about anything and everything to help him with his sadness. The horses had always meant a lot to him and he'd treated them as if they were human. Now she wondered what their lives were going to be like on a battlefield with all that noise and horror surrounding them. Well, she hoped they did a good job and helped to win this terrible war.

When Beth arrived a week later, she and Henry had news. 'I'm going to have a baby, Ma.'

'Eeh, lass, you're making me into a granny! Ta, both of you, I never saw meself as a granny, but I'm ready for the job.'

The hugs and kisses were full of mixed emotions.

'So, it is that you have to go, Henry?'

'Yes. I'm proud to be doing so, as I know I can contribute by saving many, but I have tried to stay with Beth as she needs me, and it breaks my heart to leave her. Of course, I saw my work in our hospital as vital now that we are taking so many injured from France.'

'I'm not for understanding their logic in sending you meself,' Tommy told him.

'Well, being there when the men come off the battleground will really help the injured men as I can carry out operations that will make an enormous difference to them, whereas travelling with the injuries that some of them have often means they end up a lot more disabled than they needed to be.'

The men's discussion went on while Tilly and Beth hugged and cried, and Tilly tried to console Beth while attempting to contain her excitement at having her daughter home and that she was to be a granny.

* * *

The first week or so was a real challenge for them all. Beth was run-down with being constantly sick, and more so with her heartache, but gradually things improved, and eventually she felt well enough for them to venture into Blackpool. As Tilly drove the brand-new van, which left them feeling as though they were riding a kangaroo, they laughed and chatted about this and that.

'By, I'm glad you're feeling better, me lass.'

'Oh, Ma, who can help to being around you and Tommy and Eliza. And this is an experience in itself – it's like going on a ride at the fairground.'

'Cheeky! I'll get the hang of it. I'm determined to. It won't beat me. But, eeh, ain't it grand, eh? I never thought I'd take to driving one of these things, but I want to be doing it all day long.'

'Well, let's hope you get better at it, or my baby will think that the world is a place where you're jolted and bumped all the time.'

They both laughed.

'Ma, I'm enjoying learning how to make the baskets. I really lose myself when plaiting away.'

'And you've a talent for it an' all.'

'Do you think so?'

'Aye, I do. You remind me of me when I used to learn from me old aunt. I were in me element and soon bettered her efforts.'

'I like being with you as well, Ma. I feel as though I'm getting to know you more and that the missing bits of our lives are being joined up ... You know, Ma, that I'll never leave you again, don't you?'

'Aye, why? What's brought this on?'

'Well . . . I have something that I have to tell you about . . . but, well . . . oh, Ma, I'm afraid of hurting you.'

'Eeh, Beth, what is it? I've felt for a long time that you had sommat on your mind.'

'It's . . . it's Jasmine.'

'What? Jasmine? You're not having trouble with her, are you? Eeh, that wicked woman, if I ever see her—'

'No, Ma! Ma, listen . . . Oh, Ma, I'm sorry. I feel as though I've deceived you, but I only wanted to save you from being hurt.'

Steering the van into a gateway, she stopped the engine and turned towards Beth. 'What are you trying to say, lass?'

'Ma, I'm sorry, but I love Jasmine and Roman . . . Oh, Ma, I tried to keep this from you, but well, they're coming up to Blackpool.'

At first Tilly couldn't take in what Beth was saying, but then it began to sink in. 'Naw! Naw! I can't bear it. How can you do this to me, Beth?' Distraught at this news, Tilly's eyes filled with tears. Somehow, she'd imagined her girls pining for her year in and year out, unhappy without her and wanting her every minute of every day as she had wanted them, not loving the evil folk who took them away from her.

'Ma, please try to understand. Me and Babs were so young. It broke our hearts being away from you, but Jasmine and Roman did love and care for us and we did come to love them.'

'Babs didn't, or why did she run away, eh? Why didn't you go with her? Maybe together you'd have made it back to me.'

'Ma, don't. I – I was afraid, that's all. And, Ma, we have to think about why Babs didn't make it back to you and what happened to her in the years before she became a nurse. Where was she? Was she hurt and alone? What did she go through? Henry and I have discussed it endlessly, and we think that our letters to her shouldn't be all about our wonderful lives and what we have done and achieved, but more caring of Babs, and telling her that we are here for her.'

This shocked Tilly to the core. 'I don't knaw what to say. Eeh, Beth, I knaw as you're right. I . . . well, we didn't think, did we, lass?'

'No. And I'm sure the reason we're not getting a reply is, as Henry says, that it might seem to Babs that everything has gone on in our lives as if she was of no consequence.'

'By, lass, what have we done?'

'We can undo it, Ma. We just need to be very careful how we word our letters.'

'Aye, we'll do one when we get into the shop. But what of Jasmine? What you said has hurt me very much, Beth.'

'Ma, think how it was for you. Yes, you missed us every day, and hoped and prayed we would come back, but you went with Jeremiah, you fell in love and married, you had two children, you had love, sadness, hope, and you achieved your dream of having the shop – in short, Ma, you got on with your life. What did you want to happen for me and Babs? Did you want us to be unhappy, poorly treated, crying for you every day?'

'Naw . . . I mean . . . Oh, Beth, I don't knaw. I've hated Jasmine and Roman for so long, and now you're virtually asking me to have them in my life, when all I want to do is kick the life out of them.'

'Oh, Ma. Try to understand. Henry loves them—'

'What? Henry has met them?'

Tears ran down Beth's face. 'Please, Ma ... please try to understand. I have to tell you something, and your reaction is breaking my heart.'

'Eeh, Beth, what is it? I have to knaw, I need to get all the shocks out of the way at the same time.'

'We – we had a gypsy wedding, as well as our—'

'Naw! Naw, Beth.'

'Ma, I love you. I love you more than I can ever love Jasmine and Roman, but the biggest part of my life has been with them.'

'Aye, and they should pay for what they did!'

Beth was quiet but for her crying. Tilly's heart was torn by the love for this daughter of hers who was going through so much, and her consuming hate for Jasmine and Roman. She couldn't believe that Beth wanted to continue as a happy family with them, that she'd included them in her marriage, and that she'd shown her love for them to such an extent that Henry now loved them too.

'I'll take you back to the farm, Beth. I have to go to the shop, but I think we need time apart.'

Beth didn't object.

Arriving late at the shop, Tilly found a customer waiting who wanted to order a set of four of the basket chairs. The order was long and drawn out and Tilly felt like screaming by the time the lady had decided on cushion material, the colours of the cane and wicker and the design on the sides.

At last she was alone. Making a pot of tea, she sat down to write to Babs. In this letter, she poured her heart out, and felt drained when finally she put the pen down. *Oh, Babs, I failed you. You did your best to get back to me. You didn't stay with the evil Jasmine and Roman.*

Wringing her hands with the anguish she felt, she almost cried out loud as the hurt ground into her. *What am I to do?*

'Hello!'

'Eeh, Molly, how did you knaw as I need you, lass?'

'I didn't, I just brought Gerry out for a walk. Whatever's the matter?'

Telling Molly helped to clear Tilly's head, but she wasn't prepared for Molly's reaction. 'It sounds to me as though you've to forgive and forget, lass. Don't you think your lasses are hurt an' all? Especially Beth, now this has happened. Eeh, Tilly, you've got them back. It was allus going to need careful handling, but think on – losing a child, as we both knaw, means they're gone forever. You lost your girls, but not forever. Don't spoil things now.'

'Me? Me spoil things? What have I done to do that? I have wanted nowt more than to have them back and have them gypsies punished for what they did to us. Now I find they have the best of both worlds – they got to have my young 'uns as their own, and they messed with their heads till they lost all sense that I was their ma and let Jasmine take me place. Aye, I can understand them needing to do so when they were little, but now they see the pain it caused me, and can see the sin – naw, crime – that Jasmine and Roman committed, you would think they'd want justice an' all.'

'Tilly, Tilly, just as you said, they were young 'uns, they were impressionable, and aye, it must have been easier to love those gypsies back and to have their love than to fight that. You're putting old heads on babbies.'

Tilly sank into the chair behind the counter. Frustration gripped her. *Why can't Molly and Beth see this from my point of view?*

'However you see it, Tilly, I reckon as you've two courses of action: forgive and forget and keep your daughters with you, or lose a piece of them to Jasmine, and who knaws, she may gradually make that a much bigger bit if she has the powers these gypsies are meant to have.'

'I can never forgive! Never!'

'Eeh, lass. I fear for you, I do. I reckon you could end up losing the girls again if you ask them to choose.'

'You mean, they'd choose Jasmine?'

'I don't think they'd want to, but I don't think they'd want her out of their lives either. Tread carefully, lass. That's all I can say. Try to find a compromise.'

Driving into the farmyard, Tilly was met by Tommy.

'Me little Tilly, whatever happened? Beth's distraught. She won't come out of her room and I've heard her crying every time I go in to check on her. I'm mystified.'

Tilly fell into his arms, mumbling between her sobs that she couldn't bear what was being asked of her.

'What? For the love of God, what?'

In the kitchen they sat at the huge scrubbed-pine table and Tilly told Tommy what had happened and how it had affected her. Then she went on to tell him what Molly had said.

'Aye, well, it is that it's not for happening to Molly. Aye, she's had her sorrows, but this – years and years of agony for you and what happened to you as a consequence – well, that's not easy to be forgetting. I'm fair shocked, so I am, that this should be asked of you.'

'Ta for understanding, Tommy. Eeh, what would I have done without you all these years, lad?'

'Well, understanding is not for solving the problem, and we can't have Beth in this state, bless her. She's a mother-to-be and a woman missing her man, not knowing if he's safe or not, besides coping with not being able to walk, so it is that we have to be looking for a way to sort this out. I'll ask her if she would be up for talking to me. I'm going to tell her exactly how it was for you, me little Tilly.'

'Not the drinking and the asylum . . . Naw, Tommy.'

'Aye. Without her having the full picture, how is it she's to know why you feel as you do, or what that evil pair did to you? Now, make me a pot of tea to take in with me, poor wee thing must be longing for a drink.

To Tilly's surprise, Beth allowed Tommy in when he knocked and asked if she would talk to him. Not wanting to wait to hear second-hand what the outcome was, Tilly stood outside the door.

Tommy comforted Beth, and then told her he knew all that had gone on, and that he understood both sides. 'But it is that your ma hasn't been for telling you all that happened to her, and the toll having you both stolen took on her – and was still having on her when it was that you came back into her life.'

Tilly held her breath against the pain evoked in her as she listened to what Tommy told Beth next. 'I know, as I was there, and I saw the strength of your ma as she worked hers and your Aunt Liz's passage out of that stinking hole. But it never stopped there.'

Tommy held nothing in. Tilly's life – sometimes a mere existence – after her little girls were stolen was told in every detail. How Tommy remembered – or even knew – some of it, Tilly didn't know. When he said, 'And so now you know, is it that you can understand your ma not being able to forgive those two as you told her today that you loved?'

Tilly waited. There was a long silence.

'Tommy, I do, of course I do, but Ma lived her life the best way she could. She went in different directions, as she had to do. I was a child. A child! I didn't have the wisdom of age, or the ability to make my own decisions. Jasmine told us that Ma had done a wicked thing and had upset the gypsies. That she was ill and couldn't take care of us. And then they both cared for us, fed us, loved us, played with us, taught us skills, and nursed me when I was very ill. And then when I wanted tuition to enable me to become a nurse, they paid for that, and sacrificed two seasons' work to stay close to me. I cannot wipe all of that out. I cannot.'

'I'm saddened to hear you say that, because to me, all of that was done for their own end, to tie you to them, and it is that they have succeeded at great cost to the woman who birthed you and was for having her heart broken by them. But a compromise must be found. Is it that you're for having ideas on how we can resolve this, me wee, Beth?'

'I have an allowance from Henry, and my pay entitlement as an army officer's wife. I was thinking that it would be best if I moved into a place of my own and engaged a live-in nurse to care for me. Then I can have both my mothers and you, my step-father, and Roman, and Eliza visit me, and neither of my families need ever see each other. It's the only way that I can see that we can make our relationship work.'

Tilly stiffened. She wanted to dash in and scream that she would never allow that to happen. That the moment she knew where Jasmine and Roman were camping, she would get her justice, but a weakness took her. Walking towards the stairs, she climbed them to her room and lay on her bed and sobbed as she asked what she'd asked of herself before: *How am I to bear it. How?*

TWENTY-NINE

Never had France had such a wet summer. The rain fell in torrents day after day. 'Eeh, Rupert, it's as if God's crying.'

'I'm sure He is, darling. I know that I do, and often.'

'Awe, I should be sharing those moments with you. I can't bear the separation, and yet being so close.'

They sat in what they now called *their* café, sipping the coffee that they once hated, but had both got used the taste.

'Well, my darling, at least we have two nights. I've booked us into a small hotel just around the corner from here so that we can walk there once we've had this.'

Rupert's parents had written in reply to his letter telling him that they were appalled and very disappointed in him and were barring him from using their suite.

> How could you? Have you lost your senses? We know how difficult everything is for you, but for you to act in such a way!
>
> Don't you think that as parents we are suffering enough just having you in the thick of the action and not knowing from one minute to the next if you are alive or dead?

Well, you don't have to denounce your title as we denounce you until you come to your senses, divorce this trollop and apologise for putting us through this.

Please do not write or attempt to visit us until you have sorted out this mess.

Rupert had been devastated. He knew they would be very cross and upset but hadn't expected such drastic action, even though he'd said he didn't care if this happened.

Babs and Rupert had had very little time together since. The odd night here and there, but while working they had been warned by Matron that though the Red Cross didn't agree with what they had done, they were badly needed in the area as work would be increasing, and so they had agreed that Babs could stay on, but if they were ever caught together in a compromising situation, they would be separated and sent to different work areas.

To say work would increase was an understatement. They had been working under tremendous pressure since the start of the new offensive in the Somme, often meaning that the staff didn't have a bed themselves as all the bunks were filled with wounded and the overflow used theirs.

But Babs wanted to forget all of that for one night. She had news for Rupert and was excited to tell him about it.

When she did, as they sat having dinner in the hotel restaurant, his face was a picture. 'My darling, Babs. A baby!'

'Aye. I'm not far gone, but I knaw. I missed a period, and my breasts are swollen and tender. Oh and horrors of horrors, I was actually sick this morning. No one knew. They were all too busy or too tired.'

'Oh, Babs. My darling. We'll have to tell. You can't work how you have done, and you definitely can't lift anything.'

'Ha, you daft apeth, of course I can. You're a doctor, you knaw as most of that is myths thought up by rich women. Us working-class women just get on with it. I've seen babbies born in the field at apple picking when we were joined by all the other gypsies. One minute the woman is working away, the next she's squatting and a new-born's cries can be heard.'

'Babs, you're not a gypsy, and I hate you talking of that time. Have you heard from your real family again, darling?'

'Naw. And I don't care if I do or not. I wish I'd never got in touch with them. They're so full of their cosy little lives, it's as if I never existed, and I'm sure they'd have never bothered to find me if hadn't found them. I lived without them for many years and got by, and now I have you and we are making our own family.'

'That's so sad. Are you sure you're reading their letters right? I mean, of course they had to get on with their lives; you did too. And it can't be easy to find someone. Where would you start? But maybe everything wasn't a bed of roses, but with you being where you are and Beth knowing what it is like, they wouldn't want to add to your troubles by telling you the real truth of what they have gone through.'

'I never thought of that, but aye, it's a possibility. And that is why I love you so much, you make me see the world differently.'

'Oh? Is that the only reason? It's not for what I have in my trousers?'

Babs laughed out loud. One or two other guests turned and looked disapprovingly at them. For a moment she thought she might have let Rupert down, but he laughed. 'Fuddy-duddies. They want to try doing what we're doing twenty-four hours a bloody day. They wouldn't be so stuffy then. Anyway, forget them, back to my question, as he and I are eager to get you into bed, Mrs Bartram.'

Giggling, Babs said, 'Stop it now, you're making me want to get up and go to bed this instant.'

'Good. I want to too. Have you had enough to eat, mother-to-be, as you need to eat for two now?'

'Aye. I'm off me food a bit – just not hungry. And eating for two ain't sommat that I'm going to have the luxury of as you knaw. Eeh, the food gets worse on that train.'

'I'm not talking about anything till I've made love to you at least twice. So, come on, I need to get started.'

Babs again laughed. She filled with happiness as they made their way to the stairs. All the hell of the train – the blood, the crying, broken men and their terrible injuries – faded, as did her heartache over her ma and Beth.

They had hardly entered the room before they were tumbling about on the bed pulling off each other's clothes in a frenzy of passionate groping and desperation, which culminated in a hurried, though deeply satisfying, giving and taking of pleasure.

Lying back on the pillow afterwards, Babs watched the smoke from Rupert's cigarette curl upwards towards the ceiling. He rarely smoked, but after lovemaking was one of the occasions when he did. 'Eeh, I'd love to knaw what's going on in your mind, me darling Rupert. I can hear it ticking away.'

'Oh, this and that. I'm thinking of my son. How will he look? Will he be clever like me and you? What will he turn out like? And then I was praying he'd never know what war was like.'

'Oh, our babby's a boy then?'

'Got to be, I'm sure. Oh, Babs, I'm so glad that we're together, and I can support you. Think of all the couples, thousands and thousands of them all over the world, who are separated right now as we lay here exhausted after making mad, passionate love.'

'I knaw. The world's gone mad. Do you think it will ever end?'

'It has to. It's been raging now for two bloody years. Surely someone will see sense and call a halt. Though it's not that simple of course. Oh, I don't know. I just hope that it does. I want to live a normal life, with my normal, beautiful wife looking after me and our many children, and you waiting eagerly for me to return from work to make more of them.'

Babs giggled. 'Many children! How many? And what's got into you? You're coming out with some funny things today.'

'At least ten, I thought. And the way I feel, all happy and silly, is down to you, the news you've given me, and well, just being alone with you, my beautiful wife. In fact, I'm going to show you just how beautiful you are as I'm going to make love to you again, only this time very slowly and sensuously.'

By the time it was morning, they'd coupled four times and neither had the energy to get out of bed for breakfast, but lay curled around each other, snoozing, and then waking, without a care in the world.

It was Babs who disturbed them, rushing to the bathroom to throw up. Rupert was soon by her side, rubbing her back and gently coaxing her to take deep breaths as even though the retching went on, nothing was coming up.

'I feel guilty now, darling. Here I was saying that I was going to put you through this ten times.'

'Don't be.' Babs swilled and wiped her mouth. 'This is natural. Horrid, but eeh, women have been having babbies since time began. We knaw what we're about and would put up with owt to have a healthy, happy, young 'un.'

'Sometimes you're like an earth mother, Babs.'

'A what?'

'It's a term for describing someone who lives close to nature.'

'Aye, I knaw, I was just surprised to hear you say it as it took me back to Jasmine. She called herself that. And I suppose I am. A lot of what I've learnt came from her and from my experiences in the convent, and my first pregnancy.'

'Oh, darling. I forgot. Is being pregnant again upsetting you?'

'Naw. I have me Mario in me heart and nothing can dislodge him. Better there than with another woman and me not being able to see him or look after him.'

'So, you do have an idea what it was like for your mother then?'

Babs felt as though she'd been given a body blow. 'Eeh, Rupert, I never thought. By, I've been wrong. I've done wrong. What you said last night about them only writing good things touched a chord with me, but to think how it were for me ma ... Of course I knaw. I've been through it. Well, the thought of it. Before I lost Mario, I faced losing him in the same way that Ma lost me and Beth.' Sitting on the end of the bed, Babs bowed her head. 'How can I make it right? It were her having other children as if replacing me, but I knaw now that's not how it were.'

'Write to her, darling. You'll feel better, I promise. Tell her good things too. About me and you, and about our son nestling in your womb. Whether my mother wants to hear about our child or not, I'm going to write to her. I've never stopped writing. I have this notion that they will get over it, and then when they meet you, they will love you deeply and all will be forgiven. Oh, I'll still not want to take my title, but just to be in touch with my family and to see them now and again is all I'll ask.'

'Eeh, lad, I'm sorry to have come between you and them.'

'You didn't – love did. Now, let's both write those letters as once we get back on the train, we won't stand a chance of doing so. Then we'll bathe and go out for breakfast. How does that sound?'

'Don't mention food!' With this, Babs ran to the bathroom again.

Once back on the train, they found all the staff had returned. For the nurses and sisters there was still time to rest, as now, they had an intake of orderlies who did all the donkey work of cleaning the train. It was a newer train than their original, with much more room on it to house these extra staff. Its interior had been specifically designed as an ambulance train – the official name they went under. But to the nurses and doctors it would always be called a hospital.

Though sad to once more be parted from Rupert, Babs was glad to get to her bed and went out like a light as soon as she lay down. When she awoke the train was moving.

'Had a good time, I take it, Mrs Bartram?'

Lifting her head onto her elbow and looking at Cathy, Babs smiled sleepily. 'Mmm.'

'Oh, I know you're a meany and won't tell. You have all the fun, it's not fair. The one eligible man and you nab him.'

Babs laughed. 'Ha, I didn't exactly nab him, I thought you stood much more chance than me, being from a more acceptable class than I am, but we fell in love, and love knaws nowt about class. So, it's all as simple as that.'

'Well, I'm happy for you . . . No, truly. Jealous, yes, but my time will come. I just don't know when in this hellhole.'

'Oh, I don't knaw, one of the handsome officers might fall for you.'

'Speaking of which . . .' Cathy waved a letter.

'Oh, I forgot about the post. Who's that from? An admirer?'

'It is, actually. Do you remember that blond-haired officer? The one with the shrapnel pretty much all over his body, but the piece near his spine being the dangerous one?'

'Aye, I do. Is it . . . Oh God, what was that?'

An almighty crash sounded. Babs stood up as if catapulted from the bed. The train shuddered, and then swung from side to side in a violent movement, throwing them both and everything that wasn't screwed down across the carriage and back again. Babs felt a bruising pain in her back. Something was on top of her, a heavy weight that she couldn't move. She tried to call out to Cathy, but her mouth filled with dust and sulphur.

Another crashing explosion further rocked the carriage. An ear-splitting screech filled the air as the wheels skidded, sending the train into a higher speed, but then another violent side-to-side movement and the carriage went crashing onto its side. Glass splintered all around Babs; smoke filled her nose and burnt her lungs. Her body had been flung to the side of the carriage, which was now the ground. Debris landed on her, slashing her skin and bruising her.

Released from the weight that had held her pinned, Babs rose, covered her face with her hands and groped for a door.

Finding a gaping hole, she went through it, only to fall, cutting and scraping her skin as she did. When she landed, she knew she was lying outside on the rails; they were hot and burnt her thighs. Crawling along towards the shaft of light she could see in front of her, she emerged from under the train. What she saw sent terror striking through her. The train was on fire. Carriage after carriage was alight. *The wards! Oh God, the men! Help me, help me!*

But no help came. Babs knew in that moment that she was the help as there didn't seem to be another living soul. She tried to call for Rupert, but her voice wouldn't work. She attempted to formulate a plan in her mind of what she could do to save anyone, but the heat of the blaze was scorching her, and she had to move back towards the other side of the track. As she did and the smoke wasn't so intense, she saw one of two people jumping from the train. One was on fire, but when she tried to run to them the heat drove her back.

Making it to the bank, she lay down exhausted, dazed and not sure of what had happened, or where everyone was.

Someone put a hand on her. She looked up at a soot-blackened face. 'Are you all right, miss? I'm one of the orderlies.'

'Aye, a bit bruised and burnt, but nowt broken. How many got out?'

'Not many. I've only seen four or five.'

'Awe, naw, naw . . . Any staff . . . the doctors?'

'I haven't seen any, but some are on the other side of the train – a few more than this side, I think. I saw Matron, but I think she has a broken leg. She could do with your help if you're up to it.'

Babs didn't know why, but she couldn't feel any emotion. It was all so unreal. 'Aye, help me up, lad.'

'You're Sister Smith, aren't you? I'd know your accent anywhere.'

Babs didn't correct him. Very few knew that she was married now.

'I'm Jim. I helped you the other day with that young man with the eye injury.'

'Glad you're safe, Jim. What happened?'

'A bomb, I think. Though there wasn't a follow-up attack.'

How is it that I can feel so normal? What's the matter with me? Where's Rupert?

'Matron's just along here.'

'Matron, eeh, you're hurt.'

'It's my leg mostly. It needs a splint.'

'Right, I'll see to it. Jim, find something to make a splint. Hurry.'

As she said this the screams, crashes and bangs going on around her came into focus. Her body began to tremble.

'Sister!' Matron squeezed her hand. 'Hold on, Sister. It's delayed shock, try to keep a grip. We're going to be all right.'

Babs didn't care about herself. 'Rupert? Cathy? Where is everyone?'

'We don't know yet. Probably over the other side. Here's Jim. Help me, Sister, please, please help me.'

The matron's cry of agony spurred Babs on. 'You knaw as this will hurt, Matron, but we have to straighten your leg, it's twisted under you. Help me, Jim. We need to pull the leg so the bone goes back into place.'

Matron screamed, and then mercifully passed out. Babs didn't know how she managed to get the splint in place using Jim's ripped-up shirt to secure it, but once it was done her whole body began to shake again. 'How'll we all get out of here?'

'I don't know, Sister. I think the explosion will have been heard for miles, so if those that hear it realise what's happened, hopefully help will come along. I keep thinking why me? Why you? How come we've escaped hardly scathed and yet hundreds must be dead?'

'Don't! Don't say that.'

'Sorry, Sister. Look, you rest here and I'll go to the end of the train and try to get to the other side to see if there are any more there that need help. I've checked them on this side. There's some as we can't do anything for and others with injuries that can wait.'

'I'll come with you. Help me to put Matron on her side so that she's safe if she vomits.'

With this done, they walked together along the edge of track till they could cross over to the other side. Here, they found bodies by the dozen. Someone was administering to those who were wounded. 'Rupert?'

Babs hurried as fast as she could, but the man wasn't Rupert, but another orderly, doing all he could. 'Have you seen Doctor Bartram? Is he injured?'

'No, sorry. You're the first medical staff that I've seen. I don't know if any of the others got out.'

'Naw. Naw.'

'Don't go to pieces, Sister. We need you. Tell us what to do, we might yet save some lives.'

This last helped Babs. That's what she did, wasn't it? Saved lives. Going back into mechanical mode without consciously making herself, she began to assess those wounded. To her horror, most were burnt beyond recognition. Others had cuts and gashes. When she came across one charred body, she knew it was Cathy. Remnants of her uniform fluttered around her body; bits of it stuck to the blackened torso. Moving on, she didn't react. Still her emotions were caged.

'We need water and bandages, Jim.'

'We have neither, but I can see a house through those trees there . . . Oh, look, someone's coming.'

The someone turned out to be about ten men and women. All carried buckets of water, sheets and blankets. Not able to speak the language, Babs tried to thank them, knowing that one word, 'Merci.'

What seemed like hours later, with the help of Jim and Stuart as the other orderly told her his name was, all those still breathing were cared for to the best of her ability and given drinks of water. 'Jim, find sommat to put Matron on and you and Stuart go and fetch her around to this side. Be careful with her, but I must check on her. And if there's anyone around there that can walk, tell them to come an' all. We all need to be together. I think one of the men has gone for help. I couldn't make out what he said but that seemed to be what he meant. We can only help where we can and await someone to rescue us now.'

Just as she said this a shot rang out. Fear zinged through Babs. 'An attack! Oh God, we're under attack.'

A man came up to her shaking his head. He gestured to where one of his fellow men stood over a body. 'German! No others. We search.'

Relief released a deep sigh from Babs. It seemed from what she understood that the men were armed and had seen a German creeping up on them. It crossed her mind that there must have been more than one, but suddenly everything crowded her, and she sank to the ground. Tears choked her as realisation came to her that Rupert must have been killed, but all she could say was, 'Cathy, poor Cathy. And Belinda. Oh God, everyone.'

No one stopped her from crying, but sobs joined hers as those around her came alive to the devastation. Along the track she saw Jim and Stuart carrying Matron on a plank of some sort. When they arrived next to her, Matron was awake but looked like death. In a fearful voice she called out to Babs.

Babs got up and went to her. 'You're all right, Matron. Rest, someone will come to help us.'

'My n – name's Polly.'

Babs took hold of her hand. 'Eeh, that's a lovely name, Polly. Now, don't fret. Take naw notice of me. I just had a moment. I'm all right now. I'll take care of you.'

Matron looked up at her and smiled, then her head flopped to the side, and she was gone. 'Naw, naw! Eeh, Matron ... Polly, don't go.' A sob came to her. She looked across at Jim; he was bent over sobbing his heart out. Stuart was trying to comfort him, but what comfort was there to give? How could anyone make this right?

* * *

Days later in the military hospital in Paris, Babs was told that her lovely Rupert wasn't among the survivors. 'My name's John, Sister. I'm with the Red Cross, arranging for you all to go home. The chap called Jim, an orderly, told me that you and one of the doctors were very close.'

'We are married. Doctor Bartram is me husband.'

'Oh? Dear, dear, I'm so sorry. But, well, the doctor wasn't among the survivors.'

Although Babs had known this deep down but not allowed herself to acknowledge it as a fact, it now hit her like a sledgehammer. A wail came from her that hurt her own ears and rasped her throat, as she cried Rupert's beloved name over and over. She felt herself disappear into a spiral of agony and no one's words of comfort could penetrate her torn heart.

The journey through France, then across the sea and to the convent happened without Babs taking part or having a say in where she wanted to go.

But once there, she was wrapped in the love of Daisy and Sister Theresa and gave herself up to their care.

Both sat with her for hours, praying for her, chatting to her and making sure she had everything she wanted. Sometime during this, Babs told them about Rupert, and her ma and sister.

Not long after this, Daisy came to her. 'Babs. Babs, love. There's someone to see you.'

Babs opened her eyes and tried to come out of the sleep she'd been in. Leaning over her was a face she knew, and yet didn't know. A face with a lovely head of raven-coloured hair framing it, and eyes that twinkled with unshed tears. The face had a smile on it.

'Ma?'

'Aye, lass, it's Ma. I've come to take you home, if you want to come, lass. Beth's here an' all.'

'Eeh, Ma, I do. Eeh, Beth, lass!'

'Babs! Babs! Ma, wheel me nearer, I need to hold Babs.'

Clinging on to her beloved sister, Babs knew that she was home. Truly home. She smiled a watery smile at her ma and stretched out one of her hands to her. 'I love you, Ma, and me Beth. Don't let owt ever part us again.'

Neither of them answered this, and Babs felt a niggle of worry enter her. Something wasn't quite right, but she hadn't the energy to ask about it. She just accepted their love and hoped that it wasn't so.

For now, she had enough to cope with and couldn't face anything being wrong with her family when she'd only just found them after so long and needed them so badly.

EPILOGUE

A FAMILY TRYING TO OVERCOME

September 1916

THIRTY

Babs found everything so different to what she'd imagined. She loved Eliza as soon as they met and felt sad not to have met Ivan, but she couldn't let in the grief she felt for him.

On the journey here, she tried to tell them all about her lovely Rupert, but always ended in floods of tears. She was fragile, and felt that she would break if it wasn't for the miracle of miracles that her baby was still safe in her womb.

'Eeh, Beth, I'm glad as I'm home. Will we share a room? We've so much to talk about. Not least our two swelling tummies.'

They were sat outside, Babs on a bench, Beth in her wheelchair, having just arrived at the farm earlier that day. The garden to the side of the kitchen was blooming with multicoloured wallflowers that smelt lovely. It was a picture of the England she remembered and had left behind, as the gardens of the convent were also lovely like this. Though they didn't have a faint tinge of cow dung hovering on the air, which was taking a bit of getting used to.

'No, Babs. I – I . . . well, I don't live here.'

'Oh, why? Beth, what's wrong? I knaws as there's sommat, I can feel the atmosphere.'

'Let's not talk about it, I don't want to upset you. Everything's all right on the surface and will hopefully get better. Ma's just a bit hurt, but I think she will come to terms with it all.'

'Come to terms with what? Why aren't you happy, Beth? Eeh, I knaw as you are missing your man. And God knaws, I knaw what that's like, but your man will come home ... Mine ... mine ...'

'Oh, Babs, I'm sorry. Forgive me. I'm so sorry. If I could bring Rupert back, I would. From what little you've managed to tell us, he sounds as though he was a wonderful man.'

'He – he was. And that's it, Beth. Gone. My world, my love, gone. But you still have your Henry. I knaw you don't knaw when you'll see him again, but he's alive. But missing him ain't all that's making you unhappy. What is it as Ma's got to come to terms with?'

'You haven't asked about Jasmine and Roman yet, Babs. Have you forgotten them?'

'Naw. And at times I miss them, but at others, I'm very angry with them and want to claw their faces ... Is this unhappiness to do with them? Are they bothering you, Beth? Has owt been done about what they did?'

'No! And I don't want it to be. I – I love them both, Babs. They—'

'You love them! What? Beth, have you told Ma that?'

Beth nodded.

'Awe, Beth, no wonder Ma's upset. You knaw what they did. Aye, they loved us and cared for us, but they had naw right to that. Naw right at all. That was Ma's job and they took it from her. Took us from our lovely, loving ma.'

Beth didn't speak for a moment. When she did, she said, 'I was with them longer than you, Babs. They never did anything to harm me, only loved and helped me. I can't just give them up.'

'So, you've broken Ma's heart, and don't even live with her? After all the years she's been without us. Even if you did feel as you do, Beth, couldn't you have kept it from Ma? Seen them secretly?'

'They've come to stay in Blackpool to be near me. I taught them how to read and write – well, Jasmine anyway – and she wrote to me to let me know as I'd given her Ma's address. I had to tell her in case she bumped into them. Besides, I . . . well, I wanted to see them openly, not keep them a secret. Try to understand, Babs. I don't want us to fall out. I've missed you every day. It was like I was just a half-person, as my other half – you – was missing. Not till I heard your voice when I was injured did I feel whole again. It's the same with Henry, only in a different way. I still didn't feel the me from my childhood was whole, only you have done that.'

'Eeh, Beth, Beth, lass. I knaw. It was the same for me.'

'Where did you go, Babs? How did you land up in that convent?'

'I can't talk about it now, Beth. If there wasn't this hanging over us all, then maybe I would have, but on top of me pain of me loss, I've this atmosphere, and I don't want the past to flood back into me an' all.'

'I don't know what to do to make things right.'

'Feeling how you do, it won't be easy, but to be honest, Beth, I think as you ought to tell Jasmine that unless she and Roman go out of your life, you'll fetch the police to them. No matter at what cost to yourself, you owe it to our ma to do that. Give her some peace, Beth. Get them out of her life an' all.'

A tear dropped onto Beth's cheek. Babs couldn't bear to see it. 'Eeh, Beth. Think about it, but you don't have to make a decision now. We'll sort it. We have to. We're all together, and we don't want owt to spoil that. Not ever, ever again.' With this, Babs felt drained of energy. She couldn't believe that this was going on and that Beth could be so hurtful to Ma. Beth, the timid one, the one who always did as she was told, being this defiant and unreasonable made her someone that Babs didn't know, or know how to deal with.

'Well, you two. Eeh, I never thought to see you sitting together in the sunshine again. I'm taken back to that meadow where I collected the vines from the hedgerows and you two sat together in the sunshine. That's sommat as has stayed with me for a long time.'

'Eeh, Ma, I remember that. I've thought about it so often. Did you, Beth?'

'I did. It seems to have been the last time we were all safe, as when we reached home everything changed forever.'

'It did, Beth. But not forever. We can get those happy times back, it'll just take us time to adjust.'

'Aye, you're right, Ma. What'll help is if we all want to. And we do, don't we, Beth?'

'Yes. It is all I ever want.'

'Awe, me lasses.'

They were all quiet as Tilly settled herself on the bench next to Babs. Putting her arm around her, she drew her into her and then put her hand out to Beth. 'Me lovely girls. We've so much to talk about. Well, Beth knaws all that happened to me, and me her, but you've yet to hear what life has been like for us both, Babs, and we want to knaw what happened to you. But only when you are ready. In the meantime, let's just be together, eh? Supporting one another. Three women your da would be proud of.'

'You knaw, Ma, I find it hard at times to remember what me da looked like. I only knaw the feeling I had when he were with us.'

Beth leant forward. 'That's the same for me, Babs, I can't picture his face but know the feeling he gave me was of love, happiness and being safe.'

'He was a lovely man. I loved him very much. He only had one fault in me eyes, and that were how he looked on women as not capable of doing owt but cooking and cleaning. Eeh, he'd turn in his grave if he could see how I run me own business and with another woman as me partner. Not that men's attitudes have changed in general, but I'm lucky to have me Tommy, who ain't for thinking that way.'

'I'm glad now that you're happy, Ma. I'm sorry I didn't write. I got a funny notion in me head, but Rupert made me see things differently. I wrote to you after that. Did you get me letter?'

'Aye, I did. And I sent you one of a different kind to the ones that me and Beth had been sending. It was Beth's Henry who made us see the right way to go about things. Did you get that, me lass?'

'Naw. But none of it matters now. I'm home. We're both home where we should have been all our lives. Well, I didn't have this farm in mind as home, I allus pictured the house we lived in afore da died.'

A glance went between Beth and Ma, but Babs ignored it. She hoped with all her heart that Beth would see what she should do. She'd talk to Ma when they were on their own, let her know that she knew the problem and try to help her ma to see a little of Beth's side. Not that she thought there was any right in Beth's side, but if this rift wasn't to get deeper, then something had to be done.

Putting her head on her ma's shoulder and extending her hand to take Beth's other hand, she felt as if they'd completed the circle that had long ago been broken of Ma and her twins.

She hoped that nothing would ever break it again but feared that Jasmine and Roman may once more succeed in doing so. But for now, there was a deep love between them that was alive and strong and gave them something to build on. As nothing must ever break this circle again. She couldn't bear for it to. Enough was enough. They'd all suffered, and that suffering must somehow cement them, not drive a wedge between them. This would be her mission in life. She'd call on her Rupert to help her. And surely the unborn children that she and Beth were carrying would help in that too. Holding her ma tighter and squeezing Beth's hand, she felt sure this would be so and was filled with great hope for the future. A future where the three of them supported each other through any trials that came their way. For though she knew that there were still a few problems to surmount, she also knew that they were three strong women and together, they would conquer anything life threw at them.

LETTER TO READERS

Dear Readers,

Thank you for choosing my book. I hope that I have been able to give you hours of enjoyment with Tilly and her family. If I have, I would very much appreciate it if you can take the time to put a review on Amazon, and/or Goodreads and Facebook for me. Reviews are like hugging an author.

Blackpool Sisters is the second in The Sandgronian Trilogy, but all of the books stand alone so if you missed the first book, don't worry, you can still enjoy reading the backstory of Tilly and her life in the first in the trilogy, *Blackpool's Angel*. The last book in the trilogy is *A Blackpool Christmas*. Tilly and her family struggle to find a way forward now they are together – tissues at the ready.

Oh, and in case you are wondering why the books are called The Sandgronian Trilogy, Sandgronian is the name given to a person born and bred in Blackpool – which Tilly and her family are. The name has many spellings, and I was taken to task by one of my old bosses, who is herself a Blackpool-born lass, as she spells it the popular way: Sandgrown'un, and yet others have told me it is Sandgrownian. So, in order not to take sides in this friendly debate, I have chosen to use the version given on the internet as the official one. I myself am a proud Blackpudlian, a name given to anyone living in Blackpool, whether born here or not.

Back titles of my books are available online or to order from all good bookshops and in your local library – also look out for current and new titles in your local supermarket.

And finally, I love to interact with my readers, and do so on a daily basis on my Facebook Page and website, would you like to join me? If so, go to:

Facebook – www.facebook.com/HistoricalNov

Website – www.authormarywood.com

Twitter – follow me on twitter @Authormary

I look forward to hearing from you

Much love to all

Maggie x

RESEARCH

I like to research in the area that my book is set in, so how lovely for me that I write books set in my home town of Blackpool.

This makes it easy for me to find street names and local places for my characters to live and work – I just go walkabout till I find the setting that I need.

For historical facts for my books – and my goodness, Blackpool certainly has a fascinating history – I rely on the internet and the following books, the authors of which I am very grateful to for their wonderful work in compiling:

Blackpool Trams, J. Joyce, Littlehampton Book Services Ltd 1985

Blackpool at War: A History of the Fylde Coast during the Second World War, John Ellis, The History Press 2013

The Story of Blackpool Rock: An interesting account of how it is made and who made it, Margaret Race, 1990

Blackpool History Tour, Allan W. Wood and Ted Lightbown, Amberley Publishing 2015

ACKNOWLEDGEMENTS

Many people have a hand in bringing a book to publication and I want to express my heartfelt thanks to them. My agent, Judith Murdoch, who stands firmly in my corner. My editor at Sphere, Viola Hayden, who is always there for me and does a sensitive construction edit, mindful of keeping my voice and bringing the story to its polished best. To Thalia Proctor and her team of copy editors and proofreaders, especially Lorraine Green, who tailor the words to sing off the page and check my research for flaws. To Millie Seaward, my publicist, who works to put my books on the map. To the sales team, for their efforts to get my books on to the shelves. To Charlotte Stroomer and Hannah Wood for my beautiful covers. And last, but by no means, least, to my son, James Wood, who reads so many versions of each book, advising me what is working and what should go, suggests edits to the draft manuscript and then helps with the read through of the final proofs when last-minute mistakes need to be spotted. All of you are much appreciated, and do an amazing job. Thank you. You all help me to climb my mountain.

I thank too: My family – my husband Roy, who looks after me so well as I lose myself in writing my books, and is the love of my life. He has been by my side for almost sixty years, and I couldn't do what I do without him or the love and generous support that he gives me. My children, Christine, Julie, Rachel and James, for your love, encouragement and just for having pride in me. My grandchildren and great grandchildren, too numerous to name, but all loved so very dearly and all give me love and cheer me on. My Olley and Wood families, for all the love, and support. Thank you to each and every one of you.

And I want to thank my readers, especially those on my Facebook page – Books By Mary Wood and Maggie Mason – for the love and encouragement you give me, for making me laugh, for taking part in all my competitions, for pre-ordering all of my books, for taking the time to post lovely reviews, for supporting my launch events, and for just being my special friends. You are second to none and keep me from flagging, Thank you.